Praise for the novels of *Dragons and Dwarves*:

"A very well done contemporary fantasy." —*Publishers Weekly*

"It's a good energetic mystery, with a complicated plot and lots of chasing-down-leads action." —*Cleveland Plain Dealer*

"A very enjoyable contemporary fantasy." —*Science Fiction*

"It's a provocative world of deadly enchantment in which the dirty game of policics remains the biggest threat of all."
—*Locus*

"Skillfully done light adventure, with more than a dash of humor." —*Science Fiction Chronicle*

DRAGONS AND DWARVES:
STORIES OF THE CLEVELAND PORTAL

DRAGONS AND DWARVES:
STORIES OF THE CLEVELAND PORTAL

THE DRAGONS OF THE CUYAHOGA

THE DWARVES OF WHISKEY ISLAND

S. ANDREW SWANN

DAW BOOKS, INC.
DONALD A. WOLLHEIM, FOUNDER
375 Hudson Street, New York, NY 10014
ELIZABETH R. WOLLHEIM
SHEILA E. GILBERT
PUBLISHERS
www.dawbooks.com

First Omnibus Printing, August 2009
1 2 3 4 5 6 7 8 9

DAW TRADEMARK REGISTERED
U.S. PAT. AND TM. OFF. AND FOREIGN COUNTRIES
—MARCA REGISTRADA
HECHO EN U.S.A.

PRINTED IN THE U.S.A.

THE DRAGONS OF THE CUYAHOGA

This is dedicated to a
poor little guy named Henry.

I want to thank all the hamsters
in Cleveland who saw this MS
and tried to improve it.

PROLOGUE

I DIDN'T witness it, but I imagine it happening like this. . . .

The name he is given in English is Aloeus. He weighs over fifteen tons. A hundred feet from nose to tail and a wingspan half again that long. Muscles ripple under leathery black skin with every wing beat, as each sweep hauls his serpentine bulk into the sky.

Aloeus is unconcerned about the fact that his soaring is impossible by the rules of Earthly physics. His flight is as much through the forces that pour through the Portal as it is through the mundane air. More than any other creature, Aloeus is a creature of those forces. His mind is knit by strands of magic, and magic—as much as muscles and sinew—holds his wings against the biting wind tearing across the sky three thousand feet above the city of Cleveland.

He sees those forces as he soars above the city. Where a human being would only see sky and clouds, a brilliantly lit skyline, and the roiling clouds by the lakeshore—the constant vortex marking the Portal itself—Aloeus saw in a spectrum that humans could barely imagine, much less perceive. The Portal is a font of mystical power, visible to Aloeus' eye, and to the mind behind that eye. Glowing, pulsing tendrils of power twist and whip out from the Portal, pouring through the streets like rivers of mana, flowing into the sky like an inverted waterfall.

Aloeus breathes the power like air, feels wisps of it glide through his mind, tugs against it with his wings.

The power has its limits, but Aloeus cannot see them this close to the heart of it all, the Portal. The irregular edges of the magical flood are far from here, just short of Canada to the north, just short of Pennsylvania to the east, halfway to Columbus to the south, Sandusky to the west, and perhaps about three miles up. If Aloeus could see the edges of the mana enveloping northeast Ohio, he would not be flying this fast. Here, though, practically on top of the Portal, Aloeus is immersed in the forces that keep him alive.

The forces that keep him practically immortal.

While it would be disastrous for him to leave the sea of magic that pools around the Portal, there's no danger of that *here*. While the turbulent flood of magic ebbs and flows around him, like the air, or water beneath the surface of the ocean, it is always *there*. It may be more or less dense and spots might temporarily deaden, but unlike the fickle edges far from the Portal, the magic never fades this close to the source. He would have to fly three miles straight up for that to become a danger.

These facts are fundamental in Aloeus' world. Very basic assumptions that he takes so much for granted that he isn't aware—or, perhaps, does not want to be aware—that they *are* assumptions.

Of all the creatures in the world, magical or not, Aloeus should know better.

Unconcerned, Aloeus tears through the night sky, black as a thunderhead, and as powerful as a tsunami. The citizens who care to look up at the cloudless sky see him only as a tiny eclipse of a star or two. A few people, working very late nights or very early mornings in some of the skyscrapers around Public Square, look west in time to see Aloeus' demonic silhouette against a swollen setting moon.

As to what his last thoughts are, no one can know and I don't care to guess. He doesn't see it coming; if he did, he might be able to do something, maneuver, avoid it. . . .

Around him, the impossible happens. A dead spot in the mana sea. Aloeus doesn't even have time to understand the enormity of what is happening. As the magic disappears, his mind dies. Aloeus' brain, the meat circuitry that regulates his physical body, is not complex enough to house his mind. The thinking part of Aloeus, his identity, lived in the mana that, until moments ago, had lived in every cell of his body.

His conscious mind is dead.

However, he is not unconscious. The higher functions are gone, the eyes that saw as much by magic as by light are now half blind, but, like any brute animal, Aloeus can feel pain.

He wears a body impossible by what human beings would consider the normal rules of biology and physics. Now, suddenly, he exists in a world where aerodynamics, the square-cube law, and the tensile strength of muscle and sinew all mean something.

The wind becomes a wall, tearing wings back, ripping joints out of their sockets, splintering delicate bone, shredding skin. The long serpentine neck snaps back, vertebrae separate and fracture, as a head the size of a human body slams into his back above the base of his tail.

His body tumbles in a spinning downward dive as overtaxed lungs separate from the chest wall and his heart busts open with the pressure of his blood.

No longer a shadow gliding across the sky, he is a plummeting missile. More people see him now, they can hear the whistle of air sliding by his body. There is the slight, horrible, chance that—as his body falls out of the dead spot and back into the mana sea—the thinking part of his brain might awaken enough to *understand.*

Then he hits.

Aloeus, one of the most private of creatures, suffers the most public of deaths. Fifteen tons of dragon slam into a gravel mine on the western shore of the Cuyahoga River within sight of downtown Cleveland.

The body hits at such a velocity and such an angle that it keeps moving. Bones turn to jelly and flesh tears away as it skids across the ground. Gore marks gantries two hundred feet up and fifty yards away. The body tears into a docked cargo ship, twisting bulkheads and steel as it tumbles off the far side and plunges into the river, finally, to rest.

And, before the last postmortem tremor leaves Aloeus' epic corpse, the dominoes have started to fall.

CHAPTER ONE

THE domino with my name on it happened to be Columbia Jennings, a whip-thin, middle-aged Hispanic woman who was the Metro editor of the *Cleveland Press*. Third in the chain of command and my immediate boss.

Don't get me wrong about this, I like my job. Cleveland, for various reasons, is one of very few places where serious print journalism is still kicking. Seniority gave me the ability to concentrate on investigative reporting and op-ed pieces. There are few times I dislike coming into the office.

All those times have Columbia's name written on them.

When I came in that morning, and sat down at my workstation, and saw a little messaging icon with her name on it hovering in the middle of the LCD flatscreen display, my first response was to look around the office to see if anyone had witnessed my arrival and could testify if I bolted for the fire exit.

When an unseen escape proved not to be an option, I gritted my teeth and clicked on the message. Meeting, her office, three minutes ago. I think my wince was barely visible.

The words, "You're late," greeted me as I opened her office door. I looked around the office. Just me and her. Bad sign. She waved at me to close the door, which was worse—if only because it confined the stale smell of cigarette smoke in the room. Columbia reeked of it, and the air around her made my eyes water.

I took a seat across from her and said, "I just got your message."

I don't know exactly how she did it, but she could radiate disapproval without changing her expression. "Have you heard any news broadcasts this morning?"

I shook my head. One of my few personal rules was not to take work home. When I was off duty, I was off duty. Between whatever point I got home to my condo, and coming into work the next morning, I avoided news broadcasts, newspapers, even C-SPAN. It only took my wife and daughter moving to California to learn me that lesson, though I doubt my ex gives me any credit for it.

The disapproval wave hit me again.

"They found a dragon floating in the Cuyahoga River this morning."

"I didn't know they could swim."

"Dead." She snapped the word.

I was taken aback. It must have shown, because she let a shadow of a smile leak from the corner of her mouth. Common knowledge was that dragons were supposedly immortal. The things were supposed to be able to take a bullet directly into the brain or heart and still keep flying—though I don't know anyone personally who'd had the balls to put that theory to the test.

Christ, there were only a handful of dragons on this side of the Portal. This wasn't just news, this was *major* news.

Which made things pretty damn obvious to your truly.

"You *know* I don't do fuzzy gnome stories."

"This isn't a fuzzy gnome story," she said, "and you know it." She was giving me a very cold look. I had the impression of an Old Testament pagan idol, the kind they fed babies to.

"This isn't my kind of—"

"Bullshit, Maxwell." She stood up. "You may have a privileged position here because you've been covering City Hall since they played football in Browns Stadium, but you can only take that so far. You still work for this paper."

I shook my head.

"You think you're too good to cover Morgan's beat?"

Morgan would have been the man to cover this story. If he'd still been at the paper, this probably would have been his crowning achievement, actual feature material.

I shook my head no.

"Good, because you are the only person on the staff who hasn't had to cover for him."

I gave a resigned nod. I know very few reporters at the *Press* who envied Morgan's beat. All the paranormal crap was, supposedly, what made Cleveland interesting. Makes sense, right? The fact was, the guy on the magic beat, ninety-nine times out of a hundred, is working the ubiquitous "fuzzy gnome" stories. All the stupid (in)human interest stuff that's filler in the paper and gives the morning dee-jays something stupid to talk about. Unicorn sightings, gremlins in the sewer line, the occasional talking frog—which never has anything interesting to say. All the kind of stuff you would have found in a supermarket tabloid before the Portal opened and the crap started actually happening.

The difference is, of course, when the hacks in the tabloids were making the shit up, they made sure it was interesting.

Morgan was a transplanted Kentuckian who was one of the few people who actually enjoyed hearing mages pontificate on the different varieties of graveyard soil.

Unfortunately for everyone, Morgan's interest in his subject had overcome a prudent professional detachment, and it wasn't just his objectivity that suffered. The stories on how it happened varied; the cleaner versions had him ingesting some elixir he shouldn't have, the more ribald versions had him intimate with something not quite human. Either way, everyone agreed that four weeks ago, Morgan broke out in a carpet of tumors all over his skin. That would be bad enough, but apparently all these warts grew tiny little eyes that started staring at him. They did an MRI scan and discovered the little buggers scattered everywhere in his body.

Even so, his prognosis was pretty good. They just had to life-flight him down to Columbus, away from the influence of the Portal.

Bad news, returning anywhere within a hundred miles of this town would probably wake up all the little bright-eyed tumors, with fatal results.

"Do we know who it is?"

"They haven't released any information yet."

I stood up. "Okay, Bea, where am I going?"

She scrawled directions on a Post-It note and handed it to me. And for a brief moment I saw something that I've rarely ever seen in Columbia's eyes.

Relief.

I did spend some nominal time on the way there wondering how it was, when a hundred-foot-long, fifteen-ton corpse with a 150-foot wingspan clogged the Cuyahoga River in the shadow of the Hope Memorial Bridge, that the *Cleveland Press'* senior City Hall reporter got the plum assignment.

Unfortunately, while I am pretty good at spotting real or imagined conspiracies in city government, I wasn't that good at seeing them at my own newspaper. In retrospect it was probably the willful blindness of a middle-aged man comfortable in his job that made me avoid asking a few key questions until much later.

I got to the scene a little after nine a.m. About five blocks from the river I was solidly wedged in traffic backed up from the bridge. I could just catch sight of police and EMS flashers at the base of the northernmost art-deco tower.

I looked up and saw a few traffic 'copters hovering above the river. Above them, reptilian shadows circled in the blue August sky. Other dragons paying their respects.

I turned on the radio and scanned through the stations. Each one announced itself with a few brief seconds of Portal-generated babble before the digital circuitry managed to decipher the real broadcast from the extraneous magical signals that ate up fifty or sixty percent of the bandwidth. The interference resolved into the tail end of a traffic report. "—nasty tie-up on Carnegie near the river. Police have closed the Hope Memorial Bridge, but that hasn't seemed to stem the tide of curiosity seekers, who've tied up traffic all the way back to the Convocation Center—"

I grunted in frustration. It had already taken me fifteen minutes to move half a block, so I decided to change modes of transportation. I cut off a rust-bucket Hyundai and pulled my Volkswagen up on the sidewalk.

It was already headed toward the nineties, so I had been driving with the AC full blast. So I wasn't quite prepared for it when I opened the door.

The smell of the decedent hit me like damp towel soaked in rancid bacon fat. The kind of smell that sort of slithers in when you inhale it. My lungs stopped in a sort of appalled shock, and I had to force myself to keep breathing.

Jesus, it's coming from the river.

During my twenty-some years as a reporter I had been close to some ripe bodies. That did not make me relish dealing with them. During my career I had done my damnedest, in fact, to get away from situations where I had to deal with them. I hadn't planned on getting close enough to the dragon to smell it.

Apparently, there was a flaw in that plan.

I could picture Columbia laughing at me. *So Maxwell's uncomfortable with magic? Let's not just hand him one of Morgan's stories, let's give him the one with the highest gag factor.*

I decided that she was pissed at me, and this was her way of showing it.

It only got worse as I walked toward the bridge. I wasn't getting anywhere near the source of that smell without a little preparation.

It landed last night! These things must rot real quick.

I stopped in a drugstore two blocks away. The place was empty except for a scrawny little Indian guy who was busy lighting the fifteenth lucky-number votive candle on the counter in front of the cash register. It wasn't doing any good. The guy's eyes were watering. I grabbed what I needed and placed it on the counter next to a Madonna backlit in red wax. "Hey, if you're staying here, you need some of this."

The guy blinked at the small blue-green package. I shelled out five bucks, tore open the box and unscrewed the lid of the small canister of Vicks Vapo-Rub. I got two fingerfuls of the gel an smeared it above my upper lip, under my nose. "Menthol," I explained.

I held my hand out to the guy.

"Many thanks," he said as he repeated my gesture. He took a few deep breaths. I could almost see his sinuses clear as he smiled. "Oh, God, thank you." He pushed my five back at me. "No charge."

My good deed for the day.

I walked out, taking my own deep breaths. I still sucked air through my mouth, the gel couldn't kill the evil slithery smell, but it prevented the smell from triggering a gag reflex or shutting my lungs down in horror.

The closer I got to the bridge, the more I had to watch my step. The sidewalk was splattered with the stomach contents of people less prepared than I.

In theory I was supposed to meet the *Press* photographer out here. Looking at the traffic, I decided that waiting for the guy was an exercise in masochism. I doubted that he would have any trouble finding carnage to digitize without my help.

So I walked up to where the cops had set up a perimeter, a few hundred feet from the bridge itself. A pair of black-and-whites lorded it over a forest of red cones that blocked all four lanes of Carnegie, diverting everyone onto Ontario or I-90. No cops immediately in evidence, so I just walked past the roadblock.

Once I passed the perimeter, I heard a car door slam, and a slightly strangled voice say, "Hey . . ."

I turned around and saw a uniformed cop coming out of one of the black-and-whites. The cop was a kid, less than half my age. It was probably some detective's idea of a joke setting the guy up here.

"You," he coughed, "can't go up t–there."

I was impressed that the guy wasn't falling to his knees from the smell. He was sweating. The druggist's eyes had been watering, but this guy's eyes were leaking down the sides of his face.

"Kline Maxwell, *Cleveland Press*." Instead of reaching for ID, I reached for the Vicks. I did it slowly, because one should never make sudden moves in front of cops in obvious physical and emotional distress. "You need some of this."

He made eyes at me as if I'd just turned into a two-headed dwarf. I could tell he was a rookie who'd never had my dubious pleasure of being too close to an overripe corpse. I gestured with my other hand, over my upper lip. It took a moment before the light dawned and he followed my lead. The few ragged breaths he took made me feel like the Good Samaritan.

"Oh, God, that's better."

I pocketed the Vicks. "New on the force?"

He nodded. "Two days."

"Tell whoever set you on that duty that they're an asshole." I said as I turned around.

"I'm sorry, Mr. Maxwell, I still need to see an ID."

I fished out my wallet and hand him a press card and my driver's license. Once we were both satisfied about who I was, he said, "I'm not supposed to let anyone up on the bridge."

"We all got our jobs to do."

"It's a crime scene, sir." The kid took my arm and steered me back toward Carnegie. I was about to make the obligatory noises about hassling the press and the public's right to know, when he said, "You know it's just luck I noticed you." He coughed. "I have to hide the car from this damn smell. If you'd just walked around the other side . . . The other car's empty." He coughed again and shook his head. "Just lucky I caught you, right?"

He gave me a pat on the shoulder as he escorted me past the nose of his car. After which he opened the door and slid back into the driver's seat.

The kid would have had to taken an ad out in the *Press* for his hint to be any broader. I walked around the back. True to his word, the rookie cop didn't notice me.

I walked down the center line, toward the knot of cop cars blocking the westbound lanes of the bridge. The sound of the traffic jam was distant, overwhelmed by the sense of stillness. First impression: the only movement was from the flashers on the cop cars, and a circling mass of black birds that were doing lazy circles over the Cuyahoga River in imitation of the dragons much farther up in the sky.

Two massive stone pylons flanked the entrance to the main span of the bridge. Built in 1932 in a style that might be called art-deco-classical-Babylonian, the godlike humanoid statues loomed impassively over the tiny human inhabitants of the bridge. Their gaze fixed on the distant eastern horizon, as if everything here was beneath their notice.

Glancing up at the northeast pylon, towering over the cops, I saw something man-sized, leathery and reptilian perched on the statue's left shoulder. I might have caught sight of a gargoylelike wing and a skull-like face, but then it skittered around the pylon, out of sight.

Whatever it was, I didn't like it.

Par for the course.

One cop broke from the herd and headed in my direction. I started angling toward the guardrail so I could get a good look at what had brought me here.

"Kline Maxwell," the cop called out to me. I wasn't that surprised that he recognized me. *I* recognized *him*.

Thomas O'Malley, SPU police commander. He was thin and dark, with a sharp face that led like the bow of a ship. He looked less like a cop and more like a Mafia stool pigeon, to the point where his voice seemed to carry a hint of New York in it. Despite his name, the only thing Irish about him was the fact that the Democratic political machine—in the guise of Adrian Phillips back when he was Mayor Rayburn's campaign manager—had got him his job.

"O'Malley," I acknowledged him as I reached the guardrail. I tried to lean nonchalantly on the rail, which was hard with the wind blowing the smell of rotting mentholated fish in my face. "Any comments about the floater?"

I noticed that O'Malley had a greasy trace of white under his nose. I wondered if it was better than Vicks. "What're you doing here?" he asked.

"Freedom of the press, hear of it?"

O'Malley shook his head. The gesture reminded me of a bird of prey tearing a gobbet of flesh from a corpse. "This is a little far from Lakeside, Maxwell—or are you doing an exposé on the city contracts to move the corpse?"

"So is the Special Paranormal Unit in charge of the investigation?"

"Did someone say there was an investigation?"

"Fifteen tons of dragon falls out of the sky. I may be slow, but that is out of the ordinary, isn't it?"

"Icky-eff, it happens all the time."

"Yeah, right." I turned to look down at what brought me here. *God, what a mess.*

"I can't see you walking the pavement unless some politician's getting his ox gored." His voice sounded distant, far away from the enormity below me.

"Morgan?" he asked.

I nodded, mute, staring.

"How is he? I heard they had to keep an eye on him."

I tried to swallow, but my throat was tight and dry. I whispered, "*Droll, O'Malley, very droll.*" I don't even know if he heard me.

The dragon did not go neatly. I had expected the body to be floating, more or less peacefully, spread-eagled in the river. That was a way too optimistic scenario. Crooked as the Cuyahoga was, it was, in retrospect, pretty damn lucky it hit the river at all.

Here, under the bridge, the river went mostly northwest for about a mile before it took a hairpin turn due west. The dragon, from the look of the wreckage, had been heading due east, and met the ground about seventy-five feet shy of the river, at the edge of a gravel-mining operation. The impact zone had just missed the loading gantries.

It was going at a shallow angle, because the body didn't go splat there and then, though there was gore on the gantries about a couple hundred feet up.

The body bounced or slid, off of the land, and tore across the cargo ship that had been anchored by the gantries. The deck buckled, machinery twisted and caved in, the great doors to the holds bent inward, everything splattered with black-red gore.

The dragon had made it almost all the way into the river. Its tail was the only thing left on the cargo ship. Muscular and black, it was caught up and twisted in a pile of wreckage on the starboard side. It looked as if some gigantic monster had taken a bite about midway down the ship, a semicircular area where the deck didn't exist anymore. It had become a satanic jungle gym of twisted girders, chain, and steel cable.

About a dozen firefighters and emergency workers were scrambling around the wreckage, and I could see four blue white sparking flares where they were cutting the tail free. Looking at the firemen, the dragon's tail was put into perspective. It was thicker than a human torso, and the part where it lay flat on the remains of the deck came up to mid-thigh on the tallest of the emergency crew.

In the river floated the rest of the body. The current was dragging the corpse north, but the tail anchored it firmly so that it pointed at an angle toward the center of the river. The wings had been shredded by impact, and were splayed out over the water like a tattered oil slick. The body seemed little more than a ragged leather sack, black mostly, but in several places there were brief glistening flashes of white where fractured bone had torn free of muscle and skin.

The neck, near a third of its length, had been twisted so far as to nearly decapitate the body. In places it was held on by strips of muscle and sinew thinner than a human arm. The head floated on its side, and it was hard to believe that the open golden eye was not looking right at me.

"The worst icky-eff since that griffin in Hunting Valley," O'Malley told me. I wondered how long it took to cultivate that blasé attitude. I couldn't manage it. I looked at O'Malley and decided that all it took was not giving a crap. "At least this time," he continued, "no one was hurt."

"Except the dragon."

O'Malley shrugged, and pulled at my shoulder. "Okay, long enough."

I resisted the pull, more out of orneriness than an actual desire to remain there to watch the carnage. "Any witnesses?"

"Witnesses?" He snorted. "Every West-Sider who was awake and outside at three-thirty in the morning. This isn't something you miss, Maxwell."

"Did anyone see what happened?"

"What happened?" O'Malley pulled me away from the guardrail and shook his head. "A dragon took a nosedive into the Flats, Sherlock. I know you aren't up on your forensic pathology from working City Hall so long, but maybe I can explain multiple blunt trauma to you as I walk you off the bridge."

I shrugged out of his grasp and kept looking over the water. There was a Coast Guard ship down there, holding position downstream from the head. Around the base of the ship the normally mud-brown waters of the river had turned a sickly rainbow-shimmered shade of black—a slick of the dragon's blood.

As I watched, a figure broke the surface near the base of the cutter. His wet suit was almost as black as the water he swam in.

Whatever they pay that guy, it isn't enough.

He gave a thumbs up to the people on the ship and a pair of winches in the back began reeling up cable. The cables slid out of

the water behind the ship, gradually growing taut between the rear
of the ship and the shoulder blades of the dragon.

"What're they doing?"

"Come on." He was more insistent, grabbing me this time.
"Nesmith is going to give a briefing. You can ask her all the questions
you want."

I kept thinking of the frogmen who had to anchor those cables.

"You've seen enough."

I pretty much had, but O'Malley was a little more agitated than
he should have been. I wondered why.

"Look, they're going to tow it to Lake Erie and sink it. The carcass
is a public health hazard. Now let's move it, Maxwell, before
I cite you for interfering with police business."

I risked on glance back at the Coast Guard ship as O'Malley led
me away. A glance whose significance flew right by me at the time.

The irony was, if I wasn't so used to the taxonomy of public officials
in Cuyahoga County, if I was anyone else—say Morgan,
who *should* have been reporting this mess—it would have hit me
immediately that Adrian Phillips was out of place on the deck of a
Coast Guard cutter dragging a corpse out of the river. Forget who,
or what, the corpse was. But whereas O'Malley had managed to
cultivate a blasé attitude about blood and carnage, the sight of major
public officials had ceased to make much impression on me unless
I was expecting some sort of wrongdoing.

To extend the irony, I was probably the only person on the staff
of the *Press* who could have identified Phillips at that distance
while he was hiding behind an elaborate gas mask.

So I glanced, noted the rotund figure of Adrian Phillips, chairman
of the Port Authority, and didn't think anything about it until
much later.

CHAPTER TWO

*O*NE *of the thirty-two dragons known to be resident in northeast Ohio died sometime between three and four in the morning today, police said. The dragon had been in flight, eastbound over downtown Cleveland, when it struck the ground on the west bank of the Flats about a quarter mile north of the Hope Memorial Bridge.*

"According to police sources, the suspected cause of death was the so-called 'Icarus Effect,' the name coined by Dr. Newman Shafran of Case Western Reserve University to describe the often fatal side effects when a magical entity strays too far from the Portal . . ."

The words glowed up from my laptop, fairly stunning in their banality.

"Icky-eff," O'Malley had said. A much more evocative term than "Icarus Effect." The latter sounded like a cheap thriller novel, the former was something you scraped off the sidewalk.

Five times I was tempted to use the cop slang, but I didn't because it seemed disrespectful—which was a damned odd reaction from someone who'd covered Cleveland City Council for nearly a decade.

Whatever name you used for it, the event described by Dr. Newman Shafran would have been catastrophic for a dragon.

I was one of about a half-dozen reporters in a small meeting room in the Justice Center, waiting for the press conference to begin. No one was making statements on-site, for the obvious reasons.

I had started my wait by trying to run off a draft of the piece on my notebook computer. When that effort stalled, I followed an impulse to start getting some background on what it was that killed the dragon. My third call directed me to Dr. Shafran, the professor who'd written the first academic paper that described what our dragon had gone through.

Shafran had been in and, to my surprise, was a source obscure enough to not yet be inundated by calls from other news agencies.

"Icarus Effect," he had repeated my words in a thick Eastern European accent. I couldn't help picturing Bela Lugosi as he talked.

"Yes, the police believe that's the cause of death."

"Interesting. So close to the source, in fact. Odd."

"Is it possible?"

The doctor chuckled and said, "Why, yes, anything is . . . *possible.*"

"Can you describe how it could happen? I thought the Portal's influence extended halfway to Canada."

"Oh, indeed, even farther. But mana, magical power you understand, it is energy—but not like light, or gravity, or any so-called force. It is a fluid. Like the air, or the sea, it seeks its own level, subject to eddies and currents."

"So how high up does it go?"

"It completely dissipates at about three miles up over the Portal itself."

"So this dragon had to be flying up pretty high, right?"

He paused. "Not necessarily."

"What do you mean?"

"As I said, the power ebbs and flows. The victim of the effect might be safely within the boundary—they *can* sense where they are, where the power is—but the power might suddenly shift, quicker than the victim can react. A point in space that was saturated with mana can abruptly become dead. Like an air bubble in the sea. Such volatility is much more likely at the edges of the Portals' influence, but is theoretically possible anywhere."

"How long would it take . . . ?"

"Before death?"

"Yes."

The picture that the doctor painted for me, in his bad Transylvanian accent, was less pretty than the scene at the river, if that was possible. Without the magical infrastructure to hold its body together, the sheer mass of the beast would tear it apart. The loss of magic would be as severe for it as the sudden loss of a skeletal system would be for a human being. Combine that with the probable speed the dragon was going when this happened— dragons have been known to break the sound barrier—and the result is akin to shooting a frozen turkey out of a cannon and into a brick wall.

"Couldn't a dragon survive that?" I had asked. "If the impact wasn't fatal?" Dragons were supposed to be able to survive lethal wounds to the brain, the heart, just about anything that didn't cause outright dismemberment.

"No," he said gravely. "The damage descends to the cellular level."

The awful smell of the corpse was because it *did* rot quickly. Unlike a normal corpse, large segments of its flesh were dead before it was. The growth of bacteria in the body was three or four times as fast as in a normal body. Instant gangrene.

Only a fraction of the corpse had rotted by the time I had arrived, but even that amounted to a half a ton of distilled putrescence to poison the air for a quarter mile in every direction.

Probably, if I was a crime reporter, covering people's dead kids for a living, I would have found the last few minutes of this dragon's life a little less affecting. But the deaths I'd covered in the last ten years were those of people's political careers, the blood largely metaphorical.

I stared at the screen on my laptop, convinced I was writing crap.

I kept thinking of the damn dragon, my hands hovering over the keyboard, unmoving. What had it been thinking? Where had it been going? Could it sense the end coming, like feeling the tidal bore before the wave crushes your body—or was it caught completely unaware? What would it be like to be stripped of your reason as the laws of nature decided to tear your body apart?

There was a chorus of chairs scraping around me. I glanced up and saw Public Safety Director Julian Nesmith walk into the room, toward the podium. Everyone was standing, and I pulled out my nondigital notebook. Most everyone here pulled out a similar pad of paper, or a palm-top organizer and a stylus. A few people pulled out digital recorders, but the printed word held the upper hand.

That was something that always struck the new people, especially in my profession. The lack of video. Even after the techies figured out how to get good quality digital imagery near the Portal, the photographic image had taken a cultural back seat in my hometown. There were only two digital cameras in evidence, in the back.

The Portal had struck a deathblow to television in northeast Ohio, which—in the chaos right after the Portal opened—was barely noticed at the time.

What the Portal does—in addition to opening the gates to another reality and giving us sprites and elves, mages and dragons—is play havoc with any recording medium. Take a pre-Portal tape recorder and try to dictate something, what will play back will sound like the taped inner monologue of a paranoid schizophrenic Tibetan monk, backward. Video, you'd get a fun-house mirror vision of hell seen by a color-blind housefly.

Luckily, digital communications had proved a little less susceptible to the interference. Even when the phone lines seemed to only produce garbled static, anyone with an ISDN line had been able to—at least half the time—get on the Internet. This apparently had to do with redundancy and error-checking. What it meant in practical terms was that now every electronic communication device anywhere near the Portal had to carry at least three computer processors to transmit multiple signals that could be combined at the other end to filter out the garbage. It also meant that video monitors had to be high definition flatscreen LCDs, audio recordings had to be on CD or silicon, the hard drive on my laptop had to have five times the space to store enough copies of my data so I could be certain to get it back along with a custom operating system with three-way redundant check sums that could weed out ghost data on the fly.

Bottom line, consumer electronics in this town were specialized and *very* expensive.

But Cleveland now has more local dailies than New York City, so I guess it's a blessing.

Because of that, Julian Nesmith was one of a select few American public officials who didn't have to stare into klieg lights and flashbulbs when she gave a press conference. She was also one of the few American public officials who would never need a microphone. An even five feet of pure adrenaline, she had one of those personalities that tore into a room like a rototiller into a vat of Jell-O.

"I have a short statement, after which I'll take a few questions." She looked at the clock on the wall, hands gripping the sides of the podium. She was perched on a step stool that was invisible behind the podium, and the posture that resulted reminded me of an old revival preacher haranguing us sinners. "We'll try to get this wrapped up by twelve." I had no doubt, with Nesmith leading the proceedings, that by twelve-oh-one this room would be empty.

"Between three-twenty and three-twenty-five this morning, several people in the Flats and surrounding areas reported seeing a dragon in an uncontrolled dive, heading for the Cuyahoga River. It struck a cargo ship, the *Huron Star*, that was anchored for loading at a facility on the west bank of the Cuyahoga River.

"A forensic examination of the body began at five this morning, concluding fifteen minutes ago. The examination was supervised by Cuyahoga County Coroner Egil Nixon. Copies of the findings will be passed out at the conclusion of this press conference. To summarize the findings; the dragon has been identified as Aloeus, resident of 1000 Euclid Avenue."

There was an uncharacteristic wave of muttering, interrupting Director Nesmith. There were a few shouts, premature questions that were ignored. She waited patiently for the room to calm down.

Aloeus was the first dragon—one of the first *anything* to come through to our side of the Portal.

When the room calmed down, she continued. "Death came prior to impact due to multiple trauma caused by leaving the immediate influence of the Portal. In the opinion of Coroner Nixon, it is death by misadventure."

There was more commotion this time, but the director talked through it. "Because the body represents a present threat to public health and safety, I have authorized its disposal. The Coast Guard is currently towing the body a safe distance out into Lake Erie where it will be chemically treated and burned. I have five minutes to take questions."

A sandy-haired kid, half my age, from the *Plain Dealer* asked, "Have there been any estimates of the amount of damage?"

Cut right to the chase, kid.

"Approximately two hundred thousand—"

My cell phone started vibrating at me. I had forgotten to turn it off. It was absolutely the wrong time, but I'm one of those guys who can't stand to let a phone keep ringing. I flipped it open one-handed and whispered harshly, "This better be good."

There was a whistle of static on the line. Piercing, like trying to talk to a fax machine. There was a chorus of voices beneath it, mumbling, whispering. It was the common static from the Portal, but it felt sinister, and it didn't go away the way it usually does when the phone finally deciphers the real signal.

When sense wasn't immediately forthcoming, I closed it.

". . . don't know as of yet. I'll direct you to the SPU liaison for that question." O'Malley's Special Paranormal Unit again. It was virtually an autonomous district within the Police Department, one of several outstanding gripes the Police Department had with City Hall. Hearing the initials made me severely pissed off that I'd missed the question.

"Madam Director," an older guy, from the *Leader*, was asking this one. "Don't you have any reservations about the method used to dispose of—"

My phone buzzed again.

I pulled it out. "Goddamn it." I kept my voice to a whisper, but some of my fellow pillars of the fourth estate turned to look in my direction.

It didn't surprise me this time when my ear was met with a piercing whine and the subliminal muttering. This time, a voice made itself heard over the babble.

"Is this a dagger I see before me?" The voice's tone and pitch warbled like an old cassette tape that kept sticking.

"What?" I whispered at it.

"The handle toward my hand?" The keening background noise increased, and the voice itself stretched toward breaking. *"Come, let me clutch thee—"*

The voice, and the other noises abruptly cut off. A few seconds of clicking, then a dial tone. The caller ID on my phone was no help, the anonymous thespian had his number blocked.

Great, someone with an unlisted number is phoning in Shakespearean quotes to me.

This time I turned the phone off.

CHAPTER THREE

*T*HE dragon Aloeus, first of his kind to reside here, has also been the first of his kind to die here. Shortly before four this morning, Aloeus plunged to his death on the shore of the Cuyahoga River. This afternoon his body was towed out to the open water and burned."

"The Cuyahoga County coroner issued a statement ruling Aloeus' death accidental, 'death by misadventure.' A victim of the 'Icarus Effect.' Dr. Newman Shafran of Case Western Reserve University, the person who first described it, explains the effect as follows . . ."

I liked this better.

With a first draft safely wired to the *Press* server, I was the last to leave the Justice Center. Most of my colleagues were off, some on what would be fruitless attempts to get comments from other dragons, others to comb the West Side of Cleveland in search of a witness or a dozen, others to pull the chains of whatever personal contacts they had in the city government.

I didn't mind being the last out. I had been doing this for way too long to engage in a panicked rush to be the "first" to get something. Instead, I had written out a first draft of the feature once I'd gotten enough material to write one. Without the deadline pressure looming as large, I was free to ponder how I was going to attack this story.

I left the Justice Center by the Lakeside exit. Across the street, beyond the park flanking City Hall and past the twenty-foot wall surrounding the old Browns Stadium, I could see the lake. In the distance, I could make out a pillar of oily black smoke on the horizon.

We sent a dragon to Valhalla today . . .

I watched the smoke for a moment. I knew I wanted to write about Aloeus. Not just the carnage in the Flats. Everyone would rehash that. I wanted to get a sense of who it was that died this morning.

I caught a whiff of ozone and heard thunder rumbling from the permanent cloud formations above the stadium. I looked up at the swirling vortex, and saw a pillar of black clouds stacked above the site of the Portal. I could see lightning flashes break across the slowly rotating mass. Except for the smoke on the horizon, the sky was otherwise a cloudless blue.

The strange weather here was not actually due to some magical aura cast by the Portal. It was plain old meteorology. The Portal didn't just let in dragons and elves and magic and such, it also let in—and out—very large volumes of air. The difference in air pressure, temperature, and humidity between the two sides of the Portal had created a standing weather front on both sides. There was always some sort of atmospheric effect marking the site of the Portal.

A few drops of moisture hit my face as the clouds above the stadium began a downpour. I was far enough away to avoid getting drenched, but it was disconcerting to watch the gray sheet of rain sluice off the stadium not half a mile from me.

Rainbows unfolded over the lake as the sun shone through the localized storm.

I looked at the stadium, really *looked* at it for the first time in a while. Where Aloeus had come from, the Portal, and the world beyond it.

I had been one of a select group who were able to see the Portal without either paying to reach it or being paid to guard it. A friend at WKYC—yes, I was a local TV news whore at one time—had to attend a funeral and had given me his season tickets for the game. I had gone to see a division championship battle. Instead, I had gotten the show of the millennium.

It had been a few months shy of ten years ago, when I had seen it open—twenty feet above the Pittsburgh thirty-five yard line. Halftime, tied game, and I don't think anyone really remembers that the Steelers went on to win the division when they played the second half at Three Rivers.

It sort of grew out of a point in the air, swelling until it sliced into the turf. It still gives me chills the way the silence in the stands grew with the sphere. It can be really scary when thousands of people are being really quiet.

The Portal was a mirrored sphere about fifty feet in diameter, rippling with rainbow shimmers of color. Mirror, but not quite a mirror, since the reflection on the sphere wasn't of the surrounding stadium, but a coliseum of a much more ancient vintage. Within moments we could all feel a breeze from it carrying the smell of damp mulch and swamp gas. Probably from the reflected coliseum which seemed to have been overtaken by wetlands and reeds.

The PA system whined, broadcasting whispered muttering. TV monitors across the stadium, and beyond, began showing strange ghost images, as if Salvador Dalí and Hieronymus Bosch had collaborated to make a Philip Glass music video.

The cameramen were the first to approach it, hopelessly trying to get the image on tape.

Then they came.

A small band of folks in ragged garb first appeared in distorted reflection on one side of the mirror, growing closer until they slipped through the surface. If you tried, you could pretend this quartet of guys were funky-looking humans. But, I think to the last of us, we knew. These folks weren't from around here.

They were all tall, six feet to a man, and had hair that didn't look quite right. The shade was off, and the way it grew around the skull followed subtle curves that didn't belong to a human face. Their ears were long and pointed, eyes narrow, chin long. Three of them had a bluish cast to their skin, one was a fire-engine red that would put Chief Wahoo to shame, and the last one was black—and not the black we mean when talking about human skin color, but black, like a shadow on the brightest day.

Elves. Fugitives from a kingdom on the other side of the Portal. A regime that must have been a true horror when you consider five guys from a feudal agrarian society—magic or not—walking into a Browns game . . .

Let's just say that they must have burned all their bridges before being prodded by microphone-wielding sportscasters and being surrounded by three-hundred-pound guys in dog masks started looking attractive.

It took about ten hours to clear the stadium. The police were the first to set up a perimeter around the field. Then around the stadium. In forty-eight hours, when some of the nasty things—and Aloeus would have been classed in that group at the time—started coming through, the perimeter became the province of the National Guard.

The next twelve months were pretty rough. No TV at all, radio intermittent enough to be almost useless. Only completely digital communications worked, and those became less than reliable. Computers would work for a time, but were subject to massive random failures. Everything was pretty damn chaotic.

The Feds tried to step in, and that gave Mayor Rayburn his moment of glory. The common legend is that Cleveland's mayor saw what the Portal meant, not just in relation to the short-term chaos it was causing, but in what it could mean for the area, long-term. Not that many appreciated it at the time.

When FEMA was all set to come in, declaring northeast Ohio a disaster area, Mayor Rayburn drew a line in the sand, saying, "This far, no farther." The nation was appalled that the city would stop federal aid at the city limits, but his explanation was terse, "I will not have this natural resource nationalized through the back door."

The President scoffed at the accusation, but subsequent efforts to claim the Portal through everything from the Defense Department to the National Parks Service showed that Rayburn was prescient. While the legal battles between city and federal government rolled up toward the Supreme Court, Congress made the point moot. The federal legislators—a majority of whom belonged to a party that wasn't the President's, and made much political hay over limiting the interference of the federal government in people's lives—saw a grand opportunity to thumb their nose at their least favorite executive without damaging their own power base. They sent up a veto-proof bill that granted the Portal exclusively to Cuyahoga County.

It was later uncovered that, during this whole time, Mayor Rayburn had established several unilateral trade agreements across the Portal that rendered FEMA assistance unnecessary.

Once Cleveland got out of that first year, Rayburn's decision began paying off. Once city and social functions resumed some sort of normalcy, the Portal began to grow us its first cash crop. Tourism. Nearly two million people the first year. All to see a place where things now existed that were never seen outside a Tolkien novel or a Grimm fairy tale. The money that came in the second year undid the damage of the first. The year after *that* helped undo the last quarter century of urban neglect. The year after that, and the census found that for the first time since the seventies, the city's population was growing. There were people who moved here simply because a herd of unicorns had taken up residence in Hunting Valley.

Magery itself became a major industry. The powers wrapping northeast Ohio could be used to do many things that couldn't be done elsewhere, everything from removing an inoperable brain tumor to giving you a whole-body makeover that could go as far as gender and species.

Last, but not least, the Portal itself was the ultimate money-maker. How much would you pay for a chance to start over on another world, one with completely different rules? A lot of people would pay considerably, and the city charged what the market would bear—slightly less than a passenger ticket on the space shuttle.

Over the course of a decade, the home of the Portal had grown more and more secure. Where the stadium was once surrounded by barbed wire and AA batteries, it was now contained within a forty-foot-tall brick wall that tried to look vaguely like a castle. The anti-aircraft batteries now stood in handsome cylindrical towers where people could ignore them if they wanted to. Not a hint of razor wire.

And every week a bus would pull into the stadium, drop off our émigrés and pick up the Portal's latest refugees.

Above, the sky was always swirling and black. Marking the place where our world ends, and another one begins. A connection between here and there. An unexplained freak of (super)nature that had become the backbone of this city's economy. And the fact that no one really could explain it, mages and scientists alike, meant that everyone here was living on borrowed time.

The door opening was chaotic enough. Something about Aloeus' death made me wonder what would happen if the door ever shut?

CHAPTER FOUR

I DECIDED that, if I was going to focus on the dragon himself, I needed to start with the dragon. I headed my Volkswagen up Euclid to see the legal residence of the late dragon Aloeus.

1000 Euclid. The address had sounded familiar, but it wasn't until I reached the light at East Ninth that I realized why.

The intersection of Euclid and East Ninth has been a financial nexus since the 1900s. The Huntington Bank Building lorded over the northeast corner, a massive gray stone pile over a century old. Across from it on Ninth was the characterless white facade of National City Bank, an architectural cipher perpetrated in the nineteen-sixties. Across Euclid from the blank whiteness of National City Bank was the brand new corporate headquarters of First Cleveland Savings and Loan.

1000 Euclid was on the southeast corner, the old Cleveland Trust Building. *Aloeus lived here?* I thought as I pulled up half a block to a parking lot.

The Cleveland Trust Building had been empty for a few decades before the Portal opened, ever since Cleveland Trust and its conglomerate successors merged into nothingness. Apparently, sometime in the last ten years, it had found a new occupant.

I felt a little chill. For many people, this kind of revelation would just wash over them. Not knowing that the Cleveland Trust Building was occupied? Why should they know?

I should know. That was my job. This building wasn't just some random empty real estate. Cleveland Trust was an inexorable part of the city's history. It was thanks to that particular bank that the city went into default in the nineteen-seventies, and since the building had been vacated, it had been owned by a succession of movers and shakers. Racking my brain, I think the last time I heard about who owned the building it had been bought by Forest Hills

Enterprises, Leo Baldassare's development company, maybe a year or two before the Portal opened.

In retrospect, it was interesting how the building never appeared to have been taken up in the economic boom that had gripped the rest of downtown. I wondered if Baldassare still owned the building.

Unlike its neighbors, the Cleveland Trust Building wasn't a high-rise, though it dominated the intersection. It was four stories of domed neoclassicism, someone's platonic ideal of a bank.

Looking at it, it still seemed empty to me. But examining it made me realize that the windows were tinted black, so there was no real way to tell if anyone was home. I wondered if a dragon ever resided there, or if the address was just a front. It was common enough for people involved in the higher levels of this city to rent properties just to have a legal address. I still remember the bad old days when Council members would have one address in their ward, and another one as far as their school district was concerned.

While I watched from the parking lot, I saw two or three people walk up and try the doors. Fellow members of the journalistic community. I saw about a dozen guys hovering about the building. No luck, apparently.

I stepped out of the Volkswagen and into the humid August air. I'd decided to give my obligatory fifteen minutes to this angle before I went somewhere else to ferret out Aloeus' history.

I crossed Ninth and headed toward the steps in front of the central set of massive entry doors. One of the people milling around called out to me, "Ain't no use, no one's answering."

I turned around and saw the sandy-haired kid from the *Plain Dealer*, the one who'd asked about property damage. He was shaking his head. "Typical. They only speak through their lawyers, and the lawyers don't speak."

I nodded and continued up to the doors. They were solid metal, decorated with embossed scrollwork, but no windows. I stood there a few moments wondering exactly what it was I was going to do. Knock? While I stood there, pondering the lack of a doorbell, intercom, or even a knocker, I heard a skittering noise above me.

I looked up and saw a leathery gargoyle wing flash from up on the roof. I was at the wrong angle to see what it was, so I backed up a few steps to get a better look at it. Before I could tell what it was, a voice called my attention back to street level.

"You're Kline Maxwell, aren't you?"

I turned around to face the kid again. "Yeah."

"You used to be big, didn't you?"

To hell with you, too, kid. "I suppose you could say that."

He held out his hand, "I admired your work all through college."

I pondered snubbing the brat, but I was slightly more professional than that. I took his hand and shook it quickly, once. "And you are?"

"Sam Barlogh. So is there some sort of political angle to the dragon's swan dive?"

I looked over my shoulder, up at the roof of the building. Whatever had been there was gone now. "There's a political angle to everything."

"What're you looking at?"

I turned back to face him. "Nothing."

"But—" I was saved from further conversation by a black Caddy limo pulling up to the curb. My comrades, Sam Barlogh included, converged on the vehicle as the rear passenger door opened.

The nexus of the attention was an older gentleman—white hair, clean-shaven, narrow glasses with gold rims, charcoal-gray suit with black armband. He had one of those expressions that made you think the owner went through life smelling something unpleasant. He pushed his way through the reporters without looking at them or speaking. He headed directly toward the Cleveland Trust Building, and the doors opened for him before he reached them.

I didn't bother trying to crack that particular nut. Instead, I looked at the limo, which everyone was ignoring. It pulled away, and I caught sight of its license plates.

"FOREST 1"

The windows were tinted, but I wanted very much to see if there had been another passenger.

After striking out at Aloeus' home base, I had done the rounds of the obvious interviews. Eyewitnesses, public servants, including an eerie conversation with one of the divers who'd chained the body to the Coast Guard cutter. The only obvious person I couldn't get hold of was Egil Nixon, the County Coroner, just voice mail saying he was out of the office. Didn't matter all that much, I had his write-up on the dragon.

At this point, late in the afternoon, my story had gone through another three drafts, and I was sequestered in the periodical department at the Main Cleveland Public Library. It was a quiet place where the computers outnumbered people. There were still microfilm stacks, which held everything up until the turn of the century, but everything recent was in a computerized database. Local conditions made digital archiving a necessity. It also made a researcher's job easier. With the combination of OCR software that could "read" just about any type of printed text, and search algorithms pioneered for the Internet, the user could parse millions of scanned pages with any keyword—not just a list of subjects that some database programmer thought was important.

Which worked well for me.

Aloeus, like the rest of his kin, avoided the press. There wasn't much about *him* in the archives. I did find one article, however, that had him involved in a strange "welcoming" ceremony with Mayor Rayburn in the first few months after the Portal's opening. This dragon was the first paranormal critter to meet with anyone in an official capacity. It was also shortly after this meeting that the city set in motion the legal mechanisms to recognize the nonhuman creatures coming through the Portal as beings with rights. That movement reached up as far as the state level so, currently, the United States—for the first time since the Civil War—had states that disagreed on the legal definition of a human being.

Aloeus met with people on several levels: city, county, state; judicial and legislature; public sector and private. Rarely did his name dominate the stories. It was always this particular official enacting some initiative, and the dragon's name would be mentioned in passing. Discussions were talked about, but rarely the contents of those discussions.

I had *written* some of these stories.

Very, very good at keeping a low profile. The perception from the articles was that his involvement was slight, almost beneath mention. The volume of text belied that. I tried to remember some of my own thoughts about some of these stories. To my embarrassment, I couldn't focus on any thoughts about Aloeus' involvement. The emphasis was always on what the *humans* were doing, what the government and the people in it were doing. Which Councilmen were winning, which were losing, what city departments were going to get money, which will lose funds. . . .

Did I ever once wonder about what these "paranormal citizens" did, or thought?

Only insofar as it became grist for the political mill on Lakeside.

I didn't like where the self-examination was going, so I buckled down and tried to find a connection between Aloeus and Forest Hills Enterprises.

Jackpot.

The thing about the legal status of dragons is that they only had rights as individuals within the state of Ohio. While other states had to recognize some aspects of that legal truth—contracts binding in Ohio were binding in California and so on—that didn't mean, for instance, that Aloeus had property rights in Nevada. Aloeus couldn't sign a contract drafted under the rules of any other state. He couldn't have personal assets in an out-of-state bank.

Since dragons liked to accumulate wealth, that was a bit of a handicap, even if they couldn't physically visit the places whose laws didn't recognize them.

The solution was to incorporate. A dragon, or any creature recognized as having legal rights under Ohio law, could form a corporation under Ohio state law and that corporation would exist under the laws of every state as well as those of the federal government. The corporation would have more rights than the person who owned it.

Dragons pioneered this technique to sidestep the nation's refusal to deal with them as people. Aloeus, Inc., was formed twenty-four hours after the governor signed the law granting Aloeus the right to own property.

And Aloeus, Inc., had a lot of real estate.

All of it seemed to have been bought through, or from, Forest Hills Enterprises. Besides the Cleveland Trust Building, there were properties dotting the city, and several thousand undeveloped acres in—of all places—Mexico. Leo Baldassare was making a lot of money off of Aloeus Inc.

I decided that I was going to have a talk with Baldassare about a dragon.

CHAPTER FIVE

L EONARDO Baldassare and I knew each other. He had been a high-level unnamed source for a number of my stories in the past. I was one of a select few who had his personal cell phone number, a privilege I never abused. Baldassare was much too valuable a resource for me, and he was very much aware of it.

In general, he was willing to talk to me for the usual reason: to stir the pot of his political enemies, and sometimes his allies. In return for allowing myself to be fed those stories, he would occasionally allow me to probe issues that were on my own agenda.

He once told me, "I talk to you for two reasons. One: I never saw you print anything that wasn't true. Two: you've never used my own words against me." The former was good journalistic practice. Always confirm your facts. The latter was due to the fact that Baldassare was too smart to hand over ammunition to a reporter. A fact that made him twice as smart as any politician that has served in this town in the last twenty years—except his political ally, Mayor Rayburn.

I think the real reason he was willing to talk to me was because I never quoted him, even as an unnamed source. Any information I got from him I confirmed from a couple of other sources before it went into print. Kept us both honest.

So I wasn't completely surprised when I called him for a comment and he invited me to his estate for a private chat. I made it down to Hunting Valley at a little after six in the afternoon.

Hunting Valley is an enclave of the landed rich. Unlike the golf-course developments that have multimillion dollar homes ready-furnished for the latest executive VP import, there's a sense of permanence to the estates here. The residents have an unbeatable combination of wealth and a desire to keep things as they are. We're talking a suburb so rich that it doesn't need to collect property taxes. A suburb where the city itself buys up property to keep it from the developers—though anyone coming to the city asking for commercial development, or even a multifamily zoning variance, would be laughed out of City Hall.

There are roads in Hunting Valley where you can drive for a few miles without seeing a single house.

The Baldassare estate was true to that model. It lived out of sight behind a split-rail fence, a row of pine trees, and about two dozen acres of horse pasture. The only indication of who lived here was a small wooden sign that said Long-Run Farms. Below that, it bore the ubiquitous Hunting Valley icon of the foxhunter in mid jump.

There wasn't a gate, or even a sign warning off trespassers. The only sign of how high class this place was, was the fact that the road wasn't gravel or asphalt, but cobblestone.

I turned down the driveway and followed it past the stand of pines. The split-rail fence paced me on both sides. A pair of horses stood off in the distance, watching me with bored curiosity from the center of the pasture. I lost sight of them when I rounded the trees.

The impact of the estate sort of sneaks up on you. When you reach the trees, you have a disarmingly bucolic setting. Then you enter the woods and drive about fifteen seconds, and suddenly the realization strikes you. This is *all* one estate. A single man owns *all* this. Then you reach the second gate.

This is the point where you realize that this guy is a billionaire.

The wall was about eight feet high, built out of stone carved and beveled like a jigsaw puzzle. The gate was wrought iron with twisted gargoyle shapes. Imbedded in the lattice of the gate itself were about a dozen semiprecious stones the size of my fist. The stones glowed faintly red in the evening light. The wards didn't need such a visual display; the glow was there to let you know that the wards existed.

As my Volkswagen approached, the gates opened inward. The benefit of being expected.

I followed the road. I emerged from the woods and followed the driveway down one side of a reflecting pool larger than my condo. I pulled to a stop outside Baldassare's house.

I was looking at concentrated personal wealth, distilled and molded into a Tudor mansion that covered more square footage than the field in Baldassare's stadium.

Somewhat incongruously, I saw Baldassare on his flagstone patio, waving from over a barbecue grill. I waved back to acknowledge him and stepped out of the car. The evening air was pleasantly cool, and the wind was blowing the odor of mesquite toward me.

Baldassare wasn't as big as his name. He was a head shorter than I was, and about fifty pounds lighter. At first glance he looked like one of those background guys that disappear through life. Then you made eye contact with him, and something about that impression changed. You had just started sizing him up when you realized he had already sized you up, decided what you wanted, what he was going to give you, and what you were going to pay for it.

"How are you doing, Kline?" he said, smiling at me. He presented the kind of aura of easy camaraderie that was unsuccessfully aped by most politicians and used car salesman.

I shrugged. "Same old, same old."

"That isn't quite true." He flipped a steak on the grill. The steak was an inch-thick porterhouse, and the grill was a cavernous stainless-steel barbecue that probably cost more than my Volkswagen. "It seems you're taking a step or two off the political beat."

"Yes and no."

He turned and pointed a two-foot-long barbecue fork toward a bar on the far side of the patio. "Feel free to grab a drink."

"Thanks." I walked over to the bar and poured myself a seltzer water. "I appreciate you seeing me."

"I was interested in where your questions were going." He tonged a steak out of the grill. "You want one? I got four going."

I shook my head and didn't ask why he was cooking four porterhouse steaks at one time. From what I could tell, we were the only ones here. He must have seen the question in my eyes, because he said. "Clara's off doing some charity thing in California, and I only get one night off a week to cook." He looked at the meat and said, "I know it's a sin to microwave steaks, but if I vacuum-pack these babies right after I grill them—and don't freeze them, God forbid anyone freezes them—got dinner for the rest of the week."

I nodded and sipped my soda water. I felt a little nervous. Baldassare was not just any source. I'd been cultivating him since Rayburn's first mayoral campaign. He was invaluable as long as I didn't alienate him.

"So, to what do we owe your change in the subject matter?"

"Maybe you heard about what happened to Morgan?"

A small grin crossed his face. "I hear he was a sight—so *you* got his beat?"

I shook my head. "No, just the dragon. Which isn't far outside my bailiwick, after all."

He raised his tongs. "Hold that thought." He proceeded to pile four medium rare steaks on a platter. "I'll just be a moment."

Baldassare walked toward the French doors that opened onto the patio with his pile of steaks. He bore a brief resemblance to a server in one of those old-world Little Italy restaurants. He left me outside to sip my drink.

He came back without any steaks. When he saw me looking at him, he wiped his hands on his apron and said, "Oh, I'd already eaten." He shut down the grill and shed the apron on the back of a wrought iron chair. He walked over and fixed himself a drink. "So, Kline, since when did dead dragons become political?"

"Since the dragon was political."

"A little outside the City Hall beat, isn't it?"

"A little," I agreed. "You knew him."

"The dragon?" For a few long moments he looked introspective as he sipped an unstirred vodka martini. "No, I didn't know Aloeus."

I arched my eyebrow enough so he'd know that I knew of his business relationship with Aloeus.

He acknowledged me with a shake of the head. "I'm not saying I didn't meet him, negotiate with him, do business with him, even. But I never *knew* him." He gave me a half smile, and I knew that he was having a chuckle at my expense. At how transparent I was and how easily he faked me out.

He gestured toward a pair of wrought iron chairs that flanked a mosaic table. The motif on the table was a reproduction of some ancient Greek artwork, a serpentine monster that undulated endless coils around a naked human figure armed only with a sword. "Have a seat."

I took the chair, and he settled in next to me. Seated, we both looked out from the patio toward a rolling hillside that ended in the Chagrin River.

"Kline, take out your notebook. For once, what I'm telling you is on the record."

"You see that hill over there? That's where we met the first time. I still don't know exactly how he found me, or how he knew who I was.

"I was coming out to the barbecue, just like you saw me. I dropped fifteen pounds of baby back ribs into the dirt when I saw him. It was just the start of an early spring, about two months after the thing opened. You know what it was like then? Yeah. It wasn't much better for me. I mean, of all the ways to lose the season. The

National Guard was parked on my stadium, and it looked like the Feds were about to steamroller through everything.

"And I walked outside and there's this lizard as big as my house sitting on the lawn and looking at me—he looked at me like my wife's cat looks at me. Head cocked to one side. And that neck—he was looking *down* on the roof. How he managed not to be seen for two months, I don't know. I suppose there was some sort of magic involved.

"What he looked like? I keep thinking of my wife's cat, this arrogant Siamese with a shitty attitude. Not that he looked anything like a cat; he didn't, but it was the body language, the way he sat and looked at you.

"Black skin, muscles rippling like a thoroughbred, head almost birdlike. He blinked slowly, like he had all the time in the world.

"His tail dragged in the water, and when he lowered his head toward me, I could feel his breath on my face. Smelled like flowers and brimstone, sort of a perfumed sulfur.

"I won't lie. I nearly crapped my pants. I thought I was going to die there and then.

"Then it opened its mouth.

"*'Mr. Baldassare, we have to talk.'*

"Now the last thing I expected from this thing was for it to talk to me. This was something out of a monster movie—supposed to eat people, not talk to them. And the voice. If James Earl Jones was a nine-hundred-foot-tall pope, he could sound like that if he was really pissed.

"Despite that, I managed to ask it how it knew me.

"*'I know many things.'*

"This was one of those moments where everything just sort of clicks. For me, this was the point when I personally realized that everything had changed forever. I backed up and sat down in the chair you're sitting in now.

"*'You know me,'* I told it. 'I don't know you.' That's one of the first rules of negotiation, never let the other side realize you're scared and intimidated. Especially if you *are* scared and intimidated.

"*'Call me Aloeus. I am the first of my kind to transit this realm.'*

"*'What do you want?'* I was doing my damnedest to stay calm with this thing's breath smelling of wet sulfur and wearing a lizard grin that had incisors the size of Mike Tyson's biceps. It wasn't easy. But I kept thinking, I've talked turkey with folks in

Youngstown who'd kill me as easy as this thing, and probably in more creative ways.

"*'You know the ruler here, the local baron?'*

"It took me a moment to get it. 'Dave Rayburn?'

"*'Dave Rayburn.'*

"'Yes, I know him. I helped get him elected. He's the *mayor*, though, not a baron—he doesn't even have any jurisdiction here—' I waved at the hills and the Chagrin River over there. 'His authority stops at Cleveland's border.'

"*'I have known mayors. His rule extends beyond that title.'*

"I didn't correct him. States of emergency do tend to amplify executive power. But, Dave had only been in office half a term, and while the Portal business solidified his support in the city initially, that was a short honeymoon. Right at that moment, Dave was probably at his lowest ebb, fighting the Feds, the state, the Council. He wanted to hold the Portal, but he was only inches from caving. I was *not* telling the dragon that. I was hoping he knew something I didn't.

"In retrospect, he did.

"I asked, 'What do you want with the mayor?'

"*'We need to discuss his future, and ours.'*

"I won't bore you with the details, but we talked through the night. He told me what the Portal could mean to both our peoples.

"What did it mean? Well, to Aloeus and his kind—and I mean kind to include the elves, griffins, unicorns—it was an escape from the tyranny of Ragnan, the realm on the other side of the Portal. To us, it was a window to possibilities that we couldn't have dreamed of before. At that point we were still dealing with the negative side effects of the Portal—Aloeus wanted to be sure we saw the positive ones.

"Yes, and he wanted the Portal to remain under local control.

"When dawn broke he said, *'Go now, bring him here.'*

"I tried to tell him that there was an emergency going on here, and pulling the city's mayor out to the suburbs might not be that easy.

"Aloeus held out a clawed fist in front of me. His hands seemed tiny in proportion to his body, but that fist was still the size of my head. He opened it, and laying in his hand was a loop of solid gold chain. *'Take this to him. He will come.'*

"I picked it up, and it was warm to the touch. At the time I thought it was from being held, but now I'm pretty sure it was the heat of some sort of enchantment. I took it as a good faith offering.

"Of course, when I managed to corner Dave in the HQ they'd set up at the Justice Center, he looked at me as if I were nuts. There were a few moments that morning when I was convinced that we'd finally parted company.

"Then I gave him the chain, which was still warm.

"I told you about the moment when everything clicks? I think that was the point where Dave had his click. He handled that chain for a few moments, and he must have felt something I couldn't, because right then was when he told the U.S. Army to go to hell.

"That had been the decision he'd been struggling with the past week or so. The federal government was moving into position to cap this Portal thing; they were just waiting for the mayor. He handled the chain, looked out the window at the stadium, and called in his aides.

"He gave them the first notice that David Rayburn wasn't going to play ball. Instead, he told them to request the governor to send in every available National Guard unit to, in his words, 'help hold the city.' It was as much to hold it against the Army, as the Portal.

"That evening, a motorcade came down here. We had Dave, about six police cars, and two Hummers carrying National Guardsmen. Dave didn't talk on the way out here, he just kept staring out the window and fondling that chain. He was looking out at what had happened to the city already. Even on the outbound Shoreway, you could see the damage. Boarded-up storefronts, boarded-up *banks*. National Guard on patrol through the streets of Cleveland—and once we crossed the border we saw some of the Army units, tanks and all.

"When we left 271, we passed through three blackout zones.

"I know he was thinking about the city. At that point I don't think he was sure that keeping the Feds out was the right thing. You must remember what it was like the first two months. Everyone—I mean *everyone*—was calling for Dave's head. The President was calling him an insane autocrat for trying to retain control of the Portal. I mean, in the third week of the crisis, Dave had to go as far as to get a federal judge to issue a restraining order to keep the Army from taking over.

"For two months he had been resisting. And it looked, then, like he had committed political suicide. I was close to the only ally he had left—and frankly that was because I had some vested interest in keeping the Feds from taking over the stadium. It was getting to the point where I felt that we were going to need to let the Feds in just to get the city under control. I mean, it wasn't money anymore, it was getting to be things like food—

"Yeah? I know about those rumors. I'm not going to venture an opinion. I have no direct knowledge that the Army was blocking aid into the city to put pressure on Dave. I know that shipments were making it into the suburbs, but not over the border. That could just as well have been the jurisdictional chaos the Army blamed it on. The Senate hearings found no wrongdoing, so I'm not going out on a limb to say there was any.

"Anyway, what I was saying was that Dave was taking a hell of an unpopular position at that point. People were starting to go hungry, and it was *his* fault. No one saw the Portal as anything other than a bizarre natural disaster. The federal government wanted to take it over, and he was the only one who saw any reason not to let them.

"Aloeus had stayed, as promised, and when the motorcade rounded the driveway, I was worried that the Guard, or the police escort, would start shooting. This huge lizard hadn't become any less intimidating while I'd been gone. Fortunately, Aloeus didn't make any sudden moves, and I doubt he considered the threat from the Guardsmen or the police as significant. Or, more likely, considering where he came from, he considered it only appropriate that the local baron have an honor guard.

"The security people didn't want Dave to leave the car, but Dave shook them off. I moved to accompany him, and he just shook his head. 'No, Leo. Just me.' The first words he'd spoken to me since we started down here.

"I didn't hear what they talked about. But it took longer than my talk with the dragon. Dave, to his credit, didn't appear intimidated by the fact that he was talking to a hundred-foot lizard with a set of jaws that could bite him in half at the waist. He paced. He waved his arms. He shouted. Just like he talks to the Council.

"No, I never got to know exactly what they talked about. But I do know he asked what the chain meant. I saw him hold it up, and I could read the question on his lips. I only heard a fragment of an answer, " '. . . *a sign of what is at stake . . .*'

"After that, Dave ordered the escort back, and after about a fifteen-minute argument with the ranking cop and the ranking Guardsman, we all pulled back out of earshot.

"It was hard to believe that Aloeus could whisper.

"Yes, it did influence Dave's stand against the Feds. It seemed to solidify his initial instincts. Of course, it didn't help his standing with anyone when the rumors started that he was talking to something that'd come out of the Portal. I mean the *elves* were still sitting in a tent city, behind a razor wire wall at Burke Lakefront.

"If Valdis, Ragnan's reigning god-king hadn't fallen about four months into it, Dave wouldn't have survived. Council was already getting together the legal machinery to remove him, and the courts looked like they were beginning to lean against him. The deal he struck with Zygmund, the rebel overlord who'd defeated Valdis, was nothing less than a political miracle.

"When food started coming out of the Portal, all of Dave's enemies were struck dumb for about a month. You know that Dave made damn sure that everyone knew that it was him, his administration, that was bringing the food in. That was when the tide turned. Especially when, after it was obvious that no *aid* was necessary, the federal government started its other moves to take over the Portal.

"It was almost two years through the appeals, and the court orders. It was scheduled before the Supreme Court before the Congress decided to decide the issue for everyone. By Dave's re-election campaign, he was a hero. The man who stood up to the Feds.

"I know, we're talking about Aloeus. I didn't have much personal contact with him after those initial meetings. I was just a middleman. I know that he was active in helping the administration draft legislation to deal with our new paranormal citizenry. The kind of thing that allowed some rights to these critters, at least on the local level.

"The deal with the stadium? That was just an arrangement to compensate me for the rights I—and the Browns franchise—had to give up so that the city could administer the Portal. I know, the city does *own* the property, but there was a twenty-five-year lease that both I and the city were obligated to. The fees I get from the stadium are simply compensation for the city breaking the lease.

"No, I don't think Aloeus had anything to do with that deal."

CHAPTER SIX

AFTER Baldassare finished his story, we both sat for a few long moments of silence. While the story itself was good background, it omitted more recent history, specifically Forest Hills and property deals. I knew the omission was intentional, Baldassare was more than adept enough to know why I was here. Either he didn't want to talk about it, or he wanted me to ask.

"I have a few other questions," I said quietly.

"I was sure you would," he said, smiling.

It was a chess game now. Baldassare had stopped volunteering information. He wanted me to probe. That way, he would get a measure of exactly what I did and didn't know. Which meant that, if I asked the wrong questions, in the wrong order, he would blithely allow me to stumble down the wrong path.

I bore him no malice for that; it was part of the game, after all. He treated prosecuting attorneys and Council committees no differently.

"You said you did business with him?" I opened.

"To be precise," he said with a bit of a grin, "I said I didn't *deny* doing business with him."

"But you did."

"His company, yes. I presume you knew that."

"What kind of business did you engage in with him?"

Baldassare steepled his fingers, "You should understand that I'm under contractual obligations. I can't just itemize business dealings ad hoc. I can refer you to the quarterly shareholder's report—"

I shook my head. "Just, in general, what did Forest Hills Enterprises provide Aloeus?"

"Aloeus, Incorporated, Kline. He may have died, but the legal construction carries on without him."

Interesting point. "So Forest Hills provided what?"

"It is a real estate development company. Forest Hills does with

Aloeus, Inc., what it does with everyone else. It buys and sells commercial development properties."

"In Mexico?"

"Forest Hills Enterprises holds properties all across North America."

"And why would Aloeus, *Inc.*, want to buy acres of undeveloped property in Mexico?"

Baldassare looked at me, "I suspect you would have to ask Aloeus that question." He sipped his drink, and I had the eerie feeling that in our little game of conversational chess I had suffered a fool's mate.

I didn't let him go at that. "Why would you think he bought property in a place he would never be able to go?"

"If I were to theorize, which I do not, I would say that the property was purchased for the same reason it was sold. To make a profit."

"You're saying that Aloeus was speculating in real estate."

"That seems to be the obvious conclusion." He set the empty glass on the mosaic table. "Do you have any other questions?"

"Do you associate with any other dragons?"

"Some business contacts. They tend to be private creatures."

And wealthy, I thought. The community of money could inspire more solidarity than nationality or—I suspected in this case—species. "Do you know any who might talk to me?" I asked him.

"Interesting question," Baldassare shook his head. "They don't line up for interviews."

"Could you set up a meeting?" I asked.

"You don't ask small favors." Baldassare said.

"I rarely ask any," I replied. In his case, it was true. In my years of our relationship, I'd never asked him to perform any actions on my behalf. Not so much as an introduction. I had always felt the dynamic between us was too fragile and too one-sided for me to push things with him.

I don't know why I asked him to introduce me to a dragon. I suspect that Baldassare was as surprised that I'd asked as I was. I suspect that what prompted it was a gut-deep instinct that he would. I don't know why I felt that way, unless it was an overall impression from Baldassare's monologue, but it proved correct.

"I *can* set up an appointment for you," he said after a long, thoughtful pause. "An associate who might be willing. Her name is Theophane. She resides in the BP Building."

"Thank you."

"Kline, goodwill is a fragile thing with these creatures. Don't make me sorry I did you this favor."

"You won't be," I assured him.

I drove away from Baldassare's estate with two conflicting emotions fighting for airtime in my head. First off, I was really pleased with myself for landing an interview with a dragon. That would be a real coup if I could pull it off. I certainly wouldn't find a better source for background on Aloeus.

But, on the other hand, I kept feeling that I'd slipped up somewhere with Baldassare. That thought kept nagging at me as I drove up the curvy, wooded road paralleling the Chagrin River. It kept nagging at me until my cell phone rang.

I flipped it open to familiar static and incomprehensible whispering voices fading in and out.

"I am determined to prove a villain—"

"Hello, who is this?"

"Plots I have laid—" Then a sudden series of clicks and a dial tone.

Christ, what the hell is this? I knew that it had to be the same person who'd called me with the *Macbeth* quote. This new one sounded vaguely Shakespearean as well. It made me wish I'd paid a little more attention in my English Lit classes in college.

Normally I hate people who chatter on cell phones in the car, but the heat of curiosity was on me. So, after I had again determined that the last caller was from an unknown number, and made sure that it was still before eight, I called up one of my research sources.

"Cleveland Public Library, archives. How can I help you?"

"Eric, it's Kline."

"Kline? I can barely hear you. Where are you?"

"On my cell phone, quick question—how's your Shakespeare?"

"My Shakespeare? What you working on?"

"Can you ID a quote for me?"

"Speak up, what?"

"'I am determined to become a villain. Plots I have laid' What's that from?"

"Can you repeat that?"

"'*I am determined to become a villain!*'" I yelled into the phone. "'*Plots I have—*'" I was just making a blind turn on a road following the edge of the Chagrin River, I looked up and suddenly there was a rider in front of me. I dropped the phone and slammed on the brakes, pulling the Volkswagen into the wrong lane and off the road.

In front of me the blinding-white animal turned and reared. I don't know how I missed it, a cloven hoof seemed to come close enough to touch the windshield.

The car came to a stop with one front tire tilted into a ditch. My neck felt as if the shoulder belt had abraded it raw. I popped the door and released the seat belt. I stepped out and almost tumbled downslope into the river.

"Are you all right?"

I turned, looking back toward the road. The rider was a young woman wearing a sea-green hunt coat and a matte-black helmet. Her steed was smaller than your average horse, cloven hoofed, golden maned, with a goatlike beard and a long spiraled horn emerging from its forehead about a handspan above its eyes.

They were both backing to a path that paralleled the road.

"I almost hit you," I said. I walked around the edge of the car, keeping my hand on the roof for balance. "Are *you* all right?"

The unicorn kept backing away. I suspect he didn't like me. She leaned forward and patted the creature's neck and whispered something. I heard enough to realize that it was the elves' language. She looked up, and I could see that it wasn't a coincidence. Her face carried the alien lines and metallic eyes of an elf.

That explained why she wasn't cursing me out right now. Elves had more reserve than any creature had a right to have. From a human viewpoint they had less passion than a lobotomized Englishman on thorazine.

"We are all right." She looked down on me from her mount. "You should watch for riders in these woods, sir."

I nodded. "Stupid mistake," I agreed. "I'm sorry."

"You apologies are unnecessary, and it was not as stupid as it could have been." Something passed across her face too quickly for me to tell if it was a frown or a smile. "What is your business here?"

I was tempted to say, *none of yours*. But Hunting Valley residents were kind of touchy about outsiders, and I did just come close to running her over.

"I had a meeting with Mr. Baldassare. Down the street."

She stared at me with alien, pupiless eyes. Trying, I supposed, to determine if I was lying. Finally she said, "I am Ysbail, sir."

She paused long enough for me to realize that I was supposed to reciprocate. "Kline Maxwell." I almost offered my hand, but when hers didn't reach to meet it, I changed the gesture to rub my abraded neck.

She nodded. "You are."

I didn't know if I liked the way she said that. I heard a small far-away sound, and remembered my cell phone. I held up my hand, "Wait a moment, would you?"

I was already thinking that an elvish perspective on the whole thing would be a neat detail I could slip in. Keeping an eye on Ysbail, I scrambled around the front of the Volkswagen and found the phone, still open, under the driver's seat.

She, apparently, didn't share my plans. Her mount turned without any visible signal from her.

"Hey. *Wait!*" I called after them as they disappeared down a path that led away from the road.

"Hello? Kline?"

I sighed, shook my head, and said a curt "Yeah." into the phone.

"What happened? I thought you were cut off—"

"Never mind that." I kept staring into the woods. "Do you know the quote?"

"Uh-huh. I found it for you. The full thing is: 'I am determined to prove a villain/ And hate the idle pleasures of these days. Plots I have laid, inductions dangerous/ By drunken prophecies, libels, and dreams/ To set my brother Clarence and the King/ In deadly hate against one another—'"

"You don't have to read the whole thing. Just tell me what it's from."

"It's from the opening soliloquy of *Richard III.*"

I pondered a moment. "That's the humpbacked king who kills his nephews in the Tower of London, right?"

"You got it."

Macbeth, then *Richard III*? There was obviously something my anonymous caller was trying to tell me. Something about powerful men, and betrayal. But who, and what . . . ?

Mind games.

Some joker who believed that this was some form of subtlety. I shouldn't be wasting my time on it. What I *needed* to do was get to-morrow's dragon story into the paper. And, tomorrow, I was probably going to get to talk to a dragon in the flesh.

After putting the story to bed, I got Chinese takeout. I pulled up to my complex after dark. My condo sat just on the Shaker Heights side of Shaker Square, part of a line of Tudor-Gothic apartment buildings built in the nineteen-thirties. The doorman—a grizzled old guy named Willie Czestzyk—let me in.

"Long day, Mr. Maxwell?"

"As long as they get," I said, holding my bag of Kung-Pao chicken close to my chest.

"What's the news?" He always asked me that question.

"The FAA is going to form a commission to investigate dragon safety."

Willie chuckled, like he always did, though I was unsure if I was being ironic or not. I mean, upon reflection, I would not be surprised.

Once up in my apartment I collapsed in front of the TV, promising myself that I wasn't going to think of anything work-related until I made it to the office tomorrow.

I had an investment in that promise. The television was easily the most expensive piece of equipment in my condo. It wasn't as hard to get video out of a piece of equipment around the Portal as it was to get video *into* it, but it was still a technological hurdle. Not only did my TV have to operate on redundant bandwidths like my cell phone to eliminate the spurious mana-related data in the signal, but the display had to be a hundred percent digital. That meant no picture tube at all. It had to be a flat screen crystal display, like my laptop.

Combine that kind of technology with the relatively low demand—after all, there were *no* local broadcast stations anymore, and the cable companies around here fell into high-speed Internet delivery out of sheer necessity—you have a boob tube that runs two and a half grand for a twenty-inch model. And, of course, after spending about a grand for a special receiver hooked up to a dish that'd give me something to watch, I had to pull the stops and get the five-grand thirty-five-inch screen model.

Being a couch potato in this city cost money. And after that kind of investment, I almost felt guilty *not* watching pro wrestling.

Anyway, that was what greeted me when I turned the set on, and I didn't switch channels since this was the kind of mind-numbing stuff I was looking for.

I was just settling into it when the phone rang. Not my cell phone, which I switched off the moment I walked into the building, but my private line. I put down the takeout and hefted the receiver with a sigh.

"Hello," I said while muting the Masked Avenger's face's introduction to Mr. Turnbuckle.

"Daddy?" said a quiet teenage girl's voice.

CHAPTER SEVEN

I'VE been trying to call you all day," she said.

"I was working." I eased back up on the couch and stared at the ceiling. The TV carved out blue abstract patterns in the ceiling. Sarah's voice was too damn close on the phone. I should be able to hear the distance from Cleveland to San Francisco. Her voice should have been echoey and small, not like she was down the street. "How're you doing, kid?"

"Awful. Perfectly rotten."

I'm a soft touch, and I have a pretty vivid imagination. For a few moments I was picturing everything from my ex's townhouse burning down to the city of San Francisco sliding into the ocean. I sat up, muscles tightening in the small of my back. "What's the matter, honey?"

"She's ruining my life," she said in a harsh whisper. *"The bitch!"*

To avoid hurting my daughter's feelings, I made every effort to keep my sigh of relief from being audible. I sank onto the couch as the possible crises reduced to those of a more manageable variety. "Don't talk that way about your mother."

"You don't know what she's doing." It was strange to hear the California in her voice. Just enough to be disconcerting.

"No, honey, I don't." I rubbed my forehead. "How, exactly, is she ruining your life?"

"I've been planning to go to this concert *all* summer, Dad."

"Uh-huh." A picture was beginning to form in my head.

"You've got to talk to her."

"*You* need to talk to your mother if you want to go out."

Silence.

I waited a beat before I asked, "Why did she ground you, Sarah?"

"*Dad.*"

"Why, honey?"

"I was fifteen minutes late. Fifteen minutes, Dad, and she's acting like I *killed* somebody."

"And this was the first time?"

Silence again. Despite the distance between us, I knew my daughter, and I knew my ex-wife. Margaret, my ex, wasn't one to lay down the law unless someone repeatedly ignored her warnings. I should know. "How many times did you violate curfew before she grounded you?"

"Dad, you don't understand, it wasn't my fault. Chris got lost on the way back home—"

I smiled and shook my head. "Sarah, it might not be your fault, but it *is* your responsibility."

"*But—*"

"But nothing. You tested your mother enough times to use up all the slack you had coming. Now you're calling me hoping that, since I haven't been present for all the sordid details, I might be oblivious enough to argue with Margaret about how unjustified her punishment is."

"*Please*, Dad," She segued into the sobby little girl voice to tug at the old man's heartstrings. "Chris spent seventy-five bucks *each* for these tickets. We waited in line for *hours*. He'll never forgive me—"

"No. I'm not going to second-guess your mother. Besides, if you ask my opinion, if this Chris guy has the gall to be angry at you for a situation *he* created—"

"He didn't—"

"You just got through telling me that *he* got lost and caused you to miss curfew. So it's *his* fault."

"But—"

"He does know to get you home by ten, right?"

There was a long pause before Sarah said, meekly, *"Eleven."*

"Young lady, I just lost any sympathy I had for you. And you better let Chris know that if he so much as gives you a harsh look over this, I am personally going to come down there and force-feed him the entire one-hundred-fifty dollars in pennies."

Long silence.

"Are you still there, Sarah?"

"Yes." There wasn't any affected sobbing now. Just a sigh of resignation.

"I'm sorry you can't go that concert. But it's not my place to get involved in this. You know that."

"I know." Another sigh. "It just meant a lot to me."

"Is this Chris a good guy?"

"Yes," she sounded surprised at the question. "Of course he is."

"Is he a smart guy?"

"Yeah."

"Does he like you?"

"What are you getting at?"

"I'm just saying that a good, smart guy who really likes you would, I think, scalp the tickets that you can't use and save the money for another concert—or at those prices, ten or fifteen movies."

I heard her try to hide a chuckle. "I'll tell him that."

"Good."

"If you don't mind, I won't tell him about the pennies."

At that point in the conversation drifted to less critical matters. I got to tell my daughter about all the weird things I was writing about in Cleveland, and I got to hear more about this Chris guy than I wanted to know. At least, more than I wanted to know when I was thousands of miles away from doing spot checks on the guy.

All in all, though, small price to pay.

After an hour-long talk with my daughter, I fell asleep dreaming about pro wrestlers named Chris.

Now, the guys who woke me up would not have made the WWF All Stars. Much too scrawny. However, the nine-millimeter Glock in the short one's hand made up for anything they lacked in the physical intimidation category.

"Mr. Maxwell," said the tall one. "I think the time for sleep is over." The tall one was *tall*, NBA territory—if the NBA could be conned into holding all their games at the Gund Arena. The guy, all eight and a half feet of him, was an elf.

I was still waking up, and trying to get the scene to gel into some sort of sense.

The TV was droning on in the background showing some sort of hyper-testosterone extreme-sports broadcast involving snowboards, dog teams, and a gasoline fire. Elf One, the eight-footer, sat on the edge of my couch, just within arm's reach—his, not mine. Elf Two, the middle one, stood off to the side where—due to the shotgun design of my condo—he could watch both entrances at the same time. Elf Three, the shortest at about six-five, stood between me and the burning snowboarders, holding the Glock pointed roughly at the half-eaten container of Kung Pao chicken between my legs.

"Mr. Maxwell?" spoke Elf One. The accent is somewhat hard to describe if you've never heard it. Very cultured, soft and breathy, and higher in timbre than it should be coming from someone that tall. An Oxford-educated Jamaican recovering from a blow to the groin. "Are you awake now?"

I doubted feigning sleep would serve any purpose. I nodded and slowly sat up.

The trio were dressed in cheap suits that hung wrong on their nonhuman frames. That and the Glock made me think "cop." Any other elves that would do armed home invasions would have the resources to get their suits tailored, and since the gun probably cost more than the clothes, it almost had to be department issue.

Elvish cops carried nine-millimeter Glocks because of their biological problem with iron. The mostly ceramic weapon not only didn't set off metal detectors, but the steel content was small enough to suffer repeated handling by elvish hands.

Though everyone here, including the guy with the Glock, was wearing gloves.

"Not that I mean any offense," I said. "But you mind telling me what the fuck you're doing barging in here . . ." I almost said, *"without a warrant,"* the cop smell was so strong. But these guys weren't flashing badges, and disclosing my suspicions might not be the best thing to do right now.

"No offense taken, Mr. Maxwell." Elf One's face was gray in the light from the TV. Its true color could be anything from powder blue to pastel rose. His eyes were metallic, with no discernable iris or pupil, nothing in them but a slightly gold-tinted reflection of myself. The face was ovoid, too angular and narrow, and surrounded by a mane of hair that—even cut short—was almost a ruff. The ears were impossibly contorted and twisting to a slightly forward curving point on their tips. While I watched, I could almost see them move in response to the noises in the room. "However, we are not here to answer your questions. I have to ask you to accompany us for a short while."

Very calm, very polite. I doubt that more than three humans alive had ever seen an elf nervous, or angry. They all talked with the detachment of a bored psychoanalyst.

"It's two in the morning. Don't you think it reasonable that I might not want to go anywhere right now? Why don't you come back at a more human hour?"

He gave me a sterile smile that showed a flash of very narrow, very even, very white teeth. "Since we do not suffer the human addiction to periodic unconsciousness, following a 'human' schedule would be an exercise in inefficiency. I think that, upon a moment of reflection, you will see the wisdom in following our schedule." He gave a slight nod to the elf with the Glock. "The wrong decision would be inconvenient for everyone concerned."

"Yeah, yeah." I stood up, gingerly placing the takeout container on the coffee table between me and the elf with the gun. The tacky sides of the container made me overly aware of the sticky feeling of my sweat-stained shirt sticking to the small of my back.

I gave the elf with the Glock an ironic smile. He didn't smile back. The bastards didn't even appreciate the effort I was making not to freak out.

I turned back to Elf One. Even with me standing, I still had to look *up* at him sitting on the arm of my couch. "You mind telling me what this is all about?"

"As I have told you," he stood up, towering over me and stooping slightly to avoid the track lighting, "we are not here to answer your questions."

We walked down the stairs, I think because the elves didn't like the elevator. Being enclosed in a solid steel box must be somewhat unnerving to them.

This time of night, Willie was long gone. There were supposed to be a half-dozen wards blocking unauthorized access to the building, but my escort walked through each magical barrier as if it wasn't there. The fact that they didn't trip a single alarm reinforced the idea that these were cops who had access to the talismans that allowed them free passage. My own talisman for the building was on my key chain, currently sitting on the kitchen table.

Elf Four was idling in a minivan out in front of my building. Probably not enough steel in it to bother these guys, mostly aluminum, plastic, fiberglass, and an acre of tinted windows.

I was hustled into the back, flanked by two elves, while Elf One took shotgun. I saw his head brush the roof. These guys needed the headroom of a van. In a normal car, Elf One would be looking out the windshield from between his knees.

As promised, none of my questions were answered, which didn't stop me from asking—occupational hazard. They didn't show any irritation, even though I was expecting a prod from the Glock at any moment to remind me who was in charge. Apparently, the elves didn't think like that.

We drove through the processed quaintness of Shaker Square, a yuppie haven of upscale restaurants, chain stores, and the occasional art gallery. Like my condo, it was built in the nineteen-thirties, and had about seventy years as a nice piece of local color before the developers got hold of it. I'm waiting for them to put in the Disney Store.

We drove through the square and took a turn north up MLK. We stuck with Martin Luther King Boulevard to where it hit Case Western Reserve University, and University Circle. Up until this point I was pretty sure that we were going to be heading deeper into Cleveland proper. I had just about assured myself that these were detectives from the SPU who were going to take me downtown for some clandestine questions.

I was physically prepared for some inconvenience, but I wasn't particularly scared . . .

Not until we made a wrong turn.

We hit the messy intersection where MLK feeds into Chester—one of the main East Side arteries downtown. We were caught at the light, and the area had a surreal feeling at this time of the morning. There were no cars anywhere, no people on the street, and the streetlights gave the whole place the feeling of a recently abandoned stage set.

The campus of Case Western loomed off to our right, the sprawling campus an aesthetic jumble of architectural styles, ranging from the Gothic church closest to us, to nineteen-sixties institutional. Floodlights illuminated the fluted stone sides of the church, and as I looked up at it, one of the gargoyles yawned.

The light changed, and instead of heading west down Chester, toward downtown, the van turned east, down Euclid. This wasn't a good sign.

"Where are we going?" I asked.

Silence.

We rolled down Euclid, the only vehicle on the street. We drove under the Conrail tracks and passed the downhill side of Lakeview Cemetery, then we came to a rather inauspicious signpost.

It said, "Welcome to East Cleveland."

CHAPTER EIGHT

EAST Cleveland is an object lesson of what *not* to do in the face of demographic change.

Around the 1900s, East Cleveland was a high-rent bedroom community for the Cleveland elite that couldn't quite make it to Millionaire's Row. There are *still* quarter-million dollar homes in some East Cleveland neighborhoods—the catch being that they'd be five to ten million anywhere else.

The 1960s changed that. During the end of that decade, middle-class blacks started buying a lot of homes in the inner ring eastern suburbs. In Cleveland Heights and Shaker Heights—neighboring communities to East Cleveland—there wasn't a panic among white homeowners, despite the attempt by real estate speculators to inflame passions.

Due to that one outbreak of sanity, both Shaker and Cleveland Heights have some of the most desirable—and expensive—real estate of any inner ring suburbs. Which sinks that oft-used chestnut linking "changing neighborhoods" and falling property values.

East Cleveland suffered no such restraint. White flight broke the sound barrier. In the space of two years, most of the existing residents sold at a loss rather than face a black face across the driveway.

The crash in property values and the exodus of population nearly bankrupted the city government, and the plummet in city services continued the collapse in property values. Abandoned properties proliferated, the crime rate rose, businesses moved out. . . .

By the time the Portal opened, East Cleveland was fighting a standstill battle against urban rot.

The Portal nailed the coffin shut and put a shotgun to the corpse. All the absentee landlords—who, even if they did nothing to keep up with the property, gave tenants and the city someone to sue—disappeared. The twelve months of chaos after the Portal opened gave everyone with a stake in East Cleveland legal ground to claim it as a loss, dumping the property on the city. The government suddenly found itself in possession of over half the property in East Cleveland, much of it uninhabitable. Everything collapsed.

In the decade since, everyone—at least everyone human—with any sense had left the floundering suburb. Some to Euclid, some to Cleveland Heights, but most back into Cleveland, where the Portal was becoming an investment magnet, and money was going to actually rebuild many of the city's neighborhoods.

Not so for the urban purgatory that was East Cleveland. The vacuum created by the city's depopulation was filled with *other* things. There's no accurate census. But any brave soul who'd stop to do a random head count would find that three out of five of those heads weren't human—or even humanoid.

Most of the streetlights were out, so as we drove down Euclid the buildings on either side were little more than looming shadows. Occasionally a storefront would be illuminated by torches or glowing braziers, and the boards over the shop windows would be scribed with arcane symbols written in paint, or blood, or branded into the surface of the wood.

Here were the mages who couldn't operate in the face of public scrutiny. Necromancers, assassins, wizards who worked with blood and bone and did not inquire about the source of their raw material. Here were also the night creatures who supplied the mages. . . .

From what I'd heard, the street value for a healthy undamaged human cadaver around here was five to ten grand.

If the elves noticed me tensing up, they didn't show it.

Two excruciatingly long minutes into East Cleveland, the elves turned the minivan off Euclid Avenue. They drove a short distance down a street that was more pothole than asphalt, and pulled to a stop outside a Victorian frame house that huddled under the shadow of the railroad tracks. When the van's headlights brushed by it, I saw clapboards whose paint had long weathered away to leave dead gray wood.

I thought I saw movement behind one of the blind, glassless windows.

Elf One got out and slid the side door open. I didn't leap at the chance to get out, and for the first time the elf next to me prodded me with the Glock. I scrambled out into the street.

The air here felt several degrees cooler than it should have. A suffocating morguelike silence muffled everything. The only sounds to break the night were twittering creatures—I forced myself to think of them as birds—whose distant calls were like insane giggles. If I concentrated, I could just make out an irregular liquid sound, almost a slurping . . .

I stopped concentrating.

If they wanted to kill you, they could have put a bullet in you before you woke up. The thought wasn't that comforting. I really couldn't read their intentions. With regular strong-arm types you could get a sense if the guys wanted to rough you up, talk to you, or finish you off. These guys could be going to a wedding, or casting a snuff film.

The three who escorted me from my condo escorted me up to the house. The driver stayed with the van. As we ascended the steps, the large oak door that led into the house swung inward releasing the moist odor of mildew and rotting wood. It made me sneeze.

I could still see the nail holes in the door where it had once been boarded over.

"You're late," came a voice from within the darkness.

I caught what might have been the flash of an ironic smile on the face of Elf One. "Our apologies. You were paid enough to wait."

"Why do you think I waited for you Keebler bastards?"

If the racial slur bothered my companions, they didn't show it. I think, though, that the human concept of a word being derogatory didn't register with them.

I still couldn't see the speaker. My escort led me into a hallway that was in almost complete darkness. All I could see was a dim sense of movement on all sides of me. The air was thick and musty, and I felt sweat rolling down between my shoulder blades. Under the mildew and rot, I could catch a hint of smoke, as if this place had burned a long time ago.

Ahead of us, a heavy curtain drew aside, revealing a bare room illuminated only by candlelight. Heavy black drapes marked the walls, and facing us was a massive granite fireplace, its mantle supported by a pair of griffins, the firebox blackened, cold, and dead.

The candles formed a circle on the hardwood floor, and complex symbols surrounded the circle. The writing was drawn in either ash or salt, it was too dim for me to tell.

I was really scared now. I did *not* want to be the centerpiece in some necromantic ritual. I turned, my fear now having fully counterbalanced my conscious knowledge of being outnumbered, outgunned, and being in the middle of East Cleveland. It speaks to either my dexterity, or the elves' confidence, that I got four steps toward the hallway before a thin, long-fingered hand put a very firm grip on my upper arm.

"Being uncooperative is not an option, Mr. Maxwell." I felt the Glock at the back of my neck. "We can get the information just as readily from your corpse—"

"Hey, hey, *hey!*" I finally saw the other speaker. He didn't fit my profile of a freelance necromancer. He was shaved bald, and wore a black leather jacket and blacker denim pants. His hands shone with rings, and gold chains hung from his neck. "You smoke that guy here, you blow the vibe in this room—"

"I am sure you can accommodate us if that is necessary—"

"Three grand more," the bald mage said. "Above and beyond. Ain't what you paid me for."

"—but it will not be necessary," Elf One concluded. "Will it?" he asked me.

At this point I wasn't one to argue. The elf with the Glock led me to the center of the circle, walking a careful path that was left through the symbols on the floor. The bald mage berated him twice for straying off the center of the path. I was left standing in the center of the circle of candles.

The elves stepped back to a shadowy corner of the room, so I could barely see them. The mage stepped forward, took a small pouch, and completed the break in the circle I had walked through.

Doing that, he looked up at me. "The mojo's been building here a couple hours. You break the pattern, boy, and it'll be like someone shoved a stick of dynamite up your ass."

He grinned as if daring me to make the attempt.

The air was heavy with the smell of melted wax and incense as he gradually filled in the pattern, walking away from me. Most of the pattern seemed to consist of Greek and Hebrew letters, and as he backed away, he was chanting softly in Latin.

I had some time to reflect on the opportunistic nature of the powers the Portal released. Magical energy was drawn to patterns and complexity—from physical form, to the abstractions of human ritual. That meant that it wasn't just rituals imported across the Portal that worked. The Portal had affected everyone from neo-Pagans to the Catholic Church.

I had no idea what this guy was doing, but even I could tell he was home-grown. I wondered why these elves had hired a local to do their dirty work. I would think that they'd be more comfortable with a mage from their own stomping grounds. Might cost more, but Elf One didn't seem overly concerned with the price of service.

The mage stood up in his own circle, drawn at the periphery of the symbols that surrounded me. He began chanting.

Despite living here, I'd never seen a magical ritual up close. I was expecting something dramatic; candles flaring, the symbols glowing, the floor cracking open over a fiery pit. Conditioning from movies and TV, I suppose.

What happened was a lot of incomprehensible vocalization in the mage's somewhat sardonic voice. I couldn't tell that anything was happening at all, at least not initially.

As the chanting progressed, I became more and more uncomfortable. At first the nervousness and the nausea seemed to be only reasonable physical reactions to the situation I found myself in. It wasn't until I felt my legs giving way under me that I realized that what I was feeling was abnormal.

Then he shouted something and clapped his hands three times.

My body jerked as if someone had just strapped me into Old Sparky and pulled the switch. I lost all motor control. My body froze, leaving me resting on my knees and the tips of my toes, my back arched, arms splayed backward. My neck craned back so far that my field of vision was limited to the ceiling of naked lath dotted with fragments of an elaborately molded plaster ceiling.

I should have been in awful pain, but my whole body had gone numb, the only sensation flickering ripples of pins and needles. My mind seemed severed from my body, watching from inside. In a panic, I tried to move my body, escape, breaking the pattern be damned. I couldn't even speak.

Voices seemed very far away.

"Who are you?" Elf One asked, or maybe it was the mage.

"Kline Maxwell." My voice sounded so eerily similar to the elf's that I had trouble realizing that I'd spoken.

"Who do you work for?"

"The *Cleveland Press*. My editor is Columbia Jennings." My voice was distant, almost into nonexistence. My thoughts had retreated to the calm irrationality that one usually only finds in dreams. I was wondering if I was having a near death experience— and if those carried any more weight this close to the Portal.

"No one else pays you?"

"No one else pays me." I was too disoriented to find the questions as interesting as I should have.

"You were at the Hope Memorial Bridge early yesterday. What were you doing there?"

"A dragon fell into the river. I'm doing the story."

"You are a political reporter, correct?"

"Yes."

"I am told that you have a talent for unearthing scandals."

There was a prolonged silence, during which I could gather some semblance of thought. I didn't know what the mage was doing, but it was damned scary. I couldn't even move my eyeballs, and all I could feel was that rippling numbness. I had a panicked thought that what they'd done might be permanent—a bullet in the head would be preferable.

"Why is he silent?"

The mage's voice responded, the tone of exasperation cutting through the distant fog I was listening through. "It wasn't a question, was it? You're not having a fucking conversation here. You ask, he'll answer—and we got about ten minutes before we drain him dry."

"Time enough," Elf One's voice. "Now listen, Mr. Maxwell. You do have a talent for scandalmongering, do you not?"

"It's called investigative journalism." I was left wondering if my words were tinged with irony or sarcasm.

"Indeed. So what is your interest in the dragon, Aloeus?"

"It's news."

"Is that all?"

"It's a major story."

"But not political?"

"Of course it's political."

"How?"

"Aloeus was a major behind-the-scenes figure in all the legal and political ramifications of the Portal. He acted as an advocate for the nonhumans that came out of the Portal. He's tied into the Rayburn administration. He's had business dealings with Leo Baldassare. Nesmith oversaw the cleanup, and Adrian Phillips was on the boat towing the corpse out to sea." I spoke in a dull monotone, each syllable as dead as the last. My distant brain registered surprise at mentioning Phillips. At the time it seemed just a footnote establishing how deeply Aloeus seemed tied to the Rayburn administration.

For the first time I heard the other elves speak. There was a whispered conversation in a language that didn't belong on this planet. It lasted a few seconds before Elf One said something harsh. The closest thing to an emotion I had heard in his voice.

"You believe that there is more than the story of the dragon's death."

"Yes."

"What do you believe?"

"There are major winners and losers. Who gains from the dragon's death? Who's losing something? If there's a power vacuum in the paranormal community, who's going to fill it?" Something in my gut turned sour hearing myself voice things so starkly. I had told myself that I was interested in Aloeus for his own sake. I didn't like the fact that, when it came down to it, I wouldn't have been so interested in him if he hadn't cut so wide a swath both literally and figuratively.

"Do you believe Aloeus' death was an accident?"

"No." My answer was flat, final, and a complete surprise to me. Whatever spell bound me was digging deep into unexamined areas of my own mind. The elf had plucked a suspicion out of my head that I wasn't even aware I'd been harboring.

"Why?"

"Aloeus should have been able to avoid it, whatever *it* was. I have a natural suspicion whenever any public figure dies in a freak accident."

More elvish talking then, "Does the name Faust mean anything to you?"

"He made a deal with the Devil. Old book."

"You know no one by that name?"

"No, I don't."

My vision was dimming, and I had lost even the numbness that connected me to my body. I kept thinking back to the mage's comment about draining me dry.

"These answers have been truthful?"

I was surprised that I didn't answer. Apparently the question wasn't addressed toward me. The mage said, in a voice now very far off and wee, "What you think you paid me for?"

"Then we are done."

Silence.

Darkness.

CHAPTER NINE

I WOKE up the next morning with enough memory of the prior night to realize that it was far from the nightmare I wanted it to be.

This was uncharted territory for me. The greatest physical threat I'd ever suffered before this was when an elderly George Forbes threw a chair at me during a press conference when I asked a question that—apparently—questioned his judgment in reentering city politics after umpteen years of retirement.

There is a considerable difference in tone between a chair wielded by a washed-up politician, and a Glock wielded by an emotionless elf cop. My pulse raced in my neck, and my mouth tasted of copper just thinking about it.

But, on reflection, the motive behind both was the same. Intimidation.

That pissed me off.

One major self-destructive part of my personality was that whenever someone threatened me to get me to abandon a course of action, I became more committed to whatever I was doing. Even if I *want* to cave, I can't.

That was pretty much what happened to my marriage. When Margaret started telling me I had to spend less time at the job or our marriage was in serious trouble, I couldn't bring myself to change. I knew better, but some adamantine kernel of ego kept me from responding. The Portal opening was the biggest story of the millennium, and, by God, I was going to cover it.

I can't say I was surprised when I came home to an empty house.

All in all, the divorce was amicable. Because, once I'd done the stupid macho shit and refused to bend, I was so pathetically guilty that I caved on every other point. As if responding to my wife's needs now was somehow going to fix it. Fortunately for me,

Margaret didn't have her lawyer feed too much on my bloated corpse.

And, if I wasn't going to let the loss of my marriage intimidate me, a cabal of armed elves didn't have much chance.

That was what was running through my head as I pushed open the door to Columbia Jennings' office the morning after. The smoke smell was as thick as ever, and she was half turned away from me, facing the screen on her desktop. I could see an image of this morning's *Press* on the flat screen before she looked up at me. "Maxwell?"

"Morning, Bea," I said as I pushed the door shut behind me.

"I was going to congratulate you. Good story. Above the fold."

I nodded. She was being way more gregarious than usual. She almost smiled. The subliminal nervousness that I'd sensed yesterday was there full force now that I knew what to look for. "Yes. It turns out to be more my line than I'd thought at first." I didn't sit. "Perceptive of you to give me the lead on this, wasn't it?"

"Thank you." She said it in a way that made it clear she wasn't sure it was a compliment.

"Why?"

"Pardon?"

"Why did you give the story to me?"

"It's your line. Like you said—"

"Bullshit!"

She stared at me, stunned at my outburst. I was a little surprised myself. I was running on instinct here, but that little reporter barometer in my gut was saying *warmer . . .*

"Bea, you *needed* to get me on that story. When I agreed without a fight, the relief in this room was as thick as the smoke. If you, for one moment, thought of this as a political story, you would have used that to sell me on it. One mention of Phillips, Nesmith, Rayburn, Baldassare, and you would have *had* me on this thing before you finished the sentence." I leaned across the desk. *"You* didn't know who the dragon was when you pawned this off on me, did you?"

She didn't answer.

"If you remember, I *asked* you who it was."

She nodded slowly.

"You had no idea of the political ties to this story when you assigned it to me."

"No."

"Why, then?"

"I have bosses, too. You think I decide everything here by personal fiat?"

Yes. However, this wasn't the place to say that. "Hackket?" I asked, naming the editor-in-chief of the *Press*.

"He's the one who gave me the news that you should cover the dragon. He has a boss, too."

Nyle Montgomery, owner of the *Cleveland Press*, a man who was probably richer than Leo Bladassare. Bea was telling me that my assignment to the dragon story had come from the top, before the victim had even been identified.

Officially identified, I corrected myself.

"Do you know anyone named Faust?"

"What?"

"Never mind." I turned and walked to the office door.

"Where are you going?"

"I've got a dragon story to cover, remember?"

I had several directions I needed to go in now. I had a dead dragon who had his talons in a lot of local pies. I had the suspicion that his death was more than an accident, the unvoiced hunch gaining a lot more credibility based on my nocturnal questioning. I had at least four elf cops with an interest in this; all probably members of O'Malley's Special Paranormal Unit since only two or three elves were cops outside the SPU. I had a human mage that I wouldn't have any problem picking out of a lineup. I had a name, Faust.

And I had Adrian Phillips on a Coast Guard cutter.

Why?

There was a tenuous connection. For a variety of historical reasons, the Port Authority had direct executive control over the Portal. It was the Port Authority that maintained the stadium, ran the buses in and out. Because of that, they also had regulatory control over the magic in this town, such as it was. Several times the Council had tried to spin off the magic stuff into its own agency, but Phillips and his Port Authority fought that turf battle tooth and nail. They were the agency in direct contact with the world beyond the Portal, so they should keep control of what came out of it.

Because of Phillips' tight rein on his own agency and what it controlled, he was probably the third most powerful person in the city government. Under his control was every mage who worked for the city, with the sole exception of the forensic mages who worked in the SPU. Even those had to work under guidelines drafted by Phillips and his agency.

Aloeus' nosedive had drawn some high-powered attention. The more I thought of it, the more Phillips' presence seemed to confirm the thought that there was more going on here than a simple accident. I began wondering if the report Nesmith passed out gave the whole story.

While I was at my desk, I tried to give the coroner, Egil Nixon, a call. Again, I got voice mail. This time the message said that he was going to be out of the office the remainder of the week. I left a message, feeling a little uneasy. I made a few more calls, found out his home number was unlisted, and used a source in the sheriff's office to get it and his address.

No answer at home.

That goes on the things to do list.

I wrote myself a note, then I called Baldassare.

"The dragon will be expecting you," he told me. "Like I said, don't do anything that makes me regret setting this up."

"Thank you," I said, writing down the meeting time under my note to check up on Coroner Nixon. Before he hung up, I added, "I wanted to ask you something."

There was a pause. "Okay, Kline. What is it?"

"Has it ever crossed your mind that Aloeus' death might have been less than an accident?"

"I don't put any credence in rumors, Kline. Whenever a public figure dies, especially a political one, there'll be conspiracies around every corner. I won't contribute to that."

"You've heard rumors?"

"What did I just say?"

"You know I had to ask."

"That's the difference between me and you. There are some questions I wouldn't ask." A beat. "Anything else?"

"Two things," Both were long shots. "I ran into someone on the way back from your place," Almost ran into, anyway. "Her name's Ysbail. I wondered if you knew her."

"You did?" Hard to read his voice, hard to tell if the surprise was real or feigned. "How in the world did you two meet?"

"By accident. Friend of yours?"

"Acquaintance." He seemed to consider carefully before he said, "Is she the source of your rumors?"

Interesting. "You know a reporter doesn't reveal sources—where would you be if I did that?"

"What was the other thing?"

"Do you know anyone named Faust?"

A very cold, *"No."*

I waited a moment, which told me all I needed. Just the denial, no question about why I was asking or who Faust was supposed to be. Either Baldassare wanted me to know Faust meant something, or I had—for the first time—really surprised him with something. My bet would be the former.

"Thanks again for the help."

"You're welcome," he said. "Just remember all this when *I* ask *you* for something."

I walked into the glassy atrium of the BP Building trying to fit several disjointed pieces together. My discussion with Baldassare gave me some impressions of what was happening. From the sound of things, my escorts last night weren't the only elves out there who thought Aloeus had suffered something other than an accident. From Baldassare's point of view, this Ysbail elf was of a similar mind.

It would make sense. If Aloeus was a political advocate for the paranormal underclass, it made some sense that the people he supported would view his death with suspicion. However, since some of them seemed to be cops, I suspected it was more than a knee-jerk reaction.

I wondered if Theophane had heard any rumors.

I walked back to where the elevators were kept. There was one elevator, separate from the others, that went to Theophane's floor. I had expected an intercom, a phone line, something—but all there was was the single call button mounted in its brass plaque in the marble wall.

I pressed it, looking around for visible wards or security cameras. I saw one recessed area near the elevator that could have been either, but I didn't have the time to examine it closely because the mirrored brass doors slid open immediately.

I stepped inside the wood-paneled elevator and turned around to see the doors close in front of me. I reached for the button for the thirty-ninth floor, and didn't find one. Where the control panel normally sat was a blank brass plate. The only controls were the key-operated fire department override, and the stop/alarm button. I suddenly had the feeling that those were there only because the fire code required it.

The elevator didn't move.

After a few moments I heard a voice. *"Who is asking for admittance?"* The voice had the directionless character that told me that it wasn't being reproduced electronically.

"Kline Maxwell, *Cleveland Press*. Leonardo Baldassare sent me."

It was a long sixty seconds before the elevator began moving. The upward acceleration was sudden, unexpected, and unpleasant. The little LED display ran floor numbers by too fast to read, until it hit thirty and began slowing down.

I rubbed my chin and looked into my reflection in the polished brass doors.

Thirty-seven, thirty-eight, thirty-nine . . .

The doors slid open.

Baldassare had said there was a moment where everything clicked, a point where it sank in how much the world had changed. I thought that I had passed that point long ago. I knew what the world had become.

But when I walked out onto the top floors of the BP building, it clicked. I realized that I knew jack shit.

The BP Building was late seventies, early eighties. The first major skyscraper built here after the city came out of default. First it was the Sohio corporate headquarters, then BP Oil bought them out and stayed long enough to rename the building. It was a high-profile address, right on Public Square, and the top floors were about as exclusive as you got as far as downtown office space went.

I had never been here before, but I could tell that the current tenant had ordered extensive remodling.

The fortieth floor no longer existed except as empty space three stories above me. In front of me was an atrium that enclosed almost as much space as the grand lobby downstairs. To my left and right were three stories of windows that looked down on the city from a dizzying height. Except for the heavy stillness in the air, the feeling was as if I stood on an urban mountain peak. The air smelled of roses and sulfur.

What affected me most wasn't the grand space, but the single occupant of that space.

She—I wouldn't have known gender if Baldassare hadn't told me—was easily half again the size of Aloeus, though I was probably too close to her for an accurate measure of size. All I saw was a wall of muscular blue-black flesh that rose above my head and slid, slowly, from left to right. In the direction of motion, the wall narrowed to a serpentine neck that arched above her, ending in a head longer than I was tall. She lowered her head, pulling her body in an undulating motion behind it, so I glimpsed an arm stretching lazily toward the ceiling. Baldassare was right about feline body language, though the clawed hand I saw could easily break an eight-hundred pound Siberian tiger in half.

I realized the wall of flesh in front of me was her back when she completed the feline stretch by rolling over—in my direction. If the intention was to impress me, Theophane succeeded. I flattened myself against the elevator doors, as her enormous form rolled to face me. She came to rest about ten feet from the column that held the elevator shaft, but my hypothalamus was screaming to the rest of my body that I was about to be crushed.

Her head came down between me and the rest of her body. She looked at me with a heavy golden eye the size of my skull. She opened her mouth, and her voice filled the humid air around me.

"Fuzzy gnome stories?"

CHAPTER TEN

"T HEOPHANE?" I asked unnecessarily.
She blinked at me slowly.

I realized she had asked a question, and was waiting for an answer. "It's slang," I told her, hoping to God I wasn't being insulting. "News stories that are predominantly about the paranormal."

"So I am a 'fuzzy gnome?'"

I closed my eyes because I didn't want to see her reaction. "Strictly speaking, yes."

I felt wet sulfur breath on my face and heard an ominous rumble. It shook the floor and I tensed, expecting to feel the dragon's wrath at any moment. The rumble became louder, and when I wasn't immediately torn limb from limb, I risked a peek.

Theophane was laughing.

She shook her head as she finished rolling to her feet. It took her body even closer, but she had enough control to avoid squashing me. She took a few steps away from me. With her stride that meant that there was suddenly about forty feet between us. I could now see most of her—a whiplike saurian body that seemed to cross a python with a T-rex. Her body shaded from black-blue on top, to a blue-white underneath. Her wings folded against her back like a cape, and her tail slid back past me and the pillar that held the elevator shaft. Her head sat on a serpentine neck that turned it to keep her gaze on me as she moved. Brimstone-scented steam rose from her nostrils as she laughed.

After a moment, she regarded me with her head cocked inquisitively, *"You do not find that amusing?"*

"I see the incongruity of the statement." *Sorry, but I'm a little too shit-scared to laugh right now.* "Where did you hear that phrase? I thought it was just some provincial jargon from the local press." I was having difficulty keeping my voice on an even keel. Somehow it'd never occurred to me that seeing a dragon up close would have this kind of effect on me. Blame that on the little knot of ego that got me into situations like this in the first place.

"I have heard that you're a journalist who does not do 'fuzzy gnome' stories."

"The death of Aloeus is more than that."

"We are all more than that." The great deep voice carried something akin to Columbia's disapproval. Just like a flamethrower carries something akin to a Zippo.

"I didn't mean offense."

The dragon laughed again in a way that made my fillings ache. *"You are only human, Mr. Maxwell. Can I fault you for that?"* I got the feeling that I wasn't completely off the hook.

I wondered again where she had heard the phrase.

"Mr. Baldassare called on your behalf last night. I agreed to meet you, knowing your aversion to 'fuzzy gnomes.'"

"What do you know about that?" I asked her.

"I make knowing things my business." She lowered her head to be at a level with me. That was disconcerting, facing her beaklike toothy mouth. *"Mr. Baldassare said you want to know about dragons."*

"I want to know about Aloeus."

"Are they not the same thing?"

There was silence for a moment before I heard a small alarm from behind her. She cocked her head. *"Pardon me a moment."*

She turned from me, the motion of her body vibrating the floor. Her tail slid by me with a soft hiss across the blood-red carpet. *"I must buy some more Microsoft shares before the NASDAQ starts upward again."*

I stood there and watched for a while, letting the past thirty seconds sink into my world view. Call me a racist, but I didn't expect a dragon with a sense of humor. Theophane seemed to be getting a lot of enjoyment out of playing all my expectations false. Which was no difficult task, since she knew a lot more about me, and humanity in general, than the sorry bits I knew about her kind—and about her specifically, I knew nothing beyond name and address.

And she wasn't lying about the NASDAQ.

When she moved aside, I could see another pillar in the vast chamber, twin to the one holding the elevator. This sole architectural feature seemed to serve as a combination office and entertainment center for Theophane. Flat screen displays covered most of the available space. Some showed CNN, C-SPAN, and other news and public affairs channels. The screens were all muted, dialogue transcriptions running across the bottom of their screens. Central to all of them was an inset display positioned at what must have been a comfortable level for her, about four feet above my head. I could catch a few glimpses of a computer display showing windowed bar graphs and columns of figures. Across the top I could clearly see a stock ticker running.

Theophane maneuvered an oversized mouse with a few well-placed claws. I don't know why I found it incongruous.

"So can you answer some of my questions?"

She shook her head as she stared at the screen. The display was twice the size of my TV, but it seemed too small for her. *"Your distraction cost me fifty thousand dollars."*

She must have sensed me backing up, because her head turned my way just as I felt the warm muscular wall of her tail along the small of my back.

"No matter, the entertainment value should be worth as much." Her head lowered to be just slightly above my level, and I had the uneasy sensation of being surrounded. *"What is it you want to know, Mr. Maxwell?"*

"I want to understand dragons."

Theophane's head drew back and tilted slightly in my direction. There was a distinctly saurian cast to her face, especially with the heart-shaped bony ridge of her forehead facing me. The nose and mouth were very like a skin-covered beak with teeth. Her voice was eerie, coming from deep inside her throat, with little help from tongue and near-nonexistent lips. I might have suspected that the sounds weren't even coming from her if not for the feel of moist breath on my forehead as she spoke.

She raised one hand and drew her clawed fingers together at its point, the gesture disturbingly human. *"An interesting synchronicity. I wish to understand humans. I feel we both may have embarked on an endless task."*

Conversing with her was helping me recover from the initial impact. With that came the feeling that she was playing with me. I didn't feel that levity—even the levity of a two-hundred-foot lizard—was appropriate. I took my notebook out of my pocket.

"Theophane, I am investigating the death of one of your fellow dragons. I need to know why he died."

"Perhaps you do, Mr. Maxwell. Do I?"

"Do you what?"

"Need to know why?"

"Aren't you concerned at all about Aloeus' death? He was one of your own."

"You are right to believe you do not understand dragons." Theophane shook her head and withdrew it. When she moved, I was no longer surrounded, and I breathed a little easier. She moved away from the video pillar, toward a vast wall of windows that overlooked the eastern city.

I walked up next to her, the view an antidote to the claustrophobia I'd been feeling. Below us, the arched glass roof of the Old Arcade flashed sunlight back up at us.

"There is no reason the death of Aloeus should concern me more than the death of anyone else." She shook her head. *"We are not social animals. We do not form tribes, cities, or religions—any trappings of such things we undertake for the sake of others."*

"I find that hard to believe."

"Of course you do. You have been trained from birth that another man must have authority over you, that other men define the codes you shall adhere to. You exist in a prison made of other human beings."

There was something very cold in the way she said that. My hand shook a little as I took notes. "You mean that dragons don't?"

There was another of her snorts that I took to be laughter. This one held less humor than her prior ones. *"Consider me, Mr. Maxwell. You look at a creature supreme in physical prowess, in intellect, in mystical ability. Perhaps that sounds immodest, but modesty is a human virtue. To have a tribe, one must lead, and others must be willingly subjugate themselves."* She drew herself up and spread wings that reached from one end of the cavernous space to the other. *"No dragon is a slave."*

This was not what I was expecting, and it didn't feel quite right to me. "You mean to say that there's no social connection between dragons at all?"

"We are not human beings."

A statement that any good newsman would recognize as a non-answer answer. She had sidestepped the question as adroitly as any politician. It prompted me to push slightly. "Aloeus' death means nothing to you?"

"We are sovereign creatures, each one's fate is his own."

"Even if it wasn't an accident?"

She looked down at me, then turned her serpentine neck to look out at the eastern horizon. *"There are no accidents,"* she said. A clawed finger touched the ground near my feet. It was disconcerting, the black talon was almost the length of my forearm. *"Ask me about dragons, Mr. Maxwell."*

There was something in her voice, a burning emotion that I could feel in her words, but couldn't identify. Rage or grief? I didn't know, and its intensity frightened me. "Tell me why you came here, through the Portal."

"This is the background you need?"

"You are a dragon. Everything I've heard says Aloeus was leading the way out, that nonhumans were being persecuted—"

"A refugee?" Her neck twisted and brought her face withing a foot of my own. Apparently, while modesty might be a human virtue, pride was universal. *"Is that what you believe?"* Her voice lowered in pitch until her consonants caused my ribs to ache.

"Why, then?"

She swung an arm back toward her cavernous rooms. *"This, little man. This."*

"I'm not sure I understand."

"You require an explanation?" She drew back and shook her head at my ignorance. *"Do you know why dragons love gold?"*

I was tempted to say, "greed." But I decided that insults weren't the best policy right now. "I know the popular image of dragons is that they hoard wealth."

"It is fact." She turned from the wall of windows and moved toward the northern edge of the building, where more windows looked over the lake, and Browns Stadium. From here the constant atmospheric disturbance was even more impressive. A twisting pillar of dark clouds towering thousands of feet into an otherwise clear blue stratosphere. From this high up, I could see the motion, like a massive slow-motion tornado set slightly off center above the roofed-over stadium. *"Many aspects of this world's myth and legend bear enough truth to lead one to suspect that the Portal is not a unique phenomenon."*

"I've heard that before," I admitted. "No one can prove it. If a portal existed in the past, it was far enough back that no one can find any archaeological evidence for it."

"Perhaps not. But it gives my kind an explanation for why humankind suddenly appeared and ran rampant these past millennia."

"So why do dragons love gold?"

"Power," she told me. *"As I said, we are supreme physically, mentally, in the realm your bizarre language refers to as the supernatural. So what is our weakness?"*

I thought for a minute, and came up with something that jibed with the stories I'd heard so far about the place they had left. "You're loners. You aren't organized. In a conflict you'll best any one human, but humans band together—facing you with a city, and army, a nation."

"That is, exactly, our sole weakness." She looked out over the water. I wondered if she had watched Aloeus' body as it was towed out to sea. *"Such a grave one that it may now overshadow our strengths. For millennia before our contact with elvish, and then human, 'civilization' it mattered not to us. The idea of 'political' power, 'economic' power—manipulating events through proxies, and symbols—were concepts long and hard in coming to us."* Theophane waved back to the pillar, where her computer was showing a stock ticker. *"Wealth is the easiest—and the most easily understandable—way to acquire that kind of power."*

I scribbled a few notes as I asked her, "You're saying that you only hoard wealth to be able to influence humans?"

"Human society," she corrected me. *"An individual human being means little to us. But the possession of wealth allows us to influence a city, a government, a church."* She gave me a long, cryptic look. *"A newspaper."*

That took me back a beat. "Are you saying that you influenced—"

"Don't ask me things you can readily discover elsewhere. Do not waste my time."

I sucked in a breath. I did not want to push this interview. I definitely wanted to leave things at a point where I could come back if I needed to. I made an effort to return to the conversation's previous tack. "Is that all you care for money, then? What about comforts—" I waved an arm to take in the retrofitted top floors of the BP Building. "This wasn't cheap."

"I left a more spectacular aerie to come to this world. What is a diamond, Mr. Maxwell, except a pretty rock? What is money here, in this world, but paper and ink—or ephemeral records in someone's computer?"

I looked back at the stock ticker. "Is it difficult?"

"What, exactly?"

"It's different here, isn't it? Back on the other side of the Portal, from what I understand, was a medieval economy. Wealth was a 'real' physical thing. A pile of gold, gems—"

Her head bobbed, a serpentine nod. *"I understand what you mean. Though I don't think you understand what I was saying.*

To us, a golden stone is just as symbolic as a piece of paper, or some accountant's record. None has inherent value, just as words on a page do not have any inherent meaning. Values and meaning are assigned to them arbitrarily, and the association is only as strong as the number of people who agree on the assignment."

"So it wasn't a difficult transition."

"Not conceptually."

"There were other difficulties?"

"The matter of agreement applies to your bureaucracy as well as your economy. Fortunately, your bizarre layers of rule here have allowed the city of Cleveland, the county of Cuyahoga, and the state of Ohio to allow me that right. And with it the right to equal protection, the right to own property, and most importantly, the right to incorporate. The right to hold assets anywhere in the world. The right to litigate."

"Aloeus, Inc.," I said. "I take it there is a Theophane, Inc.?"

"Much more than that, Mr. Maxwell." She looked over her shoulder, back at the pillar. *"At that workstation, I have won more battles against your kind than had ever been fought on the other side of the Portal. With a single e-mail, I can send armies from a dozen corporations into motion in any country on this planet. That is power, Mr. Maxwell. That is why I came here."*

CHAPTER ELEVEN

I LEFT the BP Building feeling as if I had just walked through a combat zone. The adrenaline was slowly leaking out of my system, and I was filled with an appreciation of the fact that I was still alive. Intellectually, I knew that I hadn't been in any physical danger. Theophane had as little need to show displeasure in a physical way as Baldassare did.

My body was convinced otherwise.

Egil Nixon was next on my list today. I was hoping that he was hiding out at home, since that was where I was headed. I really wanted to talk to him about what he had seen, and why Adrian Phillips was on that boat. I also wanted to see his eyes when he answered. Whatever he did say, my experience is that most people—outside the professions that require it—make rotten liars.

Faust.

The name rang in my head as I drove the Volkswagen through the working-class Slavic Village neighborhood that Egil Nixon called home. The place was in the midst of gentrification, and the houses were split evenly between places that had served as family homes for twenty years, and brand-new spit-shined renovations that went for twice the money to young couples or singles who had no family. No kids anyway.

Nixon lived in one of the latter.

Theophane's response when I asked her if she knew anyone named "Faust," her response was *"Faust is no dragon."* That struck me as a nondenial, but I hadn't been able to get her to elaborate. For all the stonewalling I was getting on the name, I was getting the sense that it was important, and related to Aloeus' death.

Nixon's car was in the driveway. I was in luck.

I pulled up in front of the building and walked up to the chain-link fence surrounding the front yard. The gate was hanging open. I pushed it open the rest of the way and walked up the path to the front door. I glanced at the car in the driveway, a late model BMW, black.

The lawn was mowed with surgical precision, the path perfectly edged, the grass stopping in a perfect circle around the base of the tree that dominated the small front yard.

The house itself was brick, the trim painted in a Victorian tricolor scheme of rose, gray, and hunter green. I mounted the steps to a brand-new front door that was mostly a beveled-glass oval. The porch was small, but neatly kept, the patio furniture arranged just so, as if awaiting a photo shoot.

I pressed the doorbell and heard it chime inside the house.

I couldn't see anything through the window. A gauze curtain was drawn across it, and the house looked darkened beyond it.

I pressed the button again, thinking I had struck out. Hell, if the city was hiding something, they could have easily bought the guy a ticket to Hawaii.

I was just about to ring the chime again, when I heard a window shatter upstairs.

"What the . . . ?" I backed from the doorway and looked up in time to see a figure leaping from the second floor, above the driveway. The black-clad figure moved as if in slow motion, tumbling through the air, to land in a crouch in front of the nose of the BMW.

It was not Egil Nixon.

He wore black leather, and his shaved head shone in the sunlight. I could see a flash of gold from several fingers. He wore a face that I wasn't going to forget.

The mage from last night.

He looked almost as surprised to see me as I was him.

"Hey—"

He was a man in a hurry. The lights bipped on the BMW and the door opened for him as he dove toward the driver's side. I ran for my Volkswagen as the black car was pulling out of the driveway. He turned left, which made me realize I'd never get my car around in time to follow him. So, instead of diving into my Volkswagen, I ran into the street to get a good view of the license plate.

It wasn't breaking and entering, because the front door was open. It also wasn't obstructing justice, because I was calling 911 as I entered the house looking for Egil Nixon. The only thing I left out of my call was the fact that I'd met the intruder before.

The house itself was pathologically neat. The sparse, modern furniture looked as if it had been laid out with a T-square and a level. That made the smell that much more ominous. A sour, ferric smell coming from upstairs.

I tread lightly on the white Berber carpeting as I climbed the steps. The smell intensified as I went.

I wasn't completely surprised at what I found, but that didn't make the sight any easier to take. Egil Nixon had suffered at the hands of the mage. Arcane inhuman writing scrawled the walls of his bedroom, spiraling up to where his body hung, suspended by spikes driven into the ceiling. His naked body had been slit from Adam's apple to groin, and the flesh had been pulled back to allow various parts to dangle. The carpet was soaked with Nixon's blood.

I turned away, walking carefully not to disturb anything, and went outside to wait for the police to show up.

Not a long wait. The first three cop cars were turning down the street as I came out. They pulled up, surrounding my Volkswagen, and when they turned off their sirens, I could hear more coming in the distance. One cop came up to the house and hustled me off the porch as another one started stringing up yellow police tape across the gate and the driveway.

As the cop questioned me about what happened, half a dozen more police cars showed up as well as a forensic van with SPU markings. My cop got the details from me and stationed me by his police car as he went to give the details to a supervisor. Once he left, I had the chance to make a call to the office.

"*Cleveland Press*. Columbia Jennings—"

"It's Maxwell. The shit's hitting the fan here."

"Maxwell? What's happening?"

"I don't know if the police are going to let me go in time to turn something in on time for tomorrow's edition. Egil Nixon's very dead."

"Wait," I heard the rustle of papers on the desk, a mumbled obscenity, then the sound of fingers hitting the keyboard. "Okay, details."

"He was staked out on the ceiling, eviscerated, apparently in some sort of ritual. A man was seen leaving the scene—" I gave the mage's description. "He's driving a black BMW." I gave the plate number. "There are cops all over the place here, I count at least ten squad cars. An SPU forensics team is going into the house right now. I haven't gotten a comment from police yet—but I might because Thomas O'Malley is walking right toward—"

O'Malley reached over and took my phone.

"Hey, O'Malley, that's private property!"

He put the phone up to his ear and said, "He'll call you back." He flipped the thing shut and pointed the antenna toward me. "Do the words thin ice mean anything to you?"

"Don't give me that."

"You just *stumbled* on a corpse, Maxwell? Egil Nixon's corpse?"

"I wanted to talk about a dragon, O'Malley."

"If you've been withholding evidence—"

"I called once I saw a B&E."

"If I find out different, you're in serious trouble." He tossed me the phone. "You saw a suspect leave?"

"Yes," I repeated the description for the third time.

"Ever see this man before?"

"I don't know him," I evaded.

"Uh-huh. You'd recognize him if you saw him again?"

"Yes."

O'Malley nodded and looked back up at the house. The upper windows were glowing blue with whatever the forensic mages were doing. I caught a whiff of ozone on the air.

"Okay, Maxwell, get the hell out of here."

"What?" I had already figured on at least a couple hours questioning downtown.

"Leave," he said. "If we need you, we'll be in touch."

I was actually speechless for a moment as he turned around. I did manage to shout out a question as he walked away. "Do you think this is connected to the murder investigation?"

O'Malley stopped. He turned around with a face so stony that he looked more like a Mafioso than ever. "What murder investigation?"

"Aloeus."

"The dragon was the victim of a tragic accident."

"Was Mr. Nixon an accident victim, then?"

"These are two unrelated incidents. Now, if you would step behind the police line and let us do our job."

"What about Faust?" I asked.

"Officers," O'Malley called to the two nearest uniformed cops. "Please escort this man away from the crime scene.

"Is Faust a suspect?" I called as I was hauled past the outer line of parked patrol cars. No response. I was unceremoniously deposited on one end of the blocked off street, effectively stranded since my Volkswagen was in the center of all that police activity.

"Maxwell, when you step in it, you really step in it."

I turned around to see a familiar face. "Cutler?"

Kirk Cutler was a fellow reporter. He looked like his name—beefy, crewcut, smoking like a chimney. He would never had made it as a TV journalist. He was a twelve-year veteran of print crime reporting, and he'd worked at a half dozen papers going back to when Cleveland was a one-paper town. He had come to resemble his subject matter.

Currently I think he worked for the *Leader*.

He leaned on a beat-up Oldsmobile that looked like a scarred veteran of a 1970s cop show. "You remembered," he said from behind a cigarette, "how touching." He smiled.

"Nixon?"

"Police scanner is a wonderful thing. Though Nixon is only part of the reason I'm here. That's why I'm waiting for you, rather than wading into that mess." He cocked his head back toward the house crawling with cops. "I got everything the police were willing to give me anyway."

"You were waiting for me?"

"Uh-huh," Cutler flung the cigarette at the asphalt by his feet and ground it out with a steel-toed work boot. "You found the body, after all."

I nodded, a little uncomfortable being on the other side of the journalistic fence.

"Also, we got a mutual acquaintance to discuss." He opened the door of the Olds and said. "So, need a lift?"

I cast a glance at my Volkswagen and nodded.

True to his reputation, he drove us both to the Crazy Horse Saloon. As topless dance clubs go, the Crazy Horse was fairly classy. It was downtown, and a good part of their clientele was the lunchtime old-boy network. Executives, veeps, lawyers from the Justice Center—the kind of folks that want their smut scrubbed clean. The dancers looked as airbrushed as a *Playboy* centerfold.

We didn't look like we fit in, but the extra bill I saw Cutler slip into the cover charge got us a choice table, in a private corner, with an unobstructed view of the stage.

I ordered a Diet Coke, while he chose a "Grog," one of the less subtle local microbrew beers. He seemed very much at home, lounging back and watching the stage. Thankfully he had the good taste not to order a lap dance.

He yawned as the latest athlete lowered herself from the

chromed pole on stage left and cleared the way for the next performer.

Up to this point, I had done most of the talking. I'd told him about the scene at Nixon's house, including the mage's escape and O'Malley's appearance. I figured that it was his turn to reciprocate.

"You wanted to talk about a mutual acquaintance?" I prodded him.

"Yeah," he said, taking another swig of his Grog. The beer had an eerie phosphorescence in the black light. It swirled and made complex patterns in the bottle independent of the motion of the liquid. Cutler elbowed me as the next dancer came up on the stage. "Look at the set on her."

I cast the obligatory admiring glance at the stage. "So, Cutler—"

"His street name is Bone Daddy."

I looked back at him, he hadn't taken his eyes off the stage. I suspected that, if he was here alone, he'd be shoving fives and tens in the dancer's garter. When you hit a certain age, have a decent job, and find yourself single, you tend to get weird with money. With me it was an entertainment system, with Cutler I think it was tittie bars.

Cutler kept talking. "Given name is Caleb Mosha Washington. Rap sheet longer than Euclid Avenue. Priors—defiling a corpse, body snatching, possession of criminal tools, a few things that haven't been crimes since the Salem Witch Trials."

"This is the guy who jumped out of the window?"

"*And* the guy who engaged in a little clandestine chat with you in East Cleveland."

I choked on my Diet Coke. Coughing, I put it on the table and grabbed a napkin to cover my mouth.

Cutler laughed. "Didn't think I knew that, did you?"

"How?"

"I've been following something big. As big as your chicken little, maybe bigger."

"What?"

"Rogue cops in the SPU."

"There've been rumors of that since they formed the unit."

"I got more than rumors. I got elves dealing with Bone Daddy. I got cash changing hands. I got Bone Daddy walking away from several airtight busts. They're in each other's pockets." He turned to face me. "You, my friend, are gold. I trailed Bone to that little rendezvous of yours, but you were in there *with* them."

"Ahh."

"You see my interest."

"And I get?"

Cutler laughed. "The appreciation of a colleague," he reached into his jacket and pulled out a CD. "You also get all the background I've already dug up on the dirty elves and Mr. Bone."

I reached for the CD, and he put it back inside his jacket. "Why don't you go first?"

CHAPTER TWELVE

IT was late afternoon before I recovered my Volkswagen and had it parked across from the old Cleveland Trust Building. I was biding my time, rummaging through the contents of Cutler's CD while I waited for the late dragon's lawyer to show.

Cutler had not been parsimonious with his bequest of data. I had in hand the results of what had to be several month's worth of investigation. The linchpin of which was Bone Daddy, aka Caleb Mosha Washington, a mage of no fixed address. The history Cutler had built for the guy went back as far as the guy's birth certificate. The notes were a combination of interview transcripts, old news articles, and public records from various sources.

Skimming the high points, I gleaned the following;

Bone Daddy was born to an upper-middle-class family in Shaker Heights. Father was a doctor, mother a lawyer. Their only son had been problematic early on. When he was six, he destroyed about eight grand worth of electronic equipment, including a laptop computer and three cell phones by throwing them into the pool. When he was eight, he responded to one of his mother's business trips by slashing the tires on her BMW, *and* on his dad's Jaguar. When he was twelve, he managed to call a travel agent on his dad's behalf and successfully cancel hotel reservations, car rentals, and a return ticket from a Las Vegas convention while his dad was still on the outbound flight. At fourteen, he was stealing his parents' cars. At sixteen, he was stealing their credit card numbers.

Whatever point he was trying to get across was never made. At eighteen he left.

Once he left home, his rebellion seemed to take a different tack. From the point he left home, until about a year after the Portal opened, Bone Daddy didn't have any trouble with the law. I was surprised, and I made the initial assumption that he just wasn't getting caught.

But Cutler's bio wasn't relying on police records. He had tracked down and talked to dozens of Bone's associates. The fact was, during the time in question, Bone Daddy's recreational activities weren't illegal. Mr. Bone was a mystic before mysticism worked. He was a practicing neo-Pagan, devotee of Alister Crowley, the Golden Dawn, and a shitload of other crap that I don't know jack about.

Now, when the Portal opens, the power that flows out of it doesn't care where the rituals come from. All that power is looking for is focus. Pattern. Bone Daddy had that in spades. From all accounts, the people on that particular fringe regarded him as an expert in the magical arts for two or three years before the Portal opened.

Bone Daddy was a black-market mage before anyone realized such a thing existed. Apparently, with the newfound power came a renewed antiauthoritarian streak. While most of the mages in town, especially those at Bone's level, were playing nice and working within the envelope provided by the Port Authority in an attempt to control what could be a very dangerous commodity, Bone would have nothing of oversight, regulation, or any legal limits on his power.

A spell called for a human corpse? Who was he to argue? Potentially lethal alchemical components? What his clients didn't know wouldn't hurt them. Violations of privacy, curses, sales of deadly potions? It was a new world, and people who weren't prepared to defend themselves from it had to be prepared to pay the price.

I couldn't help but think of Morgan and his eyeball tumors.

What made Bone Daddy all the more interesting was, despite all his arrests—as Cutler said, a rap sheet as long as Euclid Avenue—he'd never been convicted. He'd never even had to stay overnight at the Justice Center. That spoke of one of two things. Either he was an informant, or cops were being paid off.

Perhaps, as Cutler speculated in his notes, both.

Cutler had compiled an exhaustive itinerary of meetings going back as far as the formation of the SPU. Even at that point, Bone Daddy was a major figure. He was in the top five underground mages. He was not the type of candidate that cops select as an informant. You were supposed to use little fish to catch big fish.

Apparently what was happening here was the reverse.

A small cabal of SPU officers, all elves, had been meeting repeatedly with Bone Daddy since the formation of the unit.

According to Cutler's notes and a few digital pictures, cash went both ways. From the looks of things, Bone handed rivals and minor annoyances to the SPU elves, and in return he was pretty much immune from the cops.

It seemed off-key to me; elves have always seemed to put a lot of stock in personal honor. Like their reserve, it seemed a racial characteristic. Enough so that I found it hard to believe that a quartet of them were dirty. But Cutler's evidence was pretty damning, even if I didn't take my own experiences into account.

The crowning bit, of course, was the fact that they were the *same* elves that'd kidnapped me.

The most chilling part was a story Cutler included about the SPU's founding, seven years ago. The article was content-free, avoiding the nasty feelings in the police rank and file about the creation of this departmental entity that, while supervised by a police commander, was essentially only answerable to the Public Safety Director. What got me was the picture that accompanied the article.

It was an artist's rendering, probably based on a couple of digital snapshots too low-res to print. It showed the ranks of the twenty-five officers that formed the initial core of the SPU. The elf-to-human ratio was nineteen to six in favor of the elves. I knew that over the next seven years the ratio would drop to nearly nil on the human end. The human cops were just too subject to the ostracism of their fellow officers while the elves could care less.

Sitting in the back were four familiar-looking, overly tall kinsmen. These were the bastards who'd kidnapped me and fed me to Bone Daddy. They had been in the unit from the start, which meant they all probably had command positions now.

I stared into Elf Number One's expressionless eyes. Looking down at the caption, I finally had a name to go with the face—Maelgwyn Caledvwlch.

I preferred "Elf Number One."

There was a tapping on the driver's side window, and I closed my notebook.

Looking at me through the glass was the man I was waiting for. I lowered the window.

"Are you Kline Maxwell?" he asked me.

"That's me," I said with a smile.

The man gave me a sour expression. His hair was white, his face clean-shaven. Narrow glasses with gold rims perched on a beak of a nose. He wore a charcoal-gray suit that could have been a twin to the one he'd worn yesterday. He still wore a black armband. "I do not appreciate blackmail," said the late dragon Aloeus' personal lawyer.

I couldn't help smiling, because what kept going through my mind was that kid Sam Barlogh saying, *"You used to be big, didn't you?"*

I let myself out of the car and looked at my quarry. His name was Jefferson Friday, and he had been a partner in one of the largest law firms in the city—one that, coincidentally, had Forest Hills Enterprises as a major client. Shortly after the Portal opened, he went into private practice which, some tentative research showed, had not hurt his standard of living despite his only having the single client. Apparently, Aloeus, Inc., paid well.

"Mr. Friday, this is not blackmail. Blackmail involves a *quid pro quo*. I was just letting you know information that I've gathered, and I'm providing you the opportunity to comment."

"You can't print things like . . ."

"Like what?" I prompted.

He shook his head. "Come on," he waved me forward, "You'll have your comment."

Having Friday lead me into Aloeus' lair within the Cleveland Trust Building was no small achievement. While dragons were notoriously insular, their lawyers brought client confidentiality to a whole new level of pathology. It had taken me a few hours on the phone, sifting through what I could find of Aloeus' employees, before I even found out who Friday *was*. There had been a dozen lawyers on Aloeus, Inc.'s payroll—but there was only one personal counsel to the dragon-in-chief.

And, while Friday could quite readily stonewall the likes of Sam Barlogh and his fellows, Sam Barlogh and his fellows weren't following quite the same paths I was. A catalog of property damage might make a splashy feature, and details of the corpse's explosive demise might make titillating copy, but those angles weren't going to raise Friday's eyebrows a millimeter or encourage him to give anything but a boilerplate comment on the death of a client. However, a tastefully composed e-mail hinting at Aloeus' powerful connections to the current administration and massive land deals with Forest Hills Enterprises, and suddenly Jefferson Friday, Esq., was a lot more interested in talking.

We stood on one of the massive stone steps of the Cleveland Trust Building, and Friday faced the elaborate scrollwork on the heavy metal door. He made a few passes with his hand and muttered something under his breath. The metal doors silently opened, revealing a marble stairway into the soft-lit inner sanctum.

He led me through a room that was all pillars, wood, and marble. The only furniture was that of a permanent nature, like the long marble partition that housed the darkened tellers' windows.

The spaces were still and silent, tomblike. The tinted windows allowed little daylight to break the gloom, and only one out of three light fixtures were in use.

Scattered over the marble floor, leading back into the darkened areas, were Persian rugs and embroidered cushions the size of my couch. There was room down here for a dragon, but I didn't see how it could enter or leave.

"Did Aloeus live here?" I asked.

"This was his home."

"How did he get into the building?"

He looked over his shoulder as he took me back to a curving staircase. "We removed a wall opposite East Ninth and Euclid." He looked back up the staircase.

I looked around and tried to see the exit as we ascended. I couldn't find it. Warded and camouflaged, most probably. Wouldn't want just any riffraff walking into your lair.

On the second floor, we passed through a massive mahogany door into an office that overlooked the intersection of Euclid and East Ninth. He seated himself behind an acre of desk that reflected the white monolith of National City back at me in shades of rose.

There wasn't a chair for visitors, and I doubted he was the type to open up to someone casually sitting on his desk, so I leaned against the doorframe.

"So," I asked as I took out my notebook, "for the record?"

He shook his head. "You have excessive temerity, Mr. Maxwell."

"I'm a journalist, Mr. Friday. My job is to report the facts."

"However distorted those facts are?"

"Mr. Friday, a distorted fact is an oxymoron."

"And what you e-mailed me were *facts?*"

"You say they aren't?" I smiled. "Can you elaborate on where, exactly, I am mistaken?"

"You are ready to print all about his involvement in mundane affairs. Human affairs. Nothing could be further from what he stood for."

"From my point of view, Aloeus was a major player in city politics. There's legislation that wouldn't have existed if not for him."

"That is my point. You do not understand. No one would."
I nodded. "That's why we're here, for you to explain it all."

Friday explained it for me, in depth, as if arguing his point to a judge. He began with the standard, though detailed, explanation of what was on the other side of the Portal.

On the other side was an empire whose name roughly transliterated as Ragnan. Ragnan was a massive state that enveloped that world's main continent the way the Roman Empire had once enveloped Europe. Ragnan was a human state, upstart by immortal standards. But upstart or not, it had about five thousand years to establish itself as the ultimate temporal power in that world.

Ultimate control of the empire rested in the Thesarch, a human emperor who not only held ultimate political and spiritual authority, but—due to the nature of magic's attraction to ritual and meaning—held massive power inherent in the office.

I knew the story. The mention of divine kings made most people think of medieval Europe. Close enough for people whose only dealings with the place was three steps removed via the side effects of the Portal. However, the reality wasn't something out of the knights of the round table. The Thesarch was a true god-king, a cross between a pharaoh and the pope.

Of course, the Thesarch wasn't universally loved. Ragnan's history was drenched with the blood of countless wars, most against nonhumans. At the time the Portal opened, Ragnan was ruled by a Thesarch more despotic than most—the Thesarch Valdis.

Valdis had reigned for a century before the Portal opened. He exhibited all the characteristics of a good despot: a conviction in his own infallibility; an unquenchable thirst for control; and a ruthless paranoia. Friday related a story that was worthy of an Old Testament rewritten by Josef Stalin: in the third decade of Valdis' reign, he issued an order for the Lords in each district to monitor the population for criticism of the Thesarch. The speakers of such disloyal thoughts were to have their property seized and ceded to the empire. One Lord Mayor refused to obey the order as being too much of a burden on the population. When Valdis learned of this, he called down a rain of fire that reduced the city and everyone in it to ashes—except for the Lord Mayor, whom Valdis left as a crippled beggar just so he'd know what had happened.

During Valdis' reign, the population of dragons in the world had been halved, a nation of elves had ceased to exist, and five of Ragnan's own cities were reduced to ash.

I nodded a lot, and took a few notes, but so far a lot of this I could have been obtained from the *Encyclopedia Britannica*. Then Friday mentioned Aloeus, and my attention sharpened.

The Portal formed in a place fortunately remote from the forces of Ragnan and Valdis. And while the great despot knew of the disturbance, he did not initially know its nature. Elvish fugitives were the first to scramble through it, a few days ahead of Valdis' mages, and few weeks ahead of his ground forces.

Aloeus saw the Portal as more than escape for a few. He saw it as the prospect of a different world, without Valdis' totalitarianism. In the middle of the night, the day after I had seen the Portal open, Aloeus flew through into our world.

At this point, the Portal was still guarded by a half dozen cops in an empty floodlit stadium. The only things to have come through had, so far, been alien-looking humanoids who spoke no English. Everyone was preoccupied with the electronic chaos the Portal's opening had caused. The Portal itself wasn't seen as a direct threat.

The sight of Aloeus unfolding his wings and rising from the top of the Portal changed that. Fifteen cops saw him unfold out of the top of the spherical Portal, a hundred feet from skull to tail, the shadow of his wings blacking out half the field.

The cops, being cops, started shooting, which did very little. Killing a dragon with a handgun is kind of like trying to kill a bull elephant with a drinking straw—it might be theoretically possible, but would require twenty years of anatomy study and complete surprise on the part of the victim.

Aloeus let out a belch of fire that outshone the floodlights just to get the point across, before he flew off into the night.

His point being that the Portal was dangerous. His goal was to throw a scare into the folks on this side of the Portal, so they wouldn't be caught completely off guard if Valdis tried to invade. It achieved the desired effect. Within twenty hours, the National Guard was ringing the stadium.

Aloeus lived here, concealed by his own magical abilities, for nearly two months before he absorbed enough of the language to communicate with the men here. He picked his first contacts very carefully, not people in the city administration, but powerful men who supported the administration. Friday didn't name Baldassare, but we both knew who he was referring to.

Friday talked about Aloeus' career as one of a diplomat, not a politician. He was very clear on that point. Aloeus had always kept a distance from human politics.

"His interest was always Ragnan, and the citizens from there." His eyes were very bright and distant behind his glasses, through his expression never changed. "Do you understand? His goal was to lead his people to a new homeland, free from oppression."

Uh-huh, Dragon as Moses. "From what I know about local history, Valdis stopped being a problem over there about four months after the portal opened."

The bright light in his eyes didn't dim. I was almost ready for him to start chanting or speaking in tongues. "A changing of the guard, no more."

I nodded. "More than that, I think. Where Valdis was blockading the Portal on his end, his successor has been much more willing to deal with us."

"With Rayburn, you mean. With the human government. Do you think the purges have stopped there, or that the expansion of the empire has ceased? No. These people need an advocate, every nonhuman citizen of that world and this. *That* was Aloeus' mission. That was why he was so . . . *political.*" In Friday's mouth the word was a curse.

Now he's Martin Luther King.

"Still, with Valdis deposed, there's free traffic across the Portal. That is an improvement."

Friday looked at me, and I had a gut feeling that there was something he was holding back.

"Did Aloeus have anything to do with the coup in Ragnan?"

"He never involved himself directly in any of Ragnan's affairs after he left the Portal."

That was a nondenial. "What about indirectly?"

"Indirectly?" Friday folded his hands in front of him and frowned. "Valdis' power was largely based on the perception of his omnipotence. When the Portal opened, he was fatally weakened."

"So, according to you, Aloeus' public life was an exercise in altruism?"

Friday nodded.

"What about the purchase of land in Mexico? What motivated Aloeus to do that?"

He leaned back in his chair and turned around to face the window. "He did not do that. Aloeus, Inc., did that."

"That's sidestepping. Outside the state of Ohio they're effectively the same thing."

"No, sir," Friday said. "One is dead."

"I apologize."

He shook his head. "The corporation is large, and Aloeus did not oversee everything personally. It was an investment opportunity one of our people took advantage of, that's all." He rubbed the bridge of his nose and said, "Please go now. If you need more questions answered, e-mail my office."

"I'll do that," I smiled and flipped the notebook shut. "I can let myself out."

Friday nodded, still facing away from me.

I started to leave, but the pressure of too many "Colombo" reruns got to me. "Pardon me, just one more thing—"

Friday turned toward me. "What?"

"You know a person by the name of Faust?"

His face went stony. "No, I do not."

"Thanks," I turned and left him there.

He was probably lying about Faust, but I *knew* he was lying about the land. I don't know why. Whatever was going on about that, it wasn't an investment. I had researched the site. The land was miles from anywhere and had no road or water access. It was the size of three or four counties, and from all accounts it was mountainous and uninhabitable. Short of some miraculous mineral deposits—large enough to justify mining there—Aloeus, Inc., would be lucky to unload it for half of what they paid.

I suspected that there was more to Aloeus' connection to the end of Valdis' reign. It just smelled too convenient in retrospect.

I also had trouble buying the dragon as a selfless messianic figure. That went counter to everything Theophane told me about dragon kind. Dragons were supposed to be motivated by power. That was right in line with all the political maneuvering that Aloeus did, while Friday's angle was almost completely opposed.

Then, again, I wondered.

CHAPTER THIRTEEN

I DON'T know if Mr. Friday would approve of my story, but I did give a fair bit of ink to his point of view. It certainly gave a different perspective on the decedent. I left out, for the time being, any speculation over the cause of death, even though the murder of the County Coroner at the hands of Bone Daddy gave me ample grounds to speculate.

That speculation took me down to University Circle, to the brand new wing of the Natural History Museum. More than a wing, it was an entirely new building somewhat removed from the old center of science and paleontology, as if the trustees wanted to make a point of separating the two. In front of the old building was a life-size fiberglass statue of a stegosaurus, in front of the new building was a life-size statue of a dragon in flight.

The old building couldn't help but be upstaged.

I walked up the crushed gravel walkway and looked at the statue. From recent experience, I could tell that the rendering was accurate. I could also tell the subject wasn't either Aloeus or Theophane. A small plaque named the dragon Phlegethon.

You walked under Phlegethon to get into the new wing, and the sensation was somewhat disconcerting. The dragon was suspended with no obvious support, hovering, its wings outstretched from one side of the facade to the other. The only sign of what kept it up there was a series of white stones carved with elaborate runes hidden in the landscaping.

I entered the building and paused a moment in the lobby to get my bearings. A small ticket window stood off the cavernous lobby to the right, flanked by a rearing griffin and a rearing unicorn. The display was designed to be reminiscent of some sort of heraldic device.

I walked over to the window.

It was fifteen bucks to get into the place, including the lecture by

Dr. Shafran. I used my *Press* American Express Card. The guy behind the counter swiped my card and gave me a ticket. I felt like I was walking into a theme park.

In a way I was.

Cleveland has always had a fair number of museums. However, even before the Portal a noticeable fission had begun. For three quarters of the twentieth century, we had places of genuine scientific, historical, and artistic value. The old Natural History Museum had genuine paleontologists doing original work in the field. The Cleveland Museum of Art had a nationally recognized collection and the best collection of Medieval and Renaissance armor and weaponry on the continent. The Western Reserve historical society was a place of genuine scholarship.

Then we went and built the Rock and Roll Hall of Fame. Now don't get me wrong, I'm as interested in Janis Joplin's psychedelic Porsche as anyone else. But there's a reason they built it on the lakefront and not in University Circle. It has about as much to do with scholarship and education as P.T. Barnum's original American Museum. Then there was the Great Lakes Science Museum, which I don't think has ever employed a genuine scientist.

By the time the Portal opened, we already had two sets of museums in this town. The old style places run by stuffy Ph.Ds and paid for by grants and donations, and the new style run by marketing MBAs and paid for by tourism.

The old Natural History Museum was the former. The new Natural History Museum was most aggressively the latter. It had been a shrewd decision on the part of the board, since the whole complex, old and new, was now self-sufficient based on the income the new wing generated.

Dr. Shafran was lecturing in one of the auditoriums to the rear of the main building. To get there, I walked past displays illustrating the flora and fauna unique to our Portal-influenced environment. I also passed a large swirling display describing the atmospheric effects caused by the Portal itself. The three-dimensional animation filled half of the room before the auditoriums. Central to it was a tiny model of the Portal. Even though it wasn't the real thing, the sight of an alien world reflected in a thing the size of a small Christmas ornament made me stop for a moment. They even had a breeze coming from the faux Portal's direction, a breeze that reversed as they illustrated temperature and pressure changes.

I slipped past the display and into the auditorium. The lecture was just about half over, and Dr. Shafran was speaking to room about half full. I took a seat in the back. The heavily accented voice was familiar, but he didn't resemble Bela Lugosi. He had, in fact, a very innocuous appearance. Something like a German watchmaker, or Gepetto. He was a small man with a fringe of white hair surrounding a balding crown. He had a mustache a half-shade darker than his hair, and he wore thick, round bifocals that he had a habit of taking off his nose and gesturing with.

". . . is a failure of reason," he was saying. "Even those in the scientific community can be guilty of such a failure. I believe that the fault lies in our semantics. We called this thing 'magic,' so therefore no rules apply. Wrong, very wrong . . ." He walked back and forth behind the podium. "The application of scientific principles, the scientific method, is as valid here as anywhere else."

He looked up into the audience. "I see incredulous stares. You do not believe this? Shall I make an analogy for you. Cooking? You understand that an egg that will boil in sixty seconds here will need to boil longer in Denver, Colorado. Do we say that the laws of the kitchen are in anarchy? Do we expect our souffleé recipe to behave the same at whatever altitude we cook. Of course not." He looked around, and I could see a few blank stares myself.

"A starker example. You light a match. Do you expect that match to light just as well underwater? On the moon. In an atmosphere of pure carbon dioxide? Of course not. But the same laws of physics apply to each match." He made a grand gesture with his glasses and then replaced them. "Just because a chant, a ritual, a *spell* works here and does not work elsewhere, that does not mean the suspension of the laws of nature here. The local conditions are *different.* Energies flow here that flow nowhere else on the planet. Just as a match will not light in the absence of oxygen, a *spell* will not work in the absence of these energies."

Dr. Shafran had me thinking, again, why Aloeus, Inc., would be interested in a huge plot of mountainous Mexican land. I couldn't see why anyone, much less someone who was limited to a geographic area about a hundred and fifty miles around Cleveland, would be interested in that land. It seemed to me that this had to be an obvious counterexample to Friday's protests that Aloeus wasn't interested in human politics. That land could only be of interest to people in the mundane would, people who could use it.

Power by proxy, Theophane called it. To Aloeus, the property wasn't a physical object. It was a symbol, only meaningful for the value that others placed in it. The dragon wanted the land, not for itself, but as a leverage with someone who *was* interested in it.

Once I discovered who had interest in that land, I had a gut instinct that I'd be a lot closer to what Aloeus was trying to do. Perhaps a lot closer to why he had died.

The way things would turn would prove me half right, and half *very* wrong.

Dr. Shafran was wrapping up his lecture. "The scientific mind should not shrink before this time and place. Never has such a broad category of unquantified and unanalyzed phenomena been presented to a civilization with the tools to explain it. There are such . . . possibilities." The doctor looked down at his watch and said, "I'm afraid I've run over, but I will take a few questions. Yes?"

A woman stood up. She wore a necklace of chunky amber crystals and an orange sundress with a Navaho motif. "You've mentioned nothing about the spirit, Dr. Shafran."

"No, I have not."

"But isn't that what the point is, here. This place is where the spirit of man is closest to the spirit of nature—"

"I am not a theologian, madam. I am a scientist. I see no reason to introduce unmeasurable forces into an environment that does not require them."

"But you've said that the human mind controls these forces—"

"I have said that these forces can be influenced by human mental activity. Repeated and ritualized mental activity. You may call that spirit if you like, but in my opinion that is simply an old human prejudice. Our brain is no more the center of the universe than our planet is. There is no reason that a properly programmed computer, or even a well-trained monkey, could not perform the same 'spiritual' feats as a human mage."

The woman sat down, looking unconvinced.

Another man stood up and asked a more interesting question. "Is it impossible then, for any magical effect to influence the world outside this Portal's influence?"

"That is a good question," Dr. Shafran took off his glasses and pointed at the questioner. "It depends on what you term a 'magical effect.' It should be obvious that any change in the physical world will persist outside the realm of the Portal. The world outside doesn't care if a rock was carved by magic or by a chisel. It becomes more complicated as the mage tries to influence the world outside directly. But the existence of the Portal itself shows that it *is* possible."

Dr. Shafran smiled, probably because he'd gotten a bit of a reaction from a relatively dead audience.

"This land was empty of any magical force, and yet, the Portal—the quintessential magical effect—opened here. Therefore it is possible. For that reason, if no other, we must study the Portal. Once that mechanism is understood, and we know what forces created it, we will be able to channel this power where we will. Perhaps even generate it.

"If there are no more questions, I should dismiss you. The museum closes in five minutes."

I walked up to the podium after most of the audience had filed out. Dr. Shafran was picking up papers and putting them in a briefcase. "Good lecture, Doctor."

"Thank you," he said without looking at me. Now that he wasn't speaking publicly, his accent had grown thicker. His brows furrowed a moment, and he turned to face me. "The voice is familiar. We have spoken?"

I nodded and held out my hand. "Kline Maxwell, *Cleveland Press*, we spoke yesterday."

Dr. Shafran smiled broadly, put down the case, and grabbed my arm with both of his.. "*Yes.* The newspaperman. You do me a great service."

"You did me a service, Doctor."

"Nonsense," he gave my arm a vigorous shake and let it go. "It is you who helps my work." He waved at the auditorium. "Mine is not a popular study."

"I find that hard to believe."

"Believe me." He picked up his case. "No one wants to hear what I have to say. The scientific community," he shook his head sadly. "Too many people dismissed what was happening here as rampant fantasy before it was documented. I'm afraid that the whole generation will have to die off before one can get an impartial jury to judge a scientific paper on the subject. And the public . . ."

"I saw the woman."

"I am doing serious work here, and what kind of questions do I get? Spirits, angels, demons, God and the devil. Do they not hear what it is I am saying?" He patted me on the shoulder. "We must leave before they lock us in this place."

He led me out of the auditorium and back through the halls of exhibits. "You do me a great service by quoting me accurately. Perhaps I can use the attention in a grant request."

"Then you wouldn't mind answering a few more questions for me?"

"Certainly."

We took a seat outside the entrance, under the dragon's looming effigy.

"What concerns you tonight, Mr. Maxwell?"

I looked up at the abdomen of the dragon above us. We were lucky that Aloeus had hit in the Flats. The kind of damage that might have happened elsewhere was frightening.

"I wanted to know if it is possible that what happened to the dragon might not have been an accident."

"How exactly do you mean? Certainly the dragon could have ended his own life in such a way, intentionally aiming to an area of fatally low power."

"No, that's not what I mean."

"You are asking if someone else could have created the conditions that killed him."

"Yes."

"It is possible."

"How?"

Dr. Shafran took off his bifocals and waved them at the air around us. "The power is a fluid. When any magical effect occurs, that power is drained for a bit, somewhere. Like siphoning water from a river. If a spell was cast, involving a massive amount of energy, a momentary void could be created."

"How massive?"

The doctor shrugged. "I do not have enough information to quantify that. Enough to spread the burden, the energy flows through the mage, like an electric circuit. Too few and the synapses would fry."

"A guess?"

"Perhaps a dozen."

Christ, I didn't think there were that many competent black-market mages in the city. "So, to engineer that, you need the collusion of at least twelve mages?"

Dr. Shafran shook his head. "No, you only need one specific mage."

"But you said—"

"The mechanics are like this, Mr. Maxwell. In a proper multiperson ritual, there is only one mage directing the spell. All the other participants are gathering and channeling the power to create the effect envisioned by the central figure. If more than one person is actively casting, they *must* be focusing on different elements. Each person's influence is different, and if you have more than one person concentrating on the same thing, the effect is to dilute the effectiveness of whatever you're trying to do, not multiply it."

"But if a dozen people cast something, aren't they all going to know what it is? At least after the fact? If you're expecting some massive effect and something *else* happens"—

"You do not understand me. The void, the power being sucked away from the river, that is a *side effect.* It is quite possible for a mage to cast some great effect and be completely ignorant of the specific geographic location the energy to cast the spell came from. For most rituals the source of the energy is local and arbitrary, but all that's required is one mage in the ritual to direct *where* the power is coming from. If a mage had wanted to kill a dragon in this fashion, he need only participate in a large enough ritual, and direct the channel from where the power came from. It would be possible to do so with none of the other participants being aware."

"So it *could* have been murder."

"Yes, it could have been. But it was not."

I had been staring at the dragon above us and thinking of Aloeus' last moments. Dr. Shafran's assertion brought me back to earth. I turned and looked at him. "Why do you say that?"

"A cursory examination of the body would have revealed it," he said. "Anyone remotely familiar with the process would have been able to tell the difference."

"What? It's the same thing, isn't it?"

He shook his head. "Only insofar that the cause of death is the same. But the differences would be as stark as the difference between death by asphyxiation and death by explosive decompression. The natural phenomenon is a gradient, the body would die at different rates in different areas, the process would be nonuniform. An artificial drain would cause a sudden, stark, absence of power. The parts of the body inside the effect would all be affected equally. Any part outside the effect would be completely unscathed." He looked at me. "Such a line of division, such a uniform degradation of the flesh, that would be as obvious as a bullet wound or a slash from a knife. The police would not dismiss such a thing as an accident."

No, but perhaps Coroner Nixon had.

If Dr. Nixon had falsified the manner of death, that gave someone an excellent motive to finish him off. Since Aloeus was now so much ash, there'd be no one left to contradict the "official" examination. I was more certain than ever that Aloeus' death was murder.

I decided to not bother Dr. Shafran with my conclusions. I thanked him for his time and stood up. "One last thing."

"Certainly."

"Have you ever heard of anyone named Faust?"

"No—"

"Thank you."

"Not recently."

I stopped in mid stride and turned back around. "What?"

"A long time ago, back in the months after the Portal opened." He seemed to be lost in thought for a moment.

"Yes?"

"Just a rumor I heard somewhere. When people were talking about elves and such taking over."

"What rumor, exactly?"

"Faust was the person who was going to lead the elvish takeover. A dozen different descriptions. All probably someone's paranoid fantasy. The elves have not taken over."

"Thank you."

One of many rumors to have spawned after the Portal opened. The doctor was right. It was probably someone's paranoid fantasy. Except for the fact that Bone Daddy and the SPU elves had been asking about him.

CHAPTER FOURTEEN

I GOT home late, and the message light was blinking on my home phone. No Shakespeare this time, just the voice of my ex-wife saying, "Call me." I set a Styrofoam box of tandori chicken on the coffee table and dialed her number, hoping that Sarah would answer the phone.

No such luck.

"Where have you been? It has to be nine-thirty out there."

"Ten-thirty," I corrected her, rolling my head to hear my neck pop.

"You talked to Sarah—"

"*She* called *me*," I said. Unlike the call from my daughter, the tone my ex-wife was using made me grateful for the distance between us.

"What did she tell you?"

I shook my head. "She told me you beat her with chains and fed her broken glass. What do you think she told me? *Sheesh.*"

There was a long pause before she said, "Do you think I'm being unreasonable?"

I closed my eyes and put my head in my hand. "Margaret, I told her that I wasn't going to pressure you on her behalf. I'm going to tell you the same thing."

"Kline, please—"

"I'm not *there*. I won't second-guess your parenting skills. I don't doubt you're a good mother, or that our daughter gave you ample justification, but I'm not getting involved in a fight between you two. Period."

"You're her father—"

"Thank you for clearing that up."

"You're supposed to back me up on things like this."

"That wasn't on the divorce paper I signed." I was sorry the moment I said it. I felt the words leave my lips and realized that she had managed to snare me in the old trap of following her up the emotional escalator.

"*Goddamn it, Kline!* Since she called you, she won't talk to me."

I sighed and took a deep breath to center myself. "Margaret, she called me to bitch about being grounded. She's a very pissed young woman."

"You're taking her side?" Her voice was escalating. Any moment now, dogs all over San Francisco would start howling in response.

"You know better than that. And my opinion has no bearing on how angry she is. Whether or not you're justified, has no bearing on how angry she is. She probably deserves everything she's getting. Do you think for a moment that makes her feel *better?*"

"You don't understand. You don't have to deal with this."

"That's exactly why I should keep my substantial nose out of the whole mess. Just step back and think of how much well-meaning destruction I could wreak if I tried that kind of long-distance parenting. You really want to debate curfews with me over the phone every week?"

"She was really upset, wasn't she?" Her voice had calmed down.

"It didn't seem unwarranted."

There was along sigh. "Sometimes I think it would be easier if you were closer."

"You're the one who moved."

"I couldn't have our child in that environment."

"It's a lot better now—"

"Kline—"

"Houses in the city are worth something now, the school system is finally—"

"Kline, *don't.*"

I stopped.

"You know better than that," she said. "Sarah's lived here most of her life now. She has friends—"

"Uh-huh. Now why don't you tell me about this Chris guy . . ."

Despite the successful deescalation of things with Margaret, my subconscious was uneasy enough to prod me with nightmares.

I am confronted with a specter of Aloeus' corpse, torn and broken worse than I had seen on the river. The body is being consumed by the unnatural rot that afflicted the corpses of slain magical beasts. It stares at me with a blind milky eye the size of a hubcap and whispers in an uneven voice that sounds like a tape recorder going bad, "Murder most foul, as in the best it is. But this most foul, strange and unusual . . ."

The voice merged with the sound of my phone demanding attention. I rolled off my couch, pissed at the second rude awakening to happen to me in the past forty-eight hours.

I grabbed the handset and growled "What?"

Even though it had been a dream, I was still surprised to answer the phone and hear the voice of Kirk Cutler and not my harassing Shakespeare buff.

"Maxwell, what happened to you? Why aren't you answering your cell phone?"

"Jesus Christ, Cutler. It's three-thirty in the morning."

"I've been trying to reach you for two hours."

"Did you hear me? It's *three-thirty. A.M.!*"

"I've been leaving messages all over—"

"Cutler, I go off duty when I come home. I turn my cell phone *off*. That means that I'm not even going to ask you why you're worked up, because whatever it is can wait until eight."

"Don't you listen to the radio? The news tonight—"

"I'm hanging up, Cutler."

I was reaching to hang up the phone, and just as I was about to set it in the cradle, I heard, very distinctly, the word, "Dead."

A feeling of dread filled my stomach as I raised the handset back to my ear. I began to wonder what would get Cutler so worked up, and why he might call *me* of all people. We had consummated our *quid pro quo* and, if anything, I needed him for my story more than he needed me for his. "What was that?" I asked the receiver, something in me wishing the connection had already died.

"I said that Bone Daddy is dead. Deceased. It was all over the late newscasts."

My words felt dry, tasting of copper. "I don't turn on the news at home."

"You missed a shitload. That BMW you spotted turned up at an intersection in Hough. A squad of SPU elves called in the plates. Mix in a liberal dose of 'allegedly' and 'according to police,' and you have a fucking massacre that looks like the end of *Bonnie and Clyde*."

I was standing, completely awake now. "Back up a minute, Cutler. You're saying the cops shot him."

"No, Maxwell. I'm saying they *slaughtered* the guy. At least a hundred shots fired, none from Bone. Which is kind of funny if you ask me, since the homeboy was packing."

I was pacing now, looking for where I'd tossed my clothes when I went to bed. "From the top, Cutler. What happened?"

"I don't know *what* happened. I know what the police *say* happened."

"Out with it."

"The story goes: Bone's sitting at a light. A squad of unidentified SPU elves—whose identity I think we both can guess—run his plate, then call in that they are making the stop. Bone does not do the sane thing and pull over. Instead, he pulls an Uzi out from under the driver's seat and draws down on the elf cops—cops, I might add, who've had no problem letting him walk from all manner of felonies before this."

"He shot at the police?"

"No, apparently he was a little too slow. Though he did have the foresight to load up the Uzi with 9mm elf-stopper rounds."

I shook my head. The thing about the SPU being mostly elves and such, is bullets don't do a hell of a lot. A lead slug will knock them down, but they're a hell of a lot more resilient than your average cop. A head shot with a normal bullet won't take them out of the picture. But then, there are so-called "elf-stopper" rounds, fully steel-jacketed hollow points that fragment enough iron content to drop your average elf.

Unfortunately for Bone Daddy, the human body was quite vulnerable to standard lead bullets.

"The Uzi was a plant," I said.

"A regular rhodo-fucking-dendron."

"Why would they kill him?"

"Why you think I'm calling all over the place for you, Einstein? The dragon shit blew this open, and the hell if I'm going to lose a story because of one of you op-ed prima donnas. You and I gotta talk."

"Yeah, we do."

"Bring your notebook, I got another CD to show you."

I met up with Cutler at an all-night diner in Cleveland Heights at about four-fifteen. Cutler was getting a refill on his coffee when I walked in. I was carrying my computer, like he'd asked me.

He waved me over to the booth and waved the waitress away—rather rudely, since I didn't get a chance to order anything myself. He ground a cigarette out in the ashtray next to him and said, "Come on, let's boot this thing up."

I put the notebook on the table between us. Before I opened it, I asked him. "What is it?"

He reached down and put a clear crystal case down in front of us. The platter inside had the blue tint of a recordable CD. "You ain't going to believe this one."

"Try me."

"I hear Bone Daddy bites it. You aren't the only one I'm trying to get hold of. I'm running down everyone I know who knew Bone and who might talk to me. *Everyone.* The fucking case of my fucking life is bleeding away, Maxwell. I gotta get *something.*"

"And you got this?"

"An old girlfriend—not even his current, this is, like, three bitches ago, but I'm running out of people who'll talk, right?—I knock on he door. She doesn't know that the cops capped her ex's ass."

I can picture Cutler at this woman's door. He wasn't exactly the soul of subtlety or discretion. This must have been only hours after the shooting, Bone wasn't even cold yet.

"So she loses it when you tell her," I said.

"Hell, no." Cutler taps the CD case. "She gives me this. Says that our wizard gave it to her three years ago, saying to give it to the man who tells her he'd been killed."

"What is it? A will?"

"I don't know," Cutler said. "It's encrypted."

I picked up the case and looked at the CD inside. I shook my head. "I hope you didn't call me here for my prowess as a code breaker." When it came down to it, there was enough hard encryption on the Internet that chances were that the CD was essentially useless, unbreakable without a passphrase.

Cutler shook his head. "No, but let me tell you this. Bone Daddy said to this chick, 'Pass this on to the man who tells you I've been killed.' He didn't say, 'when I die.' he said 'killed.'"

I shrugged. "Not a tough call in his line of work."

"Kline, this guy was an eye, a fortune-teller. He *knew* he was going to end badly. And, three years ago, he knew that someone was going to bring the news to this babe he was shacked up with."

"Fat lot of good it does anyone if the CD's encrypted."

"She told me that he knew that the guy who was supposed to see this thing would know the password."

I shrugged. "So if this guy is—was—such a seer, why don't you know it?"

"I don't think it is meant for me."

"Pardon?"

"I've tried passwords six ways from Sunday. Like I said, he's *good*. He'd know what passphrase to use to let it fall into the right person's lap. Not me. *You*."

I looked at the CD. "*Me?*"

"The CD is tied up with Bone's death. Not coincidentally, we're talking magic here. The guy it's for, he's tied up with it, too."

"What've I got to do with his death, Cutler?"

"You're the last person to see him alive, outside his killers. You gave the cops the plate number of his BMW. You were in his presence and in the presence of the elves who would kill him—"

"We're *assuming* they're the cops who shot him."

"Do you think we're wrong?"

There was something about Cutler's manner that I was starting to find unnerving. "I think you're reaching about this CD. You were a lot more tied in with Bone Daddy than I was."

"A day after you become involved his pet elves turn on him? I think there's a connection." He slid the CD across the table. "Try it." There was an uncharacteristic note of desperation in his voice.

I opened the notebook and slipped the CD inside. "I don't know what this is worth even if we could read it. It's three years old." I typed on the keyboard, trying to access the CD. Predictably, the only result was a little gray box asking for a passphrase. "How good a seer *was* this guy?"

"Damn good," Cutler said, lighting up another cigarette.

The password box stared at me. The guy who was supposed to see this thing would know what to type.

On impulse, I typed, *"Murder most foul, as in the best it is. But this most foul, strange and unusual."* The little text box filled with asterisks. My finger hovered over the return key.

"Cutler, I've got a question for you."

Cutler looked at my hands, still hovering over the keyboard. "What're you waiting for? Afraid it won't work?"

More likely, afraid that it will . . .

"How did you know I was the one who gave the plate number of his BMW to the cops?"

"Damn it, Maxwell—" he reached over and actually pressed the return key for me.

I grabbed his wrist. "What the fuck do you think you're—" I was interrupted by a beep from my notebook as a small gray window notified me, "Loading . . ." with an ominously slow-moving progress bar.

"Cutler, if this is a virus—"

"Christ. You got the passphrase in one shot? I spent hours with that mother before I called you."

I felt the sweat on my back freeze into solid little balls of ice on my spine. If this wasn't a practical joke on Cutler's part, I just guessed a sixteen-word passphrase, punctuation and all. That was better than a billion-to-one shot. The only explanation was that Bone Daddy had left this CD for *me*, and had divined my guess at a passphrase over three years ago.

The way that bar was moving, and the CD was rattling, I hoped the guy divined my processor speed and the space on my hard drive as well. I looked up at Cutler, "What did you give me?"

"I told you, I don't know." He looked up from the screen of my computer. "The CD *was* meant for you. Why the hell would he be giving *you* messages? After all the crap I went through—"

The questions weren't right, and his expression was all wrong. Tense, strained, muscles taut, eyes darting, a few beads of sweat by the hairline and the upper lip. His wrist, which I still held, was shaking very slightly.

"How," I repeated, "did you know I gave the cops Bone Daddy's license plate number?"

"You told me you did." The voice had lost a lot of confidence, and a note of pleading had entered it.

I shook my head. "We talked about dragons, about kidnappings, about questionings. Never once did I mention what I talked to the cops about."

"Lucky guess, then." I saw Cutler's hand drift toward his chest, and stop. I saw fear in his eyes.

"What's going on here?" I stared at the spot on his chest where his hand was moving. There was a slight bump visible beneath the thin cotton shirt. "Christ, man? Are you wearing a wire?"

I stood up, pissed and confused. I smelled a setup. Cutler raised his hands, and I saw panic in his eyes. "Kline," he whispered. "Don't, they're watching."

I don't know exactly what possessed me. I supposed, from Aloeus' death until this point, everything had been a step removed from me. Even my abduction had been dreamlike, not as threatening as it should have been. So, instead of sitting down and playing it out like I should have, I bent over the table and pulled Cutler's shirt open.

No wire.

Hanging on a chain around his neck was a small charm the size of the last joint of my index finger. In a half second my brain registered what it was—

"You stupid bastard!" Cutler was reaching for me, fury in his eyes. His hands were almost at my neck as I realized the charm was a forty-five caliber bullet covered with intricate engravings that were just starting to glow.

I was deafened by the sound of a gunshot. Cutler spasmed away from me as flecks of gore erupted from the sudden crater in his chest. The odor of smoke was rank as I watched Cutler slump backward into the booth. The casing from the charmed bullet bounced off of the table and struck my right hand, burning it. My left hand still held part of Cutler's shirt. I let it go.

Someone screamed.

CHAPTER FIFTEEN

*N*O, *no, no. This shit is not happening.*
    I looked up, and everyone in the diner was backing away from me. I silently mouthed my innocence, knowing, already that it wouldn't do any good.

Worse, out the windows, I saw the blue of police flashers. Too soon. They'd been waiting. There wasn't any time. Normal course of events, I'd patiently wait for the cops. After all, I was obviously unarmed, and forensics was bound to get a lead on the magic bullet from the engraved casing.

This *wasn't* normal. Those blue flashers probably belonged to the folks that'd just cashed in Cutler, and I saw a good likelihood that—like the late Bone Daddy—they'd shoot me and plant an appropriate weapon on my corpse after the fact. My gut told me to run, and I've always been good about following my gut.

I grabbed the notebook off the counter and ran for the back of the diner. I reached the emergency exit in the back before I had the thing closed. A siren started when I slammed through the door out into the parking lot in back of the diner.

There was no real cover. The cops were out front, and the diner was a single building surrounded by parking lot. Running right or left, I'd expose myself. The blue flashers were sweeping the cars in the lot to my left. If there were four of them, like last time, there would be two going into the diner, and a pair in the car to move around back. If they were smart, one got out of the car, and they were flanking me.

I ran straight back, toward a tall fence that separated the parking lot from the residences on the other half of the block. It was a twelve-foot wooden privacy fence, which I didn't have hope of climbing without help. Fortunately I had help in the form of a Buick Century parked next to a minivan that was backed in by the fence. The cars were almost straight back.

I'm no athlete, but adrenaline and fear can do some surprising things. I sprinted flat out for the Buick, and I reached it before I heard the warning whoop of the cop car's siren. I half jumped and half stumbled onto the hood and managed to keep moving.

Behind me I heard an elf-accented voice say, "Freeze."

Call me an idiot, I didn't freeze. Instead, when I scrambled on the roof of the Buick, I tossed the notebook up, over the fence. I didn't know what was on that CD, but I knew I didn't want my elvish adversaries to have it.

As I jumped for the roof of the minivan, I heard a gunshot. Something shattered underneath me. I cursed as I rolled on to the top of the van, the luggage rack gouging my shoulder. I didn't let myself stop. I got into a crouch like a sprinter, gasped as I felt the effort in my groin and my left knee, and sprang toward the fence.

The top was just in reach, which was good because the protests my lower body was giving me meant I wouldn't be able to make any substantial jump. I slammed into the flat face of the fence, slivers tearing into the meat of my hands as I grabbed its irregular top. I pulled up, trying to swing my right leg up as I kept a precarious foot on the roof of the van.

Another gunshot. It wasn't a warning shot. It barely missed, and I could feel the impact shake the fence. The shot of life-and-death fear that gave to me was enough to convince my forty-three-year-old body to pull itself over the top.

That almost finished the job for the elves. I flipped over the top, and couldn't hold on. I rolled off, and would have fallen the twelve feet straight down if a stand of pine trees weren't growing up right next to the fence. I rolled off into a tree, the trunk slamming into my lower back, sending a shock through my kidneys that made me forget the splinters in my hands and the burning muscles in my legs.

The branch beneath me snapped under my weight, spilling me down onto another branch, and another, thrashing me like whips for six feet or so, before I ended folded over a branch too thick for me to break.

At this point, just about every part of my body was screaming "bad idea" at me.

I heard the branch beneath me strain. I took it as my cue to finish my descent. I tried to lower myself by my hands and drop gracefully, but the bark tried to grind the splinters deeper into my hands and I couldn't hold myself up, even momentarily. As soon as my weight was supported by my arms, I fell.

It was a little less than six feet, and this time my fall was somewhat controlled. I hit with my legs, which buckled with the impact, not because that's the way to absorb the impact of a fall, but because my legs were having third thoughts about supporting my weight.

This wasn't part of my normal work experience. The most physical I ever got was about every other month when I got guilty about my lifestyle and used the gym at the *Press* building for about twenty minutes.

The ground here was lower than the parking lot, and graded away from the fence. I rolled through a bed of pine needles into the trunk of another tree. I finished facing upward, in time to see the blue lights of a cop car washing the tops of the trees.

"Fuck."

It had reached the point where I was pissed off that I hadn't broken any bones, which would give me a legitimate excuse just to wait here for the elves. Instead, I sucked in a breath and pulled myself up as quickly as I could manage. As I did, I whipped my head around looking for three things: pursuit, my notebook, and an escape route.

The first thing I saw was the notebook. It had hit the ground out of the shadow of the fence, where there was some light from the streetlights in the parking lot. The bad news was that the three-grand machine was now in about four separate pieces. Another thing I was going to have to justify; the machine belonged to the *Press*.

I half stumbled and half ran past the remains. I grabbed the lower half of the base unit, now just a plastic slab with a circuit board bolted to it. The keyboard was off elsewhere in two pieces, the screen even farther away. That didn't matter right now. This section of the remains had the two important bits, the CD unit, and the hard drive.

I heard some commotion behind me, and I burst into a limping run through the backyard of the house in front of me.

By all rights, the bastards should have caught me. I wasn't making good time on foot, and they had seen where I had jumped the fence. I'd almost considered ditching the remains of my notebook, because it seemed so inevitable.

But I eluded them. When I managed to slow down enough to think about what happened, I came up with the reason why.

These guys, while they might be cops, only had the one car. For a foot pursuit, you need backup. Cops don't outrun suspects, they flank them. The guy chasing you is radioing your position to a second car that's moving to cut you off. If these guys were who I thought they were—which was a guess, since I hadn't taken the time to look back at them—then they had to radio some Cleveland Heights cops for backup. Not only would the Heights cops not immediately be in position to cut me off, but the jurisdictional issues would probably add at least a minute or so to the response time.

My getaway vehicle was a blue-and-white Americab summoned via cell phone and met in a church parking lot. I gave the guy everything in my wallet to get me downtown, which amounted to a fifty to keep his mouth shut.

As I rode, I had time to attempt a coherent explanation for what happened.

Bone Daddy was a black market mage with a long criminal record and no small ability. Cutler was investigating his connection with a quartet of SPU elves. Bone Daddy and the bent elf cops had some interest in the demise of Aloeus, and my investigation of it.

They killed Egil Nixon, presumably to cover up the fact that Aloeus was murdered. Dr. Shafran had made it clear that a murder would be impossible to mistake for an accident.

Then Bone Daddy winds up dead, presumably killed by these same SPU elves. Cutler was right that a coincidental falling out was pushing the bounds of probability. He also seemed to have access to an inside source, since it seemed pretty certain that it was these bent cops that were holding his fatal leash.

I was also becoming certain that he wasn't telling the whole truth about the origins of the CD. I suspect that it was more than likely that the elves on the other end of that bullet handed the CD to Cutler, with marching orders to get it into my hands, preferably in a public place where they could see the keystrokes as I entered the passphrase.

Given the way he died, I doubt the elves were willing to have any unapproved data floating out there with Bone Daddy's name on it.

I had the cabbie let me out by a bank machine, where I got a large cash advance from my *Press* Amex. Then I proceeded to disappear for a few hours.

Bone Daddy sat on a leather couch pointing a remote at a digital video camera. He wore nothing but a pair of jeans that rode on his hips. He had a muscular torso and wiry arms, both of which were covered by black tatoos, dozens of circular charms made of Greek, Hebrew, and Latin text.

The hand with the remote was trembling slightly, and the other hand carefully set a bottle of amber liquid on the glass coffee table between him and the camera. He ran his hand over the skin of his scalp and shook his head.

"Man," he whispered. The remote clattered to the table.

Bone Daddy looked up into the camera and smiled—lips pulled tight and muscles locked. "Hello, Will," he said. "I'm going to call you that cause I don't know who the fuck you are. Chances are, you don't know who the fuck I am either." He grabbed the bottle and took a swig, then wiped his mouth with the back of his hand. "Ain't the Oracle a bitch?"

He stood up a little shakily and started pacing. "Word of advice, Will. Don't ask questions about your own future. Especially don't ask how you're going to die. The Oracle ain't going to lie to you, and the bitch ain't going to tell you anything you can change." He was quiet for a few moments, staring into the middle distance between him and the camera.

"You want to know what this is about, don't you? Well, I'm dead—smoked by some motherfucker I'm supposed to trust. And, no, I don't know who. If the bitch let me know *that*, I could do something about it, and she can't screw a perfect record, can she?" He grabbed the neck of the half empty bottle, lifted it up, and slammed it back down on the glass table. The table shattered, leaving him holding the bottle hovering over empty space.

He stood there a moment, staring at the remains of the table. Then he let the bottle drop.

"What you are, Will," he spoke into the camera, "is the guy most likely to fuck up the shits who killed me." He crouched, bare feet crunching the broken glass, and stared into the lens of the camera, leaning forward as if he could see the person he was talking to. "That's what you're going to do." He pointed a trembling finger up at the lens. "Fuck up these shits."

Every muscle in his body was tense. Sweat shone on the surface of his arcane tattoos. His eyes were wide and the pupils were points, nearly invisible in the iris. Reflected in the iris was a small image of the brick-sized digital camera pointing at him.

"I know you, Will. I spent three hours with that cold bitch, and she told me things. Not your name, but I know you're searching. Looking to find out something these shits don't want you to know. Don't know what, just that either you'll find it, or these shits will kill you, too."

He grinned. "Ain't life a bitch?" He shook his head. "Just in case you're thinking of dissing what I have to say—remember your quote, Mr. Shakespeare? Ironic one, too, ain't it?"

He shifted his weight to the sound of crunching glass. If he felt the glass under his feet, it didn't show in his face. "Anyway, I expect you understand, I know my shit. I think you also know you're in a world of trouble, too. You're at a nexus, Will. Right now, or very shortly, you're going to be in the sights of powers you only brushed against till now. You're not a powerful man and you threaten powers a lot greater than yourself." Closed his eyes and muttered to himself, "Fuck, as if I'm telling you shit you don't already know."

He reached for the camera and looked down at it. His face held a haunted expression. "I'm a dead man, Will. I got wasted and wanted to know more than I should. This message might seem fucking weak, but damn it all, I tried not to seal your fate the way that I did mine. I didn't ask if you'd succeed or fail, if you'd live or die. You still got the freedom, Will, and fuck Fate—" He stood up and walked with the camera. "I got three things I busted my hump for. You *better* use them."

He was holding the camera right up to his face, staring into it, looking into the eyes of the person who would view this record. "You got three enemies, Will, all badasses. A villain of deeds, a villain of thoughts, and a villain of words. The first will kill you if given the chance, but he is the least of your opposition. The second is the mastermind, driving plots that others follow to your undoing. But the last is the greatest threat, for with only a well chosen word he will destroy one man, or empires unborn."

He held up a hand with two fingers extended up to the camera. "Your path has been chosen for you by forces you've known and have not seen, and they fear your allegiance because the masters you serve are not theirs. The alliance they offer will not be an easy one."

A third finger extended. "Finally, Will, there are many hands, but no head."

He blinked and lowered the camera. "That's all we got for you. Good luck, you poor bastard," Bone Daddy said as he switched off the camera.

I was watching Bone Daddy's auto-eulogy at one of the PCs in the Cleveland Public Library. You weren't supposed to load outside software on these things, but when no one was looking, I'd slipped Bone Daddy's CD into the base unit, and called it to life. It took me a few tries this time, I couldn't remember the exact punctuation and capitalization that I'd used the first time.

I watched the grainy digital movie three times trying to intuit why the elves would kill over this. The whole setup with Cutler had to be to get me to unlock this CD.

I had a room at the downtown Raddison, paying cash along with another generous bribe to buy silence. I had managed to clean myself up somewhat, and get most of the crap out of my clothes. I had slept until noon, which meant that the desk clerk hadn't phoned the cops on me.

When I had emerged, I didn't gather too many stares. My slacks were dark and didn't show the stains from sap, dirt, and blood. Most of the bruising was beneath my shirt which, while it had sustained a few tears and lost a button, was casual denim so it didn't show the damage so blatantly. The remains of my notebook had made it into a dumpster behind a restaurant I passed on the way to the library.

The only thing that made me look the fugitive were my hands. The effects of splinters and pine bark had made them a bloody mess. They were mostly scabbed over now, but they had been bad enough that my bloodstained jacket had joined my notebook in the dumpster. They'd be all right if I didn't try to make a fist.

At one-forty-five I checked for people watching me and slipped the CD out of the PC.

I still couldn't quite get what was up with the SPU cops. If it wasn't a bunch of elves, their actions of the last thirty-six hours would've struck me as desperate, even panicked. But elves were too damn cold to be panicked. The interrogation struck me as an elf job, but not Bone Daddy's execution. That was sloppy. The little setup with me and Cutler was even worse, messy, witnesses, and not only did I make it out in one piece, but with the CD they seemed interested in.

I slipped the enigmatic disk into my pocket.

He had made it pretty clear that there was more than one power at work here. *There are many hands, but no head.*

"Well," I whispered to myself, "did we ever really believe that this thing was *just* the elves?"

I pushed away from the table and looked out the window.

The sane thing to do was to turn myself in to some clean cops. I actually knew a few. Staying on the lam like this was borrowing trouble. I knew that there'd be no way to make the charges stick, even if they'd tampered with the evidence any competent pathologist was going to be able to tell that Cutler hadn't died from a conventional gunshot wound.

Yeah, then why don't I?

I flipped open my cell phone—which had survived the night intact—and hit the third autodial button.

After a moment, a familiar, stressed voice said, "City desk."

"Miss me yet, Bea."

"Holy sh—" Her voice lowered. "What the hell are you doing? There're cops crawling all over here."

"I didn't do it, Bea."

"Christ, I know that. But we have policemen here, with *warrants*. They've already taken fifteen boxes of paper, your workstation—"

I knew how she felt. In spite of all the voyeurism inherent in the profession—or perhaps because of it—journalists are incredibly sensitive to invasions of privacy.

"Look, Bea, I am on to something. Big."

"Big enough to get Cutler killed?"

"And me, if I'm not careful."

"Where are you? I'll send a car."

"No, not a good idea. I just need to know, is the SPU there?"

"What are you into?"

"Are they?"

Whispered this time, "There's an SPU detective here, why are—"

"What's his name?"

"Caledvwlch."

"Thanks," I moved to turn off the phone.

"You better be on to something, or I'm personally going to—"

"Stand in line, Bea." I flipped the phone shut.

CHAPTER SIXTEEN

I DIDN'T stay on the line with Columbia because, at this point, if they didn't have a trace on her phone, they probably had one on mine. Zeroing in on a wireless phone was difficult, but well within the SPU's capabilities in a normal police investigation.

I had called in some vain hope that the outlaw cops wouldn't allow there to be a normal police investigation. I was hoping that they'd want to keep it intimate. I was holding some pretty damaging info, they wouldn't want me hauled in by cops that weren't in on their particular scam.

I had either overestimated their caution, or things had gotten too big for them to bottle up. The Cleveland Police had a warrant out on me, and at this point I could either cut and run, or try to get myself into the custody of some non-SPU cops.

I came to a decision. The Justice Center was within spitting distance of where I was standing. I knew Caledvwlch and the rogue elves were crawling all over the *Press* building. All I had to do was slip into the DA's office, or maybe internal affairs. These bastards were deadly, but if I got firmly embedded in the system and, most importantly, got what I already knew into the record, it would be very difficult to get rid of me without implicating themselves.

When I left the library I took the rear entrance, to cut across the mall toward the city buildings clustered around Lakeside. I passed by a hot dog vendor, scattering the pixie things that hovered in the garlic-scented steam from the hot dog water. The little alien humanoids, all of an inch in height with a shimmering wingspan no bigger than my outstretched hand, gave me a wide berth. They probably saw it coming before I did.

I didn't know I was in trouble until I saw a van pull to a stop at the intersection ahead of me. I was a little too slow in reacting. I kept walking, turning to watch the van, both the exactly wrong things to do. By the time my legs got the message and started turning, tensing to sprint, it was too late. The door was sliding open on the side of the van, and I was suddenly flanked from behind by two muscular gentlemen with navy suits and earth-tone ties.

"You have to come with us, Mr. Maxwell," said the suit with the brown tie, as the pair of them grabbed my arms and ushered me quickly to the idling van. I might have fought them, but I felt a hard pressure over my right kidney wielded by the suit with the mustard-yellow tie.

I knew right off they weren't local cops. They were too polite, too obviously concerned about making a scene. Local boys would have done one of two things; a cowboy would have tackled me, sworn a lot, and read me Miranda while he ground my face into the pavement, while a good ol' boy would call it in, and watch as five or six cars drove in to pick me up.

I was shoved inside the van, which was moving before the door had slid completely shut.

And who the hell are you guys?

"Where are you taking me?" I asked as we crossed the river on the Main Avenue Bridge, going west. I noticed a few of them, notably the guy with the mustard tie and the guy riding shotgun, watching to our right as we passed the stadium. It was the kind of look that let you separate the tourists from the natives—though the look Colonel Mustard was giving seemed more like a general sizing up an enemy army. The gun he still held on me must have contributed to the impression.

Mr. Brown watched out the opposite window. "We'll be there soon enough, Mr. Maxwell."

"What do you guys want?"

"We want you to be quiet until we get to the safe house," said the man I thought of as Professor Plum—glasses and gray hair made him look slightly bookish.

Safe house?

Over the river, the driver—whom I labeled Mr. White because he was a black guy who bore a passing resemblance to a former mayor of the same name—called back, "We got a critter on our six o'clock, pacing us."

"Fuck it," Colonel Mustard said as he squinted out the back windows of the van. "I don't see a tail."

"Up," said Mr. White.

I followed Colonel Mustard's gaze upward and saw what Mr. White had been talking about.

It was some sort of flying creature, about half man-sized, with leathery wings and a skull-like face. A demonic gargoyle creature that, I now realized, had been following my movements since I'd arrived on the Hope Memorial Bridge. I'd seen it perched on a bridge, on a church while the elves kidnaped me, and I'd caught a glimpse of it on the Cleveland Trust Building. I wondered what my score on the oblivious meter was.

"Can we lose the familiar?" asked Professor Plum.

"Sir," said Mr. White, "it flies. I can't lose it in traffic."

There was a pause, then Professor Plum flipped open a cell phone. "This is mobile one. I need a car at," he flipped open a notebook and, after a moment, said, "Rendezvous green-seven, third level. Ten minutes."

He flipped the phone shut without listening for any response. He looked over to Mr. Brown and Colonel Mustard. "I want to know what that thing's following." He looked at me and said, "Have you seen that creature before?"

This is where I get overcome with the self-destructive urge for resistance. "You bastards just kidnapped me off the street, why should I help you?"

Professor Plum smiled. "Mr. Maxwell, you're intelligent—but shall I spell it out for you? You're a fugitive, wanted by the police for questioning for a murder that was most likely committed by people who will have no hesitation in killing you as well. How many friends do you have? How sure are you that the thing following us is one of them?"

"Answer the man," Colonel Mustard said, pressing the gun into my side to make sure I got the point.

Bone Daddy's words echoed in my head, *many hands, but no head.*

"Yes," I said, finally. "I've seen it before."

"Christ, it's tracking him." Colonel Mustard didn't sound pleased.

"More than likely," agreed Professor Plum, "some charm planted on him." He pulled a small silver chain from his pocket. A stone dangled from it, rough and unfinished, resembling a piece of coal. He handed it to Brown. "Check him out."

Brown held the chain wrapped around his hand and mumbled a few words. Then he passed his hand over me. When his hand passed over my left jacket pocket, it glowed slightly—an evil greenish glow that made the eye hurt.

"Got one," he said and pulled my cell phone out of my pocket.

"Hey," I said.

Professor Plum took my phone from Brown. "Your phone has been subject to some sort of enchantment. I don't have the ability to determine what, right now. But it has probably been acting as a beacon for our hitchhiker."

I wanted to argue, but I couldn't. I had been receiving odd calls on my phone—could you phone in an enchantment?

Mr. Brown also liberated Bone Daddy's CD, and my house keys. Both apparently held magical signatures that our follower could track.

We were deep into Lakewood now, and Mr. White took us into a parking garage, drove up three levels and pulled in alongside a Lincoln Town Car that was idling and facing in the other direction. Doors opened before the van had stopped completely.

"Move," Plum said, "before that thing can see what's happening."

Mustard and Brown hustled me into the back of the Lincoln, Plum took shotgun again. White stayed with the van and started it again, driving up the ramp to the next level. The enchanted items Brown had identified were still sitting inside it.

The Lincoln started down, back out of the parking garage.

Mustard watched out the rear window for our follower. "Yes," he said. "It's with the van."

I could glimpse it, very high up, circling the parking garage as we pulled away.

Our destination wasn't in Lakewood, which made some sense. You wouldn't want to lose a tail very close to where you wanted to go. It was about twenty minutes before we pulled into the driveway of an anonymous white ranch deep in the wilds of Berea.

Brown opened the door just in time to let in the sound of a 747 on approach to Hopkins. I looked up to see the belly of the jumbo jet blacking out a quarter of the sky. It made me want to duck.

"*The house!*" Brown yelled at me over the sound of the engines.

I nodded, looking around at the place. The lawn was weed-shot and half-brown. The back of the property was marked by a twelve-foot tall chain-link fence topped with razor wire. There were trees behind the fence, attempting to screen the view of the airport and failing because they'd been cut uniformly down to twelve feet in height.

To the left, right, and across the street were vacant lots. I suspected that the only reason this building still stood was due to oversight, some accident of zoning. This place really shouldn't have survived the last airport expansion.

They escorted me up the concrete walkway, past empty flower beds where the mulch was in bloom. We reached the door in time for a departure to pass over our heads. A smaller three-engine jet this time, but close enough to rattle the aluminum storm door in its frame. I also noticed small metal amulets riveted to the inside of the door, where they wouldn't be visible from the outside.

One would be an adequate ward for most people. I knew my apartment had three. I didn't know much about magical security systems, but I did know there was a separate charm for each kind of protection—intrusion alarm, antiscrying, repelling certain types of creatures.

I counted seven amulets on the inside of the storm door before Colonel Mustard got impatient and pushed me through with the point of the gun.

I stumbled through into a dingy living room, followed by all my escort except the driver. When the door shut, it was surprisingly quiet—enough that my ears popped with sudden relief from the aircraft's rumbling.

One wall, to our left, held a dead gas fireplace inset into a faux stone wall smeared with enough black soot that it seemed that someone had tried half-successfully to burn wood in the thing. The other walls were papered with mylar with a green velvet nap patterned on it. The mylar was gray-white with water stains and age, and the floral pattern had, between waist and shoulder level, had been worn away by three or four decades of human touch.

"Nice place," I commented. "I like the blue shag carpet, it adds just the right—"

"Shut up," said Colonel Mustard, "You're wanted in the rec room."

I shrugged and followed his lead. I expected to be taken to a wood-paneled room with a bar and a pool table, with an acoustic tile ceiling.

I was wrong about everything but the acoustic tile.

Brown and Mustard flanked me as I stepped into a room about ten feet square, off of the kitchen. The walls and ceiling were paneled with acoustical tile, except for a mirror about five feet long on the wall opposite the entrance. There was a single metal desk and three office chairs. On the side of the desk that abutted the wall sat a small bronze Buddha. A small curl of aromatic smoke rose from a cone of incense in its lap.

Sitting on one side of the desk was a middle-aged Asian gentleman. His hair and mustache were still jet black, but the skin on his face was deeply lined and the joints on his hands were swollen with the obvious signs of arthritis. He was rubbing his hands as we entered, and he gestured to one of the chairs. Brown and Mustard placed me into the seat, a little forcefully.

"Gentlemen, please. That isn't necessary."

Mustard snorted, "This guy's a Clevelander, sir."

"Which isn't a crime."

"Perhaps you two should wait outside," said Professor Plum as he walked in behind us. He took up the remaining seat.

Mustard grunted, but both he and Brown backed out of the room, closing the door behind them. This side of the door was covered with soundproofing tiles as well. I glanced at the walls and noticed talismans mounted near the ceiling at the four points of the compass.

I looked down at the new guy. "So what Agency are you with?"

The Asian smiled. Professor Plum looked slightly nonplussed, "What makes you—"

"Mr. Maxwell has simply taken note of the resources expended on his behalf, and the nature of this safe house, and has come to certain conclusions."

"My only real question is what government you work for." I cast a glance at the Buddha.

"Simply a serene influence." He pulled out a billfold and opened it on the table in front of me. "Special Agent Ts'ao Kuo, Federal Bureau of Investigation."

I looked over at Professor Plum. He said, "I'm Doctor Roy Blackstone." He didn't provide an ID.

"Uh-huh?" I shook my head. "When does the FBI start kidnaping people off the street?"

"You're wanted for questioning," Agent Ts'ao said.

"By the Cleveland PD—and if you were going to charge me, why aren't we at the Federal Building?"

The doctor steepled his fingers and said, "There are matters of National Security involved here."

That was just what I needed. "And who do you work for?"

He glanced over at Agent Ts'ao and said, "I'm a special adviser on this case."

"And exactly what case is that?"

CHAPTER SEVENTEEN

IT didn't surprise me much when they weren't immediately forthcoming about their investigation. "What prompted you to start investigating the dragon Aloeus?" Dr. Blackstone asked me in answer to my question.

"Funny thing," I said. "Last I checked, my copy of the Bill of Rights said I don't have to talk to you."

"Son, you better—"

Agent Ts'ao raised his hand and said, "Mr. Maxwell is quite right. He doesn't have to say anything." He reached down, picked up a briefcase, and set it on the table between us. "We both respect the Constitution, don't we, Mr. Maxwell?"

I wasn't quite sure where he was going with this. "Goes along with my job."

Agent Ts'ao nodded. "And despite certain impediments to law enforcement, it goes along with ours." He opened the briefcase and started removing folders. "The doctor and I agree, our current job is the protection of that document. He was not engaging in hyperbole when he mentioned a threat to national security."

I shook my head. "I've worked a political beat for a decade. I might not work in D.C., but I know that 'national security' is in the eye of the beholder."

Agent Ts'ao handed a stack of folders to the doctor and closed the briefcase. "It's fair to reserve judgment."

I watched Ts'ao's expression grow grave and the smell of incense in the air was heavy and stifling. "You weren't brought here to be hassled, Mr. Maxwell. You are here because I believe that we need each other."

"Interesting premise," I said. "Care to elaborate?"

"You've been close to the people we've been investigating," Blackstone told me. "You're going to help bring them down."

"I see," I said slowly. I looked from Ts'ao to Blackstone. "What exactly do I get for my civic mindedness?"

Blackstone gave Ts'ao a look that said, *I told you this was a bad idea.*

"You get two things, Maxwell," Ts'ao said. "The first is a federal shield against anything that comes out of your unfortunate meeting with Mr. Cutler." He leaned toward me. "You also get your heart's desire, Mr. Maxwell."

"Which is?"

He nodded slightly to the folders in Blackstone's hands. "Information."

The air in the meeting room was so still, it was almost stagnant. There was little or no air-conditioning, and if there was any ventilation, it was hidden so well I couldn't tell. I raised my hand to loosen the button on my collar, wincing as my injured hands fumbled with the button.

To be honest, I was stalling. The wheels in my brain had shifted gears so many times in the past seventy-two hours that I felt like my mental transmission had been stripped. Objectively, I shouldn't be hesitating; I *had* been on my way to the cops when they hauled me into the van. If anything, I should prefer the Feds, since no way in hell would they be tied up with a bunch of corrupt elven cops. All these guys had going against them were a traditional Clevelander's bias against Feds, and the strong-arm method they'd used to pick me up.

"What kind of information?"

"You asked about our investigation. You're interested in the death of a major public figure. Perhaps you're also interested in what the Port Authority and the Rayburn administration are really doing with the Portal." Ts'ao leaned back.

Your path has been chosen for you by forces you've known and have not seen, and they fear your allegiance because the masters you serve are not theirs. The alliance they offer will not be an easy one.

The Feds? Why not. I leaned back. "I'll tell you what I've found out. But I won't go into the identity of any sources."

Blackstone started to say something but Ts'ao cut him off. "That's no problem. We understand about sources and methods, don't we, Doctor?"

Doctor Blackstone nodded, but he didn't look happy about it.

I must have winced again, and Ts'ao leaned forward. "You're injured."

I pulled my hands down and said, "It's nothing."

Ts'ao leaned forward, over the table. His arms were long enough to reach for my hands. He turned them palm upward. "I think we need a first aid kit in here."

I don't think they were consciously doing good cop, bad cop. I don't think Blackstone counted as a cop anyway. I think that the doctor was just naturally an uptight asshole, and Ts'ao was simply a little more subtle. Of the two, Ts'ao was the more dangerous. Like Baldassare, he had the glad hand down pat. He came across as genuinely sincere, and the fact is that he probably was. That did not, however, mean you could trust him. He'd be the first to tell you that the job came first. If he had to throw you to the wolves to do his job, he'd do it in a heartbeat. Though he'd probably apologize.

However, I played the cards as they were dealt to me. I gave them the story of my life the past three days as Colonel Mustard did a field dressing on my hands. I told them the truth, and didn't leave out anything except my interview with Baldassare and Theophane's name. I gave them everything I'd learned about Bone Daddy and the elves. In the end, everything I had was going to make it into print anyway.

After engaging in an hour-long monologue, I decided it was time for some *quid pro quo.*

"Your turn," I said.

"Now wait a minute," Blackstone said. "There are a few points I need to have clear here—"

"No," Ts'ao said. "Mr. Maxwell's right. He's been cooperating, and we should thank him for that."

Blackstone folded up his own notebook. "You've made it clear it's your show."

Ts'ao turned to me and said, "What do you know about the way the Portal is currently being used?"

"The city uses it as a source of income; there's a steady flow of immigration both ways. There's enough demand for tickets out of this universe to charge ten grand a pop. The Ragnan government has a similar setup sending people to this side. The city runs a quarantine camp at Burke Lakefront . . ."

"You know of the prisoner release program?" Agent Ts'ao asked.

"I've seen a few cases where they were given the option. It's voluntary, more power to them."

Ts'ao nodded slowly. "Council gave judges the power to give

nonviolent offenders a fresh start. A one-way ticket, though." He leaned forward and said, "Where have the homeless gone, Mr. Maxwell?"

"There's been a dramatic upturn in the economy—"

"You've never heard the rumors?"

Of course I had. "Do you have any evidence of people going through the Portal against their will?"

"As a reporter, I assume you realize that such a charge is difficult to substantiate." Ts'ao told me. "The alleged victims leave nothing behind. And the city officials doing this are those least likely to break their silence. The fact remains, Mr. Rayburn's administration has the power to disappear people, Mr. Maxwell. The right paper, signed by a local judge, can make someone cease to exist. No oversight, no appeal, no way to even determine if the choice isn't made under duress." Agent Ts'ao pulled a paper from one of the folders the doctor held. "We've made some studies— average time from sentence to Portal, three hours. Eighty percent plea the option without trial. Sixty without legal representation. More than half on misdemeanor charges that would mean probation in any other city." He slid the paper over. "Care to see? It would make any third world dictatorship proud."

I picked up the paper. Needless to say, I hadn't seen any statistical studies like this coming out of the local government. "This can be backed up?" I asked.

"All public records," Agent Ts'ao said. "Though as a reporter you might have a long wait before the city government responds to a FOIA request."

I shook my head. "No one has picked up on this story yet?"

"You know why," said the doctor, and he didn't sound pleasant. "The interests it serves have the power to suppress any story they want in this town."

I shook my head. "There are other news outlets—"

"Disney is negotiating with Cedar Point to put a theme park in Sandusky. They've got several billion poised to create a real 'Magic Kingdom' here. None of their news media outlets will ripple those waters. AOL Time Warner has too much invested in Disney's programming to start another feud that threatens their cable interests. Enough Microsoft stock is owned in this area—"

"I get the picture."

"Do you?" asked the doctor.

"Yes," I told him. "That's the same argument about corporate newsthink that I was hearing when I started in this business. It's bullshit."

"And you're part of—"

Agent Ts'ao raised his hand, cutting the doctor off. "Let's not go off on tangents here. The story is not necessarily being suppressed. Perhaps *overlooked* is a better word in this context."

It galled me being patronized like that, but I didn't say anything.

"There is more, Mr. Maxwell. Shall we hand you another journalistic coup? Doctor?"

Doctor Blackstone laid one of the folders on the table in front of me. "Are you old enough to remember the Cuban boat lift? Castro's last great, 'fuck you!' Rayburn and his equivalents across the Portal are doing a reprise."

The doctor opened the folder. I looked, half expecting what I saw: a full-color eight-by-ten glossy of a dead woman. Cops are nothing if not predictable, and typically throw horrible pictures in front of someone they're questioning in an attempt to shake something loose.

"Murder," the doctor said unnecessarily.

The woman had been violently abused and dumped in a woodland setting. The color of the clotting blood and the deep bruises showed too smooth a transition for a digitized image. The photograph had been taken outside the area of the Portal's influence.

The doctor followed it with others, "Rape. Assault. Assault with intent. Reckless endangerment. Kidnapping. Murder. Murder. Assault. Arson. Aggravated robbery. Rape." File upon file dropped in front of me, glimpses of criminal acts only subliminally registering. Finally, he looked up at me. "Shall I continue?"

I looked over at Agent Ts'ao and shook my head. "You're going to tell me that there is a point to this?"

Ts'ao nodded and drew the latest folder forward and held it up. "This one's Osric, being held in San Francisco for severely beating a prostitute when she demanded payment for her services." Another folder. "Maynard, hospitalized after attempting to fend off a NYC cop with a broadsword." Another. "Learoyd, attempting—I quote, 'to fulfill an oath of vengeance to erase a slur on his character.' He torched a club in Dallas after the bouncers ejected him." Ts'ao looked up. "These men are all immigrants from the Portal."

"Wait a minute," I said. "None of those incidents happened anywhere near here."

"Pointedly," Ts'ao replied. "For every criminal exile that Rayburn's administration sends across, another one comes back through. And unlike your elves and dragons and unicorns, a human being can leave the influence of the Portal."

The doctor slapped a hand on top of the stack of files. "These aren't just criminals. They are the dregs of a society that doesn't value human life, sees women as property, and sees violence as the first resort in a dispute. These men don't know the rule of law, and what does the Rayburn administration do with them? Put them in quarantine at Burke, where they have a show camp for all the exotic characters that can't leave the area anyway? No, because that would overflow the city's resources. You know what's done with them?"

I shook my head, though I did have some idea. It was common knowledge that the Port Authority helped relocate people who could live outside the influence of the Portal. One of those little details that you never paid much attention to.

"They're given a change of clothes, fifty bucks, and a ticket on the next bus out of state. There isn't even a cursory attempt at orientation and assessment."

"So you have a problem," I looked at the two of them. "Shouldn't the INS be dealing with that?" I knew the answer, but I wanted to hear their take on it.

"Congress has," Ts'ao said, "in it's wisdom, passed a law that—currently worded—places the Portal and everything 'inside' it under the jurisdiction of Cleveland and Cuyahoga County."

"Annexing an entire universe and making it part of the United States," The doctor concluded.

I nodded. "So these immigrants aren't legally immigrants, are they? They're U.S. citizens."

The doctor frowned. "Because of a badly worded law, hastily passed."

What they were telling me wasn't really news to me. It was fairly well known that there were a few "problems" coming across the Portal. But a Ragnan native committing murder wasn't much more of a story now than anyone else doing the same thing.

Now if you start adding the courtroom statistics and the hint of a deal letting Ragnan send their criminals across, we started to get into interesting territory. "You said there was a deal?"

Ts'ao nodded. "Are you familiar with Article Two of the Constitution?"

"You're going to point out that only the president—with advice and consent of the Senate—can enter into treaties and conduct foreign policy."

"Two things that Rayburn and the administration have been doing with Ragnan since the beginning," Blackstone added.

I nodded. It was a well trod argument. The Supreme Court had already decided under current law, the Congress effectively annexed the Portal and made it part of the United States. And, as far as jurisdiction went, the Portal and its "contents" were inside the Cleveland metropolitan area. Until that changed, Rayburn has as much right to negotiate with Ragnan as he does with Lakewood. I told them as much.

Ts'ao raised his hands to his temples. I think I got him. "Do you understand the threat the Portal represents?" He pulled the Buddha toward him and frowned. "On the other side of the Portal is a foreign country of uncertain motives and alliance. The courts may not view it as a nation, but it still has the capacity to conduct covert activity that is against the interests of the United States."

"What are you getting at?" I asked.

"The worst threat to this nation since the fall of the Soviet Union," Dr. Blackstone said. He actually sounded serious.

I couldn't help but chuckle. "You mean China?"

Neither of them seemed to appreciate my humor. "It is a fact, Mr. Maxwell, which I don't think you'll deny, that the dragon Aloeus was fleeing an oppressive regime in his homeland," said Agent Ts'ao. "And he was a key figure in establishing Mayor Rayburn's policy toward the Portal."

I nodded.

"Followed, shortly afterward, by the fall of that regime," he continued.

"What are you getting at?"

"Aloeus was no refugee. He was the highest-ranking guerrilla in a civil war. He negotiated with Mayor Rayburn the delivery of arms and advisers from the Ohio National Guard, arms that were used to overthrow a foreign government."

I shook my head. "How the hell could that be kept a secret?"

"During the initial chaos after the Portal's opening, it was easy enough to keep things under wraps—including the disappearance of a whole unit of National Guard troops, three Apache gunships, and four Abrams tanks." Dr. Blackstone looked as if he was enjoying the look on my face. "You're wondering why none of the Guardsmen gave their story to CNN? They were debriefed by Army Intelligence when they came back, and the whole episode was classified. Those men represent one of the few intelligence assets that our government has on what's on the other side of the Portal."

Agent Ts'ao looked at me, sizing up my reaction. "The omnipotence of the Thesarch was tied to a vulnerability—an inability to anticipate the speed at which the invaders could move, and the damage that could be inflicted by nonmagical means. The tanks, the guns, the helicopters weren't enchanted, so they weren't a threat. His command and control was vulnerable, overt, and easily targeted because they were immune to any magical threat. In two days the Guard traveled to Ragman's capital city. The battle lasted twenty minutes." Agent Ts'ao steepled his fingers. "The guerrilla organization that masterminded that coup didn't disband after that victory. They've remained in place, on this side of the Portal, engaging in espionage and political subversion."

"That's a lot to swallow," I said. "Why would the Guard invade a foreign territory like that?"

"Orders from the governor," agent Ts'ao said. "After a two-hour meeting with Mayor Rayburn."

"Okay," I said, "you still haven't—"

Agent Ts'ao raised a hand. "Shall I explain the threat to you? We have elements of a foreign regime in place here, a regime created by a violent overthrow aided by rogue elements of our own military. Despite the presence of magic, our own technological and military advances operate on the other side with a few exceptions—while the 'magical' advances of theirs fade in effect the farther one gets from the Portal."

Dr. Blackstone leaned forward. "We're a gold mine to them. It isn't a backward civilization we're dealing with. It is as sophisticated as our own. If you hand them an AK-47, they're capable of reverse engineering it and fabricating a copy. With magical aid they can sidestep the issues of machine tooling—in fact, with the right engineering knowledge, they can duplicate anything they want."

"Including weapons of mass destruction," Ts'ao said.

"Now you're reaching," I said.

"We're talking about an empire that has undergone unchecked expansion for millennia, and whose leader is traditionally just this short of an absolute god." Dr. Blackstone looked grave. "Combine technological espionage that can bear fruit in months and weeks rather than years, with a sophisticated grasp of magic. If they get a foothold here—"

There was a solid thump, and the Buddha rattled on the table.

"What was that?" Agent Ts'ao asked.

CHAPTER EIGHTEEN

B ROWN burst into the interview room. "Sirs, we got a problem." There was another thump, louder now that the door was open. It was an odd sound, heavy, but not like an impact—more like a rush of air.

Agent Ts'ao and Dr. Blackstone got up and went through the door, which Brown held open for them. I craned my neck to look beyond the three of them, but all I managed to see was an unnatural character to the light. A flickering quality that felt ominous.

Brown let go of the door as they went toward the front of the house. I saw no incentive to meekly wait for their return, so I stood up and grabbed the edge of the door before it had swung completely closed.

I heard Agent Ts'ao's voice, for the first time raised in anger. "Damn it, Blackstone! You said he was clean—"

"We checked—"

"Obviously not well enough."

I edged down the hallway between the "rec room" and the living room, to get a view of what was going on without interrupting the argument. I needn't have worried. The sight out the picture window was taking all of everyone's attention.

The thumps, which were more sustained and rhythmic now, *were* from a rush of air. A wall of it, rushing by the front of the house, glowing a peculiar orange in the sunlight.

"We weren't tailed here," Dr. Blackstone objected.

"Then that," Ts'ao waved toward the window, "is one hell of a coincidence, Doctor. You grandstanding Company spooks have done nothing but screw up since you got here. You probably got one of our assets killed—"

"Sir—" Brown's voice sounded strained.

Ts'ao shook his head. "Now you've blown the cover off of the *only* magically secure safe house we have."

"Sir—" Brown was pleading.

"Do you know how many man-hours it took to make Feng Shui look this crappy?"

"Sirs, *what do we do?*" Brown shouted at them.

Ts'ao looked out the window, gave a half smile, and shook his head. "About that? Nothing."

Dr. Blackstone looked appalled. "What do you mean, nothing? We're under attack."

"I've confidence in the building's security. If there was a breach, they would be exploiting it."

I looked out at the moving wall of force. I saw debris swept up in it, trash, paper, mulch—all darkening it like an approaching storm. Occasionally it would swell and seem to sweep toward the glass, but it would pull away before it touched.

"No," Ts'ao said. "The wind isn't the threat." He glanced at Brown and Mustard. "Break out the guns. And vests."

The way he said it let me know he wasn't talking about pistols.

Doctor Blackstone looked befuddled.

"Doctor, out there is a distraction. Very high profile covering fire meant to pin us down for the real attack." He looked out the window. "Which is going to be soon. No one can keep this up for long. You better keep an eye on our guest."

For some reason—probably complete obstinance—I backed away from the living room and slipped behind the first door that wasn't the interview room. Turned out to be a bedroom that, fortunately, was unoccupied.

Damned if I knew what I was doing, but I had a pretty good idea who the fireworks were for. Somewhere along the line I picked up information, or someone thought I had picked up information, that was worth pulling out all the stops to keep a secret. Elvish discretion or not, these guys were panicking. Whoever was in charge had completely lost any sense of proportion. I could not see anything I knew as being important enough to make a frontal assault on a bunch of Feds.

All I knew is that I'd seen Egil Nixon's corpse and I was not making plans for a similar end.

I ran over to the window. It was shaded by heavy drapes that I drew aside. I was looking toward the back of the house, but I saw the same swirling wall of air. No escape that way. I stared into the maelstrom, watching the wind growing darker with accumulated dirt and debris. I knew enough not to open the window. The charms at every opening in this place gave this house an unbroken circle of protection. That was what kept the winds outside. Once that circle was broken—

"*Maxwell*—" came a voice from behind me.

I looked behind me and saw Dr. Blackstone standing in the bedroom doorway. "What the hell are you doing?" he snapped at me.

"Figuring my odds on getting the hell out of here."

"You're not going anywhere, son," Dr. Blackstone said.

"I don't remember being charged or Mirandized." I stared out the window. If I agreed with Ts'ao's tactical assumptions—which I had no reason not to—when our opposition was ready to assault the house, the winds would drop to let the attackers in.

"It's not safe by the window," Blackstone said. "You need to come back to the interview room."

"So what do you do for the CIA?" I asked him, staying by the window.

Blackstone stayed silent.

"You don't strike me as a field agent. You're more an analyst type, right? Must be quite a legal Gordian knot to have you guys working on Ragnan when it's supposedly part of the U.S."

Blackstone grunted.

"That's why you're with the FBI, isn't it? Because you don't really have jurisdiction here—you need them to make it all neat and legal."

"What the hell are you doing?"

What I was doing was babbling at Blackstone while I tried to engineer my escape. The problem was how many people we'd have to deal with in the attack. Would they have enough to hit every opening? Would they have snipers?

I was betting that the attack would be limited. The bastards had a lot of magical resources at their disposal, but I doubted that they had a lot of spare warm bodies. They didn't have enough to flank me after the meeting with Cutler, they probably didn't now. I suspected that was the reason for the windstorm. They had to pin us all down, because they had limited numbers to devote to the attack itself.

That probably meant snipers.

I had studied the window and saw all the protective charms were attached to the storm window. That meant I could slide the inner window open without breaking the protection.

"Jesus, Maxwell—"

Blackstone wasn't doing anything. He was an academic type,

and he suffered the flaw that, if no one automatically succumbed to his authority, he didn't quite know what to do.

I had a plan now. It wouldn't work until the winds dropped, but it gave me a chance.

Blackstone finally got over the fact that I wasn't listening to him. He grabbed my arm and said, "What do you think you're doing?"

"Self-preservation," I said.

Blackstone backed up and pulled a gun on me.

"You really want to shoot me?"

"Don't force me to make that decision."

I looked him up and down. "You'd do better to train that gun on the window."

"You're coming back with—"

The wind stopped suddenly. The sound ceased as if someone pulled a switch. Almost at the same time there was the sound of gunfire. Blackstone ducked and suddenly didn't know where to point the gun. I ducked to one side of the window frame and looked outside. I didn't see anyone prepping to enter this way. Good and bad. Good, because they didn't have the manpower to cover every entrance. Bad, because that almost certainly meant that they had a sniper covering the area.

I threw open the inner window, and heard more gunshots.

"Christ," Blackstone said.

I looked back at him as the sounds of breaking glass and wood came from the front of the building. "We've got to get out of here," I told him as I tried to get the storm window off its track, while exposing myself as little as possible.

"What're you doing?"

The door into the bedroom was raked by a series of oblique bullet holes near the top. Splinters showered over Blackstone, and he dove over by me. He held his gun upright and divided his attention between the door and the window.

"The charms on the window," I said. "They'll probably protect us until we reach cover."

"You don't think—" Machine-gun fire interrupted him.

"I can't stop you from coming," I said as the aluminum storm window came free of its track. "You've got the gun."

My theory was partly confirmed as the inside window was suddenly peppered with gunfire. Again, it was oblique, the sniper shooting from off to the left somewhere. I stuck the storm sideways through the opening, and the shots stopped hitting the window. I could still hear them, thudding into the wall above the window frame.

That was all the confirmation I needed.

"*Maxwell*—"

I dove through the open window trying to simultaneously keep the charmed storm window between me and the sniper, and to present as small a target as possible. I didn't land well. My left knee decided to remind me of what happened last night and buckled. I spilled to the ground, my bandaged hands losing their grip on the window as I plowed face first into the wound of raw earth left by the magical winds.

The storm window fell across my back. Lucky for me, the aura of protection provided by the charms worked for a diameter of about seven feet. Bullets that should have been kill shots were plowing divots in the ground about two feet in front of my face.

I heard Blackstone mutter an obscenity as I heard something hit the ground on the far side of me from the sniper. I felt the storm window lift up, and the sound of gunfire was much closer.

"Get up," Blackstone said between shots.

I did, and saw him standing next to me, holding the storm window with his left hand, as if it was a riot shield. His gun was pointed in the general direction of the unseen sniper. He fired another shot and yelled, "Get moving!"

Twenty-five feet to the airport fence, Blackstone moving slowly to keep from overtaking my limping lope. Every few steps, he would take a shot and mutter something like, "Fucking bullshit."

In front of the fence was an overgrown drainage ditch filled with a foot of black stagnant water. We took shelter in it, crouching behind our magic window.

"Fuck, fuck, fuck," Blackstone said. "Now what, genius?"

"Through the fence," I said.

Above us a jumbo jet took off, rattling fillings and drowning out the gunshots. I backed up, down the trench, away from the sniper. I risked a look back at the not-so-safe house, but I really couldn't see much of anything through the weeds. About ten yards down I found what I was looking for. A muddy stream fed runoff under the fence, into the ditch I was wading through. Despite the pain in my hands, I dug into the muck to clear a space under the chain-link.

"*Blackstone*," I yelled above the engines of the passing jet. I started under the fence without waiting for him. I crawled into the woods on the other side of the fence, and started running directly away from the house.

Blackstone was on the other side of the fence, with the window and its protection, but I was running on pure panic now. The fact was every instinct was screaming at me to put as much distance between me and the gun as possible.

The cover didn't last long. In a few seconds the sky opened above me and I was running through knee-high grass at the end of "White's Elephant," the ten thousand foot runway built as one of the last grand projects of the eponymous mayor before he left office. It was long enough to accommodate nonstop flights to the Pacific rim, at a time when there wasn't more than a single flight out of Hopkins that left the North American continent. The runway's extra length was unused and unnecessary until the Portal graduated from natural disaster to tourist attraction.

I ran toward the runway. The asphalt cut the air with heat ripples, and the sound of taxiing aircraft was a pressure trying to squeeze my head inside out. When I cleared the grass, my feet slid on gravel that flanked the edge of the asphalt. I fell down next to the concrete base of a runway light.

It felt like I'd slammed into a wall. I wasn't in great shape to begin with, and the past few days had taken their toll. When I got my breath knocked out of me, it was hard to get it back again. I rolled over, stunned, for a moment unable to do anything if the sniper decided to target me.

It seemed an hour where nothing moved. The thrum of jet engines so loud it wasn't really a sound any longer, just a throbbing pressure. Above me, the sky was cloudless and just starting to purple with evening.

Then, suddenly, Dr. Blackstone's face appeared over me as the silver belly of a 747 slid by above. He still had the gun. He pulled me up and started dragging me toward the terminal. The sniper didn't reappear.

CHAPTER NINETEEN

I DON'T know what Blackstone flashed at airport security, but it made them very deferential, right up to providing him with a private interview room and coveralls to replace the wreck our clothes had become.

"This is a fucking nightmare," he told me when we were alone. "What the hell happened back there?"

Every joint in my lower body ached, and I, for one, wasn't feeling very conciliatory. "Someone screwed up," I told him.

He nodded vigorously, though the skin on his face had turned a shade just this side of purple. "Yeah, you're a smart one, aren't you?"

"It doesn't take a genius to realize that your cover was blown back there."

Blackstone didn't look pleased at my assessment, but he didn't disagree. He looked at me and shook his head. "The whole situation here's blown. We need to get you out of the city."

"Hey," I said, "wait a minute. You don't have the authority to do that."

"You have no idea exactly what authority I have," Dr. Blackstone said. "I'm giving you a choice. Gracefully accompany me on a flight to Washington, or go there in handcuffs."

I got up. "You can't just kidnap American citizens."

"You'd be amazed at what one executive order can do."

Blackstone escorted me out into the terminal. I was good, and therefore didn't rate the handcuffs. However, the fact that I didn't try to ditch him and lose myself in the crowd had more to do with the idea that there were some very powerful people out there ready to do me physical harm than with any sense of cooperation.

While we walked down the terminal, Blackstone pulled out his cell phone, which had survived the mess. After a few moments of trying to get it to connect, he grimaced and closed it.

"Didn't get a Cleveland model?" I asked.

He muttered some obscenity and moved us toward a pay-phone."You have no idea how sick I am of this town."

I looked at the phone, then at him, and said, "Do I rate a phone call?"

Blackstone sighed. "Calling your lawyer?"

"My daughter."

For once I saw the starch in his expression soften a little. I guess there was a human being in their after all. "Okay, I'll give you five minutes." He pulled out a credit card. "You're going to use a secure account. And I'm standing right next to you. You don't say where you are. You don't mention anyone's name. You don't say where we are going—"

I picked up the receiver and took the card. "And I don't mention the safe house, etc., etc." I used the card to dial California. It looked like a regular long-distance calling card, but there were a lot more clicks and whirs and electronic noise than seemed usual.

Hell, it was a government account, there was probably a recording being made in the NSA's basement for every call made with this account.

With Blackstone hanging over my shoulder I heard the phone on the other end pick up. "Hello?"

"Sarah?"

My daughter sounded surprised. "*Daddy?*"

"Yeah, honey."

"What's happening? You're all over the news. Are you hurt? What happened? Are you all right?"

Oh, shit. For some reason I was hoping the whole mess with Cutler was just going to be a local story. Silly me.

"I'm all right—"

In the background I heard a very pissed voice say, "Is that your father?"

Better and better.

There was a muffled commotion and the phone rattled as it dropped on the floor. I was suffering a pang of severe guilt that this was the first moment after the mess started that I'd thought of calling my expatriate family.

"What the fuck do you think you're doing, Kline?"

"Margaret, it's all right. There's just a little jurisdictional mix-up."

"Mix-up? The anchor on CNN said you're wanted in questioning for a murder."

"It's a misunderstanding. I didn't do it—"

"Christ, I *know* that. Why the hell are there cops looking for you, then?"

"It's jurisdiction. I'm cooperating with—" Blackstone placed his hands on the phone, ready to hang the thing up. "—the cops," I finished. Blackstone moved his hand away. "They're just not local. Cutler was dealing with dirty cops in the city here, and I didn't want those people involved."

"Why's CNN saying you're a fugitive?"

"The local cops don't know I'm working with another law enforcement agency." I looked at Blackstone, and when he didn't appear concerned, I went on. "They might not know until charges are filed."

I heard Margaret sigh. "Are you all right?"

I glanced at my hands but decided not to mention it. "I'm fine. I'm safe."

"You said it was getting better."

"This doesn't have anything to do with magic," I lied. "Dirty cops, this could've happened if I was working in San Francisco."

"Then why don't you?"

"Margaret—"

"If you can do the same work here, why don't you move closer to your daughter?"

"Can you put Sarah back on the line?"

There was a rustling, then a voice that said, "Dad?"

"Yeah, honey."

"You're not in bad trouble, are you?"

"Not really," I lied again. "Your mom will explain it to you. I'm fine. CNN just doesn't have the whole story yet."

Blackstone touched the watch on his wrist. Christ, I had not planned blowing my time arguing with my ex. "I'm sorry, honey, I've got to go."

"But, Dad—"

"I love you. I'll call back soon."

"I love you, too. But, Dad—"

Blackstone hung up for me. He looked at my expression and said. "I gave you more than I was obliged to. You can talk all you want after we've debriefed you."

I stepped back and handed him the receiver. He pulled out a different card, made a call—and with the power of a government expense account—we had a pair of business class seats on the next outbound Continental flight to Dulles Airport. The plane left in two hours. He made another call after he got his flight. "It's blown . . . Yes . . . three agents . . . I had local authorities informed about the mess . . . no, I have the subject here . . . I'm taking him in for de-briefing . . . I've made arrangements, the flight leaves in two hours . . . Yes . . . Yes . . . I understand."

He hung up and started hustling us toward the gate.

"Hey," I said. "The rush is over, you got your flight, calm down." He looked at me as if I'd just suggested that he consummate an un-speakable act with his mother. "We'll have about ninety minutes be-fore they start boarding. I haven't eaten a thing all day, aren't *you* hungry?"

"*Christ.*" He looked at me as if my suggestion was singularly in-appropriate, but he said, "Yes, we can get something to eat."

He pushed us into the first place that we passed, a McDonald's where some mental giant had contracted someone to construct full life-size simulacrum of some of the more creepy denizens of Ronald McDonald's world. A life-size blue-furred hump of a mon-ster watched us with eyes that were too human.

He sat me down at a McTable and was interrupted by an elec-tronic beeping. He pulled out his cell phone again, listened, shook his head and cussed it as he threw it down on the lemon-yellow table. "Useless . . . Hold up your hand, Maxwell."

I raised my right hand as if I was about to take an oath. He slapped one end of a pair of handcuffs on me, and before I could register an objection, he had the other end attached to the back of the chair next to me. "I thought we weren't going to resort to hand-cuffs."

"I don't trust you, Maxwell. And right now you're one of the few things I've got to salvage from this operation." He looked back at the counter and asked, "So what do you want?"

I ordered the generic burger-fries-and-soft-drink, just because what to eat wasn't high on my list of things I wanted to spend time thinking about. Dr. Blackstone went to stand in line, and I made a cursory examination of the McChair, which was fiberglass and bolted to the floor. It looked possible to break the cuffs free of the chair, but not in any unobtrusive way.

While I was contemplating the chair, Blackstone's phone rang.

I looked at it. A small black rectangle, slightly rounded. The Motorola logo across the top without any of the trademarks for the kind of multichannel digital encryption that made phone traffic pos-sible around the Portal. The only thing anyone would be able to get on that phone would be a cacophony of magical interference.

It rang again.

The thing shouldn't even be receiving enough of a comprehensible signal to know someone was calling it.

A third time it rang.

I reached out for it, a familiar feeling twisting in my gut. I raised it to my ear and activated it. I was greeted by the now familiar sound of whispering babble led by a voice that was like an old-fashioned tape player going bad.

"—I come not to praise Caesar—"

"*Who the hell are you?*" I whispered harshly into the phone. My anonymous Shakespearean *had* to be a magus of some sort. I couldn't figure anything else. How else could this guy know to call me on Blackstone's cell phone? Not to mention that his phone number was probably unlisted, and this phone didn't have the electronics for normal operation near the Portal anyway. Magic would be the only way my someone *could* make a call . . .

The voice continued with the quote.

"Damn it. Stop playing the enigmatic Oracle. I get your point—" This time the voice didn't cut off, it faded into the din and the babble took over. "Who are you? What do you want?" The transmission faded into nonsense. After a few more fruitless moments, I shut the thing off and tossed it back on the table.

Blackstone came back with our food and sat down. He still looked pissed, though now it was a pissed without a specific target. He kept looking toward the entrance and watching the crowds press by the terminal, as if he expected to be jumped.

I didn't blame him after the last hour or so.

"So what do you intend to do with me?" I asked him.

"You're going to be debriefed."

"CIA?" I asked again.

"Threat Assessment Office," Blackstone answered. "It's an inter-agency organization."

"What threats are you assessing?" I asked between bites of my hamburger.

"What do you think?" Blackstone asked, keeping an eye on the concourse outside. "The Office was established in response to the Portal."

"So the federal plan to take over the Portal has spawned an entrenched bureaucracy."

Blackstone shook his head. "You can be glib if you want, but this is more important than a battle over local turf. Do you have any idea of the danger the Portal represents?"

"You've made that point—"

"One mage," Blackstone said, "one person with the arcane knowledge, and access to blueprints, can manufacture a nuclear device."

"Is that what you're worried about?"

"I've seen studies. I've *conducted* studies. It's possible for a mage—given enough effort—to create elemental matter. Nothing prevents their access to fissionable material." He turned to look at me. "No tooling necessary, no weapon plants, just one man with the will and the power. Same can go for chemical and biological weapons."

One thing I'll say for our government's intelligence agencies. They have no problem coming up with nightmare scenarios. I shook my head and ate a few fries.

Pointing one at Blackstone's nose I said, "There's something you're leaving out."

"Yes?"

"What exactly do I have to do with it?"

"You know something important," Blackstone said. "You have managed to stumble across something that this conspiracy—this magical fifth column—is willing to go to any length to prevent us from finding out."

"This is the conspiracy that Aloeus was part of?"

Blackstone nodded.

"Well, good luck, because I don't even know what that is."

"It can be anything, Maxwell," he said. "A name. Someone you've seen. Something that would allow us to uncover exactly what's happening, and who is involved."

I shook my head. "All I have is a dead dragon, a bunch of crooked cops, and a guy named Faust."

Blackstone leaned forward. "And exactly what do you know about Faust?"

Ah. This is what interested the doctor. I wouldn't lay odds against this being one of the things that Blackstone had wanted "clarified" after my first run through in the rec room.

"Nothing other than the elves were interested in him, and that he was a rumor that Dr. Shafran had heard about."

"More than a rumor."

"Why don't you tell me about him."

Blackstone shook his head. "No, that was why I was against Agent Ts'ao lending you information. There's no better way to contaminate the intelligence from a subject than to tell him what you already know." He looked at me. "Not that I disagree with him entirely. If you remain as cooperative as you have been, I don't see any reason not to answer your questions. *After* we debrief you."

I nodded. "You would like a story about all this crap, wouldn't you?"

"Let's just say that it would help us if public opinion started to move in our direction." He reached over and undid the handcuffs."Come on, Mr. Maxwell, we have a plane to catch."

I hadn't finished my food, but I didn't see much point in arguing. So I grabbed the leftover burger to finish on the way to the gate. At this point I was kicking over story ideas in my head.

We were halfway to the gate when Blackstone stopped and said, "No, you've got to be kidding me."

That brought my attention back to the here and now in the concourse. I took a bite of my hamburger and looked around to see what Blackstone was complaining about.

It would have been hard to miss.

Coming down the central corridor of the concourse was a line of blue uniforms, their wearers watching us with grim attention. I looked behind us, and saw another five officers approaching from the rear.

At this point I was suffering from law enforcement overload and couldn't produce enough adrenaline to panic. Blackstone was looking back and forth with a dumbfounded expression that was almost amusing. "What?"

I finished my hamburger, dropped the wrapper on the floor, and slowly raised my hands and locked them behind my head. "There's a warrant out for me, remember?" I took a few sideways steps away from Blackstone. If he did something stupid, I didn't want to be caught in the aftermath.

The ranks of blue converged on us from both sides. I was somewhat relieved to see that they were all run-of-the-mill Cleveland cops supplemented by airport security. No SPU officers.

Blackstone recovered somewhat and addressed the lead cop, "What's the meaning of this?"

I was somewhat surprised, though only somewhat, to see that the head cop here was Commander Thomas O'Malley, looking more like the mafia hood than usual. "Doctor Roy Blackstone?"

"Yes, I can show you my identification. I'm conducting a federal investigation here."

O'Malley nodded. "Uh-uh." He didn't look impressed.

Blackstone reached for his ID.

O'Malley raised his hand and shook his head. "I know, Doctor. One of Langley's little 'experts.' PhD dissertation on the geopolitical implications of the Portal, worked the Cleveland desk at the CIA—Christ, don't look so surprised. You thought the FBI was the only Agency that kept files on people?"

"This is a matter of national security, sir. I need to take this man back to Washington D.C."

"I'm sure that's the way you see it," O'Malley said. He waved a hand and three officers converged on a sputtering Blackstone, one on each arm and the third patting him down and taking his gun.

"You're making a big mistake," Blackstone shouted at O'Malley.

"No, Dr. Blackstone," he said. "It was a mistake when an academic CIA desk jockey decided he wanted to play James Bond in my city." He took Blackstone's gun from the officer who was patting him down.

"When word of this gets to Washington—"

"You'll probably be put on six months unpaid administrative leave," O'Malley finished. He looked at Blackstone and shook his head. "Shall I draw you a map? There's a burning ranch at the end of a runway. There're at least two bodies. A lot of gunfire. Then we have you, a federal employee with no police powers, aiding and abetting a suspect wanted for questioning in a felony investigation, taking him on a flight out of state."

"You can't—"

"Did I say that anything you say can be used against you?"

Blackstone shut up.

O'Malley turned to look at me. "Maxwell?"

"O'Malley," I replied.

"Not the smartest thing you've ever done."

"I didn't have much choice." I shrugged, my hands still locked behind my head. "Besides, is there a law against poor judgment?"

O'Malley shook his head. "We don't have prisons that big. But obstruction of justice might do for a start. Leaving the scene. Failure to report."

"You're saying I should invest in a lawyer?"

"Maybe in some common sense."

The majority of the officers started leading Blackstone away, one of them finishing the litany of rights that O'Malley had started. I watched him go and looked at O'Malley. "So you knew about him?"

O'Malley looked back in Blackstone's direction. "The Threat

Assessment Office? Yes. As if we could keep the Feds from rooting around in our backyard." He turned back and looked at me. "And get your hands down, will you? We need to go downtown. Some people want to see you."

CHAPTER TWENTY

O'MALLEY rode in the back of an unmarked squad car with me as we took the freeway downtown. They didn't cuff me, and looking at O'Malley I had trouble reading if he was going to charge me or not.

He surprised me by saying, once we were underway, "Damn shame you got involved in this, Maxwell."

"My job, O'Malley."

"Is it?" he asked. He was gazing out the window at the sound barriers sliding by. "You stepped into a hornet's nest, my friend."

"Did I?" I decided to throw my cards on the table since I didn't seem to have anything to lose. "Was it investigating Aloeus' death, or was it when your SPU elves decided to do some extracurricular legwork? Or maybe it was set up with Bone Daddy? Since when do SPU units do traffic stops?"

O'Malley shook his head. "I suppose you have an answer already?"

"I know something corrupt is going on in the Special Paranormal Unit. I know that Aloeus was prominent in the decisions that Rayburn and company made about the Portal—with a *quid pro quo* that, in exchange for disaster assistance, some national Guard troops did some social engineering on the other side. I know the federal government is worried about influence across the Portal, stopping just short of accusing this city of harboring a fifth column bent on the overthrow of the U. S. government . . ."

O'Malley was shaking his head. "The Feds are a sideshow. Have been since the Portal opened." He looked across at me, and I noticed, for the first time, that he hadn't shaved and looked as if he hadn't slept in days. In short, he looked like I felt. "Maxwell, you're smart, and I think you realize this; you have no real idea what's going on here."

"Care to enlighten me?"

He shook his head. "That isn't my job."

* * *

We drove to Lakeside, but not toward the Justice Center as I expected. Instead, we went half a block farther, and pulled into the underground parking garage of City Hall itself. I could almost sense the tension, as if some sort of static energy had rubbed off from the nearby Portal.

The car rolled down three levels underground, past ranks of city vehicles, then down a narrow one-way concrete ramp that read, "Authorized Vehicles Only." I saw expensive-looking digital cameras, as well as crystal wards set into the concrete walls.

The car drove another level down and into a nearly empty parking lot. The only light was a flickering fluorescent hanging roughly in the center of the space. Beneath the light, incongruously, sat a boardroom-sized table with about twelve executive leather chairs.

The driver shut off the engine, and the lock on my handleless door popped open. The driver got out and opened the door for O'Malley, who walked around and opened the door for me. I stepped out and shivered. This place was about ten degrees colder than the day outside. The only sound in the whole space was the sound of an electric motor lowering a rolling metal barrier across the ramp we'd just driven down. It finished with the echoing clatter of metal locking home.

"Welcome to the War Room, Maxwell," O'Malley said.

I had heard the rumors that Rayburn had established some ultrasecure meeting place in the early days of the Portal, back when the Feds were a military threat, not just a political one. I had taken the rumors, as had every one else I knew, as equal parts fact and exaggeration. Now I looked around at the space and decided that I, and the people I knew, probably lacked sufficient imagination.

I could barely see the near walls in the light, but what I saw was covered in small inscriptions. Mystic text no larger than the type on your average printed page. The floor, too, was covered with inscriptions. Concentric rings centered on the conference table. Unlike Bone Daddy's magic circles, these words were permanently inset in the concrete, each symbol cast in gold, silver, or some semiprecious stone. The feeling in this place was like standing next to the main transformer at a nuclear power plant. The hair on my arms wanted to stand on end.

O'Malley walked me toward the center of the room. I kept flashing back to a memory of Bone Daddy warning me, *"The mojo's been building here a couple hours. You break the pattern, boy, and it'll be like someone shoved a stick of dynamite up your ass."*

I wondered how long the mojo had been building up in this room. Fortunately, someone would need a jackhammer to break the pattern.

O'Malley sat me down in one of the chairs at one end of the long table. He backed away, out of the light. My dark vision was shot now, and all I could really see was the conference table, the chairs, and the long fluorescent tubes above me. I heard a car door slam, and an engine start—

I turned and yelled, *"Hey!"* into the darkness.

I heard the car drive away, and the ratting metallic sound of another door closing.

For a few long moments I was left alone here, wondering exactly what the hell I was supposed to do. I squinted out at the darkness, trying to make out any sense of movement. The only sound now, the electric hum of the fluorescents. The air was heavy, cold, and carried the humid smell of mildew—perfect atmosphere for a dungeon.

Then there was the sound of a large electric motor, the sound so sudden in the enclosed space that I jumped. *Elevator,* I thought. I listened to its descent for what seemed an inordinately long time. Then the motor stopped and I heard the doors slide back. I also saw a narrow rectangle of light slowly open on the far wall across the conference table from me. The space revealed was huge, taller than the room I was in, and wide enough to take two cars abreast. All similarly embellished to the room I sat in.

Three human figures were dwarfed in the revealed space, and the capacity of the elevator made me wonder if they ever met dragons in this room.

The trio exited the elevator, and due to the ill lighting and misleading cues to scale, it wasn't until they entered the domain of the fluorescent light that I saw for sure who they were.

To the left was the five-foot blonde landmine that was Cleveland's Public Safety Director, Julian Nesmith. To the right was the pudgy and somewhat taller form of Adrian Phillips, the chairman of the Cleveland Port Authority. The man in the center overshadowed the other two, both in physical stature and in impact. Mayor David Rayburn stood six-six, and had shoulders that made it look as if he could break your average elf in half. He had huge peasant hands, blocky, the hands of a laborer—even if his dad put him through law school. He owned a legendary smile that he was choosing not to use at the moment. It might have been the light, but

I think I saw a little more gray in his close-cropped black hair than I'd noticed the last time I'd seen him.

The trio sat without ceremony, Rayburn taking the seat opposite mine, the length of the table between us. "I think we can forgo the introductions, Mr. Maxwell." His expression was grim.

I nodded and folded my hands in front of me, on the table. "What can I do for you, Your Honor?" I managed, barely, to keep my voice in line with a fiction that I had come here voluntarily.

"I'm informed that you had a recent run-in with some local Federal Agents," the mayor said.

"I think that is, perhaps, an understatement."

Nesmith slid a small stack of eight by ten glossies toward me. "These the men who abducted you?"

I reached for the photographs. They were all slick black and whites, apparently cribbed from whatever official IDs these men had owned. No names were attached, just file numbers. I riffled through them and tossed back Mr. Brown, Colonel Mustard, Agent Ts'ao, and the two drivers. There were a couple of other pictures in the stack of people I hadn't seen before. I studied them—just in case I ran into any more Feds.

"You're missing Doctor Blackstone," I said.

"We're aware of that," Nesmith snapped. Struck a nerve there. *They didn't know him until today, until that fiasco at the safe house.* Nesmith continued after pausing to look at the photos I had sent back. "These were the only agents you saw?"

I nodded.

"What did they question you about?"

I looked at the trio and got an uneasy vibe. Almost as if the Cleveland home team was on the same fishing expedition the Feds were. I answered the question, giving them a brief on the Feds' tune. It wasn't as if there were any privileged communications involved.

As I continued, the trio facing me grew graver.

When I finished, Mayor Rayburn folded his hands in front of him. Adrian Phillips leaned forward and said, in a squeaky voice, "Is that what you believe? After all this administration has done for—"

The mayor held up a hand, and Phillips fell silent. "Don't attack the messenger. Mr. Maxwell is simply relating a belief held by some in the executive branch of the federal government."

"Yes?" Phillips asked slowly. "But what's *his* view?"

I was about to answer, but the mayor spoke for me. "His views aren't the issue here. What side he takes in this turf war with the Feds is, at the moment, completely beside the point." Rayburn waved a hand at me. "You're not here because of your politics."

I couldn't decide if that was a good thing or a bad thing. "Why, exactly, *am* I here then?"

Rayburn leaned back in his chair and steepled his fingers. His collar shifted and I caught a gleam of gold around his neck. *The chain Aloeus gave him?* I wondered.

"The dragon." The mayor spoke softly, almost a whisper. "You know something about his death."

"Something. I wish I knew more."

Adrian slammed a palm on the table and looked at me with distaste. "Why are we bothering with him?"

"I know the pressures you're under, Adrian," Mayor Rayburn said. "But allow the man to speak. Tell us about what you do know."

Again, I gave them the story I gave the Feds. I studied them for reactions as I talked. To my surprise, none of them reacted when I talked about Cutler and crooked elf cops. Phillips himself was fuming.

When I'd gone through to my liberation from Dr. Blackstone, Phillips turned to face Nesmith and said, "Your people already established he wasn't on to anything. Why aren't your elves doing something productive, like finding Faust?"

The name "Faust" fired a switch in my brain, recasting everything that I'd been going through to date. No wonder O'Malley thought I didn't have a clue. *"Your elves?"* I leaned on the table and stood up. "Those were *your* elves?"

Nesmith looked at me with a slightly pained expression, the kind of face I'd expect to see on a mother when she learns that her six-year-old son has found out about sex. "Please sit down, Mr. Maxwell."

"These corrupt SPU elves that kidnaped me and fed me to the late Bone Daddy, they're yours?"

"Mine, actually," said Mayor Rayburn. "They're not corrupt, and they're very, very dedicated. Sit down please."

I shook my head and sat down.

Nesmith started, "That episode was outside normal channels—"

"No shit," I muttered.

"—because the people we're looking for have sources, perhaps even a mole, inside the administration. If we had brought you in for a formal questioning, your life might have been endangered. Even if you knew nothing, the appearance would have been that you did."

"Thank you so much, it worked so well. I'm sure Mr. Bone Daddy would agree—"

Rayburn leaned forward. "Let's dispense with the recriminations."

"Okay, let's." I said, glaring at Nesmith. "So what the hell was Cutler investigating? I have transactions between these guys and Bone Daddy since the start of the SPU."

Nesmith looked at Mayor Rayburn, who nodded at her.

"I will tell you this, Mr. Maxwell, only because Mr. Caleb Washington is dead. The gentleman you refer to as Bone Daddy was the best undercover cop this city ever had."

"What?"

"Caleb Washington was the first recruit the SPU ever had. We spent years building his persona, all the more genuine because he was one of the most talented native mages in the city. We knew about Cutler's investigation. He labored under a mistaken assumption. We used him to help maintain Washington's cover."

Suddenly, everything over the past three days took on a surreal cast. "No, wait a minute, Egil Nixon—"

"Died less than three hours after he went home the day of the dragon's death." Nesmith shook her head. "Through his own means, Mr. Washington had followed a trail to Mr. Nixon's corpse."

"Why the shootout?"

Nesmith shook her head. "It was a decision O'Malley made. Washington was ambushed by someone, probably the people responsible for Nixon's death, before he could meet with O'Malley and pass on what he had discovered. O'Malley decided to preserve his cover by planting the weapon and manufacturing the story . . ."

"Jesus." I whispered. The guy was a cop.

"The same people more than likely set up the episode with you and Cutler." She shook her head. "These same people may have set Cutler after Washington in the first place. Washington was getting very close to them."

"Faust?"

I was answered by a silent trio of nods.

CHAPTER TWENTY-ONE

"PERHAPS you begin to understand," Mayor Rayburn said quietly. "There have been threats that, up until now, it hasn't been in the city's interest to acknowledge publicly. To do so would have been to hand ammunition to the forces that want to remove local control of the Portal."

"What, exactly, do you mean?" I asked him.

"The Feds have been as reluctant to publicize their operations here as we've been to acknowledge the threat you named 'Faust,'" Nesmith explained. "Their contact with you has shown that their attitude has changed. That is why you're here, and not in the Justice Center."

"What are you saying?" I smiled and shook my head. "You offering an exclusive interview?"

"I am offering you a deal," Mayor Rayburn said.

"Over my objection," Phillips said, mostly to himself.

"What deal?"

"Help us get Faust," Nesmith said.

"Pardon?"

"Their activity has risen to an unprecedented level," she said, "centered on you."

"Now wait a minute—"

"They are giving us an opportunity to flush them out."

"Using me as bait?" I stood up. "Thank you, no."

"What did I tell you?" Phillips said. When he shook his head, his whole body moved. "This whole exercise is pointless."

"Please sit down, Mr. Maxwell," Rayburn said. It was the kind of voice I associated with Charlton Heston as Moses—after the bush incident. I stood my ground and looked Rayburn in the eyes.

"I think the discussion's over," I said.

"I don't think you want to leave just yet," Rayburn said.

"Is this where you start threatening me with criminal prosecution?"

I snapped at Nesmith. I could feel the old self-destructive stubbornness strike. I did not like to be threatened.

Nesmith surprised me. "No. If you don't cooperate with us, you're free to go. No strings."

The silence filled the cavernous room. From somewhere water dripped. A vent kicked on and began to suck a mildewed wind across my face.

"What?" I said, slowly sliding back into my seat.

"We have no grounds to hold you," she said. "You witnessed a felony, that's all. You could walk out the door right now, if you wanted to."

"Then why don't I?" I asked Rayburn.

"Self-interest," Rayburn replied.

In the end they had me, and they *knew* they had me. Rayburn knew from the beginning. That was why he was the mayor, and I was the one doing features on him.

The deal, which wasn't really a deal, was simply this—

I cooperate, agree to be their stalking horse, I get a little limited Q&A with the Cleveland triumvirate. On the record.

I walk, and not only do I get to go without that particular interview, but I get to face an unknown quantity of killer mages without police protection—and with decent surveillance the cops still get to use me to flush the bad guys.

So, in the end, it was a no-brainer.

I pulled out my notebook and tried to get my money's worth.

Nesmith did answer most of my questions. I got some limited background on Faust. The name began as a legendary figure, a native human who sold his soul by working with the mage underground. The rumors were born in the first few months, when the primary reaction to the Portal—and the things coming out of it—was one of fear.

The name became associated with secret societies, and what Nesmith described as a government-in-exile—almost as if Cleveland was a staging area for operations on the other side of the Portal. Faust and company could certainly communicate across the Portal, and the existing exchanges made it possible for agents to slip in and out.

I asked about the National Guard and forays into Ragnan, and got a predictable "no comment." When I asked why the Feds shouldn't be in charge of the Portal, with everything that was going on, I got a bombshell of an answer.

The Portal was not a natural phenomenon.

This thing that had been confounding scientists and mages for a decade had a very specific origin. The dragon Aloeus.

Not only was the dragon influential in shaping policy. Not only was he a primary source of intelligence about Ragnan. Not only was he a source of knowledge to work with mages and protect against them.

Aloeus was the last defense against the fifth column the Feds were worried about. He had created the Portal, and knew the mechanics of how to close it. As long as the dragon was friendly with the administration, the city didn't have anything to fear from an invasion. It was possible for Aloeus to shut the door.

The idea that Faust murdered Aloeus was enough to send waves of panic from Lakeside Avenue all the way to Pennsylvania Avenue. Such a blatant stroke made it almost certain that there was going to be some sort of push from the other side of the Portal.

Which made everyone all the more desperate to find these guys.

By the time I got to this point, I think I was using up the information faucet. I tried to get confirmations or denials on a lot of the Feds' accusations, but they weren't about to comment about National Guard involvement in a coup. Or disappearing homeless, for that matter.

One question I asked did get a rise from Phillips. Not that he said anything, he remained mute through the whole Q & A. But when I brought the questions around to Aloeus' business dealings. Rayburn, quite adroitly, pointed out that it was none of the city's business what Aloeus, Inc., did with its money. Phillips, however, looked uncomfortable.

I asked how they knew there was a mole in the administration. It boiled down to timing. Faust and company knew too many things. The fact that Nixon suppressed forensic data. The location of Bone Daddy's meet with O'Malley. The location of the FBI's safe house. Cutler's investigation . . .

I looked across at Phillips. "You've been quiet."

"I do not agree with the decision to use you, or to talk to you."

"Why is that?"

"I've explained my reasoning to the mayor. I do not need to do so to you. Suffice it to say that I believe you're a risk the administration can ill afford at this time."

"Why were you on the Coast Guard cutter, Phillips?"

"My job required it," he snapped. "I think you've wasted enough of our time."

Rayburn glanced at Phillips, and his hand went to the chain at his neck. He turned back, as if reassured by the touch of the chain. "Mr. Phillips felt that his presence was needed on site. You don't need to question his loyalty to this city and this administration."

Was that what I was questioning?

I was about to say something more when the mayor went on, "I trust the people in this room, Mr. Maxwell. Strangely enough, that includes you. But the time for questions is over."

I left the bunker under City Hall in the back seat of a minivan escorted by my old friends, Elves One, Two, and Three.

Elf Three still held the Glock, and Elf One still did all the talking.

"Mr. Maxwell," he said by way of greeting.

"Maelgwyn Caledvwlch," I said, butchering the name.

If I'd hoped to rattle him by knowing his name, I was disappointed. He looked at me impassively, and said in his breathy near-Jamaican accent, "*Detective Sergeant* Maelgwyn Caledvwlch, Mr. Maxwell."

I looked over to the elf with the Glock. At least he wasn't pointing it at me.

As we rolled out of that bunker I knew that Nesmith was drafting a press release to be faxed to all the papers in time for the a.m. editions. A press release calculated to make Faust and the Mage Mafia rabid to get me. I was pretty sure it went something like, "Kline Maxwell, recently wanted for questioning in the murder of Kirk Cutler, has turned himself over to the police. He has been cooperating with the murder investigation, as well as several other related ongoing investigations. At the moment he is not a suspect in any criminal wrongdoing, and is being held in police custody at an undisclosed location for his own protection." Something to rehabilitate me while simultaneously making me look threatening to Faust. That was how I'd write it.

"So where are you taking me, Detective Sergeant Caledvwlch?" I asked, expecting pretty much as unresponsive a ride as I had gotten to Bone Daddy's ministrations.

"We're taking you home, Mr. Maxwell," he responded, confounding my expectations on several levels.

"Home," I repeated, for a time unsure if he was referring to my home or his.

"You are in protective custody," he told me. "We will remain with you until you are no longer in danger."

"Uh-huh," I said. "You're painting yourselves a mighty big target, aren't you?"

He didn't respond to that.

The minivan rolled out of downtown, east, through neighborhoods of new townhouses and small strip malls. It was hard to believe that, at one time, the area around us had been some of the most depressed real estate in the county.

I felt backed into a corner, and I didn't like it. For all their talk that I could just walk away, either choice I'd make essentially amounted to Rayburn and Nesmith throwing me out to draw the hunters. I didn't like the fact that their scenario about Faust didn't add up—a gut feeling, but a powerful one.

My doubts did have a foundation, albeit a shaky one. If Nesmith was correct in her theories, Aloeus was killed for something he *might* do, because he represented the administration's control of the Portal in a crisis situation. I'd always found it much more likely that people are killed for what they *have* done, or what they *will* do.

As the night slid by, I asked, "So were you the cops the late Bone Daddy supposedly drew down on?"

Caledvwlch, as usual, was the one who answered me. "It was unfortunate."

"More so for Bone, don't you think?"

"It is the nature of mortal beings to die." He paused a moment, as if in reflection. "The timing, in some cases, is inconvenient." It was hard to tell if he spoke with anger, regret or some other, less accessible emotion.

"You work with him a long time?"

"An instant," Caledvwlch said, making a gesture of dismissal. It rang false to me, even through the enigmatic elven reticence. I didn't get the feeling that there was affection there, but I sensed that there might have been some sort of camaraderie that Caledvwlch wouldn't want to admit. "He was useful for the work."

" 'The work?' " I asked. "A rather pious way to put it. Or are you more than a city cop?"

"Our unit has a special role, Mr. Maxwell. Caleb Mosha Washington aided that role."

We hit University Circle. As we drove through, I looked up at the Gothic cathedral at the edge of the Case campus. Trying to see the gargoyle that had yawned at me. I didn't see anything but inert stone.

"What is your 'role'? Do you guys have some sort of mission statement beyond 'serve and protect'?"

"You are looking for hidden agendas, Mr. Maxwell."

It wasn't a question, so I didn't answer it. "You—the SPU—were formed to be specialist cops, like Vice, or Homicide. Doesn't look as if that's the way things worked out."

"We are police officers."

"You're doing covert black bag jobs for the administration. That night with Bone Daddy wasn't your first midnight questioning of an unwilling subject."

"Perhaps." The minivan slowed to a stop outside my building.

They led me out of the van, and I hunched my shoulders, expecting an ambush out of the night. Three elves accompanied me inside, the driver staying with the car, as always.

Once we were in the stairwell and I felt a little safer, I asked, "How close was Cutler to what was really happening?"

Caledvwlch's voice echoed hollowly, and somewhat ominously, in the stairwell, "Mr. Cutler asked the wrong questions."

I had a real bad feeling. What were the *right* questions? Why did Cutler have to die? Why did they want me dead? Coroner Nixon? Bone Daddy? Several things that had been nagging at me began surfacing as the elf led me up to my condo. Nixon wasn't killed to hide the dragon's murder. Nesmith and company *already* knew, they had just invented an accident in an attempt to play things down. The city was doing Faust's job in that respect.

Nixon was killed for some *other* reason.

Faust had a mole in the administration . . . .

I looked at Caledvwlch and asked, "How did Caleb Washington die?"

He looked at me and said, "Mr. Maxwell, Caleb Washington held a fellow officer, a human officer, at gunpoint. We had no choice but to shoot him."

The air around me began to leach the heat off my skin. "Nesmith said—"

"Ms. Nesmith does not know."

When I stared at him for a few moments, he repeated, "We had no choice," as if I had missed the point.

Before I could ask him anything more, he had the door open and we were walking into my condo to face the hunched form of Thomas O'Malley. The elves flanked me and stood, almost at attention until O'Malley nodded and gestured them at ease. Caledvwlch was silent, and it started to strike me that, like Baldassare, this person I'd been pumping would never tell me a thing unless he had a concrete reason to do so.

As Commander O'Malley stood to greet us, I began to wonder exactly what that reason was.

CHAPTER TWENTY-TWO

"WELL," I said, "make yourself at home." The bad feeling in my gut had just deepened several notches. What Caledvwlch had said in the stairwell didn't sync with what Nesmith had said about Bone Daddy, unless O'Malley here was part of it.

How much of this did Cutler have right?

O'Malley shook his head. "I would have thought you'd be flattered at the attention." He gave me a humorless grin. "You're under 'special police protection.'"

"The elf squad isn't special enough?"

"We all follow Ms. Nesmith's lead, don't we boys?"

"Sir," replied Caledvwlch. He was echoed by his two henchmen, the first time I had heard their voices. The feeling in the room was unnerving. I couldn't read the elves, beyond the fact that they had become even more reserved upon entering the room—as impossible as that seemed. O'Malley on the other hand, radiated unease like the heat from a compost heap. His posture was tense, and he eyed the elves more than he eyed me.

I looked at the tableau in my living room, all back-lit by my wide-screen showing some nature documentary. The tension was taking its toll on me; I needed space to breathe, to think.

After a few long moments I said, "Okay, folks, if you all don't mind, I'm going to take a long-overdue shower."

I had just got my airport coveralls unzipped, an effort the way my hands still pained me, when Detective Caledvwlch opened the door.

I stood there, the coveralls half dropped and hanging on my hips, staring at him in numb disbelief. *"Come on."*

Caledvwlch responded by settling his ungainly form on the john. He reminded me of a spider, the way his overlong legs bent past his lap. Even so, he managed to look gracefully imperturbable.

"You are not seriously going to watch me take a shower?"

"Mr. Maxwell, our duty is to protect you and neutralize your attackers."

"Yeah, right." I waved an arm around the windowless bathroom. "You think someone will attack me in here? There's no way in. You can sit by the door."

"A magical attack can ignore physical barriers."

I sighed, stood there a little longer, and finally dropped the overalls. If privacy was a little much to ask for, I was going to have to settle for getting myself clean.

"Enjoy the show," I said, and continued with my mission to feel like a human being again. I considered making a joke about dropping the soap, but a joke is wasted on an elf—and it was the kind of reference that would probably mystify him.

While I cleaned myself, I asked through the shower curtain, "What's the deal between you and O'Malley?" With the door shut and the water going, my question wouldn't carry outside the bathroom.

For a time, I thought Detective Caledvwlch's comparative gregariousness earlier had been a fluke. I didn't hear anything for a minute or so, so I resumed scrubbing.

It took so long for a reply that when it came, I did end up dropping the soap.

"Mr. Maxwell, I fail to understand your question."

I snorted. It seemed an overly trite way of being coy, and I was about to say so, when it struck me that he might truly not understand. "There's no love lost between you, is there? You might be cool to me on general principles, but around him it's like you're all sucking on dry ice."

"We owe fealty to him," he said in a flat voice.

"Don't like your boss?"

"From him to Ms. Nesmith, from her to Mayor Rayburn." I actually had to turn down the shower, his voice had become so low. "But *first*, to him."

Okay, he's got chain of command down pat. But his words began to ring an uneasy chord in my mind. In the twenty-first century United States, archaic feudal codes of honor were way out of place. But Caledvwlch wasn't born, or in any real sense raised, in the twenty-first century United States. Would patterns of behavior, definitions of right and wrong, be so easily swayed by movement from an agrarian society of noble-born landowners and serfs to a post-industrial service economy?

"*. . . a society that doesn't value human life, sees women as property, and sees violence as the first resort in a dispute. These men don't know the rule of law . . .*"

Blackstone was speaking of the dregs when he said that. How such a world created for us a new breed of criminals and rapists. However, I began to realize that the effects might be manifest in ways more subtle—and more corrupting to the principles the Feds were supposed to be fighting for.

I turned off the shower and pulled the curtain aside. Caledvwlch wasn't looking at me, but I was thinking of the way he had said— right before we entered the condo—that he "*had no choice.*"

I was beginning to see more than one way to interpret that phrase.

"Who was Bone Daddy threatening?" I asked.

"I cannot say," Caledvwlch responded in the same flat voice, answering my question without answering it.

"O'Malley?" I asked.

"I cannot say." He didn't turn to look at me.

My elven escort followed me as I shaved, bandaged the cuts on my hands that'd reopened in the shower, and when I went to the bedroom to get dressed. While I pulled on some clean clothes, Caledvwlch kept up his silent presence, not looking at me.

He stood in the doorway, slightly bent because of his height. The silhouette of his head against the light of the hall was obviously nonhuman. His eyes had a slight glow to them that I hadn't noticed before, lifting them out of his shadowed face. His right hand touched his left shoulder, almost an expression of mourning.

It wasn't right. He seemed more out of place here now than he ever had. His cheap cop suit hung on him as oddly, and as disrespectfully, as a pair of dirty overalls hung on the statue of David. I've never used the word beautiful to describe another man, but in Caledvwlch's case, the word fit—a lot better than the suit.

"Why did you come here?" I asked him.

He answered in his breathless island-flavored accent, a few notches lower on its inhuman register. "I am supposed to protect—"

I shook my head and interrupted him. "Not here, my condo. Here, Cleveland. Why did you come through into this world? Why pass through the Portal?"

He turned to face me and looked as if no one had ever bothered asking the question. "What interest is it of yours?"

"You're out of place here."

"Everyone is out of place here." He turned away, looking down the hall, back toward O'Malley and the other elves.

"Why are you here?"

"Mortals have a great advantage," Caledvwlch said. "That's why Ragnan is the only empire of any consequence for the past thousand years. So fragile . . ."

He trailed off, and I didn't say anything. I didn't know where he was going with this.

"Mr. Maxwell," he turned to face me. "You might think that I might be more 'in place' were I to go home. You presume that a home still exists for me." Caledvwlch shook his head. "We are a dying race. We started dying when mortal man took the first step into our world. Valdis simply consummated the inevitable with the destruction of our noble houses."

The aspect of mourning became concrete, the gravity of his past drew on his posture more than it did his words. "I and my fellows were raised for the honor of serving a noble lord. I have done so longer than any of the petty nations on your world have existed. Valdis took that last honor from us, with everything else." He looked upward and for the first time I saw a trace of emotion. His right hand clenched on his shoulder, bunching the material of the suit so tightly that I thought it might tear.

"They have the temerity to tell us that we're free now. *Free?*" The hand relaxed. "How can I be free, Mr. Maxwell? My native language doesn't even have a word for the concept."

His voice never wavered.

I stepped up, feeling the need to say something. It was a misplaced urge, and I realized it as the words came out of my mouth. "It must be a difficult adjustment."

He looked at me as if I was a disease-laden insect that had just landed on his shoe. "Adjustment? You are a fool if you believe it possible for us to be as inconstant as you. Honor and duty are not malleable virtues to be reshaped at a whim. If what is right is only right as long as it suits you, there *is* no right."

"I didn't mean that."

"What did you mean, Mr. Maxwell, other than that we adopt your 'freedom'? What purpose have I without honor? I have sworn myself, and that cannot be unsworn." He turned away from me, and his voice was very low now, almost as if he was talking to himself. "Even should I want to abandon myself, do you think I can be so easily changed? We do not change. We are not mortal. We are supposed to be incorruptible, eternal. What we are is permanence. To change is to die." Then, very quietly, "Not to change is to die."

Then he looked over his shoulder at me, as if he was waiting for me to follow him down the hallway. He said something that I found very disturbing.

"There is no word in my language for suicide either."

He walked me out to the living room where O'Malley was sitting watching my big-screen TV. On the high-definition flat screen, a lioness was chasing after a wounded gazelle. The other elves were gone.

"So where is everybody?" I asked him.

"Sent them to cover the rest of the building," O'Malley said. There was a tumbler of amber liquid in his hand. "You're important, Maxwell." He took a sip as the lioness ran the gazelle to ground and sank its teeth into the animal's neck.

"Uh-huh," I said.

I glanced over at Caledvwlch for a clue as to what was going on. The situation didn't feel right to me. Caledvwlch was no help, he had become solidly impassive again.

"You and the detective get to know each other?" O'Malley asked. "That's good," he added without pausing for an answer. "I know that Caledvwlch has a lot to get off his chest." He looked over at the elf and shook his head. "Take it from a good Catholic, confession is good for the soul."

"What's going on here, O'Malley?"

O'Malley chuckled and shook his head. "Sit down, Maxwell. Detective, stand by the door."

I didn't sit as Caledvwlch obediently stationed himself by the entrance to the condo. "This isn't right, O'Malley. What's going on here?"

"Oh, God, what isn't right about it?" He put the glass down roughly on my coffee table, and I was reminded of the image of Bone Daddy putting a bottle through the glass tabletop. "Sit yourself the fuck down, Maxwell."

I stepped in front of my lounge chair, but I didn't sit. I looked at O'Malley on the couch and, for the first time, I noticed that he had his gun out, resting on the arm of the couch opposite me. "What are you doing here?"

O'Malley stared at the screen where a trio of lionesses were tearing gobbets of flesh from the deceased gazelle. One white leg stuck straight upward, as if in some plea for mercy. "I wish I'd never heard of the damn Portal. I wish I'd stayed a damn beat cop. I wish I never had to deal with this crap."

"What are you talking about?"

"I didn't have to have this job, I volunteered. The Special Paranormal Unit. I thought it was so fucking interesting. Police work that no one else had ever done. Fucking idiot."

"O'Malley?"

"I did not start out to run a goddamn Gestapo. And now it's gone way past the point where I can go back." He reached for the gun.

I backed up. "O'Malley, this is not a good idea."

He moved slowly, picking up the remote and shutting off the television. "I didn't want this," he said as he stood up. He wasn't even looking at me.

"We can talk about this, O'Malley. Come to some sort of arrangement."

"Left hand doesn't know what the right is doing, Maxwell." *Many hands and no head.* "It's like trying to ride three horses, this job. Everyone's got a piece of me. All panicked over this Faust." He finally looked at me. His eyes were empty. "Some more panicked than others."

I raised my hands. "Let's not—"

"Do something rash? Irrevocable?" He shook his head and took out a silencer and began attaching it to the end of his gun. "Way too late for that Maxwell. It was too late when that goddamn dragon plowed into the Cuyahoga."

"Christ, O'Malley—" I looked back and saw Caledvwlch impassively guarding the door. Is that why he was so forthcoming? Because he knew I wasn't going to live through this? "At least tell me *why?*"

"*Why?* You know why. Didn't Nesmith explain it to you?" He shook his head. "If that bitch knew—so many fucking idiots. You know the chain the mayor wears? Tells him who lies to him, who's loyal to him—and the poor bastard thinks that means he knows what's happening."

I swallowed and thought about Bone Daddy's CD. "It wasn't Faust, was it?"

"Fuck, it was *always* Faust. Faust plans to destroy Rayburn and everything he's ever built. We can't let that happen, can we?" O'Malley shook his head. "We have to do anything to prevent that, don't we?"

"Aloeus . . ."

"Was working with Faust," O'Malley said. "Had to be stopped."

The whole sick situation was beginning to fall into place. The attack on Aloeus wasn't an attack *on* the city. The murder of the dragon required a *lot* of mages in a concerted effort. When it came down to resources, the city employed more mages than anyone else.

"Bone Daddy knew, didn't he?"

"Such a fiasco. Right hand, left hand again. Nesmith didn't know about the action to neutralize Aloeus. Didn't come off of her desk—but then, of the three, she's the least likely to do something that stupid. She also wasn't one to take things at face value. She knew it wasn't an accident despite what that poor little bastard Nixon was told to say."

I could smell his breath. There was enough scotch there to give someone a contact high. I looked down at the gun. "Why don't you set that down. We can figure out a way out of this together—"

I don't think he even heard me. "She sees it as a movement by Faust, all hell's going to break loose. Sends out Washington, our lone good cop. The one guy we actually got in close to Faust. Of course the shit starts flying—"

I stepped forward, "Why don't you give me the gun—"

"*Don't you fucking move!*" Scotch and spit flew from his lips as the shaking gun slammed barrel first into my chest. He shook his head and the eyes that looked down on me were those of a different person than the O'Malley I knew. "You think I *want* this? I'm a goddamn cop. You think for one moment, if Washington couldn't talk his way out of it— *Fuck!*" He slammed the pistol across my face and my vision blacked out as blood stung my eye.

"I recruited him. I handpicked him for this job. And he has to buy it because if it gets out how the dragon died it would be worse for Rayburn than if the beast had lived. Of course, since the stupid bastard sending the orders *loves* Rayburn . . ."

I rolled over and blinked up at him. A blurred form held a shaking gun at my head. "No contest, Maxwell. I don't even *like* you."

I braced for the shot.

The phone rang.

CHAPTER TWENTY-THREE

IT rang again. O'Malley looked over at the phone.

You want me to get that? I thought, but I managed not to say it.

It kept ringing, the electronic beeping cutting through the silence like a knife. I could tell that O'Malley wanted the person just to hang up, but the caller wasn't cooperating. Five, six, ten rings.

I did say, "Might be Nesmith."

My vision had cleared enough to see O'Malley's mouth harden into a bloodless line. "Get that, Detective."

Caledvwlch walked away from the door and picked up the phone. It was hard to read his expression. "Hello?" After another moment he repeated, "Hello?" After a half minute he hung up.

"Who was it?" O'Malley asked.

"'The play's the thing,'" Caledvwlch quoted, "'Wherein I'll catch the conscience of the king.'"

"What?" O'Malley wore a puzzled expression.

I was in a sprawl facing O'Malley, and the windows to the street. Streetlights shone against the curtains, and while I watched, a shadow passed between the window and the light. I took my Shakespearean caller as a cue to dive for cover.

I rolled behind the lounge chair as the window exploded inward. The hairs stood up on my arms as the wards on the condo let go, trying to stun the intruder. Unfortunately for O'Malley, the wards only carried enough punch to KO something the size of a human being.

O'Malley turned around to face the window, bracing his arm. The gun fired, the silencer making the shots sound like a sledge-hammer slamming into a bag of wet cement.

The intruder stood on the remains of my coffee table. The thing stood as tall as Caledvwlch, even in its perpetual hunch. The black leathery batwings folded behind it added a foot to its height. Its arms were long enough for the knuckles to scrape the floor, its legs thick and half the length. The face was twisted and skull-like, all toothy jaws and deep black orbits for eyes.

My shadow.

O'Malley emptied his automatic. To his credit, even caught completely off guard, I saw about half the shots find a tight grouping on the gargoyle's chest. Fat lot of good it did O'Malley. The holes the bullets punched in the thing's flesh didn't even bleed, they only released a little steam.

The gargoyle's response was slightly more effective.

A long arm, ending with a hand full of foot-long talons, swatted O'Malley like a windshield wiper taking out a horsefly. Just as effective, and a lot more messy. O'Malley's body sailed into the entertainment center, shattering the wide screen and knocking it off the wall. His head didn't quite make it that far.

I did the sensible thing. I ran.

I had forgotten about Caledvwlch. I only made it halfway to the door when the elf clotheslined me. Flat on the ground, I coughed and opened my eyes to see Caledvwlch pointing a Glock down at me. "Are you nuts?" I coughed. "That thing—"

Something was wrong here, because the gargoyle should have decapitated both of us by now. I looked back, and it hadn't moved from its station in the middle of my living room. It opened its mouth, and spoke *"Place the gun on the ground, brother."* It was like the voice of the dragon, deep enough that I felt it vibrate behind my sternum.

"Do not approach, or your prize will die."

The creature spread its arms. *"You do not trust me?"*

"You killed my liege." Caledvwlch pulled back the slide on the Glock.

The creature laughed, and the sound made me sick to my stomach. It didn't help that Caledvwlch looked ready to shoot me to spite this thing. *"You would call a **mortal** liege?"*

"I have honor. I have duty."

"You debase yourself. Do you imagine your 'liege' saw your noble fealty as more than a tool to control you?"

Caledvwlch shook his head. "This is not what was agreed—"

"Consider it a favor," the thing said, gesturing toward the pile of meat that had been O'Malley.

"Go," Caledvwlch said, "the others will be here soon."

"Not without him."

Caledvwlch shook his head. "Not after what you've done. I cannot accept this."

"Who are you serving now, brother? O'Malley's ghost? You know the evil they've done."

"I cannot trust you with him."

The Glock moved away, and I sat up a bit. "Don't I get a voice in this?"

"You keep him in city custody, it is only a matter of time. You believe I would harm him after what we've gone through already?"

Caledvwlch wavered. For myself, neither option seemed all that appealing. The standoff seemed primed to endure indefinitely, then a pounding started at the front door. When no one answered immediately, the sound changed to someone slamming into the other side, trying to break the dead bolt.

Caledvwlch looked at the door, than at the remains of O'Malley. He lowered his Glock and shook his head. "This cannot be allowed to continue." He stepped away from above me. "You wanted to *know*, Mr. Maxwell. So you shall. Go with the creature."

"Is this a good idea?" I asked as I got to my feet.

Caledvwlch raised the Glock again. "Go," he said.

I heard the doorframe crack. So much for caution. I ran over to the gargoyle. It didn't give me much choice. Once I was within reach, those long arms took me into an ice-cold embrace, holding me to the unyielding flesh of its chest.

The thing held me in an iron grip, and I had a few brief moments to contemplate the idiotic things people are capable of doing when a gun is put to their heads. I felt movement, but I couldn't see past the thing's shoulder. I managed to turn my head just as the whole world went topsy-turvy on me. I saw a brief flash of ceiling behind me as the gargoyle sprang backward. Then a starless expanse of sky twisted around us as my inner ear decided that it was time for me to throw up.

We fell like a stone; a dive that nothing should've been able to recover from.

Fortunately for both of us, the gargoyle was a magical entity and the laws of aerodynamics need not apply. It unfolded its wings beneath its plummeting body and managed to pull out of the dive a few feet above the sidewalk. We narrowly missed the power lines for the nearby rapid transit tracks as we shot upward.

By now the sense of vertigo from all the movement was making my head hurt. I managed one passing look at the flood-lit quad of

Shaker Square—from about three hundred feet up and at a sixty-degree angle—and screwed my eyes shut.

The thing moved so fast that it was hard for me to breathe. The wind whipping by us tried to snatch the breath from my mouth.

Okay, someone remind me why this was preferable to being shot . . .

I could feel the remains of this afternoon's McFood backing up on me. I think the only thing that kept me from actually throwing up was the thought that it might encourage this thing to drop me. I risked a few glances as we flew, looking downward. We seemed to be heading northeast, though that was only a guess based on sighting the downtown skyline, and not from anything below or the sense of direction that I had abandoned during that dive out my condo window.

Thank God no one is shooting at us.

My one glad thought was quickly followed by the mental image of Aloeus. We were, apparently, escaping from the folks responsible for that. If they decided to reprise that with my gargoyle . . .

I spent the rest of the flight imagining myself plummeting to the ground embraced by three or four tons of inanimate stone—or whatever this thing was made of.

It felt as if we were airborne for an eternity, though it was actually only a few minutes before the gargoyle began its descent. I risked a look downward and, for a few moments, I thought we were falling, upside down, into the sky.

Below us was black, inky darkness. It was even darker than the sky, when I realized the sky was still above us. The blackness was bordered by broad avenues and streetlights, but the interior was a vast unlit space. We had already descended too far for me to see the extent of it.

The gargoyle set down on a dark lawn in the midst of the darkness. It let me go as soon as it landed. My legs weren't ready to support me, and my inner ear wasn't quite sure of the direction of up. I tumbled down at the gargoyle's feet. I had to sink my fingers into the grass to convince my body that I'd stopped moving.

I agreed with my body; down was good.

I lay there for a few long moments, waiting for the flight-induced vertigo to recede enough for me to open my eyes without setting my head spinning.

When I felt well enough, I pushed myself off of the ground. My legs were a little wobbly, but they supported me. I blinked a few times before I realized that I was face-to-face with an angel. A few more times before I was convinced that the angel in question was made of granite and perched atop a rectangular monument whose front read "Drummond" and whose side bore a carved shield with the text of the 23rd Psalm engraved in it.

It was dark, but I could see ranks of headstones surrounding me.

At least I knew where we were. Lakeview Cemetery was the only near east side necropolis that covered this much real estate. I turned around to face the gargoyle. It stood, impassive and unmoving.

"So?" I asked it. "We're here?"

No response.

"Now what?"

Nothing.

"Damn it, I know you can talk—" I shook my head. "Did you fly me all the way over here to abandon me in a graveyard?"

"No," came a feminine voice from behind me. "And it cannot talk without someone to animate it."

I spun around again, staggering a bit because I did so too quickly. "Who?"

"We've met before, Mr. Maxwell," she said as she walked out of the shadowed woods beyond the graves. She wore a dark hood that made her form nearly invisible in the shadows. I only caught sight of her because of the sense of movement toward me. She lowered her hood as she approached me, and her pale face stood out against the darkness, her eyes glowing slightly as Caledvwlch's had.

"Ysbail," I said.

She gestured in a half bow, half curtsy.

I placed my hand on my head and closed my eyes. "This is a long way from Hunting Valley."

"One of many places of power."

"What the hell's going on here? Why did your pet—pet *thing* over there—grab me?"

"You would prefer being killed like their mage?" She walked up next to me and stared at the gargoyle. She spoke several lines quietly in her native tongue, and the misshapen thing jumped straight upward, unfolded its wings, and disappeared into the starless sky.

"You've had that thing following me since this started."

"Imperfectly," she said. "And initially it was watching Commander O'Malley."

"Why?"

"Accompany me, Mr. Maxwell, and I will explain." She started walking away, and the fear that she might leave me here was more than I needed to convince me to follow.

I walked after her, through sparse woodlands, toward a mausoleum set back into a hillside, facing partly away from us. "You were singled out the moment Aloeus fell from the sky. Set upon the twisted path that led you here." We walked around to the front of the mausoleum, where green bronze doors were held shut by a rusty chain. Ysbail made a hand gesture and the chains rattled to the ground.

"Uh-huh," I said as the doors to the tomb opened of their own accord. "Who did the singling out?"

The doors stood open before us and, inside the tomb I could see only an inky blackness. Ysbail walked up the steps and said, "Come with me."

She walked through without looking back. Her form disappeared into the darkness and I hesitated until the doors began closing again. I slipped through before they had shut completely. I felt a sudden drop in temperature as a cool wind beat at my face. I felt for the walls, so I'd have some sense of direction, but my hands didn't find any.

I walked into light, as if a curtain was drawn aside.

For a few moments I was blinded. I blinked a few times, and the first thing I noticed was the unfinished stone floor.

I looked up to see Ysbail standing against a curving stone wall. The wall was unfinished stone, like the floor, and inscriptions in some alien language were carved into the rock. Light came from a Coleman lantern that hung incongruously from a bronze sconce set into the wall.

I looked around and saw no trace of the mausoleum we had entered.

However, hanging in the air behind us was a sphere of inky blackness that seemed to hold a reflection of some space that wasn't *here*. As I watched, the sphere shrank, as if it was deflating or fading into the distance. In a moment, it was gone.

I turned around to face Ysbail.

"Welcome to Ragnan," she said.

CHAPTER TWENTY-FOUR

I SHOOK my head. "No. Don't play games with me. Where are we?"

"The catacombs beneath the city of Galweir. I assure you that I am not playing any game."

I looked back to where the sphere had disappeared. "Was that what I think it was?"

"A Portal? Yes, though a short-lived one."

"That's not supposed to be possible."

"Many from your world wish that were so." She picked up the lantern, and the shadows shifted around us. "Come," she said, leaving me with little choice. She led me through twisting corridors of stone, all inscribed, most with niches in place to receive the dead. The air here was cool and dry, and—now that the mini-Portal was gone—still.

I looked at the skulls piled into some of the niches, and it didn't seem so far-fetched that we had left the shores of Lake Erie.

"Why are we here?"

"Because the people who threaten your life are not here." Ysbail said it as if she was explaining things to a child. She followed a narrow staircase upward.

"What's my life to you?"

"We used you. Invested what was left of our cause in you." Her voice changed tone slightly. I didn't know if it was the elvish equivalent of compassion, or irony, when she said, "We bear some responsibility for your safety."

"Used me?" I said. "Everyone and their brother have been using me."

"Yes," she agreed. I could swear she gave me the ghost of a smile. She pushed open a large oaken door and led me out into our partner universe. I don't know exactly what I was expecting.

What I saw was decidedly surreal.

The sky was just purple with dawn, which allowed me to see the mountain first. It towered over us, a rocky mound covered by trees until, about halfway up, someone had decided to turn the mountain into art. The bluff on which we stood, and looked upward from, turned into a muscular leg. The ridge where it led toward its sister mountains, became a tail leading into a serpentine torso. One wing still rose on the far side, but on our side, the stone dragon's remains were buried chest-high in rubble, on top of which lay a carved head the size of a five-story building.

I looked around and saw our surroundings were in similar disrepair. We stood on flagstones that could have once been inside. Stone walls on either side of us were draped in vines and moss and only seemed to go halfway up. Behind us I saw the shell of a ruined tower, collapsed so all that was left of the upper levels was a semi-circular wall whose concave side faced us.

"What is this place?" I asked.

"Our capital," Ysbail said. "The home of the elves."

I looked at her, and I could see the same aspect of mourning that I had seen in Caledvwlch. I looked back toward the catacombs we had walked through. "You're supposed to be immortal."

For the first time in my life, I heard an elf laugh. It was a quiet sound, and somewhat sad. "Your word, Mr. Maxwell. Not ours. We do not age, but all but the most prideful of us know death is no stranger to us. To one as short-lived as you, we must seem forever unchanging, eternal. Our greatest sin was believing that was so." She cast an arm back toward the catacombs. "Our ancestors, and their ancestors. Generations before memory."

"What happened here?"

"You did."

"What?"

"Mankind. Mortals more familiar with death, and much more willing to face it. They could not abide us, so they destroyed us. Our people are so scattered now that in a few of our generations we will cease to exist." She reached out and took my arm. Her fingers were long, pale, and cold. "Come see."

She took me to the edge of the flagstone courtyard, which was once a great hall, and stopped at the edge, where the floor fell away. We stood at the top of a hill that sloped downward about a mile. There was a road coming from what must have been the front of this place, snaking down the hillside to a city.

The road had once been lined with statues, but the sculpture lay in dismembered piles along the gutters. Large segments of the road had fallen away into gullies that now dug into the hillside. The buildings, whatever remained standing in the town, were roofless. Most had only two or three walls left. Plants covered the stone, giving everything a weathered, softened appearance.

I expected to smell death here. Perhaps my psyche needed that kind of tangible sensation to bring home the gravity of what I was looking upon. The world, of course, didn't cooperate. The smell here was the smell of a meadow at dawn, dewy grass and wildflowers. The mortal wound inflicted here happened too long ago to leave such a sign. The ruins here were centuries old.

Still, I asked, "Valdis?"

"No," Ysbail said. "He was only the most recent."

"How long has it been like this?"

"An instant—" she turned away from the dead village. "I remember when these halls smelled of incense and lavender and proud men argued about the most enduring values of aesthetics."

"Why haven't you rebuilt?"

"Here? No. The magic here is alive with the atrocities still. To remain here overlong would be death. To build here would be to desecrate a tomb." She shook her head. "Elsewhere? Until now, it has been all that we could do to survive in the face of the human realm here."

"Until now?"

She nodded. "To begin again—that has been what has made such bitter enemies, Mr. Maxwell. The great beast, Mankind, cannot forgive us for refusing to die, or be forgotten." She turned to face me, and I could almost see tears on her cheeks, though her voice didn't change timbre. "Your world as much as mine."

I was a journalist again, asking questions, taking notes. Ysbail, for her part, was like any partisan who'd suffered the loss of land, home, people. I don't know if she'd appreciate the comparison, but the voice that came from her belonged to every dispossessed person I'd ever heard. Croat, Irish, Palestinian, American Indian—it only really varied in intensity, which was a function of memory, the severity of persecution, and of the individual personality.

Ysbail's personality was cool, but more passionate than any elf I had ever met. If she'd been a human, I would have assumed that she was still in shock over the events she described, that any moment, when the reality sank in, she would break down.

Maybe that's it, the entire species is still in shock.

Before Ragnan existed, when humans were still grubbing in the

mud, killing their food with well placed stones, this—Galweir—
was the soul of civilization of this world. It was a city of philoso-
phers, scholars, mages, artists, and poets. It existed in peace for
uncounted millennia, unchanged. Even the anarchic dragons paid
tribute to study from the hoard of knowledge Galweir represented.

This place was so far removed from the lands of men that even
the most learned among the elves thought that mankind would
never become a threat.

According to Ysbail, it was the elves' inhuman pride that kept
that belief alive long after it was apparent that mankind was growing too fast beyond anyone's ability to contain it.

The citizens of Galweir had been convinced of their own invul-
nerability even as their city was falling down around them. The men
were ruthless in their slaughter. To the humans, death was an in-
evitability. To the elves, any death was a ghastly accident. Every elf
who fell in battle was a festering wound cut into the body of their
kind. Their choice became surrender or extinction.

Those whose choice was surrender were the only ones left. The
damage, however, was already done. The scars ran deep into the
elvish psyche. Their nobles were executed, individuals who had defined the elves' destiny for centuries. Their cities ruined, so soaked
in the blood of their immortal dead that if any elf stayed there for
any length of time the spirit of the place would drive them mad.
Their people scattered so that the elvish community no longer existed, only singular individuals humbled by defeat and guilt-scarred
by their own survival.

According to Ysbail, not one elvish child had been born since
the fall of Galweir, while half of these supposedly immortal creatures had since died.

"There is no word in our language for 'suicide.'" Her voice was
thin and hollow in the wind. Dawn was leaking over the ruined
dragon, the light reflecting off of the skull, picking out what might
have been gems encrusting the massive sculpture.

"Caledvwlch said that."

"A motto," said Ysbail, "for those of us who want to survive.
Many of us saw this," she motioned to the ruins below, "as our end.
To them, we are already dead and all that is left is the wait for the
inevitable."

"You and Caledvwlch?" I asked.

Ysbail shook her head. "My brother is not me. He sees salvation
in holding on to the old ways in the face of everything. He sees the

survival of our culture as the survival of ourselves. Even if he has to call a human Lord."

"He is your brother?"

"In the ways that matter to my kind."

"You don't think he's right?"

"Pretending this did not happen does not undo it. He sees himself—all those who do as he does—as preserving us."

"And you?"

"I know better. Caledvwlch is simply looking for a way to die with some dignity." Ysbail turned to face me. "I do not accept our end. I rebel against it. I will fight it as a wounded she cat defending her young. I do not care about our dignity." She had grabbed my upper arm. The touch was light, but it shocked me, as did the sudden violence of her words. "I do not care to leave a dignified corpse."

She looked at me, and the expression on her face could have been that of a fanatic, or a visionary. The eyes, metallic and expressionless, could have hidden either.

"What does this have to do with Aloeus' death?"

The hand left my arm as she turned to look at the broken dragon. "The elves were first. But the dragons suffered as well. Even though each dragon was a nation unto himself, by then, mankind had great experience in subduing nations. Aloeus gave us an alliance, a chance to bridge the gap between worlds. To find a sanctuary."

I shook my head. "My apologies for the state of that sanctuary."

"You misunderstand. Cleveland was never the destination. The term in your language that best fits our purpose there would be 'reconnaissance.'"

"Recon . . ." My voice trailed off as switches began flipping in my brain.

Fact one, the Portal was not a natural phenomenon, as the general public seemed to believe.

Fact two, Aloeus created the Portal to give the elves a homeland. Cleveland, Ohio, while adequate, had the disadvantage of being populated by the mortal types who'd been giving these people the shaft.

Fact three, ten years to these creatures was a very insignificant span of time.

Fact four . . .

"Mexico," I whispered, looking at the mountains surrounding us. A plot of land the size of Cleveland with no commercial value, no easy access, little in the way of natural resources. A property completely worthless to Aloeus, Inc.

Until you opened a Portal to it.

"He was teaching us, Mr. Maxwell. Helping us. He had been since he opened the doorway into your world."

"Helping who?"

"The few remaining elves who want to survive." Ysbail looked away at the ruined dragon. Dawn was cutting the sky into ribbons of red and purple. "The land was ours. More than enough to rebuild our city. Enough to serve those who are left."

I suspected the answer, but I asked anyway. "You can move now, can't you?" I waved back to the catacombs. "You don't need the Portal."

Ysbail shook her head. "We learned enough from him to open a temporary doorway. It lasts hours at most . . . We cannot survive in a world devoid of magic, Mr. Maxwell. We need a permanent source."

Aloeus' death, his *murder,* made too much sense now. There were dozens of interests involved in having the Portal as a monopoly. *Everyone* in the city, from Rayburn on down, had a stake in our Portal being the only game in town. Christ, what would happen to the tourist money if an entire nation of elves decided to open up shop south of the border? What would be the draw if there was the same thing available in a better climate, and without the remnants of the twenty-first century hanging around obscuring the magic. Disney was ready to drop billions to build that kind of environment out by Sandusky.

To the person who, in O'Malley's words, panicked the most, the natural progression led to an even worse possibility: The second Portal wouldn't be the last.

"No one wants competition for the Portal," I said. One goose laying golden eggs is worth something, but more than that and the eggs start depressing the economy.

"Centuries of work were wiped out with Aloeus' death," Ysbail said. "It might mean the end of our species."

"*Centuries,*" I whispered to myself. I thought of something Caledvwlch had said, *"You are a fool if you believe it possible for us to be as inconstant as you."*

I thought about that for a moment. I was walking in a world where allegiances shifted slowly, if at all. That was important, maybe the key to what was happening here.

When Aloeus formed an alliance with Rayburn to keep control

of the Portal local, helped engineer the attack that ended Valdis' reign, and continued his influence on the administration—during all that time, he had been working with the elves.

"You are 'Faust,' aren't you?"

"Your kind can be very loose with names. The same term can apply as much to many as to one." She looked at me. "I am of the many, but I am not the one."

I decided to count that as a confirmation. Nesmith was right. There was a mole in the administration, and someone had decided to do something violent about it. They were also correct, in a way, about "Faust" attacking the city and the administration. Their interests were certainly at odds with the long-term goals of most of the political and business community in Cleveland. From the look of things, though, the terrorism seemed pretty one-sided.

"Tell me about what Aloeus was doing with you."

She obliged.

The Portal was not intended solely as a doorway. It was to be an extension of their world into another, a foothold around which the elves could build their new capital. It required years of effort to produce the permanance of the Portal. It took, had been taking, ten times as long to teach those skills. The temporary Portal that Ysbail had led me through was just a small manifestation, a temporary doorway whose creation was made easier by the proximity of the other Portal.

The difference between that, and creating a new, permanent Portal was the difference between driving down the interstate and *building* the interstate—*and* the car to drive on it. Ysbail's little portal was simply pulling the energies from the permanent Portal and opening another space to walk through. It wasn't even possible to do it outside the influence of the permanent Portal.

And, unlike the Portal that Aloeus opened, the little portals could only be opened into places the mages—and apparently there were several needed to do it—themselves had seen. At least one member of the ritual had a sole duty to visualize the destination.

The Portal that Aloeus created suffered no such restriction—of course it would have been useless if it had. Aloeus could cast a Portal to a world no one had ever seen. That gave them the ability to escape Ragnan, but made two Portals necessary for their mission. One for reconnaissance, the other once a suitable site had been found for permanent settlement.

The decision to solicit the National Guard's assistance was

simply a tactical decision on Aloeus' part, to remove Valdis and buy time on the Ragnan side of the Portal.

Once the political situation on both planes had stabilized, they needed to find their final target on this world. A target they found with the help of Leo Baldassare.

I asked about him.

Ysbail told me, "He has been a friend to our cause since Aloeus arrived in this world."

"Hasn't helped with the administration?"

"We've both required privacy in our dealings."

"He knows about 'Faust'?"

"Yes."

I knew Baldassare kept things close to the vest, but this was surprising, even for him.

"Where do I come into this?"

Ysbail and her people *knew* that the Rayburn administration had Aloeus assassinated. There wasn't a question in their minds. With their plans wrecked with the dragon's death, their only real hope was to make the administration's actions public in such a way that it couldn't be covered up. Then, maybe, they could convince the government, the courts, the public—someone—to consider reparations.

That kind of proof was problematic. Especially as the administration and the SPU seemed to be moving to place the blame for the assassination on "Faust."

They needed someone credible, someone *human*, someone with no obvious connections to the paranormal citizens involved. They needed that person to voice the crimes of the Rayburn administration.

"You were chosen by the one 'Faust,' himself. He knows your works, and knows that if you call Mayor Rayburn a murderer, those who read your words will know it is truth."

"Baldassare," I said. "You had him pressure the *Press* to put me on this story."

"To the other journalists, it was not a political story."

I shook my head.

"We granted your guidance."

"What do you mean?"

"The term in your language is bibliomancy," she said.

It took a moment to realize what she was talking about. "You're the damn bard!"

"Not exactly," she said. "I could not establish any immediate link to you, magically or otherwise, because you were so well watched. I could, however, create an independent floating enchantment that could warn you, guide you, long after my connection with the spell had been broken and could not be traced."

"You're saying a *spell* called me?"

"I cast the spell on the web of electronics that makes up the phone system in Cleveland. The spell moved from point to point, confounding any attempt to trace it."

"What's with the quotes? Why not something useful, like 'your life's in danger.'"

"An oracle does not work like that. It needs a matrix, a form, to cast its information from. It can be runes, dice, cards, bones . . . I chose a form that would be easiest for you to interpret, and easiest for you to receive through the medium I selected."

"You expected me to go up against Rayburn for you."

"We believed that you would willingly publicize his crimes."

I nodded. "There's one problem with that plan, Ysbail."

"What?"

"Rayburn didn't have the dragon killed."

CHAPTER TWENTY-FIVE

YSBAIL turned to say something, perhaps an objection, but she was interrupted by a presence. There was a sudden feeling of imminence in the air, a sensation that set the hair on the back of my neck on end. I turned away from the ruined vistas of Galweir and back toward the flagstone courtyard we had emerged from.

The air rippled above the stone, and I could see a tiny speck floating there. As I watched it grew to a dot, then a ball, then a rapidly expanding sphere. This was the third Portal I had seen in my life, and the impact wasn't diminished by the fact that I was expecting it.

It certainly was a good way to cut any possible pursuit, just sidestep into the next dimension and wait for your comrades to rendezvous. I looked at Ysbail and asked, "How close are we to the original Portal, on this side?"

"Thousands of miles."

I looked at the slowly stabilizing sphere. "But someone can only *make* these temporary things near the permanent Portal, right?"

"The caster has to be within the permanent Portal's influence."

"So what were you planning on doing if the ride home didn't show up?"

"We would have had a long journey in store for us." She stepped forward. "Come, it only remains a few moments."

I took a step toward a curving image of a huge building in a wooded glen. With no sense of transition at all, I found myself stepping away from the shore of the Chagrin River. In front of us, rising out of the bluff overlooking the river was the massive Tudor pile of Leo Baldassare's mansion.

I got the weird feeling of coming full circle.

The air was thick with the smell of incense, and a quartet of exhausted looking people sat on the grass between us and the mansion. The two elves, I expected. The humans, I didn't. The man I hadn't seen before was long-haired with a beard and gut worthy of a Hell's Angel, with more cryptic tattoos.

The other one was Mr. Friday, the man whom I'd taken to simply be Aloeus' lawyer.

"You're a mage?" I asked.

He looked up at me as if I still carried an invisible, disgusting odor, "You are surprised?"

Ysbail walked up and looked over the quartet , examining each member as if checking for damage. Perhaps that's what she was doing. Friday seemed the least fatigued by whatever happened here. Perhaps he just showed it less.

The Hell's Angel type got unsteadily to his feet. "You," he said, pointing toward me. The look he gave me wasn't that friendly.

"Me?" I answered. So far, a stellar conversation.

"You're why they killed Bone." The finger collapsed into a fist about the size of my face.

I took a step back, and the guy stepped forward, about halving the distance between us.

"I think you're making a mistake," I said.

"You made the mistake. You tipped them off to Bone," he told me. "When this is over, I'll have your liver for lunch."

"Angor and Einion need to rest," Ysbail interrupted us. "We need to go inside." Ysbail helped the two elves up and started toward the mansion. Friday stood up and looked at me, then at the biker, and shook his head.

The biker was still standing in my way, staring me down.

I started, "I don't think you understand—"

"It's simple. Bone was fine with the cops till you showed up. Then something tipped them on to him." He slapped his open hand on top of his fist as if he was trying to drive a knife into someone's chest. "Your fault, ain't it?"

To the guy facing me, the question was rhetorical. For me it was less so. Yet another datum added to my evolving portrait of Caleb Washington. He had, as O'Malley said, gotten very close to this Faustian network. From the looks of things, all the way inside.

I suspected that this guy would not take well to the news that Mr. Bone Daddy was a cop, and had been one for years. The biker would probably be even less pleased with the info that Bone wasn't killed because the cops caught up with him. He was killed because he knew who was behind the demise of Aloeus, and made the mistake of taking the information to O'Malley, rather than to his little underground group.

The irony was, this guy might, in a sense, be right. Bone Daddy had been ventilated after interrogating me. I suspected that something he heard while questioning me set him on the path that got him killed.

I even had a good idea what that was.

When I didn't answer the biker immediately, he turned and followed Ysbail and the others up toward the house. I followed in time to see Leo Baldassare holding the door open.

He looked at me as we all walked into his wood-paneled sanctum, and his expression held no trace of irony. Not that I expected it. He'd always been one of those guys who knew exactly what he was doing, and left it to others to speculate about what that was.

"Kline," he said by way of greeting.

"Mr. Baldassare."

We had gathered in the massive library. There were more than enough overstuffed chairs, and the two-story ceiling gave enough headroom even for the elves. The bookshelves covered three walls, ten feet up to a balcony that held more shelves all the way to the ceiling. A massive semicircular arc of windows faced the river and the clearing we had walked from.

Everyone sat, with the exception of Baldassare and myself. I stood next to a long, wide desk that seemed designed explicitly for holding large volumes flat. Quite a few were open on it. I saw a few non-English titles, a book with mostly Hebrew text amidst circles and linear diagrams, and something that was authored by Alister Crowley.

"I suppose you have some questions," Baldassare said as he closed the door.

"You know me," I said. "I always do."

"You know I support Rayburn, always have. But you probably know by now that the administration has some strange ideas about my friends here."

I nodded, walking down the long desk, flipping a few pages here and there at random. I stopped at one ancient-looking tome as thick as my arm and about three feet tall. The writing was hand-lettered in a text I couldn't recognize from any human alphabet.

"A fifth column," I said. " Elements of an invasion that may or may not come. A threat to the city government on several levels. At the least, a justification for deeper federal involvement. At worst, agents of unregulated and possibly competing access to Ragnan." I closed the book. The cover was black leather from some animal I didn't recognize. "I'm wondering what's your angle, involved in this."

Baldassare smiled. "It really isn't very arcane. I'm a businessman, not a politician. I provide them with logistical support, planning, staff," he glanced at Friday. "They find their homeland, and I receive sole rights to control human access to that homeland. Sole licensee to export goods from that homeland."

Right now Baldassare only received a royalty for each person passing through the Portal. He didn't have any control over it, didn't receive anything from tourism, or the goods and services that exist because of the Portal.

Take what he has now, and add two or three zeros on to it.

"That's an incentive," I said.

"He has been the one human of any temporal power who's been sympathetic to our purpose," Ysbail said.

Baldassare shrugged and was atypically self-effacing in the way he said, "For all the good it's done."

I looked at Mr. Hell's Angel, and thought about Bone Daddy, and asked, "How many are in this little underground of yours?" I directed the question at Ysbail.

She was comforting the two elves, who seemed to be suffering most of the aftereffects of our little rapid-transit exercise. I saw one look at her and shake his head. I preempted her response. "No, I know, let's keep numbers out of it. But a lot, isn't it?"

"Some might say so," Ysbail said.

I looked back at the biker and said, "We're not just talking an elvish homeland, are we?"

It was Friday who answered. "The Portal created a new underclass. Any mage has two choices here—accept dictation from the government, or suffer marginalization. The 'Faust' fantasy perpetrated by the administration is a threat because it—we—represent mages who aren't under their control. Therefore, we must be brought under submission."

Voting with their feet. There was a mage underground here that people on Lakeside dismissed as criminal, a ready source of people who would be candidates for relocation to a place free from the politics and bureaucracy of this city. For all the forces in place that brooked no changes to Cleveland's control of the Portal, I started to see that there might be as many—if not more—forces who would like to see northeast Ohio's monopoly on the paranormal come to an end. Which, of course, would contribute to making the former much more strident in their opposition.

"So, Mr. Baldassare, from what I know, no one here is doing anything illegal. You seem to agree that Mayor Rayburn and company have some wrongheaded ideas about your project. You're on a first name basis with the mayor. Why haven't you just walked in his office and set him right?"

To his credit as a politician, he was expecting the question. "It's not that simple, Maxwell."

"Come on," I said. "That chain you gave him, from Aloeus, it's a lie detector. He'd *know* you were telling the truth."

Baldassare nodded. "The Dragon Stone."

"So why don't you?"

"You're assuming that politics fundamentally changes when you cannot lie," Baldassare said. "Truthfulness is different from honesty, and facts can always be dismissed, even if their accuracy is not in question. Shall I paint you a scenario? I confront my old friend, the mayor. I give him the unvarnished truth. He then asks me how I know Faust's motives. How I know I'm not being duped—"

"And, of course, you risk alienating one of your chief political patrons."

Baldassare didn't bat an eye. "I'm not just a sugar daddy for this project. Political connections are important. I lose David's ear, and the whole project loses."

"With what happened to Aloeus, it seems like you've already lost."

The biker muttered something like, "Fucking bastard." Ysbail was a study in mournful silence.

Baldasare frowned, "Don't think I haven't second-guessed myself since that happened. But when it comes down to it, if Dave was fanatic enough to have someone—to have a *dragon*—killed over this, then there was no way I was ever going to talk sense into him."

"Maxwell believes," Ysbail said, "that Rayburn didn't have Aloeus killed."

For once, Baldassare looked a little surprised. The expression didn't wear well on him. His persona was so consciously crafted that the contrast of seeing a truly uncontrolled emotion break the surface gave the feeling of seeing the first crack appear in the ice over a rushing river. He recovered from his lapse quickly enough to make me wonder if I had imagined it.

"I would like to believe that," Baldassare said. He walked over to the grand windows and looked out toward the dawn sky. "I'd always thought of him as a friend. It isn't pleasant thinking him capable of such an act."

"You believe it, though?" I asked.

"I *know* it," Baldassare said. "He began ruthless, and he's only become more so over time."

"He also inspires great loyalty, doesn't he?"

Baldassare chuckled and wrung his hands behind his back. "Inspires? Not quite."

"The chain," I said. "Aloeus' gift. It assures him loyalty . . ."

"It assures him that the people he employs are the sycophants he wants." There was a trace of bitterness in his voice, letting me see how he could end up supporting people that were so at odds with the administration. He turned around. "David has always wanted control. He never could tolerate dissent. Giving him that chain gave him the keys to Pandora's box. It allowed him to question everyone's loyalty, and anyone with imperfect belief in the Rayburn administration was shoved aside for someone with absolute loyalty."

"His appointees all support him, unquestioningly," I said.

"If he has his way," Baldassare said, "they worship him."

Baldassare was probably right. Rayburn was the wrong person to give that talisman to. It might have enticed him to negotiate with the dragon, and be unsurpassed as a gesture of faith, but it was a mistake to give such a tool to someone convinced of his own righteousness. Even before the Portal, there was Rayburn's way, and the wrong way. Leaders like that tend to need the balance of opposing views in the people around them. But with Aloeus' gift, Rayburn had the unprecedented ability, not just to employ people who said what he wanted to hear—but *believed* what they said.

"Then," I said, "it isn't unlikely that if someone in Rayburn's administration perceived a threat to Rayburn, he or she might go to extreme lengths to deal with it."

"Of all the fucking bullshit," the biker sneered at me. "That's what happened? Rayburn's goons killed Aloeus, killed Bone, killed that fucking jerk-off reporter of yours?"

I nodded. "Not Rayburn."

"Not Rayburn," Baldassare repeated. He looked at me with an expression that seemed to acknowledge what I was about to say.

"Someone inside the administration has gone out of his way to protect Rayburn's interests. Gone so far that he's had to protect Rayburn from the knowledge of what was happening."

"That's bullshit," said the biker.

"It's called plausible deniability," Friday said.

"Yeah, it's still bullshit. You telling me that anything goes on without Rayburn knowing? He's got that damn chain."

"I suspect quite a lot happens without his knowledge," I replied. "Once you've surrounded yourself with people of unquestioned loyalty there's great temptation to trust their judgment. Rayburn is probably so convinced of his infallibility that it hasn't even occurred to him that his own people might be responsible. No one has to lie to him if the right questions are never asked."

Baldassare nodded. "It's possible, he's cocksure enough."

"How the hell you know this, is what I want to know." The Hell's Angel stood up and was glaring at me. "You working for him?"

"They were going to assassinate him," Ysbail said. "Mind yourself, now."

"Oh, the great one speaks for herself. You know, I've been minding myself for, what? Seven years?" He pulled his beard. "I was impressed with you poor fucks, I went along. You promised me a new city, a goddamn new world. What you been delivering is all been bullshit and fuckups—"

One of the other elves, still recuperating, pushed himself off of the couch. I didn't remember if he was Angor or Einion. "Do not talk to the Lady like that."

"I ain't one of you Keebler bastards, I'll talk to the bitch any way I want."

The elf got steadily to his feet and interposed himself between Ysbail and the biker. In his eyes I saw something like rage. It was the first genuinely violent emotion I had seen in an elf.

"Stop this," Ysbail said. There was a resignation in her tone that was fatal for any sort of leader. If it wasn't clear before, her voice, the plea for calm, confirmed the fact that this alliance was falling apart. It probably had been since Aloeus plunged into the river.

"Don't you get it?" the biker said. "It's *over*. The grand plan is shit and best we can do is cut and run." He looked over at me. "And off anyone who can rat us out."

"You will apologize," the elf informed him. The demand seemed rather ludicrous coming from someone who was barely holding himself upright.

Ysbail tried again. "No, Einion, he will not."

The elf turned to face her and said, "My Lady—"

"His anger is his own. I will not have you make him deny it." She looked over at the biker. "You are free to leave us."

The biker looked somewhat surprised. "Yeah? And what about him?" He pointed toward me.

"He is not your concern," she said.

"Oh? I'm supposed to walk away so that he can tell Rayburn's goons to vent my ass? I don't think so." He sat himself down and folded his arms.

Einion shook his head and took a step toward the couch and half collapsed into it. Ysbail stood and helped place him back on the couch. "Too much effort," she whispered to him. "Rest." She brushed her hand against his cheek.

"What happened to them?" I asked.

"They bore the brunt of forming that portal you walked through," Baldassare said. "The energy had to be channeled through the people who had walked the ground they were connecting to. The others were basically life support."

"You better be worth it," the biker said.

Baldassare walked forward and looked at the two nearly comatose elves and said, "If he is correct, he might just be." He looked up from Ysbail and Einion and said, "It's a legitimate question, Kline. How do you know? You've provided a plausible theory. But it is just that, a theory. One that absolves the mayor of what happened. How do you *know* it was one of his subordinates?"

CHAPTER TWENTY-SIX

IT took a while to tell them, going over my encounters with the upper echelons of this city's political machine, and going over O'Malley's last words. The way O'Malley had it, neither Nesmith nor Rayburn knew what had actually happened to the dragon. The attempt to frame Faust was for their benefit as much as the public's.

The person who ordered Aloeus neutralized had ties to O'Malley, and had control of enough mages to assassinate the dragon and set up attacks on the Feds' safe house. Mages that weren't—given the elvish markings on the bullet that killed Cutler—native to Cleveland. This person had to be loyal to Rayburn, close enough to be unquestioned, and fanatical enough to plan to "neutralize" Aloeus. It also would make sense that, by doing so, he was preventing a direct threat to his own power base.

"Who do you mean?" Baldassare asked me.

"Adrian Phillips."

The only one who did *not* give me a blank stare was Baldassare. The others, perhaps, could be forgiven for not knowing the chairman of the Port Authority—though they should've. Phillips was the executive in charge of "maintenance" of the Portal. His agency ran the quarantine facilities at Burke Lakefront that housed new arrivals. His agency employed the most mages of any city department. He was part of Rayburn's political machine, was his campaign manager in his first reelection bid after the Portal. He was adept at finding positions for political cronies; one such was the head of the SPU. He got O'Malley his job.

I had little doubt that O'Malley was loyal to the Rayburn administration, and to Phillips in particular. And because of the elves' fealty, the elves were loyal to O'Malley. So, even though the SPU was a police unit under the command of Nesmith, Phillips would be able to run it as a private fiefdom.

Phillips had spent a lot of time taking the "Faust" rumors and casting "Faust" as the devil. Ysbail and her followers were threats because they weren't under city control. When he discovered their plans, and the dragon's part in it, the dragon had to be removed. A new Portal not only threatened Cleveland's economy, but Phillips' own power base. He would no longer be able to control who came and left between the worlds.

He used the Port Authority mages to assassinate Aloeus. Then he used O'Malley and the SPU to attempt a sloppy cover-up.

Unfortunately for him, Rayburn and Nesmith had taken his beliefs about "Faust" to the obvious next step. They saw Aloeus' death as a first move in a coming attack from Ragnan. Combine that with the Feds pushing into the jurisdiction, and they needed to come up with "Faust's" head on a plate.

"Nesmith wants 'Faust,'" I said to Ysbail. "She's pegged you as the prime suspect. And that's why Caleb Washington was assassinated by the police."

My choice of words got the biker's attention.

Bone Daddy was a mole for the cops. He was looking for "Faust" and had been for along time. Everyone here probably had two things to thank for the fact that a squad of SPU elves weren't breaking down the door right now.

First was, I assumed—and Baldassare confirmed that I assumed correctly—that the network I was looking at was formed of independent cells like any sane guerrilla organization. Bone might have made it high in the echelons, but he hadn't got far enough to have real contact with the leadership. No Faust.

Second, and more important, Bone was a *real* cop. He wasn't into what O'Malley referred to as "Gestapo tactics." Caleb Washington wasn't going to go out of his way to report details on an organization that wasn't breaking any laws. Instead he spent his time giving the SPU any black market necromancer and two-bit mage who was dealing with illegal shit.

The biker, as I had thought, didn't take well to this.

"You ain't telling me he's no fucking cop . . ."

"That's exactly what I'm telling you."

"I should fuck you up for saying that."

Ysbail held up her hand toward him. "Allow Mr. Maxwell his say."

"Of course, when Nesmith lets on to Bone that Aloeus' death is less than an accident, and that Faust is suspect number one, Bone Daddy is off on his own investigation. He has a major advantage over everyone. He's pretty damn sure, judging from the reactions he's seen within the Faustian community, that 'Faust' is the *least* likely suspect. Especially since—if he hadn't known beforehand, he would realize now—Aloeus was, in at least some important sense, 'Faust.'

"Going into his investigation, he questions yours truly and finds a fact that really doesn't sit well with him.

"Adrian Phillips was present while they dredged the dragon out of the water. Adrian Phillips was present during the medical examination by Egil Nixon. A medical examination that was falsified to show the death was an accident. Falsified by order of someone other than Nesmith, since her later comments showed she believed the report the honest opinion of the late Coroner Nixon.

"Unfortunately for Bone, Nesmith didn't believe Nixon.

"Unfortunately for Nixon, Phillips couldn't allow him to disclose exactly what went on aboard the Coast Guard cutter.

"I don't know what Bone discovered on his own, but I suspect it was whatever had killed Nixon. Phillips had already shown himself to be an imperfect tactician. Everything from the dragon's death onward showed no planning, just reaction. It seems quite likely that during the examination Phillips let slip something that identified him as the person behind the dragon's death. It could have been a mistake as simple as ordering the murder covered up before Nixon gave him his actual findings . . .

"Whatever Bone found, he didn't count on O'Malley being Phillips' creature.

"Unfortunately for O'Malley and Phillips, the snowball was already rolling downhill. Cutler was checking on Bone Daddy's movements before his death, and had got too close.

"I suspect that the real reason that Cutler got the CD was because the SPU handed it to him, right after putting that bullet around his neck. Something about that CD made the SPU think it was meant for me, and since it was from Bone, Phillips wanted it cracked. It could hold damaging information. After I opened the CD, they could finish me off in a righteous shooting once Cutler's chest blew open.

"I think it might have been less luck that saved me then, than the fact that Caledvwlch was already disillusioned with his liege at this point. The elf had worked with Bone for a long time; being ordered by O'Malley to kill him was enough to shake the foundations of his belief system. Not enough to ignore orders at that point, but enough, maybe, to miss.

"By this point Phillips was panicking about what Bone Daddy

might have known and when. When the Feds nabbed me for questioning, it had to be the worst of all possible worlds. He had gone to the mat to 'protect' Rayburn. Letting the Feds pick my brain could be a disaster. He set up 'Faust's' attack on the safe house, and when that didn't finish things off for me, he had O'Malley pick me up when Blackstone tried to take me out of the city."

"Then why didn't the bastard take your sorry ass out right there?" quipped the biker.

"He seized me from a Federal Agent in a public place. They might have been becoming more reckless, but not *that* reckless." It must have been nerve-racking for Phillips during that triumvirate meeting. He probably had a near stroke when I asked about the Coast Guard cutter. Lucky for him that Rayburn was willfully blind.

"O'Malley was setting my death up as another one of 'Faust's' victims. He probably had his evidence all lined up." I shook my head and chuckled. "It's ironic really; you gave Phillips the best evidence he could want, with O'Malley's corpse."

"That was unavoidable," Ysbail said with the barest tinge of regret.

"I'm not complaining," I told her. "That gargoyle probably saved my life."

"Fat lot of good it's done us," said the biker. "They got O'Malley's death to dump at our feet, along with Aloeus and that reporter. And fuck if they ain't right this time. We *did* kill O'Malley. For what? So we can listen to exactly how we've been screwed?"

"He's gong to help us," Ysbail said flatly.

"Yeah, right. How?"

Baldassare looked uncustomarily grave. I suppose he had a lot invested in the success of this enterprise. "Lady Ysbail, I am afraid I do have to agree. While he has given a laudable analysis of the situation," he nodded in my direction, "I fail to see exactly how he is supposed to help."

"What you going to do? Write about it?" I got a sneer from the biker that was acid. It was an expression I knew. Two of the most lauded virtues in the old school of my profession were objectivity and detachment. We do not become part of the story. The point is not to right wrongs, but to illuminate them.

It wasn't Ysbail who spoke, it was Friday. "Caleb Mosha Washington was why we saved him."

"Bone didn't know this guy from Adam."

"His gift knew," Friday said. "It knew when he saw this man."

"There ain't no fucking savior. Not for the elves, not for us. He's a goddamn reporter, for Christ's sake."

"It is him," Ysbail said quietly.

Baldassare shook his head. "You're jumping to conclusions."

This had gotten cryptic enough for me. "What conclusions?"

"Don't worry, you ain't him."

"Show him the message," Friday said.

"While we're at it why don't we just tell him our life's story?" The biker looked back across at me. "That's what all this is to you, an effing story."

Of course.

I didn't say it, though.

Baldassare walked out of the library, leaving me alone with five rogue mages. I didn't realize until then how reassuring his presence was, the one player in this drama who I knew, who I thought I understood.

Ysbail sat, caressing the brow of one of the elves, the one who had defended her from the biker. The biker walked up to her and lowered his voice. His bearing suddenly had a trace of deference to it. "Lady, look I ain't subtle, and I ain't polite, and I sure as hell don't pretend to know all this shit. But, damn it, what the *hell* is the point of all of this? We've been keeping ourselves under wraps, and for damn good reason. We're just supposed to spill everything to this guy? What's he got at stake?"

"He is Caleb's man," Ysbail replied.

"Uh-huh? And what if he isn't? You're just going to let him splatter our secrets, our *names,* on the front page of his rag?"

"If he isn't, what reason have we left to hide?"

Baldassare returned with a notebook computer in tow. I had a strong feeling of déjà vu. He set it on top of the desk next to the large incomprehensible tome. He flipped it open, the blue LCD screen glowing ominously.

He struck a couple of keys and the CD player whirred.

"He left this with a lawyer," Baldassare said. "It was delivered the day after he was shot."

The blue background switched to black, which suddenly changed to an extreme close-up of a blinking eye. The eye backed away until we saw a shirtless Bone Daddy standing in a living room that was all too familiar to me. I noticed that the coffee table and all the broken glass was gone. He also looked a little less strung out. The arcane tattoos rippled across his back as he walked away from the camera and sat down on the couch.

"Greetings from the great beyond." He even smiled somewhat as he said it, but his voice was flat and carried little in the way of emotion. He probably blew most of it on making the previous movie. At the very least, he had blown most of his inebriation. "I thought a lot about not making this tape. You should know that I *am* severely pissed off. That comes from divining that a good friend of mine is going to betray me. The fact that one of you all might be the one to off me sort of chilled my enthusiasm for trying to help you bastards out."

He leaned forward toward the camera. "Of course I kept trying to find out who the bad guy is, but you all know the Oracle. Can't let me know that, it might keep me from getting killed. So I did find out a few things you can't do anything about either." He held up his index finger. "Your great plans for a homeland are pretty much doomed. Sorry, I would have told you, if it could have done any good. Sometime in the week they bury me the whole thing is going to fall apart. Death, destruction, evil deeds, betrayal, the whole enchilada." Second finger. "A man of great temporal power holds your existence—I mean *all* of you—in his hands. He can destroy you or not, at his whim. This man is connected with the man who killed me, and may be responsible for my death. He is male, human, and is—big surprise here—involved in the political leadership of this city." Third finger. "There is another man, someone of great honesty who is threatened by the same forces. He is the one person I see who can get your butts out of the fire. Again, don't ask me who he is, I just know that he's got the best chance of sticking it to the shits who killed me off."

He lowered his hand and stared in the camera. I felt as if he was looking directly at me. "Call him Will."

CHAPTER TWENTY-SEVEN

MY instincts wanted me to leave, told me I was too close to this little band of revolutionaries. Looking at the biker and Ysbail after Bone Daddy's last self eulogization, I knew that it wasn't altruism that prompted them to pull me out of a life threatening situation.

However, at this point, my options were limited. I faced the same Hobson's choice that I had been given in front of Rayburn's triumvirate, though no one here explicitly stated so. I could go along, or I could go out alone to face a threat that had shown no reluctance about violently dispatching people with too much information. Phillips could have every mage in the city's employ hunting me down. My only reprieve right now was the fact that Baldassare's estate was very seriously warded against magical intrusions.

I needed Phillips stopped as badly as anyone did.

But as badly as anything, I needed to rest. I felt as if I hadn't slept in weeks.

Baldasarre led me to a bedroom bigger than the living room in my condo, and I collapsed on a mahogany four-poster king-size bed. My body screamed for sleep, but my mind kept spinning along out of sheer momentum.

I lay on Baldassare's sheets and tried to think of how Bone Daddy's Oracle thought I was supposed to save the idea of an elvish homeland.

Call him Will.

"Bastard," I answered my mental image of Bone.

With that one phrase he tied me inextricably to his little prophecy. Even if I'd kept quiet about the CD that had been sent to me, word of it had made its way ahead of me. Apparently a familiar gargoyle had salvaged my hard drive from the dumpster I'd stashed it in. And there was enough decrypted data on it for Ysbail and company to scry the passphrase, and Bone's home movie.

The Oracle's second message to me: *Your path has been chosen for you by forces you've known and have not seen . . .*

That fit well. I had known a lot of players here—in Baldassare's case, years—without "seeing" the whole. And, according to Ysbail, it was Baldassare who pressured the *Press* to put me on the dragon story.

. . . they fear your allegiance because the masters you serve are not theirs . . .

Again that made sense. Probably more so than it did with the Feds. In the elves' case I had no doubt that they had a literal "master," possibly in Ysbail.

. . . The alliance they offer will not be an easy one.

I closed my eyes and whispered, "You pegged that one, brother."

It wasn't just that these people were unashamed partisans, and I was a supposedly objective journalist. I had done enough op-ed pieces to know that unbiased reporting was generally an oxymoron, and reporters have been getting involved in their own stories ever since Councilmen started throwing chairs at people.

No, what really worried me was the fact that I was standing with the losing side. Not just my opinion, mind you. These folks believed that they were on a death watch and it was only a matter of time before the darkness closed in on them. I had seen the fatalism in everyone's eyes—except, of course, within Baldassare's carefully crafted expression.

It was hard not to picture everyone here suffering the same fate as Aloeus. However careful they had been, it was only a matter of time. Despite Phillips' botched manipulation of the SPU, there were certainly more conventional investigations going on over Aloeus' death . . .

. . . and Bone's.

. . . and Cutler's.

. . . and O'Malley's.

All of it, given the nature of the quarry, would be tainted by SPU involvement. All of it, with the SPU's help, subject to manipulation by Phillips.

If I had the luxury of time, an explosive exposé would be just what the doctor ordered. As nice as that thought was, there was no way this was something I could just phone in to Columbia. You can't go around accusing major public figures of murder in print without sources and documentation lined up from here to Lakeside Avenue. To get this into print without a criminal investigation would require more evidence than it would to convene a grand jury.

I'm sure, as clumsy as Phillips had been, the evidence was out there. I just didn't have the weeks to collect and itemize it.

I kept coming at the problem from every angle, and kept getting the same simple, and the same ludicrous, answer:

Despite Baldassare's reservations, my—and by extension, the Faustians'—only hope lay in getting me a face-to-face with Mayor Rayburn.

The mayor might be adept at fooling himself, or cultivating blind spots where his cronies were concerned, but I doubted that he'd be as willfully blind when someone introduced the possibility that one of those cronies was going off half-cocked without his authorization. It was Rayburn's nature, there'd be no possible way he could tolerate that kind of challenge to his authority—no matter how loyal Phillips might be.

Easy.

I could picture the headlines the next day. "Newsman slain in foiled assassination attempt."

Rayburn never went anywhere unguarded. There were always cops, SPU officers, and mages shadowing the mayor to protect him. Any or all of them would be under Phillips' thumb. Worse, even to set up a meeting alone, assuming Rayburn would be willing, there was no way he'd be able to avoid telling his security team. That would, in turn, let Phillips in on the meeting. God only knows what he'd do then.

The only place that I'd ever seen Rayburn without an extended entourage was in the secret meeting room they had set up under Lakeside.

Eventually, I slept.

The sun had come and gone, its light fading from the windows when I opened my eyes. I sat up and looked across to see Ysbail standing in the corner next to the windows, watching me with her metallic eyes.

"How long have you been there?" I asked.

"Does it matter?"

"What do you want?"

"You know what I want."

"What if Bone Daddy is wrong?"

"Is he?"

I rubbed the sleep from my eyes and swung my feet off the bed. I had not had a restful sleep. My racing thoughts and the heat of the day had kept me awake. But I did now have the embryonic glimmerings of a solution to our shared dilemma.

I told her about it.

"It has to be me," I said "Baldassare has the contacts, but he doesn't believe. Or, if he does, the best he could say to Rayburn was, 'This is what Maxwell said.' It would be easy to dismiss secondhand, especially after he admits his relationship to you."

Ysbail nodded.

"You all suffer that credibility problem. Even if Rayburn *knows* you're telling the literal truth. He can always tell himself that your beliefs are skewed. That's even if you could manage to meet with him, and I'm sure Phillips is watching that line of attack."

"Perhaps it is as you say. But what good is it for us for Rayburn to know that Phillips is corrupt? We have lost our Portal."

"You've lost *a* Portal," I corrected her. "Once Rayburn discovers what Phillips has done, is doing, he'll be driven to distance himself from the guy. He'll have to establish that the policies that Phillips was trying to advance are not the administration's." I looked up. "I think you'll be able to deal with him, if only to give him political cover from Phillips' covert activities."

"You sound very certain."

"I'm not certain of anything. This role was forced on me, I didn't volunteer."

"Perhaps," Ysbail said. "But we have learned to respect Caleb Washington's gift."

"Uh-huh." I shook my head, telling myself that—if I survived—there was going to be one hell of a story out of this. "As far as getting me and Rayburn in the same room before Phillips gets to do anything about it . . ."

"Yes?"

"You need to tell me, exactly, what is involved in casting that mini-portal of yours."

"You've got to be kidding, Maxwell," Baldassare told me after I'd explained to them all the details of my plan to, in Bone Daddy's words, pull our butts out of the fire.

"At least he's got some balls," said the biker, whose name I'd learned was Boltof. He was, unlike Bone and Friday, an immigrant from Ragnan.

Of course, Boltof couldn't let a compliment leave his mouth without hunting it down and killing it. He added, "Unless he's really a spy and this is all a setup."

"He is not a spy," Ysbail insisted.

"Besides," added Friday, "there would be easier ways to inform the administration who we are. The phone comes to mind."

"Yeah?" Boltof shook his head. "He's smart enough to know that I'd slice him open if he pulled something like that."

"We all know," Baldassare said. "Can we all dispense with the posturing?" He turned to me. "Had Ysbail explained the implications of what you're suggesting?"

I nodded. "To open a temporary portal somewhere, you need someone who has been there—"

"Someone to visualize the destination," Ysbail corrected me.

"In this case it is the same thing. I'm the only person we have who's been there," I finished.

"You did see what it did to the elves?" Baldassare said.

I nodded. "Ysbail explained it. The spell needs someone to act as a lens, to focus the spell."

"Someones," Baldassare corrected. "This is no simple task. The energies involved are immense."

Friday rubbed his hands. "Mr. Baldassare does have a valid point." He said it as if he found it distasteful to allow the man that much. "The last Portal was the first we attempted with as few as two. Angor and Einion nearly collapsed focusing the energy."

"Exactly," Baldassare said. "And they were mages, and benefited from an inhumanly tough constitution. A human, especially an untrained one, would have died in their place."

Boltof chuckled, "Hey, if he wants to—"

"I told you, I discussed this with Lady Ysbail," I said. "There's a risk, but it isn't a suicidal one."

"You think you'd be better at this than Angor or Einion?" Baldassare asked.

"No," Ysbail answered for me, and everyone turned to face her. "He realizes he is a novice. You all are forgetting the significant difference between creating a Portal to Galweir and what Mr. Maxwell proposes."

It only took a moment for Boltof and Friday to get it. Friday nodded, as if it suddenly all made sense, and Boltof just gave a caustic grin. Baldassare frowned and asked, "Will someone enlighten me?"

"In going from point A to point B, there are two things that stress the person guiding the destination," I told him. "The distance from the source, and that person's affinity for the target. While Angor and Einion might be adepts, and have an unmatchable affinity for Galweir, the distance from Galweir to the Portal on the Ragnan side was several thousand miles." I looked into Baldassare's eyes and tried to gauge his reaction. All I saw was a calculated concern. "My destination lies less than half a mile from the Portal, and lies in a place—at least beneath a place—that I have unquestionable affinity for. My inexperience might cost me, but the other elements we have going for us should make up for it."

Baldassare nodded. "You are talking about one of the most magically secure places on this side of the Portal."

"Designed by people who have no idea that Ysbail and her mages can do this. It is also one of the few places I know that Phillips won't be able to penetrate with his own mages. Once I'm in, the wards are going to protect me."

"You are *sure* that Nesmith will meet with you?" Friday asked me.

I nodded. "She's going to want to hear from me, especially after what happened with the gargoyle."

"Without Phillips?" Friday pressed.

"She has no reason to involve Phillips. This is a law enforcement matter, and she's the chief law enforcement officer in the city."

Baldassare nodded. "On this point, I agree with Maxwell. Phillips can't blatantly insert himself into Nesmith's turf without exposing himself, and Nesmith seems unlikely to invite a political rival into something that, from Maxwell's description, is her show." He smiled grimly. "I won't pretend to like this, and while I'm not a hundred percent convinced that you're right about Rayburn, things have descended to the point that some sort of negotiation is the only real option—whatever dangers it might open up."

"Then why the fuck don't we just set up the meet with Hizzoner himself?"

I shook my head. "Rayburn's security is an issue. If he goes anywhere alone, it might tip off Phillips. I'm betting the same attention doesn't apply to Nesmith. And if *she* sets up a private meeting with the mayor—"

"Lot of ifs," Boltof said.

"But the reasoning makes sense," Baldassare asserted.

"Great, so you're behind this guy now?"

"I've yet to hear a more coherent suggestion." Baldassare walked up and took my arm. "You're taking a risk."

More than you have. But then you know that, don't you?

"How do you want to set up the meeting?" Baldassare asked.

"That's a sticking point." I said. "Contacting Nesmith directly has the same issues as contacting Rayburn directly. Any official channel is likely to alert Phillips."

"I have some 'unofficial' channels to contact people in Rayburn's administration," Baldassare said.

"I was hoping you would."

CHAPTER TWENTY-EIGHT

"IF we're going to do this," Baldassare said, "we have to do it right."

I had no illusions that I was dealing with a democracy here. I had a fair certainty that whatever Lady Ysbail said was the rule, despite eruptions from Boltof. Even so, I could feel the political weight in the room shift with Baldassare's somewhat reluctant endorsement. It was interesting to see how Baldassare could move a room without so much as asking for anyone's support. The man had a gravity that drew even chaotic personalities like Boltof after him.

Even a genetic aristocrat like Ysbail could feel it.

I felt it, too, at first without realizing it. My initial reaction was simple gratitude at having his support. I had blown most of my intellectual capital in answering his arguments. Somehow, though, through some sort of rhetorical judo, Baldassare was suddenly center stage, laying out exactly how we were going to do this.

It wasn't until we were fifteen minutes into the details of the plan—a plan I had developed and introduced to these people—that I realized that I hadn't made a significant contribution since Baldassare had agreed to contact Nesmith to set up the meeting.

"Night would be the best time for this. Better chance that Nesmith will be unobserved during her off time. Lakeside will be pretty much empty except for a few cops, none of whom should be hanging around the meeting area." Baldassare kept going on, as if it had been his idea. At this point it seemed as if it was.

Watching him, I decided that it was the fact that he never seemed to stop thinking. He was always questioning, hypothesizing, figuring the angles. It was impressive, and scary.

"I'm going to have to set this up as close as possible to the meeting as we can get. The longer lead time we give Nesmith, the more chance that she might, voluntarily or involuntarily, let this slip to Phillips. Two, three hours, at most. And I shouldn't be anywhere near you people when you do your magic—and you shouldn't be anywhere near here."

Heads nodded, mine among them.

"When can your people do this?"

Ysbail looked at Boltof and Friday, "With the three of us—"

"You're going to have one novice more than you should doing this. How long before Angor or Einion can back you up?"

Ysbail shook her head. "Days. Weeks."

Baldassare frowned. "You must have other mages who can do this. Back you up. You're going to need all the help you can get."

She looked across at Baldassare and seemed to be weighing something. I noted a look of concern cross Boltof's face. He shook his head and said, "We're exposed too much."

"There are others," Ysbail said quietly.

Boltof shook his head. "This is a mistake. They're underground for a reason."

"They have learned at our knee," Ysbail said. "To deliver us. This must work, or our purpose is lost. They will aid us."

"You made the right decision," Baldassare said.

I wondered.

Twenty-four hours later, I got a slight amusement out of the fact that Boltof loaded us into a minivan that was the twin of the one used by the SPU elves. The van had spent those hours as a target for nonstop scrying wards. We might only be on the road for about fifteen or twenty minutes before we entered an area where the wards wouldn't be necessary, but each minute of that time was a risk. If Phillips' mages zeroed in on us—

That didn't bear thinking about.

Baldassare was in downtown Cleveland preparing to contact Nesmith, and it was about three hours short of my own personal zero hour.

Boltof drove the van off of Baldassare's estate, and that gave me the option of either worrying about leaving that permanently warded haven, or worrying about the fact that Boltof was native to a world without the concept of speed limits.

The van blew through the night, racing at seventy along dark, curving, rural roads, while Boltof stared forward with an expression of manic ecstasy.

I gripped the seat, telling myself that our destination was close. We were headed due north of Hunting Valley, toward the

Metroparks. Toward an area of wild enchantment that would make it very hard for anyone to follow us.

It was there that our quartet was to meet up with a trio of elven mages. It was an assemblage that would gather together almost all the people who had any knowledge how to open a Portal—all there to thrust me into a meeting with Nesmith.

The roads the minivan swerved through were pitch-black and hemmed in by the silhouettes of trees. No streetlights broke the darkness as we passed a large green sign saying, "Warning: You are entering the North Chagrin Reservation. Enter at your own risk."

Officially it was still part of the Metroparks system, but, since the Portal opened, it had become something unto itself. The woods here had changed. Neighboring developments in Willoughby Hills and Mayfield Heights had been overtaken by trees. Owners of half-million dollar vinyl monstrosities built on clear-cut lots would wake up to suddenly find their three-acre chemically treated front lawns home to a half dozen century-old maples and elms. New sewer lines would be clogged with roots, and wildlife from raccoons to skunks and deer would be making homes in garages, pools, and porches.

In a decade the enchanted wood had doubled in size, spreading northeast and southwest. The interior of the reservation—with the exception of a few human artifacts, like the road—had taken on a primeval character. Creatures were rumored to live here, sprites and dryads much more furtive than any elf.

Ysbail had picked this place for a reason.

Professor Shafran had explained to me—it felt as if it were a long time ago—that the magic flowing through the Portal was a fluid. It flowed and found itself concentrated in places, often at man's whim, sometimes at nature's. The North Chagrin Reservation represented such a concentration. For some reason, the geography here, the nature of the land, attracted the mana and kept it from flowing away, the woods becoming one of the densest concentrations of mana east of the Portal itself.

I could feel it hanging in the air. The sense of the sound just after, or just before, the portentous word is spoken. It ate into me with every breath I took, the weight behind the trees. It was almost as if we drove underwater instead of under a moonless sky.

Every so often we would pass an area where the trees were slightly thinner, and sometimes the headlights would catch the reflection of some pastel-tinted vinyl sagging off of the remains of a swaybacked house half eaten by vines and moss. Soon, even those traces were gone, and the van rocked on the broken asphalt as it edged into the heart of the wood.

There were no signs left. The wooden Metroparks signs had all rotted away, and the local park service hadn't replaced them. It had been a long time since anyone had jogged here, walked their dog, or had a picnic.

Apparently, one human structure remained, and—according to Ysbail—it was one of the half-dozen highest concentrations of mana within the Portal's influence. Anything cast there would have that much higher a chance of success. This one, in particular, was the choice for our ritual because it was the least accessible. The other places that offered as much of an advantage—Browns Stadium, Public Square, the reflecting pool in front of the Art Museum—all were much more public.

Squire's Castle, on the other hand, had done all it could to remove itself from human ken.

"They say it moves," Boltof said, by way of conversation. "Won't let people it doesn't like near it." He looked at me and I wondered if he was trying to make me nervous.

The castle had been built by Mr. Squire, vice president of Standard Oil, back in the 1890s. The stone structure was intended as a gatehouse and caretaker's quarters for an estate that was never built. By the time it passed into the hands of the Metroparks as a castellated turreted picnic shelter, it was little more than a shell. Proving that in the U. S. it only takes us half a century to reduce a castle to the state of ruin that Europe takes five or six hundred years to achieve.

I found it hard to believe it moved, magic or not. But I did know that it had, over the past decade, slipped rather quietly off the list of Cleveland landmarks anyone talked about.

Abruptly ahead of us, the headlights picked out a solid wall of trees blocking off the road. The van braked, coming to a graceless stop on the crumbling road.

"Here we are," Boltof said, sliding aside the door on the mini-van.

With the engine silent, it gave me a chance to hear how quiet the woods were. No insects, no bird calls, not even the leaves rustling in the still air. If it wasn't for the quiet ticking of the cooling engine, I would have thought I'd been struck deaf. The scent of mulch and rotting leaves hung in the air.

"Have you ever done any meditation," Friday asked me. "Any visualization exercises?"

I shook my head as I wiped my palms on my shirt. The air here was very still, as if the forest around us was locked in a single moment. If I didn't know better, I would have had the impression of a forest unchanged for a thousand years.

The headlights died, plunging us into darkness.

"You need to hold the image in your mind," Friday told me. "Concentrate on it. That's your part. We do the spell, you concentrate on where we're going."

I nodded.

"Don't let anything distract you," he said.

I heard Boltof slam the door of the van, and one of the humanoid shadows around me spoke in Ysbail's voice, "This way."

I had no idea which way she meant, but someone grabbed my shoulder and led me. I think it was Friday.

We walked into the woods, and the way was clearer than I had expected. In the stark glare of the headlights, the way had looked impassable in every direction. The road appeared to be hemmed in by a wall of trees on every side. But, as my eyes adjusted to the darkness, the wood was not as dense as it had looked from the van. The trees were old and tall, and they didn't crowd each other. At least not where we stood.

I thought, for a moment, I caught a whiff of woodsmoke and roses. Then I lost it under the damp smell of the leaves under my feet.

Once we had walked for about ten or fifteen minutes, and I could see enough not to walk into a tree, I got the eerie impression that, just beyond us, on every side, the woods crowded into impenetrability again. It was obviously an illusion, because we kept walking and the woods, if anything, thinned out around us as the trees got bigger.

Despite that, I knew that if I was separated from the others I would be hopelessly lost. I had heard the stories about these woods, and I could fathom how Boltof's legend of the moving castle might have grown.

These woods were enchanted, and I suspect that their enchantment warped the way the woods were perceived. The magic locked in these anachronistically ancient trees radiated an aura that made me see them as menacing and impenetrable, and once I was in the woods, they filled my senses with a forbidding dread. The trees said I didn't belong here. They said to stay here was to die.

It made panic seem like a viable option. Two things kept me from bolting and trying to make it back to the safety of the van.

First was the fact that, if I bolted, I knew that my warped perception of the woods would have me lost within a few steps. The second reason was that I had the same sense I'd had during Bone Daddy's ritual, that the emotions I felt weren't my own. I knew that they came from the trees.

"This place," Ysbail spoke quietly, barely above a whisper. But I heard her clearly. "Across the Portal, little like it is left. Such concentrations of wild magic were challenges to the authority of the Thesarch."

"What happened to them?" I asked.

"Valdis, and his predecessors, would burn the woods and salt the ashes," Ysbail told us. "Much of our world is desert."

Somehow, even given the menace of the woods here, I found the statement by Ysbail more chilling. I'd always thought that our world had held the monopoly on large-scale, man-made environmental disasters.

I noticed that Ysbail and Boltof seemed to be checking landmarks. The things they looked for were mostly invisible to me, though once or twice I could catch a glimpse of something—a pile of debris that could have been weathered asphalt, a dead piece of moss-covered wood that could have been an old Metroparks signpost, a mound of earth just rectangular enough to mark a man-made foundation.

Sometimes it was too easy to pretend that the Portal hadn't changed anything essential. I had spent most of the past decade avoiding the idea that the nature of my hometown had changed in a fundamental way. As we walked on, enveloped by the silent trees, I realized that the way I had been looking at things was wrong. The Portal, magic, the elves, the dragons, the mages—all of these things—I had seen them as simply additional layers on the city I had been covering all of my professional life. They were *additions*. As long as I saw them as separate from "my" city.

It wasn't until we broke into the clearing that it sank in exactly how far I'd had to come. I stood in a woods that had, somehow, decided that mankind had not touched it for centuries, and had the power to rewrite its own history so that it was so. The land itself had changed, become something alien to me. The effect of the Portal wasn't just a modification, an adjustment to what was already there. It wasn't a demographic shift, like East Cleveland, or a flood of new investment, like Cleveland proper. It wasn't the introduction of a new species, or a new discipline, or a new kind of technology, or the effect of interference.

These woods had *changed*. The land I walked on wasn't the same as it had been a decade ago, the trees weren't the same, even the air I breathed wasn't the same.

And, when the scent of roses and woodsmoke returned, when we emerged into the clearing around Squire's Castle, I could see that the *castle* wasn't the same.

What I saw, lording it over the hillside, wasn't the gatehouse that Mr. Squire built in the nineteenth century. It wasn't the empty shell that had been used as a picnic shelter for the years before the Portal opened.

The castle had grown. The style had stayed the same, the stone walls still echoed an English baronial hall, but the walls had doubled in height, the turrets trebled and multiplied. The glow of firelight lit every window in a flickering orange, even in the upper stories where, in the original structure, there had been no floors. I saw shadows move and dance in the windows, as if the castle was occupied.

In the silence of the woods, I thought I could hear them. I heard songs in an unfamiliar tongue, heard the clatter of silverware. I could just barely perceive the perfume of an unearthly feast.

"What is this?" I whispered.

"The Folk," Friday responded. "The denizens of these woods. This is the home of their king. The center of their kingdom."

"How did they come through the Portal," I asked, "without us knowing?"

Ysbail shook her head. "They are closer to the magic," Ysbail explained. "Where it is, they are."

"But—" I started.

"Like the woods," Boltof said. "The mana made the woods here, the woods made them, they made the castle."

Ysbail walked us up the hill, to the castle. She saw me hesitate and said, "We have permission."

She didn't say it in a reassuring manner.

We climbed the stone steps, the sounds of banqueting and revelry getting louder. As we mounted the steps I asked, "Are these our other mages?"

Boltof chuckled.

Ysbail said, "The Folk *are* magic, they do not use spells as we do. They are capricious."

We walked in through the open arched doorway, and I looked around to catch sight of the Folk themselves. It didn't happen. The moment we stepped through the arch, the sounds of revelry ceased;

the odor of a banquet and of roses was gone on the wind. The silence of the woods descended again, and I looked through an entry hall that was empty of anyone.

"They're gone?"

"No," Ysbail said. "They remain, but they prefer to watch us rather than have us watch them."

I could feel them watching us. I think I'd been feeling it since we'd entered the woods. "Okay, where are we going to do this?"

Ysbail looked up. "The turret."

I followed the others up a stone staircase that spiraled six stories up a tower that was three times as high as the original castle. The woodsmoke smell grew as we ascended. On the stone walls, ornate sconces held torches whose smoke curled straight up.

There was an odd feeling of anticipation in the air, as if the cold stone walls waited expectantly. We followed the stairs to a rough wood trapdoor in the ceiling that let us out on the roof of the turret. Outside, it was about thirty feet square, a wood floor hanging between waist-high castellations. About every five feet along the walls, a torch burned, casting a flickering orange light on the rough-hewn roof.

The wood had been covered with tracings in ash and salt, words in an alien language. The look was familiar to me from the glyphs on the casing of Cutler's bullet.

Three figures stood waiting for us. Two were elves whom I didn't know. The last was a human in a hooded robe. I could catch glimpses of the jaw of a disfigured face in the firelight, almost enough to recognize.

"No . . ." I whispered.

But the cloaked figure nodded in disagreement. "I'm afraid so." The man raised gloved, knobby hands and lowered the hood so I could see his face. He had once been handsome, and he still had a pair of innocent blue eyes that were as likely as not to send any girl this side of puberty into heat.

The problem was, now, that tiny twins of those blue eyes blinked at me from dozens of lumpy growths on his face.

"Morgan?"

"Maxwell," he said. "You're a sight for sore eyes."

CHAPTER TWENTY-NINE

"YOU?" I said.

"Me," Morgan said. "You look surprised."

I shook my head. That was an understatement. "You're working with . . ." I waved at Ysbail, and at the elves.

Morgan smiled, and the way it twisted the tumors on his face made me turn away. "Is the distaste in your voice because you don't approve of the cause, or because you don't approve of a journalist being involved in this subject matter?"

"We do not have much time," Ysbail said. "Everyone get in place for the ritual."

Boltof led me to the center of the markings. I turned to Morgan, who had replaced his cowl. "You're a mage?"

"You know a better person to cover my beat?"

I kept shaking my head, trying to place this new bit of information in my world view. "You set me up," I said finally.

"I did toss your name in the ring. What? You thought you were Baldassare's first choice?"

No, maybe I wouldn't have been. We knew each other too well.

I looked around me, at the view past the torches. Beyond the immediate blackness of the trees, there was a glow from city streetlights. It was dim, though, as if I had stepped halfway out of the world.

"You're going to need to concentrate," Morgan said. "We've pulled out all the stops for the spell itself, but you have to tell it where to go."

"Why?" I asked him.

"Why am I part of this," Morgan said, "or why did I come back?"

"Take your pick."

"We really don't have the time. Let's just say the Morgan you knew was as much a fiction as Faust ever was, and if the possession infecting my body must progress to achieve our purpose, it's a price I'm willing to accept." His tone lowered. "Now, you need to imagine our destination. Make it clear in your mind."

I tried to do as he asked, closing my eyes and picturing the sanctum in the sublevels of City Hall's parking garage. I tried to mine all of my memory's resources for every small detail. The subliminal buzz of the single fluorescent fixture. The micron or so of concrete dust that marred the sheen of the table. The pebbled texture of the executive leather office chairs. The shape of the words carved into the concrete walls. The smell of confined air. The tang of exhaust fumes and oil. The feeling I felt through the soles of my feet when the access door slid shut.

Around me, the soft tones of a spoken ritual began. The language wasn't one designed for a human voice. The alien syllables wormed inside my ears as if they were burrowing for a warm place to lay their eggs.

I was afraid of what was going to happen. For all my assurances to Baldassare, I didn't know a damn thing about what I was doing. All I understood about the spell that was about to be cast was that I was going to be in a position of channeling all the energy massed by the ritual.

And, in order to improve the success of the spell, there was going to be a lot of energy involved.

I pushed the fear away with images of arcane symbols etched in concrete.

The chanting continued, and it was a struggle to hang on to my memory of Rayburn's bunker. The words that filled the air around me threatened to fill every empty space in my brain. God only knew what the result would be if I allowed that to happen, and let my mind lock onto sounds without any concepts or connotations to them. Would a portal open? If so, to where? Could a portal be opened onto an abstraction?

I forced myself to think of the bunker. The feeling of the chair as I sat in it. The coolness of the still air. The smoothness of the table. The sound of dripping water.

An ache began behind my eyes, and spread through my sinuses into my jaw. I felt blood pulsing beneath my scalp, and the hair on my arms and legs bristled against my clothes. The air around me was no longer still. It carried the scent of electricity and ozone.

I screwed my eyes shut even tighter against the distractions. I didn't move, my muscles frozen in place for fear of disrupting the tenuous mental image. I imagined increasingly fine details of the room. The small cobweb I had seen at one end of the fluorescent light, the black husk of a dead insect suspended in it. The way the grain in the table's surface made a pattern somewhat like a human face near the end where Rayburn had taken his seat. The way the mechanism of the chair caught slightly when I had turned it to the right, and how the casters it rode on ground slightly with concrete dust caught in bearings designed for use on a quite different surface.

Something was rushing through me. I felt a vibration that seemed to originate in the core of my body, the marrow of my bones. It was as if my flesh now hung on a superstructure constructed out of an overloaded water main. My teeth hurt. Every muscle in my body began to contract against the force, tearing itself into a tiny ball. I felt the sensation of millions of tiny insects running across my skin. The sense unidirectional, originating in the soles of my feet, shooting upward. The insect feet became pins, then razors, then claws tearing my flesh upward, pulling it toward the sky, the same direction the vibrating pressure inside me was going.

There was a small crack in the veneer of the table, I remembered. Humidity, perhaps, had made the edge pull away from the rubber bumper that wrapped the edge of the tabletop. Above was the shine of mahogany grain under a light coating of dust, but for a small space, no wider than the base of my thumb, the veneer had separated allowing a view of the particleboard beneath. The top was dark, shiny, ordered—but the true nature of the table, revealed by the flaw, was light, dull, and a chaos of wood splinters suspended in some sort of caked adhesive emulsion.

I collapsed, my legs giving way beneath me.

My hands had stuck to the arm of the chair, the skin peeling away from a surface that I realized was only vinyl that was textured to look like leather.

My breath came in gasps. My body shook, a seizure that slammed my legs, my arms, my head into the wooden floor. I couldn't feel the impact through everything else, but I heard the hollow thumps as my skull slammed into the wood.

Rust spots on the white reflective underside of the fluorescent—

Burning now, as if a torch had been taken to my trembling skin.

The glint off of the golden inscription beginning with the Hebrew character aleph—

The pulse of blood in my ears—

The chunk of the elevator's motor starting up—

Fingernails cutting into my palms—
The drip of water in the distance—
Blood—
Concrete—
Burning—
Flickering—
Choking—
Rayburn's face . . .

Suddenly, the pressure broke, so abruptly that I thought an artery had exploded, spilling all the pain and feeling, as well as what was left of my life, onto the ground. No more chanting, no more wind, no more hideous internal pressure. All that was left of my body was a burning ache and a terrible heavy fatigue.

The floor was cold and hard beneath me. I slowly unclenched my fists and took a few deep breaths.

The moment I tasted the cold, slightly stale air, I opened my eyes. Above me the world was twisted and distorted into a shrinking spherical reflection. I could look up into Ysbail's eyes and the sphere shrank, seeming to withdraw via a direction I couldn't perceive. Through the sphere came torchlight that illuminated the space where I found myself.

Concrete walls embossed with arcane inscriptions. A meeting table surrounded by executive office chairs. A single suspended fluorescent light fixture that was, at the moment, unlit.

Then the sphere was gone, and I lay on the concrete floor in total darkness.

I could have blacked out. The effort of what I had just done had sapped every ounce of my strength. It had tapped resources that I didn't know were there until I found them missing. The thought of not moving at all was tempting. I had done my bit, I only had to wait for Nesmith . . .

Of course, it probably wouldn't make much of an impression if she found me out cold on the floor, and it would probably blow my chance of talking to her without the possibility of Phillips overhearing or intervening. And that *was* why I was here.

I sat up slowly. My flesh felt so weak that it seemed the sheer weight of my skeleton would tear my bones free to clatter on the ground under me. My brain spun with a sick vertigo when I sat up, my mind tumbling in a viscous black liquid with no sense of up or down. My gut spasmed as I tried to heave up the contents of an empty stomach.

When the world stopped moving, somehow I was on my hands and knees. Spots darted in front of my eyes, as if I were squeezing them shut, but they were open—which I confirmed when I ran my hand over my face.

Pushing myself upright was like fighting hundred-pound weights draped across my shoulders. My knees threatened to buckle as I stumbled toward the table. My hand found it by slamming into the edge with a knife-sharp blow that felt as if it—in my weakened condition—could snap my bone.

Fortunately, my body's structural integrity hadn't been compromised by the spell, just my sense of it. I didn't suffer a compound fracture, just a numbed and bruised hand.

I leaned against the table and inched along until I bumped into one of the chairs.

I didn't want Nesmith to find me on the ground, but I lacked the strength to stand upright—even long enough to find the light switch. I slid into the chair feeling as if I only weighed fifty pounds, all held together with tissue paper.

I rubbed my hand; at some point during the ritual the dressings had come off the old wounds. My palms were moist, probably with my own blood.

I waited.

My one fear was that I was so close to collapse that I might lose consciousness before Nesmith met with me. Her reaction would probably be to hospitalize me under police guard, which would give Phillips an opportunity to finish the job that O'Malley started.

I couldn't leave this room until Nesmith had heard everything. Until I had got her to set up a meeting with Rayburn. If we could do it quickly enough, it wouldn't matter how secure it was, Phillips wouldn't have time to react.

Until then . . .

It felt as if I'd been sitting, waiting, for hours. The darkness made time expand, stretching out into an infinity of fatigue before and ahead of me. I might have blacked out again, but I had no way of telling in the unchanging environment.

Then an explosion of light washed the world with blinding whiteness. The light slammed into my eyes like a blow, grinding my retinas into the back of my skull. I blinked and turned away from the fluorescent that had come on.

I turned the chair toward the direction the elevator had been. I couldn't see the doors; my night vision had been assassinated by the light. But I could hear the whir of the elevator's motor starting up.

I could feel the pulse in my neck as I straightened in my seat. My fatigue was forgotten for the moment.

It seemed another hour after the motor started before the doors slid open, spilling light into the darkened corner of the chamber. The light backlit three silhouettes, just as before. With one exception: these silhouettes were different.

These silhouettes were also *wrong.*

None of them was short enough to be Nesmith's. Two were so tall and angular that they could only be elves.

The round one in the center was the most wrong of the bunch. The trio stepped forward and Adrian Phillips walked into the circle of light thrown by the fluorescent. Behind him, the elevator doors slid slowly shut.

"It's almost a shame to have to kill you," he said by way of greeting.

CHAPTER THIRTY

I WAS so drained that I couldn't even muster up a decent response. Somehow, Phillips had caught wind of the plan and had beat Nesmith here. I should have been shocked, afraid, at least a little pissed off. There was only an empty hollow inside me where my emotions should have been. I squinted at Phillips' sweaty, pudgy face , and all I could think of was at least it was over.

"No comment?" he inquired. "That's ironic, don't you think?"

"Nesmith?" I asked. I don't even know why I said it. Reflex, I think. I was in some sort of psychic free fall, and I wasn't really aware of the meaning of the word until after I spoke it.

"I regret she wasn't able to make it. Fortunately, I was able to intercept your contact with her."

Obviously.

I looked at his escort. The elves were familiar to me. Caledvwlch looked a little more gaunt, and the one I knew only as Elf Three had his Glock out. *What's going through your mind, Caledvwlch?*

"Where is she?" I asked, closing my eyes.

Phillips' words washed over me, leaving little of themselves behind. "Mr. Maxwell, since you've obviously become an agent of Faust's, or at least you're under his influence, it is only prudent that the Safety Director send trained officers of the SPU to bring you to her."

I shook my head, smiling. "At your suggestion?"

"You're a smart man, Maxwell." He shook his head and turned away.

His turning away pulled me out of my stupor, at least to the point where I could feel my own anger. "Why are you here?" I sputtered. My jaw ached and the muscles felt slack on my face, slurring my words. "Let your boys do the dirty work." I pushed myself upright, and the chair slid aside and upended.

Phillips turned around.

"You get off on it, don't you?"

"Maxwell—"

"The idea you can order someone killed gives you a raging hard-on, doesn't it?"

Phillips' hand was white and pudgy, and came at the end of a flabby swing that had more inertia than muscle behind it. It still managed to cave in my nose and make me topple backward. I sprawled at the foot of Phillips' bulk, his gray eyes glaring down on me.

If he expected the blow to shut me up, he was disappointed. Somehow the shock of the impact seemed to shake the remains of the stupor from my brain. "That's why you had to be on that boat. You had to see the dragon burn—"

Phillips shook his head. *"No."*

"Bone Daddy—you look at the autopsy photos? You get a rush when you realize you did that?"

His foot connected with the most sensitive part of my lower anatomy, and that did shut me up. It wasn't pain so much as a burning numbness and a paralyzing clenching of the muscles that bent me double. I didn't have any idea what I was doing, or even if there was some kernel of strategy in it.

I think I might have just stopped giving a shit.

"You don't *know.*" He leaned over and I could smell alcohol on his breath. "I was given the responsibility for this thing. A trust. To manage it, to support the mayor, to benefit the city. I could not let them do this thing. *Could not!*" I must have turned away, because a pudgy hand grabbed my jaw and forced my face toward his. My nose had swollen shut now, and I was forced to breathe through my mouth.

"God forbid we have any competition," I whispered between ragged breaths.

"You naïve bastard. You think that was it? No, Aloeus brought the Portal here for one reason. If he had achieved his goal, it wouldn't be competition, it would be the end. The end of economic recovery, the end of Mayor Rayburn's administration." His hand clamped on my jaw as he leaned forward. "It would be the end of the Portal. He had the power to shut it down, and once another existed, nothing would prevent him from doing so."

"You're trying to justify murder," I said.

"Aloeus was a traitor to the city, a realm that he helped create." Phillips shook his head and let my chin go. My head slammed back onto the concrete floor. "The mage was a traitor." He stood back up, wiping his hands on his suit. "So are you."

"So is anyone who threatens your private fiefdom—"

He shook his head. "This is Mayor Rayburn's city, not mine."

"He knows what you're dong?"

"The mayor's constrained by politics. It would prevent him from acting in his own, or the city's best interest." Phillips shook his head. "No, Maxwell, I do not like the necessities of the past few days. My responsibilities forced them on me and I would not be worthy of that trust if I did not act."

"A power trip, and you get to pretend to be noble at the same time," I spat. "You're living a fascist wet dream."

"Enough. Despite your accusations, I'm not here to relish the violence. I'm simply present to make certain that," he looked at the elves, *"this time,* the job isn't botched.""

"Your whole world view is botched." I said, even though Phillips didn't seem to be listening anymore. "You think that killing me will accomplish anything? You've gone so far over the top that you'll never be able to keep it quiet."

"If you would finish the job here," Phillips turned to the elf with the Glock.

This was not how I'd planned things. For all my romantic notions about the press, I never saw dying for my profession as a particularly glamorous way to go. Several thoughts ran through my mind. First was a nice little daydream about me overpowering the elf with the gun, a slight possibility when I was in perfect shape. Then I thought about the consequences of killing someone in this inner sanctum. Bone Daddy had been concerned about it disrupting his magical environment. Would this place's more permanent nature make it more or less disruptive? I also idly wondered who Bea would get to replace me on my beat. It'd be ironic if Morgan could land the job.

My musings lasted long enough for me to realize that the fatal bullet wasn't immediately forthcoming.

Caledvwlch held his hand on top of the other elf's Glock. "I am afraid we cannot, Mr. Phillips."

Okay, what's happening here?

"What do you mean? You took an oath to serve this city. That's supposed to mean something to you."

His posture and tone didn't change, but somehow I could tell that Caledvwlch didn't like the implication. "Do not fault our honor, sir. We serve the mayor and the city. We follow the commands of our liege."

Phillips waved toward me. "Your 'liege,' O'Malley, one of the most faithful cops in this city, is dead because of him—"

"There is no honor in killing an unarmed man."

I chuckled and Phillips whipped around to face me.

"I guess you get to do it yourself—"

Phillips grabbed the Glock from Elf Three, and aimed it toward me with a shaking hand. I tensed as he squeezed the trigger, even though nothing much happened. He didn't know enough to switch off the safety. He grimaced in frustration, and I was halfway between pissing my pants and busting up in laughter.

"Sir," Caledvwlch said quietly.

"Goddamn gun."

"Sir."

"How're you supposed to—"

"*Sir!*" The act of raising his voice erased every other sound from Caledvwlch's presence. It was a sound of such clear crystalline fury that it felt as if the concrete walls should crack just from hearing it. Caledvwlch held his own weapon on Phillips. His arm was arrow straight, and his hand was not shaking.

Phillips turned to face him, shock and anger rolling across his face like waves over a breakwater. "What is the meaning of this?"

"Put the gun down."

The sound of Caledvwlch's voice dried my mouth and made me push away from Phillips, the focus of it. Phillips sounded truly amazed. "He's the enemy. You know that. You serve—"

"We serve the Honorable Mayor David Theodore Rayburn. Our honor, our service, our duty became his when his servant, our liege, was taken from this life."

Phillips nodded.

I got it, what Caledvwlch was saying. Phillips didn't

"You see, then," Phillips said. "He's a threat to the mayor. To the city. He has to be stopped." He turned toward me and steadied his own gun.

"Put the gun down, Mr. Phillips."

Phillips shook his head. "We're serving the mayor here. You can't interfere." He found the safety at last, and cocked the weapon.

The gunshot was like a cannon going off in the enclosed space.

I could smell it, an acrid burning, as a hole erupted in Phillips' forehead. Phillips collapsed as if his body had turned into a sack of so much wet cement. He fell across my legs as blood sprayed from the hole in his skull.

"Shit," I pushed away from the corpse, pulling my legs back and trying to get clear of the spreading pool of blood. For a moment, everything was still except the blood. Even the gun smoke seemed to hang suspended in the air, frozen as if in anticipation.

The hair on my arms began standing on end.

Magic is a fluid thing, I've been told. It has eddies and currents. It follows the curve of reality, finding gravity in points of complexity, order, and ritual. It can concentrate in places, objects, even people. While we manufacture our own rituals to manipulate it, ultimately it is its own master.

I could feel the potential filling the air, like a static charge, like the hum of an overcharged transformer. There was even a smell to it, a slightly sour, tinny odor. The elves were stepping back from the body.

Phillips had fallen inside the central circle. The perimeter was etched in gold, embedded in the concrete. The blood spread across the concrete until it touched the circle.

The warning from Bone Daddy crossed my mind, *"The mojo's been building here a couple hours. You break the pattern, boy, and it'll be like someone shoved a stick of dynamite up your ass."*

There was an arc when the blood touched the circle. The sound was somewhere between an electrical sizzle and a relay being thrown. A blue-green light began to radiate from the metal of the circle, sweeping around it in pulsing waves from where Phillips' blood touched it. The greenish light spread to the glyphs etched in the floor, in the wall, and from details I had never seen before in the ceiling.

The fluorescent light exploded in a cloud of sparks and dropped, sputtering, onto the meeting table. By that time there was enough of the glow to see.

I tried to push myself up, but Caledvwlch shook his head, "No." He may have said something, but the room was filled with the sound of electrical sizzling. Arcs leaped from the circle to the inscriptions, and back. Tendrils of blue-green energy erupted from the concrete walls, like lightning, but smooth, curved, and slow. The energy had a terrible feeling of potential. Just looking at the glowing snakes gave me an impression of energies an order of magnitude above what had passed through me when we cast the spell that had brought me here.

Caledvwlch was warning me to stay in the circle. Inside the

glowing ring, free of the display that tore the air apart outside. We seemed to be in a bubble that didn't quite reach the ceiling. Arcs and tendrils slid over an invisible dome around us, sometimes making slow-motion splashes against it.

Closer to me, Phillips' blood was sizzling. The pool of blood had turned black and was charring. Where the blood had touched the circle, the gold wasn't glowing. I could see green filaments of energy, slipping across that dead-black break, like probing roots.

The edges of the bloodstain started burning, jets of flame reached around from the edge of the circle and followed the now black stain. When the flames reached Phillips, they raced around the edges of the corpse like a chalk outline from hell.

The green energy was slower; it flowed out from the break in the circle, covering the black stain in a net of crackling light. It reached Phillips' head as the flames fully encircled him.

The green followed the blood; it crawled up the side of his head, the flesh charring and releasing smoldering jets of flame underneath its touch. It spilled into the head wound.

When it reached the interior of Phillips' skull, something fundamental changed in the room. The random electrical sounds were replaced by the sound of a great wind. The filaments that reached into Phillips grew, merged, became a thick, pulsing, green conduit. It began racing by, whipping up and down like a garden hose out of control—though the motion was reversed, the energy flowing *into* the stationary hole in Phillips' skull, the source whipping around the surface of the invisible dome around us, sucking power into itself.

The body jerked.

Caledvwlch and the other elf had got on the ground themselves, staying out of the way of the whipping tendrils of energy that fed into Phillips. The circle seemed no protection now; power arced from outside, splitting into several sources, all feeding into Phillips' skull.

The body shook, the back arching and the limbs flailing in a seizure. The skin was turning black.

Phillips may have been dead, but he screamed. The sound of the prolonged cry drowned out everything. An agonized keening that went on long after living breath would have expired.

His back snapped back, and suddenly, impossibly, Phillips was on his knees. His arms flung forward and up, as if to embrace the energy spilling into his skull. His head bent and twisted side to side almost too fast to follow. Fire ate his clothes as smoke rose from the exposed parts of his carbonized skin.

Every scrap of the green energy fed itself into the corpse until all light in the room died. For a few moments the darkness was complete. The room was silent except for a quiet sighing. In a few moments, I could see a ruddy light, a crackling glow that seemed to form an outline where Phillips' body knelt.

I distinctly heard the words, "*Oh, my God.*"

It was Phillips' voice.

Then came the explosion.

An eruption of red light, fire, and smoke tore from the remains of Phillips' body. The light shot upward, tearing a hole in the ceiling as a cloud of tar-black smoke unrolled in its wake. I was still on the ground, but the force of the blast pushed me back about four or five feet, spraying me with burning embers whose nature I really didn't want to think about.

I lay there, stunned and coughing, as sensations from the real, normal world began leaking in. Above me I could hear the sound of dozens of car alarms. I could also hear the spray of water from the sprinkler system. Somewhere a klaxon sounded a fire alarm, and as I looked up, through watering eyes, I could see the mercury-white glow of emergency lights shining from the ceiling—more exactly, from where the ceiling had been.

"Mr. Maxwell?"

I looked up and saw Caledvwlch standing there, looking unmoved despite the fact that his cheap cop suit was charred, stained, and spattered with blood.

"Yeah?"

"Perhaps we should talk."

It was like emerging from Dante's Inferno. The elves had to help me up out of the hole; the elevators were out of service. They escorted me through the levels of the parking garage, the lower two levels awash with water, courtesy of the sprinkler system. Another two floors up, and we passed fire crews going in the other direction. Another floor, and a trio of uniformed cops met us, but Caledvwlch flashed his badge and we continued on our way.

"Phillips was a traitor to his liege," Caledvwlch told me on the way up.

"No argument here," I said. My voice was hoarse and ragged, and all I wanted to do was to lie down. My eyes burned, and my body felt as if it had aged about thirty years. My clothes smelled of smoke and ozone, and my shoes were covered in blood, causing the soles to stick to the concrete as I walked.

"Our oath was to O'Malley," Caledvwlch continued. "Perhaps that was an error. But we served until he died."

I nodded. "So why—" I shook my head. "I have no objection about what you did. But why intervene for me, and not for Bone Daddy? I presume the situations were similar."

"No," Caledvwlch said. "O'Malley had our fealty. Our duty was to follow him. Anything he required, we had to give. That is the nature of the duty." He looked down on me and said flatly, "Were he alive, and ordered me, you would not still be living."

"Then I guess I'm glad he died."

"As am I," Caledvwlch said. "

"Hey? Isn't that a little traitorous on your part?"

"A traitor is defined by acts, not thoughts. My duty required me to obey O'Malley, not to love him." Caledvwlch looked across at Elf Three, who nodded solemnly. "The killing of the mage was an evil, criminal act, that we were powerless to prevent. Our fealty takes precedence over any other oaths."

"Including an oath to uphold the law," I said. "You went through the standard cop initiation, didn't you?"

"Yes. But our honor places men before abstracts."

"Yeah," I said, "but, as they kept telling us in civics class, this is a nation of laws, not men."

"That may be so," Caledvwlch said. "But I have told you, we are not so easily changed."

"So what happened to you guys after O'Malley died?"

"Mr. Phillips did not understand—"

"Obviously."

"—he assumed that since we belonged to O'Malley, and O'Malley belonged to him, that we became his."

We walked up the ramp to the sounds of sirens and red-and-blue flashing lights. The sky was still black above us. I noticed that a few streetlights were out, and that a patch of lawn on the park to the north of Lakeside, next to City Hall, had turned black and ashlike. In the distance, the permanent clouds swirled over the Portal, and it might have been my imagination, but I thought the clouds had a greenish inner glow to them.

"You obviously didn't."

"Our fealty is an inviolate bond that cannot be severed, and certainly cannot be traded. We must give such loyalty, it cannot be taken. Mr. Phillips' attitude, that we were employees who owed him the same duty that we owed O'Malley, was an insult. The only man who holds such a claim to us now is the man who allowed us our pledge in the first place."

"Mayor Rayburn?"

"The ruler of our adopted land."

I shook my head and looked up at the sky. No stars, too many lights. "Why did you wait until Phillips had a gun on me?"

Caledvwlch was quiet, and I looked down and saw a contemplative look on his face. His pastel skin was alternately rose and aqua under the flashes from the emergency vehicles. "Dare I say that we have learned some things here of law and politics? Assassination is not a viable way to remove your liege's enemies. The act poses more threat than the individual could. But if such a man dies in the commission of a criminal act—deadly force is appropriate in a case where police or civilian life is in immediate danger. No matter who the man is." He looked over at me and might have smiled. "As you said, this is a land of laws, not of men."

A couple of paramedics came over. "Sir, I think we should look at you."

"No, I'm all right." I shook my head—a little too fast, it made me dizzy.

"No, you are not," said Elf Number Three. It wasn't until that point that I realized that he had been supporting me during the walk out of the parking garage. He made his point by ever so slightly lowering his arm from my shoulders. My knees felt my full weight and began to buckle.

The paramedics saw me start to collapse and got on either side of me. Caledvwlch and the nameless elf let them take me. By the time they got me to a gurney, my mind had already spun away, eager to be free of the effort of controlling my body and keeping myself awake.

My last thought was that Caledvwlch might not have the wrong idea about how to deal with this new world we shared.

EPILOGUE

IT was five weeks after I got out of the hospital before I returned to Hunting Valley. It took me that along to get the various facets of my life back in some semblance of order. This not only meant giving depositions to the cops, to the Feds, and writing my own stories for the *Press*—suitably mauled by three layers of editorial oversight—it involved insurance claims on my condo, replacing my entertainment center, and dealing with building management to get a contractor to fix the damage. It also included a week of vacation and a long needed flight to San Francisco, where I got to take my daughter to a concert.

It was mid-September now, fall was starting to nip at the air, and the story of Phillips' little conspiracy had begun fading. The elves did Rayburn a favor in more ways than one by killing him. Not only was Phillips gone—a good thing in and of itself—but the lack of a warm body meant no trial, and less prolonged coverage. It also gave the administration a convenient scapegoat on whom to hang every query the Feds were on to. Phillips was in charge of the Portal, and any unpleasantness associated with the Portal, from prisoner dumping to disappearing homeless people could be blamed on his criminal mismanagement of the department.

Hearings were being held, but with everyone's cards on the table, it was hard for the Council to stick anything on Rayburn. Everything had Phillips' prints on it, and it was evidence of Rayburn's political mastery that he had co-opted the elvish cause. Somehow he had got on the other side of the issue, and there were talks about constructing a reservation out in Lake Erie.

The Feds had lost the rhetorical war once Ysbail held a press conference at City Hall.

Of course, Phillips' position in the administration was still vacant. The Council had to go through all its hearings on the Port Authority before Rayburn could fill the job. The word was that there weren't a hell of a lot of people willing to step anywhere near Phillips' bloody shoes.

However, any good newsman has his sources, and one of my better placed sources gave me a short list of Phillips' possible replacements. At the top of the list of possible candidates was a familiar name.

One of many reasons I decided to pay my old acquaintance a visit once my own life was in order.

It was funny, how the approach to his estate seemed a little less intimidating than it had before. The mansion seemed a little smaller, the Tudor architecture less grand.

I suppose it was the memory of Galweir. Baldassare's realm suffered by comparison.

He was sitting on the patio again, the barbecue off. He stood up as I climbed out of my Volkswagen. His calculated smile and easy manner seemed more obviously artificial to me now. Looking at him, I knew he wasn't the one who had changed.

"Kline, good to see you."

I nodded, but I didn't take his hand. "I wanted to talk to you," I said. "I saw you were on the short list to replace Phillips."

"I shouldn't comment on that." His smile said that he thought otherwise. "I don't even know if I'll take the job."

"Oh, you'll take it."

The smile lost a little of itself. For all his political savvy, I don't think he understood, until that moment, why I had come here. The fact that the smile stayed at all meant he was still too cocksure to care. "Okay, shall we drop the pretense? Why are you here?"

I smiled myself, and shook my head. Baldassare was the only person here engaging in pretense. "I have a story and I wanted to give you a chance to comment."

He looked me up and down, measuring me again. Perhaps he was trying to figure out what it was I wanted.

"You've followed the stories about Aloeus?" I asked.

"Where are you going with this?"

"The public has just about sainted him. A martyr for nonhuman civil rights. With the elves stumping for Rayburn, the Feds are backpedaling so fast that you'd think *they* killed the dragon."

"Dave's always been adept at seizing political capital."

"All of which has made your own political capital rise."

Baldassare shrugged, "I didn't become involved with the elves for political gain—"

I shook my head. "No. That is *exactly* why you became involved."

"There's no call for—"

"Aloeus was no saint leading his people to the promised land, no matter how we'd like to read it that way, or how the pundits would like to spin it that way. Aloeus was a *dragon*. Altruism is a human virtue, a virtue of a society."

Baldassare shook his head. "His actions speak otherwise."

"To whom? My experience with Phillips has taught me that you cannot ascribe human motives and values to an alien creature. But I'm sure you understood Aloeus' motives perfectly."

"Did I?"

"Aloeus wasn't *escaping* Valdis. He wanted to *replace* him."

Baldassare nodded. "Interesting, but I've noticed you haven't printed that."

"Some editorial decisions are out of my hands."

"Come," he gestured toward the river. "Let's walk."

I followed him, waiting for some reaction.

When we had gone a way from the house, Baldassare asked, "Why does this disturb you, then? So Aloeus didn't have pure motives by human standards. He wasn't human. He made a cool decision that he could achieve some advantage, creating a Portal so that the elves could escape persecution. Would you condemn him because he saved the beings he sought to have serve him?"

"You've mistaken me."

"How so?"

"I don't condemn Aloeus," I told him. I turned around and faced him. "I condemn you."

To his credit he didn't seem surprised. "I suppose you have an explanation for this?"

"How did Phillips know?"

"Know what?"

"Know *anything*," I said. "The man was a fanatic. A loose cannon. He was inept and stupid. Seriously prone to overreaction. Aloeus hadn't changed allegiances since the Portal opened. Someone had to have tipped Phillips off that Aloeus was planning a new Portal somewhere." I looked over the river and wondered what it had looked like when Aloeus had flown over this river. I wondered if what had attracted him was the presence of a like-minded individual.

"Are you accusing me?"

"Bone Daddy gave me a message from his Oracle. 'A villain of deeds, a villain of thoughts, and a villain of words.'"

"You aren't expecting me to take this seriously?"

I didn't care if he did.

"Deeds was O'Malley, the one who'd kill me—but Bone called him the least of my opposition. Thoughts, twisted as they were, that was Phillips. The mastermind plotting my undoing."

"And I am words?"

"Fits you like a glove. You're a master of the glad hand, the spin, the rhetorical twist. You can talk someone into knots, and you could certainly give Phillips his share of encouragement. In the words of the Oracle, 'with only a well chosen word he will destroy one man, or empires unborn.'"

"You give me a lot of credit."

"How did Phillips know enough to ambush me?"

"He had mages—"

I shook my head. "No, he didn't use a mage to zero in on me. If he had, he would have been ambushing me at Squire's Castle, or trying to. He couldn't have found me in the 'war room.' The place was designed to be completely impenetrable to any *known* magical force. By definition, if Phillips or his mages had access to any arcane knowledge, they warded the place against it."

Baldassare had stopped smiling.

"He knew. He knew because you briefed him."

"I hope you don't intend to print this." For the first time in my life, I heard a hint of threat creep into Baldassare's voice. At one point that would have intimidated me. Not right now, though.

"It got to you, didn't it?" I asked. "Being so close to the administration, and losing control of the Portal to a dim bulb like Phillips."

"You think I had a dragon murdered over a civil service job?"

"Power." I said. "It is all about power. You joined in with Ysbail and the rest not out of altruism but because Aloeus had become closer to the administration than you were. I suspect you relished the idea that Aloeus' goal would marginalize Phillips as he had marginalized you."

"Then why would I have the dragon killed?"

"Because Aloeus wasn't human," I said. "For all your Machiavellian political manipulations, the dragon was a colder, more manipulative motherfucker than you could ever hope to be. You never even realized that you were the one being used. I suspect that you believed you were to hold some powerful position when

Aloeus opened his new Portal. Maybe the chief liaison between his new kingdom and the rest of the planet. Am I warm?"

Baldassare was silent.

"Was it when the land deal was finalized? Did it start sinking in then? You were dealing with a creature who only understood gratitude and loyalty as tools to influence people."

He shook his head. "You don't understand."

"Don't I? Aloeus had decided, like Rayburn, that he didn't need you anymore. You decided you didn't need him anymore."

"Did you come here expecting some sort of confession?"

"No."

"You're not going to get one."

"I didn't think I would."

"You don't believe you're going to get any of that garbage into print."

I laughed. "I can't substantiate any of this. And I know enough not to push a story that'll be pulled out from under me. I know if you could get my paper to assign me to a story, you can get them to pull one just as easily."

"Why are you here, then?"

"You ever imagine it?"

"What?"

"The last few moments. The plunge to the ground. Your body shredding to ribbons around you—"

Baldassare snorted, shook his head, and turned away, leaving me by the edge of the river. Very cool. I'll give him that.

"You know what the worst part would be?"

He kept walking. Apparently he was tired of our little game.

I yelled after him. "You know the worst part?"

He stopped.

"Seeing it coming," I told his back. "Seeing it coming and not being able to do a damn thing about it."

He turned around very slowly.

"You wanted to know why I'm here?" I said.

He stood there facing me. One of the most powerful men in the city. And I saw a twitch.

I smiled. "You betrayed a powerful group of *very* patient people."

"What do you mean by that?"

"I just wanted to see your face when you realized that." I turned around and started walking to my car.

He was silent until I'd almost made it to my car.

"Powerful . . . patient . . ." Hearing Baldassare trip over a word was worth more than several thousand expressions. "What did you tell them. *What did you tell them?*"

I got into my Volkswagen and slammed the door. He still stood, halfway between his house and the river. He repeated, *"What did you tell them?"*

I lowered the window and called out to him, "Ask them when they catch up with you, in a year or so. Detective Sergeant Maelgwyn Caledvwlch can be quite the conversationalist."

As I drove away, I left the window open so that I could smell the hint of early fall in the wind.

THE DWARVES OF
WHISKEY ISLAND

Dedicated to the citizens of
Cleveland, Ohio

PROLOGUE

WHAT I know—what anyone knows—of Dominic Lloyd Mazurich's last few hours, is pieced together from police and forensic reports, a few witnesses, and public records. It goes something like this . . .

Mazurich holds his last press conference at Cleveland City Hall at about 6:30 in the afternoon. It is in a small meeting room off of Council Chambers that is packed with reporters. The scene of the press conference, as was the City Council session that preceded it, is more hectic than usual. The Supreme Court has just issued a ruling against the city about jurisdiction over the Portal, which happens to be the city's prime—pretty much only—natural resource. The expectation, of course, is that Mazurich will issue some sort of statement about impending federal annexation of northeast Ohio's golden goose.

That is not what is on Mazurich's mind.

Mazurich is a large man in every conceivable dimension. Tall and wide, with an expansive personality. He started as a union organizer, and he retains that blue-collar air. He can stand at the head of a roomful of a thousand people and make everyone feel as if he is one of them. He can give anyone the impression that he is on their side, if he wants to.

He walked out of a shutdown West Side steel plant two decades ago, and walked into City Council with a promise that he would pull his ward out of the economic depression the steel collapse had left it in. In his first three years, he pulled off a minor miracle, halving an unemployment rate that had started at nearly forty percent. By the time the Portal opened, the decommissioned steel plant had been replaced by a high-tech office park—built largely by the local labor force.

When the chaos from the Portal hit, he hooked his star to Mayor

Rayburn, and managed to get the companies in his ward a major slice of the city contracts rebuilding the information infrastructure in Cleveland. When the dust settled, two years later, the unemployment rate in his ward was below the city average for the first time in a quarter century.

When Rayburn won reelection, Mazurich was elected as council president. He's been council president for eight years, and the current consensus is that the only thing that might keep him from serving eight more would be a successful run for the mayor's office.

Mazurich walks in frowning, an uncharacteristic expression. He steps in front of the lectern, facing the room of reporters. For a few moments, the assumption is that his displeasure is due to the Supreme Court ruling. No one in city government is happy about it. The federalization of the Portal represents a loss of jobs, money, and power for the city of Cleveland.

Mazurich clears his throat and pulls a dirty, wrinkled piece of paper out of his pocket. He glances down at it and says, "I only have a short statement, and I'm afraid I will not be taking any questions."

He takes a deep breath and deflates a little. His tie is somewhat askew, a detail picked up by many political cartoonists. Suit and tie have never worn well on Mazurich's large frame.

"Effective 7:30 PM today I have resigned my position on City Council."

There is, perhaps, a second or two of shocked silence. Something rare in the journalistic profession, complete, sincere, and universal surprise. There have been no rumors, no leaks, no hint of anything like this on Lakeside Avenue or off.

"Brenda Carlson will be acting councilwoman in my absence, and I have directed my staff to work with the next council president to effect a smooth transition. I have served my ward for twenty years, and it is my deep regret that I cannot serve them any longer."

Then, of course, the questions. Everyone shouts at once in the vain hope that Mazurich—who'd been, up to his announcement, the second most powerful man in Cleveland—might break and answer a question out of frustration, if nothing else. People ask him if he plans to run for mayor, if he consulted with Mayor Rayburn—or anyone—about his decision, and, of course, everyone wants to know—

Why?

Mazurich stares at them. His expression is odd. He's a career politician, but he looks shocked and slightly afraid, as if the attack of journalists is a surprise to him. He stands at the lectern as if dumbfounded, a state so incongruous that the questions slack off a bit.

To the consternation of his audience, Mazurich doesn't utter a single word more. He turns and exits the room without any further acknowledgment. As the door closes behind him, the sound of shouted questions is replaced by electronic clicks and beeps as the reporters rush to make cell phone calls and e-mails to catch the next edition, and in a few cases, the next broadcast.

Mazurich dismisses all his staff around 6:45 PM. They are all loyal, and have been working for him for over a decade in some cases. The feelings range from betrayal to despair. No one understands what he is doing, and the impact leaves the half dozen city employees shell-shocked and mute. Most of them end up in a bar down the street from City Hall and remain there for the next four hours.

Mazurich's secretary, Pam Lebowitz—who's worked for him the longest, close to eighteen years—doesn't join the others at the bar. At 7:00 pm, she walks into Mazurich's office to see him sitting at his computer. Mazurich looks up at her and closes the briefcase on his desk.

"Why are you doing this?" she asks.

His answer is abrupt and uncharacteristically cold, "I've said all I'm going to say on the subject."

"You owe me, all of us, an explanation."

"Owe you?" Mazurich shakes his head. "*Owe* you? I've given my life to this city. I lost a marriage and two kids. I gave and gave until this thankless job is all I have left. Now I've given *that*. How dare you. Owe? *Owe?*" He slams a large fist down on the desk, and stands up, toppling the precariously balanced briefcase. It tumbles to the floor spilling papers and CDs. "*This city owes me!*"

His dumbfounded secretary looks down at the spilled briefcase and bends over. "I'll get that, sir."

He steps in front of it and says, "You'll get out. I don't want you in here."

"But."

Mazurich's expression softens. "Please, Pam. I can't tell you what you want to hear. It's over. Leave it at that."

"But—"

"Let an old man go home."

Pam knows him well. She senses the pain, which only adds to her own confusion. She's run this man's life for nearly two decades, set up his meetings, his travel plans, rallies large and small. She's been a part of every decision he's made in his public life—except this one.

"Please, Pam. You can't help me anymore."

Something in his voice causes her to back away, a decision she will regret the rest of her life. "Dominic, please, if you need to talk . . ."

He just nods.

"I'm your friend. We all are."

"I know. I just need to be alone now, please."

Pam leaves him as he picks the papers up off of the floor. Behind him, the screen of his workstation is flashing block letters on an otherwise blank screen, "Format Complete."

At some point before 8:30, he drives though his hometown neighborhood, and pulls into the driveway of his two-story frame house. The house belonged to his father, and his grandfather, both steelworkers and union to the core. Twenty years ago, you could have seen the stacks of the steel plant from the front porch.

No lights greet him as he pulls in the driveway. His two children are grown and his wife is separated from him—has been for three years now. The only thing preventing their divorce is the fact that both of them still hold Catholic beliefs.

He sits in the driveway of the empty house for some time. According to a later statement to investigators, a neighbor walks his dog past Mazurich's house and sees him sitting in the darkened vehicle at 8:30, then at 8:45.

A little before 9:00, Mazurich walks into his house. He doesn't turn on any lights, and he doesn't lock the side door behind him. At this point, he knows what he's doing. He walks upstairs, feeling his way in the dark. In the bedroom he sits down on the edge of the bed, by the nightstand. He takes off his shoes and sets them neatly on the floor by the nightstand. He loosens his tie and slips it off over his head, hanging it on the corner of the headboard. He takes his wedding ring off and sets it on the nightstand. He places his wallet next to it.

Then, he opens the drawer to the nightstand and pulls out a thirty-two caliber automatic. He takes out the magazine and removes every bullet except one, setting the ammunition neatly back in the drawer. With one bullet, he replaces the magazine and chambers the round. He places the barrel in his mouth.

Sometime before 10:00 PM, he pulls the trigger.

CHAPTER ONE

"WE must never forget that Cleveland is a *city*."

Gregory Washington stood at a podium at the head of the Lakeside Baptist Church. The rally was deep in his home territory on the East Side—"Energizing the base," as political wonks like myself would say. I sat in a front pew reserved for local press, keying shorthand notes into my PDA with a stylus.

The man oozed charisma, and had the presence of a young James Earl Jones. There was a fair bit of lay preaching in his background and it came out in his speaking voice without devolving into parody.

"Let me say again. Cleveland is a *city*. Homes. Businesses. People. Too long our leaders have bowed down before this 'Portal' which has appeared on our shores. The city's budget has tripled in ten years. Have you seen that money?"

A chorus of "No's."

"Have your schools seen that money?"

"*No.*"

"Is it in the roads? Is it in the fire department?"

"*No.*"

"You know why? Because almost all that money has been fed into the Portal. We've paid lawyers millions of dollars to help us to keep this thing that's costing us tens of millions. Last year, half our city budget—*I said half*—went to expenses related to the Portal. Let the federal government have it."

I made a silent promise to myself that I would be the one political reporter this election who would refrain from using the phrase "paradigm shift" in an article. The rhetoric that Washington was using would have been politically inconceivable two years ago. The Portal, a mystical phenomenon about twelve years old now, had been the raison d'être of city government for a decade. The Portal had granted Cleveland, Ohio, an association with the supernatural so pervasive and widely acknowledged that my hometown's relationship to elves, dragons, and sorcerers was as fundamental as gaming was to Las Vegas, technology was to Silicon Valley, and politics was to Washington D.C.

However, some politically disastrous moves by the administration of the outgoing Mayor Rayburn, followed by a series of new Supreme Court rulings, had cast the relationship of the Portal to city government in a whole new light. The fact was, the Feds now had physical control of the Portal and passage through it, and the world had not ended. The streets of Northeastern Ohio were still awash with mana, mages still brokered their potions, and dragons still flew in the nighttime sky.

Of course, when federalization happened, people started asking the obvious questions; what was the big deal? Why did we waste all that money on lawyers? Even Gabriel Clifton, Mayor Rayburn's spiritual successor and Washington's only real opposition in the race for the Democratic spot in the next mayoral election, did not go to the mat defending the city's stand against federalization.

Even Rayburn himself didn't much talk about it anymore.

The fact was, what marked Cleveland's economic boom wasn't the Portal. It was the supernatural radiation flowing out of it. Immigration had been important, at least at the beginning, but while the novelty of passage to another universe initially commanded prices usually reserved for tickets into suborbital flight, the income from that had been surpassed by income from tourism within two years. It was always the case that more people wanted to visit the circus than there were who wanted to run away and join it.

So even with federal regulation of passage, customs, and a drop in ticket prices that made the cost closer to a one-way flight to Europe than a seat on the space shuttle, the hit to the northeast Ohio economy was practically nil.

Even if the Feds ever shut the door completely, a dozen years of near-unlimited passage from the universe next door had given Northeast Ohio enough local color to last into the next century.

So, despite the protests from the folks who ran the city, in pure economic terms it was pretty much irrelevant who had physical control of the Portal. One councilman had put it this way, "If we gave the Feds immigration control over the Sun, it wouldn't make our streets any darker."

People linked to the current administration were having a lot of trouble explaining how they had been on the wrong side of that argument.

Washington's rival for the Democratic nomination, Gabriel

Clifton, might have the establishment's blessing, and the support of the man who was, at one point, the city's most powerful and popular mayor, but people had been talking about "Rayburn Fatigue" for six months before the current mayor made the announcement that he wasn't going to run for reelection. And there wasn't enough daylight between Gabe Clifton and Dave Rayburn to grow a mushroom.

And, given the state of the Republican Party in Cuyahoga County, that meant that there was a pretty good chance that I was watching the next mayor of the city. Unlike Clifton, Washington had both street cred and the currently enviable position of being a complete outsider. That gave Washington, a relative unknown, a better-than-even chance to win the nomination, and—barring a massive screwup—the election.

"Do we want a city government that gives away millions in tax 'incentives' to corporate cronies? Two billion dollars—I said *billion*—two billion dollars in new construction downtown. Office buildings, hotels, malls. Do you know how much of that pays back the city any property taxes? *Any?* Fifteen million."

There was a chorus of hoots.

"Ninety-nine percent of new construction since the Portal opened has been built under an 'emergency tax-abatement incentive' begun under the previous administration. Don't you think the emergency is over?"

"*Yes.*"

I shook my head. His figures were a little dubious. A hell of a lot of that two billion figure represented construction by the city itself for city facilities, including the containment structure around the old Browns Stadium and the Portal inside. That probably accounted for a quarter of that figure.

Still, he did have a point. A lot of the executive bureaucracy of the city was a patchwork of ad hoc measures and emergency provisions that, when examined as a whole, made little sense. The blanket tax abatement was a case in point. The Portal opening had been an economic disaster in the short term. No one had been thinking about what things would look like a decade hence; the worry was about the social and economic collapse of the city.

But, while the emergency was long since over, it's a fact of politics that it is a lot easier to get a tax abatement passed than it is to get one repealed.

About the time Washington began delving into a comparison between the growth rates between the city budget as a whole, versus the budget for the city schools—along with the same figures for various outlying suburbs that *still* outperformed the city in proficiency achievements and graduation rates—my cell phone started vibrating at me.

I spent a moment assessing the likelihood that Washington might deviate from the speech he distributed to the press, and whether any extemporaneous comments might be newsworthy, before I slid out of the pew and headed toward the back of the church.

When I was back and off to the side, I pulled the phone out, flipped it open, and said, "Kline Maxwell, *Cleveland Press*. Make it quick."

"Mr. Maxwell, I wish to meet with you."

It wasn't a voice I recognized. I glanced up toward Washington. "I'm on assignment at the moment. You can call the main desk at the *Press* and leave me a message."

"Please. I expended much effort to contact you. You, specifically."

The voice had an accent. I couldn't identify it, because my caller was disguising his voice. All I got was the occasional too-hard consonant. Middle Eastern, dwarven, or German, I couldn't tell.

"I'm flattered," I said. "Tell me who you are and what you want to discuss, and we'll see if I can accommodate you."

"I cannot over the phone. My life is in danger."

Not German . . .

"You have to tell me something if you want me to take you seriously. Why should I be interested?"

The crowd in the church broke into a standing ovation. I had to turn to the wall and cover my other ear to hear what my caller was saying.

"What?"

"—Mazurich."

Mazurich?

"What about him?"

"Why did he die, Mr. Maxwell?"

I grunted. "My friend, you are the latest in a long line of conspiracy theorists. I have more letters on who killed Mazurich than you'd ever care to write. I could write a dissertation of the cover-up using theories more creative than you could think up—"

"Mr. Maxwell—"

"You also want to know what I have? Police reports, forensic reports, digital images of the scene. The man killed himself. If there was anything to any of these conspiracy—"

"Mr. Maxwell—"

"I'd be the first to report it—"

"*Mr. Maxwell!*"

I stopped talking for a moment.

"Mr. Maxwell, I am not delusional. I offer you nothing that cannot be substantiated. I am aware that he killed himself."

"What then?"

"*Why* did he kill himself?"

I remained quiet.

"Mr. Maxwell?"

"Okay," I said, "Why did he?"

"Not over the phone. I've talked too long already. Meet me in the Old Arcade, mezzanine level, at 6:30."

"How will I know you?"

"I will know you." The phone clicked. I switched it off, turning around. As I watched Washington basking in the glow of potential constituents, I told myself that the call was a wild-goose chase.

I also knew where I was going to be at 6:30 tonight.

When I left the rally and returned to my Volkswagen, someone had brushed the snow away enough to slip a neon-green flyer under my windshield wiper. I had parked only a block away from the church, so I wasn't particularly surprised when I pulled it free. On the cover was a stylized whirlpool graphic around which swirled the phrase "God's Plan or The Devil's Handiwork?"

The question was rhetorical for anyone who had seen one of these pamphlets before. The whole trifold was a warning how the Portal was a threat to my immortal soul and a gateway to hell itself. The inside showed a crude graphic of Satan lording over it the Cleveland skyline, surrounded by half a dozen quotes from "Leviticus" and "Deuteronomy."

"Give no regard to mediums and familiar spirits; do not seek after them, to be defiled by them: I am the Lord your God."

I looked around at the other cars parked down the street. All had Day-Glo flyers tucked under the wipers. I wondered if the author was independently motivated, or was part of Washington's base. Attitudes might be shifting, but I was pretty sure that the voters in this city were still a few steps away from condemning the Cleveland Growth Association to "the lake that burns with fire and brimstone."

I pocketed the evangelical pamphlet and got into my car.

The drive back to the *Press* offices was a little rougher than usual. In addition to a short flurry of lake-effect snow that unloaded during the rally, an accident on the Shoreway tied up pre-rush hour traffic downtown in both directions. A semi had jackknifed on Dead Man's Curve trying to avoid a griffin. The guy on the traffic report speculated that the griffin had been a brand-new arrival out of the Portal, which was pretty close by, and it didn't know about interstates, and that a semi wasn't a good choice of prey.

While it was true that the griffins that had been here any length of time knew enough to hang out in the Metroparks and thin out the deer population, the idea that the victim of the accident had just popped from the recently federalized Portal implied that the Feds didn't have as tight a lid on things as the Port Authority had had, which was kind of scary.

I passed by the mess, where the cops had traffic downtown narrowed to one lane. Not pretty. The griffin carcass had been removed, but the signs remained. Blood and feathers covered the eastbound lanes like a voodoo ceremony gone horribly awry. Police wreckers were still trying to remove the semi, the front of which was caved in as if it had run into the business end of God's own place kicker.

The driver had probably taken the curve going fifty, and from the looks of things, the ill-fated heraldic beast had been diving in the other direction, from the lake, just on the wrong side of an overpass for the driver to see him in time.

As I inched by the scene, the radio informed me that the driver had lived, and had been life-flighted to Metro Health Medical Center.

Well, I knew what the lead Metro story was probably going to be. The driver's miraculous survival cinched it. The Portal might have killed local television and TV journalism, but the ascendance of blogs and print hadn't changed the dynamics of local news coverage all that much—and the only thing better than a gory accident, was a gory accident with survivors. Gave you someone to interview.

Back at the office, I wrote my piece on Washington's political destiny. I even managed to work in a bit of evangelical politics, a nod to the serendipitous pamphlet. I would probably be the only reporter to give even a passing mention to the born-again vote, given the fact that Cuyahoga County was one of the most aggressively liberal pieces of real estate between Boston and San Francisco, but there's always something to be said for the organization and passion of a vocal minority in the political process.

As I typed, I heard with half an ear people talking about griffins. Someone walked up to my desk and said, "Say, Maxwell, who's the prof at Case, the guy you used on the dragon story?"

I kept typing. "Shafran, Dr. Newman Shafran."

"Thanks."

I muttered something polite, keeping my annoyance in check. I was a political reporter, but one story about a dragon's murder and I was the expert on any supernatural critter that met an untimely end. I had been dealing with this for the past two years.

Even if it had been, arguably, the biggest story to break out of the Portal after the Portal opening itself, I didn't want to be the dragon expert, or the elf expert, or the talking frog expert.

We supposedly had a reporter on the "fuzzy gnome" beat. It was unfortunate for me that the position had a high turnover and the people Columbia Jennings, my boss, tended to pick for the job tended to creep out the other reporters.

"Mr. Maxwell?"

Speak of the devil.

I looked up to see Nina Johannessen standing next to my desk. The current *Cleveland Press* journalist on the supernatural beat. She was a Nordic blonde suitable for a Wagner opera, or a lite beer commercial during the Superbowl. The only disconcerting note were eyes that were nowhere near shallow enough to make the average male comfortable talking to a woman that attractive.

"Please tell me that you don't want to talk about griffins . . ."

She gave me a puzzled look and shook her head. "Why would I?"

"I wouldn't know . . ."

She reached over and picked up the neon-green pamphlet off of my desk. I felt slightly embarrassed when she opened it. Considering the kind of sources she used for her stories, it was sort of like having one of my Jewish coworkers pick up a neo-Nazi tract from my desk.

She stared at the devil picture for a long time and I mentally prepared a long explanation about Washington's candidacy and changing attitudes toward the Portal.

She set the pamphlet devil faceup on my desk. "Has anything strange happened to you lately?"

"No, what?" I was left conversationally disoriented by a question I wasn't expecting. She looked at me deeply enough that I had the uncomfortable sense that she was seeing much more than I was saying. "What do you mean?"

"Unexpected changes or influences? Anything new or threatening?"

I was suddenly looking for sinister influences in every part of my life over the past few days. It took a bit of an effort to rein myself in. As a reporter I was naturally paranoid, but that impulse did quite well enough without outside help.

"Nina, the only thing I can think that might match that description is that question."

"I'm sorry, I didn't mean to disturb you."

"The only thing disturbing me is wondering why you're asking in the first place."

"A vision." She tapped the pamphlet. "It wasn't completely clear, and I thought it might involve you."

"Might? You don't know?"

"Sometimes the Oracle is unclear."

"And how would you know?"

She shrugged. "Have you seen Death or the Devil recently?"

I had the feeling she wasn't kidding.

CHAPTER TWO

I SHOULD have known better.

Hell, I *did* know better. At quarter to seven I was staring up at the vast glass canopy that roofed the Old Arcade and telling myself that I never really expected anything to come from my anonymous caller. I sat back in one of the chairs lining the railing of the first mezzanine level and looked at my little neon-green pamphlet.

The author had certainly gotten his money's worth out of me. Something about it had me thinking about the backlash coming against the Portal. What exactly would happen when the author's point of view became a majority position, or even a plurality?

Federalization might be the least of our worries.

A shadow glimpsed out of the corner of my eye brought me back to the here and now. A very *tall* shadow. I looked up and saw an elf standing by my table. Not just any elf either.

"Maelgwyn Caledvwlch," I said, still butchering the name after two years.

"*Commander* Maelgwyn Caledvwlch," he responded with none of the irritation that a human would lend to the correction. His voice was cultured and much too light for someone eight-and-a-half feet tall. His accent carried a hint of the West Indies, though the magical influence of the Portal would keep him from ever traveling any farther south than the edge of Columbus before the life drained out of him.

When I first met him, under less pleasant circumstances, he was a senior detective in the Special Paranormal Unit. He had since graduated to running the whole SPU, which made him probably the highest ranking nonhuman in the city government.

But his suits were still cheap, and they still didn't fit right.

"What can I do for you?" I asked. I reached over and picked up my coffee, trying to remain casual in front of Caledvwlch. It took an effort. Not just because he was physically intimidating; he ran tall even for an elf, and his eyes were featureless metallic reflections that hid any slight emotion that might pass over his impassive face. What really made me ill at ease was the fact he was a cop, the SPU commander, and in two years he had never once said one word to me that was not part of some official communication.

For one brief moment I thought that he might have been my anonymous caller. But that wasn't Caledvwlch's style, and he certainly would not have any issues contacting me whenever he wanted.

"I wish to ask you some questions in connection with a police investigation." He drew the seat away from the other side of my small table. He folded into the seat without asking my permission. Even seated, I had to look up to see his face.

Reading his expression was hopeless. I took a sip from my coffee and asked, "Am I a suspect, a witness, or a victim?" I told myself not to be too worried. For the past two years my brushes with the law had been largely benign, limited to two speeding tickets, contempt of court for not revealing a source, and one bogus trespassing charge brought by a councilman who felt I shouldn't be spending time watching city employees unload kegs of Miller Lite behind a bar owned by the councilman's brother.

"Witness, Mr. Maxwell. I need to know what you know about a gentleman named Ossian Parthalán."

"The name doesn't ring any bells."

"Perhaps, then, you may recognize his face."

Caledvwlch reached into his breast pocket and pulled out a picture. His long fingers covered it as he slid it facedown across the table.

I looked down at the white glossy back of the picture as his hand withdrew. Fresh inkjet print on cheap paper, still curling a little, as if it had just come out of the printer.

I set down the coffee feeling a little trepidation as I lifted the picture, half expecting what I saw.

Cops, even elven ones, are nothing if not predictable. If Ossian Parthalán had meant anything to me, looking at a picture of his mutilated corpse probably would have provoked some incriminating reaction. I was very aware of Caledvwlch watching me stare at the gruesome crime scene picture.

Someone really did not like Mr. Parthalán. They had cut out his eyes, sliced his mouth open, and chopped off his hands, among other things. The blood was so bad that it took a moment for me to realize that Parthalán wasn't human.

I lowered the picture to the table and said, "Dwarven?"

"Yes."

"I don't know him."

"Look again, please. Mr. Parthalán knows you."

I lifted the picture reluctantly. "Dwarves," in this case, referred to the humanoid race that came over from the other side of the Portal. Dwarves weren't squat humans. Their skin was different, wrinkled, thick, the color and texture of weathered leather. Their skulls were flatter and wider, a thick jaw usually hidden behind a thick beard. There were a whole litany of subtle differences in internal organs and skeletal structure . . .

"Who'd do this to someone?" I whispered.

The body was sprawled on a hardwood floor. Blood had spattered everywhere. The camera looked straight down, framing the body. There were few other details visible. I looked up at Caledvwlch and asked, though I already suspected the answer, "How does he know me?"

"The last time we know Mr. Parthalán contacted anyone while he was alive was one phone call he made at 12:45 PM today."

"And you know who he called?"

"You, Mr. Maxwell. He called your cell phone."

I looked back down at the body. This was the person I had come here to meet. The person who knew why Council President Dominic Lloyd Mazurich put a gun in his mouth and pulled the trigger.

What did you know? What were you going to tell me?

"I got a call," I said.

"What did Mr. Parthalán talk to you about?"

"He wanted to meet with me. He didn't give his name."

"Why did he want to meet with you?"

I looked up at Caledvwlch and felt a little uneasy. I had been dismissive about conspiracies involving Mazurich's suicide, but the dwarf's death lent substantial weight to whatever suspicions he did have.

However, while Caledvwlch was one of the few cops in the city I could say for certain wasn't crooked, that didn't mean I trusted him.

"How did you find him?" I asked. "What happened?"

"The investigation is ongoing."

I slid the photo back across the table. "You know us humans, we tend to have faulty memories."

Caledvwlch shook his head. "I know humans, Mr. Maxwell. I know you. What did Mr. Parthalán discuss with you?"

I sipped my coffee. I have two personality traits that, in most professions, would be self-destructive. The first was a cultivated paranoia that, in my more self-aware moments, I told myself was a natural journalist's instinct not to take people's motivations at face value.

The second was, whenever anyone attempted to pressure me to do anything, I tended to behave in the exact contrary manner.

"You know me," I said. "And I'm under no obligation to continue this conversation with you."

"I cannot detail our investigation—"

"No, but you can give me enough facts about the case to satisfy my curiosity."

Caledvwlch retrieved his photograph and replaced it in his pocket. "There are very few facts. Mr. Parthalán died two hours ago. He was killed in rooms above a tourist bar, the *Nazgûl*, on the West Side of the Flats. Authorities there for an unrelated matter became aware of a disturbance and broke into the room Mr. Parthalán had locked himself inside. He was dead when they found him. In the room was the phone he had used to call you."

"Locked from inside?"

"Yes."

"Was any sort of ritual involved?"

"Dwarves do not use magic," Caledvwlch said. "They cannot manipulate mana, and are largely immune to its effects."

"That's not quite an answer to my question."

Caledvwlch stared at me. "You have not answered mine. Do you wish to, or shall I leave you now?"

Despite my contrary streak, I saw no good reason to obstruct a police investigation. "He said that his life was in danger, and he wanted to talk to me about Mazurich."

Very, very slightly, an eyebrow arched on the elf's face. Given their almost pathological reserve, I counted that as the equivalent to a human expression of stunned disbelief. Nothing altered in the timbre of his voice, so I might have imagined it. "Council President Mazurich?"

I nodded. "One of the hundreds of conspiracy theorists out there. He said he knew something about his death but couldn't talk about it on the phone. That's pretty much it."

Caledvwlch nodded and stood. "Thank you, Mr. Maxwell. I will contact you if we need to discuss this further."

He turned to go, and I asked again, "*Was* there a ritual involved?"

"Perhaps we will talk later," Caledvwlch walked away without looking back at me.

I sipped my coffee.

One of the hundreds of conspiracy theorists . . .

True.

But the only one I knew of who had been murdered.

I drove home thinking of the late Councilman Mazurich, and about dwarves.

Mazurich was union to the core, the kind of traditional working-class Democrat that didn't even have to ask the locals for support. It just sort of happened. So it made sense that dwarves had an interest in him.

Dwarves were labor personified. One of the dwarf clans in Cleveland was responsible for most of the construction that Gregory Washington had been complaining about. The dwarves at the local Ford plant were, to my understanding, the most productive workers on the North American continent. During the exodus of skilled labor in the chaotic years following the Portal's opening, dwarves had slid into dozens of niches in the economy, from plumbing to civil engineering.

And, while a lot of dwarven individuals were part of the Teamsters, or the UAW, and so on, the dwarven clan system was more powerful than any union. You cross a dwarf, you'll not only lose your dwarven employees, but your clients will lose theirs. And their dwarven customers. Down to dwarven contractors abandoning construction sites if the owner was too cozy with someone on their shit list.

I was certain that dwarves would have a political affinity with Mazurich. A lot more so than with the opposite pole of Cleveland politics, Mayor Rayburn.

Rayburn was, according to his critics, autocratic, authoritarian, elitist. . . . A top-down type of politician whose view of the world was more in sync with elves and dragons.

Mazurich, to the same people, was populist, egalitarian, a small "d" democrat . . . a man whose grass-roots politics would certainly be more in tune with the dwarven clans.

I sighed to myself. I was a political reporter, but the politics I reported on were almost universally human. It was inevitable, I suppose, a white journalist in the Deep South during the days of Jim Crow wasn't going to be very good at discerning the internal politics of the civil rights movement. I was in the same position, trying to understand a culture—a series of cultures—I wasn't a part of.

However, when I parked behind my condo, I had enough professional sense to realize that all my speculation up to that point was just that. Speculation. Nonhuman politics happened behind closed doors, out of view of the media.

I stepped out of my Volkswagen, raised my collar against the snow, and walked around my building to the front entrance.

Willie Czestzyk—the doorman for my building who looked at least as old as it was—let me in to my condo.

"Long day, Mr. Maxwell?"

"Longer than some, shorter than others."

"What's the news?" he asked, like always.

"Old politicians never die, they just become the focus of conspiracy theories." I shook my head and walked into the lobby. I didn't like that I was still thinking about the dead dwarf. Ever since my divorce I had made an effort to leave my job at the office—as if I was still trying to fix my marriage.

The sad thing was that I did a pretty good job at it once my marriage wasn't on the line.

So, trying to think happy thoughts about my daughter's coming visit this weekend, I gathered my mail and took the elevator up to my condo. I noticed a new set of charms riveted to the doors as they slid open. Building management must be upgrading security again.

My condo lived on the third floor of a line of buildings built in the nineteen-thirties. Originally intended as apartments for professionals commuting via the brand new light-rail line downtown, it sat just on the suburban side of Shaker Square. My place was one of the lesser residences, some of the suites here ran larger than some good-sized houses, with an inflated mortgage to match.

I had one of the more reasonable condos, four rooms if you counted the bathroom, five if you designated the living/dining room space as two separate areas.

I let myself in and collapsed on the couch that dominated half of the living room area, and scattered my mail on the coffee table. Bills mostly.

I checked my watch and saw that it was still before five on the West Coast. My daughter usually didn't call until after she ate dinner, so I picked up the remote, intent on watching something brainless on my new fifty-inch Panasonic LCD flat-screen. I powered it on and waited while the electronics between it and the satellite dish established a reliable digital connection and filtered enough of an incoming signal through the Portal interference.

While I waited, I saw that one of the envelopes I had brought up wasn't a bill.

I set down the remote and picked up the envelope. It was an odd size, and a little lumpy. My address was written across the front in an elaborate cursive hand. The postmark was local, a post office downtown, dated yesterday. Two fifty-cent Ronald Reagan stamps. No return address.

The television was flashing a "signal error" message at me. I shut it off.

Okay, are we paranoid yet?

Holding the corners of the envelope, I walked to the kitchen with it. I set it down in the basin of the sink and pondered what to do with it.

Unfortunately, I work in a profession that is a lot more likely to receive dangerous things in the mail than most.

I went into the bedroom, grabbed a table lamp, stripped off the shade, and carried it into the kitchen. I plugged it in and turned the thing on.

Then, feeling like an idiot, I grabbed a pair of tongs and picked the letter up by the corner and held it up between me and the incandescent bulb. I stared at it, lit from behind.

The good news: no wires, no electronics. It contained a folded piece of paper with some writing on it in the same hand as the envelope. The lumpy bit was something else, rectangular, about the size of the two stamps on the envelope. There seemed to be some transparency to it. When I tilted the letter, it stayed in the same place, as if it was taped there.

There didn't seem to be signs of anything loose inside the envelope.

I set it down on the counter.

"So?" I asked it. "Are you safe or not?"

The fact was my self-destructive curiosity was getting the better of me. I figured I was safe from most hostile magic, I certainly paid enough for the wards in this building, a nasty enchantment shouldn't have made it through the front doors. Mundanely, there didn't seem to be any surprises inside this letter.

Even so, I got a pair of latex gloves out from under the sink and dug out the sharpest paring knife I could find. With the envelope flat on the table, I very carefully slit open one side of the letter. Then I backed up and spread the opening with the end of my tongs.

Just a folded letter with something taped to it.

Figuring I was safe, I drew the letter out of the envelope. Still wearing the gloves, I opened it and laid it flat on the table.

What the hell?

The letter was a single line long:

"This is why he killed himself."

Somehow, I had a pretty good idea who "he" was.

The object taped to the letter was a small ziplock bag that contained a few grams of some granular white substance. I looked at it and shook my head.

"What were you into, Mazurich?"

CHAPTER THREE

THE letter stayed on the counter, slipped back into its envelope, and the envelope, in turn, isolated in the biggest ziplock bag I could find. I figured that there was a good chance it was evidence of something, and I didn't want too much contamination from myself or from my apartment on the thing.

Not that I was about to turn it over to the cops.

Not yet, anyway.

What I did do was grab a beer from the fridge and settle down in front of my TV. I turned it on and it was still having signal difficulties.

"Damn it."

One would think that with a dozen years working on the signal problems in this city, they could come up with a reliable television. I had paid almost double the national standard to get a TV and satellite hookup that had the custom electronics to work within the Portal's influence—and the damn thing couldn't lock on a signal.

I leaned back and sighed.

I couldn't bitch too much. The Portal's influence on data transmission was why I had a job in the first place. The interference, the inability to transmit or receive video without special equipment, was why there were no local broadcast or cable TV stations around the Portal. That meant no local TV news. That meant the revival of print journalism to the tune of five local dailies in the Greater Cleveland area along with hundreds of regional weeklies.

TV in northeast Ohio was an elitist luxury.

It was still annoying.

I shut it off again and walked over to the windows. I looked out at the purple sky where a swollen yellow moon competed with the streetlight glare off of Shaker Square. Signal blackouts usually happened because of weather conditions, storms, thick cloud cover . . .

The sky was perfectly clear.

The phone rang.

I walked over and picked up the phone, "Maxwell."

"Dad?"

"Hey there," I said, staring up into the cloudless night sky. I effortlessly forgot Mazurich, dwarves, and political conspiracies as I slid into Father mode. Something I've gotten a lot better at in the years since me and Margaret split. "All ready for this weekend?"

"More than ready." I could pick up the exasperation in her voice all the way from California.

"What's the matter?"

"Nothing."

"What particular nothing is it this time?"

"Oh, you know, Mom."

She wasn't a little girl any more, but I could hear the child-like frustration in her voice—probably half calculated to catch my sympathy. A long veteran of long-distance parenting, I asked, "So, why are you upset with your mother?"

"She can't stop it with telling me what to do. I'm seventeen, Dad. I'm not a kid who needs to be told how to cross the street."

"She just worries about you."

"She's acting like I'm going into a war zone. Like goblins are going to eat me or something."

I hoped my sigh wasn't audible. When the Portal opened up, the whole area was thrown into chaos for a good eighteen months. Everything from power outages and the failure of most of the electronic infrastructure of the city, to a federal blockade and a small invasion by magical critters of every description. It was the story of my career, and I didn't have the good sense to listen to my wife's concerns about living in the epicenter of all this. I've never been able to blame her for that, which is one of the reasons that up until now every family visit I've had involved me buying the ticket.

This time around, though, Sarah had insisted on visiting *me*. She wanted to see the town where she had been born.

This, of course, drove her mother nuts.

"Sarah, your mother has very bad memories of this place. Try to understand where she's coming from."

"She's being irrational. She wants me to lock myself in your condo until I take my return flight."

"I'm sure you're exaggerating."

"You think so? I said I wanted to see the Portal, and she went nuts. She almost tore up my boarding pass . . ."

"Sarah, there's no reason to bait your mother like that."

"I have a right to see you, Dad—"

"Correction. *I* have a right to see *you*. You have a right to do whatever your parents tell you."

"Dad."

"Don't 'Dad' me. Just because your mother has buttons doesn't mean you have to push them. Just be happy she's letting you come here for once."

"Okay, but you don't have to live with her."

At this point, that was probably a good thing.

"Anyway, I got a surprise for you, Dad."

"Oh, what?"

"Hey, that would be telling."

The paternal instinct kicked in. "Is this a surprise I'm going to like?"

"Uh-huh . . ."

"Why do you sound uncertain about that?"

"It's just . . . I haven't told Mom yet."

Okay, now I was really worried. "Tell me."

"I wanted to tell you in person—"

"Honey, unless you want me to have nightmares about you eloping with a biker with a ring through his nose, tell me what it is."

"Ick. Okay, if you promise not to tell Mom."

"Sarah, you know I—"

"I'm going to tell her, I just need to let her calm down first."

"What is it?"

"I got an acceptance letter from one of my college applications."

"Hey, that is good news. Congratulations!" As I said it I began to realize that there was more going on here.

"What aren't you telling me?"

She sucked in a breath and said, "It was my application to Kent State."

"You applied to Kent?"

"And Oberlin."

"Uh-huh?"

"And Antioch, and Case Western . . ." She rattled off a list of a half dozen other schools.

"Is there a university in Northeast Ohio you didn't apply to?"

"Cleveland State."

I placed my hand on my forehead. "Did Margaret let you send out those applications?"

"Uh, no."

"Did she know you applied to these places?"

Silence.

"Honey, you aren't eighteen, wasn't a parent supposed to sign your applications?"

"She did . . . sort of."

"You didn't forge your mother's signature, did you?"

"Not really."

"Sarah!"

"I filled out a stack of twenty or thirty, Dad. I just slipped a few more in when she was signing them for me. Can I help it if she wasn't reading closely?"

I tried to stifle a laugh.

"Dad?"

I gritted my teeth and said, "You have until this weekend to come clean with your mother."

"You're angry with me?"

"I will be if you continue this feud with your mom. Think of who's going to be paying for half of this education. She has a right to be part of that decision."

"You know how she feels—"

"And you're making assumptions. If you don't want me talking to your mom, do it yourself. She might surprise you."

"I doubt it."

"Perhaps, but you're a year away from having the right to make those decisions unilaterally." I walked away from the window, holding the phone.

"Okay, I will."

"Promise?"

"Yeah, I—"

"Honey?"

"—ble hearing you, Dad." Her voice was small and weak. I could hear the distance in it now.

"I think we're losing the connection."

"—is weekend—ve you, Dad."

"I love you, too."

A rattle, a hiss, and a shaking dial tone. I turned off the wireless and tossed it on the couch.

"Kent State?" I muttered to myself, smiling. I was going to catch hell from Margaret about this one. She would think I put our daughter up to it. And, knowing my daughter, I doubted that there was anything Margaret would be able to do to keep her from moving up here.

There were God knows how many parents of God knows how many teenagers living perfectly normal lives here. More all the time.

However, despite all the times I had told my ex that things were okay up here, now that the possibility was staring me in the face, I wasn't sure how I felt about it.

CHAPTER FOUR

As soon as I hit the office, I spread the competition across my desk. The *Herald,* the *Leader,* and the *Plain Dealer,* all had at least some ink devoted to the late Mr. Ossian Parthalán. The *Plain Dealer* had little more than a police blotter, but the other two pretty much confirmed what Commander Maelgwyn Caledvwlch had told me.

At Club *Nazgûl,* at about six-thirty yesterday, they found the corpse of our dwarf. The one detail I picked up from the stories that Caledvwlch hadn't volunteered was the fact that the "authorities" who broke in on our decedent were FBI agents, not local cops.

Of course, the glaring omission in every story was what Federal agents were doing there in the first place. After plumbing the record, such as it was, I decided to check the *Press'* own resource.

Reggie Sommers had been a veteran of the crime beat longer than I'd been paying attention to politics, much less covering it. He'd been a rookie back in the Danny Greene era and probably had the numbers of more mob guys in his head than were in the Youngstown phone book.

He looked like the guys he covered; squat, beefy, snow-white hair, with a cigar—always unlit in the nonsmoking building—clamped in his mouth.

He looked up as I stopped in front of his desk. "Hey, Maxwell, what brings you to my side of the tracks? Another kickback story?"

"No." I pulled up a chair. "Murder, actually."

Reggie arched an eyebrow and took the unlit cigar out of his mouth. "A little off your beat, isn't it? They didn't find another dragon, did they?"

They're probably going to carve that story on my tombstone.

I shook my head.

"Thank God for that."

"No," I said, "this was a source. Well, he might have been a source. . . . Someone killed him before we met."

"That sucks."

"I want to know if you heard anything. I got a feeling that the FBI might have had my guy under surveillance."

"This guy wouldn't have just turned up dead in a Goth nightclub, would he?"

"Ossian Parthalán."

"Holy crap. I knew I had a bad feeling about that one."

"What do you mean?"

"The guys I usually talk to, they might hire mages here and there, but they have a good Catholic fear of the kind of voodoo that flies out of the Portal. The nasty stuff, they don't want to touch."

"A ritual killing, you think?"

Reggie laughed, "You see any crime scene pictures? Kind of thing that can make a forensic mage lose his lunch. This was a dwarf thing, and the dwarves in this town are up to their little skulls in the nasty stuff."

"I thought dwarves weren't involved in magic."

"Well, I can't count the stories of guys who crossed the wrong dwarf and ended up like your friend Parthalán. Guys a century removed from the old country will give you the evil eye if you mention dwarven business."

"So no one's talking about Parthalán?"

"I didn't say that."

"So what have you heard?"

Reggie leaned forward and lowered his voice. "Now, I didn't hear this from who I heard it from, and you didn't hear it from anyone. The wise-guy gossip is that your dwarf had left the reservation. He was selling out someone, and this was payback."

"Who?"

Reggie shrugged. "Someone involved with the clans, and big in the dark side of things."

"Things a good Catholic mobster doesn't mess with?"

"You got it." Reggie looked at me with a little concern. "And, frankly, if he was talking to you, I'd watch your back."

I grunted a "Thanks," and changed the subject. "So you have any idea what the FBI was doing there?"

"I haven't got a clear answer from anyone, but there are rumors about some sort of dwarven smuggling operation." I thought of the little plastic bag of white crystals. "My guess is they were tailing the dwarf, and considering how he was cut up, probably a good chance that he was about to become an informant, if he hadn't already."

I nodded.

"So want to tell me what he was a source on?"

After a long conversation with Reggie, I slipped out to have lunch with one of the few good, reliable contacts I had on the investigative side of law enforcement.

Like any good reporter, I cultivated cops for sources. But I'm a political reporter, and that skews the people I cultivate. All the cops I dealt with were either in the city administration or in the union hierarchy. Basically old guys with a lot socked away for their pension and within spitting distance of retirement. Folks whose secure position made them reluctant to openly criticize anything, but, ironically, made them more likely to be my unnamed source. The guys I usually talked to weren't going to be the first ones—or the last ones—at a crime scene.

However, there was one guy I knew who was still actively involved in criminal investigation more than politics. The guy wasn't even a cop. His name was Dr. Russell Kawata, and he was a forensic pathologist. I'd met him over a liquor store shooting a few years ago. It wasn't something I normally get involved with, but it was a high profile case with some racial overtones—which meant that someone decided to make political hay out of what happened. Speeches, public trial, all very ugly. Kawata had been offended at the way some public figures were misstating the facts of the case, and fed me details on what *really* happened.

It wasn't often that a political reporter needed the help of a forensic pathologist, and it had been over a year since I talked to him about a story, but, thankfully, he was free for lunch at a small deli downtown. He was waiting for me when I walked in.

"Maxwell, how're you doing?"

"Good. Thanks for meeting on such short notice."

He held out a beefy hand and I shook it.

Kawata was dark and round, with black hair and Asiatic features. He spoke with an accent unfamiliar to most Midwesterners. He told me once that about half the people he met thought he was Indian or Pakistani, the other half thought he was some weird Puerto Rican half-breed. He actually was a full-blooded native Hawaiian. I never asked why he came to Cleveland, but I suspect it had something to do with the Portal.

"No problem, Maxwell. I was thinking of you the other day. I saw the story about the bar."

I nodded. "I was hoping that you could do me a favor."

"What?"

I pulled out my letter, contained in its Ziplock bag. I placed it on the table. "You do drug tests when you do an autopsy, right?"

"Yes?"

"So if I asked you to, you could identify what's in this envelope?"

"If there's enough for a spectral analysis." He picked up the bag. "We just got a new toy. They finally bought us a mass spectrometer that gives accurate readings."

"There was a problem with the old one?"

"I never told you? Same problem every TV had. Analog signal. Up to now we had to ship tests to an out-of-state lab, or take about twenty-five readings on one sample and average out the noise. Got a brand-new machine now, though, does all that for us."

"Glad to hear it."

"Only took a decade . . ." Kawata held up the bag and looked at it. "Addressed to you?"

"Someone sent me a present."

Kawata nodded. "You know, all I'm competent to do is a chemical analysis. If you want anything more thorough—handwriting, fingerprinting . . ."

"I have a good idea who sent it."

"Okay."

"But you should probably treat it like crime scene evidence, just in case."

He lowered the envelope. "Is it?"

"I don't know yet."

When I got back to the office, I tried to research what I could about Ossian Parthalán. Mazurich aside, Ossian Parthalán's life and death already counted as a minor news story even if he was just a dwarven conspiracy buff blowing smoke out his ass.

I sat at my desk, running searches through my computer through periodical databases at the *Press*, at the local library, and at two subscription services, as well as the basic Internet search engines.

The pickings were slim. In two hours of searching, I only had three solid hits, and only one of them directly concerned the dwarf in question.

The direct hit was a minor story from about three years ago

about a legal battle between my Mr. Parthalán and State Farm insurance. It seems that Ossian Parthalán made a trade out of auto bodywork. He worked out of a small garage on the near West Side called *Thor's Hammer.* State Farm wasn't compensating my dwarf for work he did because, apparently, he did too good a job. State Farm thought the claims were fraudulent. Their adjusters were convinced that, based on the damage done to the cars involved, they wouldn't be salvageable.

Mr. Parthalán won that case.

The first indirect hit was from almost ten years ago. It was someone's attempt to do a story about dwarven politics. My caveat about reporters on the outside looking in applied here in spades. The article was mostly a description of some sort of dwarven council meeting that was held in the Tower City Hilton, the mechanics of which the reporter obviously wasn't privy to. The whole story amounted to little more than saying: "the dwarves here have a clan-based system that has something to do with blood relation, and after a lot of raucous infighting, one of these clans is dominant."

The picture accompanying the story showed a half dozen dwarves yelling and pointing at each other around a circular meeting table. By the caption, third from the left was my guy, Ossian Parthalán.

So my guy was active in dwarven politics at one point. I wondered at what point that interest carried over into Cleveland City Council.

The second indirect hit was from one of my Internet searches, and at first look the Web page seemed to have nothing to do with my dwarf at all:

The Dwarven Armorer:
Highest quality arms and armor. Serving the Midrealm for ten years. If your marshal doesn't pass it, we'll take it back!
　　Specializing in:
- Full Plate
- Chain Mail
- Functional Historic Reproductions

Gauntlets to Gorgets and everything in between. Reasonable prices, financing, Master Card and Visa accepted. Prop. Sir Thorndyke of Dover (mundanely Teaghue Parthalán)

It was located at another West Side address. I would have passed it off as simply a coincidence of names, but the address was only a block or two from the *Thor's Hammer* body shop, and—when you think about it—there is some similarity between making plate mail and doing auto bodywork.

At least there seems to be, to a reporter looking for leads and who knows nothing about either.

There is some truth to the argument that once you cross the Cuyahoga River you are entering a different city. When Kipling wrote, "West is West and East is East," he could have very well been talking about my hometown. A lot of people simplify the thing by pointing out the racial fault lines. It's easy to do, since Cleveland is—even post-Portal—one of the most segregated communities north of the Mason-Dixon line. But the differences go a lot deeper than that.

The histories of the two halves of Cleveland over the past hundred years have been radically different. The East Side had the race riots in the '60s, while the West Side had its working class communities plowed under and split in half by interstate construction. Almost every museum was built east of the river, every factory built on the west. The East Side has Case Western and University Circle. The West Side has the airport. Hispanic people drift west. Middle Eastern people drift east. Rayburn was a solidly West Side mayor, and Gregory Washington was firmly East Side.

On the East Side we've got elves.

The West Side got the dwarves.

I was thinking of the Portal's contribution to the yin-yang nature of this city as I left the Shoreway and started looking for *The Dwarven Armorer.*

It was hard to miss.

If the heraldic banners flapping in front of the doorway didn't give it away, the suit of plate mail standing in front of the shop was a dead giveaway. I found a parking spot across the street and looked at the building. It wasn't a regular storefront. The building was a low red-brick structure with large garage doors set in the side. A small lot on one end was surrounded by chain-link. The snow-covered lot was piled high with scrap metal of every description—old plumbing, wheel rims, twisted rebar still dangling fragments of concrete, and the occasional engine block.

We were obviously zoned for light industrial here, and I wondered what the building used to produce. I suspected that it was a machine shop of one sort or another, which probably closed up when this town's last steel mill shut down for good, about twenty years ago.

I got out and walked to the door and its metallic guardsman.

I was impressed. I've seen the medieval armor displayed at the art museum here, the best collection in this half of the world, and you could place this guy's work right up there with it. All it lacked was the patina of age.

Teaghue Parthalán also did something a bit unusual. Every suit of armor I'd ever seen had been in a static upright display. This one was mounted on some sort of articulated skeleton that allowed it to be posed in the midst of delivering a blow to an unseen attacker. It helped show off the mail underneath and the way the joints moved.

Apparently, you had a much wider range of motion in one of those things than you'd expect.

I slipped under the broadsword and pushed through the door into the shop.

If the showroom was any indication, business was pretty good. There were glass-fronted display cabinets on every wall, and a couple taking up floor space in the center of the showroom. While there were a couple of full suits on display, most of the space was devoted to individual pieces. Helmets, gauntlets, shields, swords, breastplates, and innumerable other metal parts whose names escaped me.

I was busy studying an intricately engraved broadsword with an eight hundred dollar price tag when Mr. Parthalán emerged from one of the rooms in back. He announced himself in a gruff voice, "Is your interest display or function, good sir?"

I tapped on the glass in front of the broadsword. "What would you consider this?"

"Display, my lord." He chuckled. "That pretty little number is meant for a wall, or for fancy dress."

"I see."

He seemed to measure me up. "What is it you're looking for?"

"A story." I turned around and held out my hand. "My name's Kline Maxwell, *Cleveland Press*."

He cocked an eyebrow and took my hand. It felt as if I were shaking hands with a cinder block. "Ahh, you didn't look like any Cleftlander I know."

"Cleftlander?"

"Barony of the Cleftlands, the local chapter of the Society for Creative Anachronism. Are you familiar with it?"

"Somewhat. I had a friend in college who would go out every Wednesday with a bunch of people who'd beat each other with sticks. I didn't think it was this sophisticated, though."

"Well, it's a little more than that. The S.C.A. recreates all aspects of the Middle Ages: arts, sciences, as well as combat. It happens to be that armory is my own particular specialty."

"If I recall, my friend's armor was mostly blue plastic and duct tape."

The dwarf laughed. "I doubt any marshal would pass that nowadays, even before the Portal opened. There are strict safety rules."

I shook my head. "So how did someone from the other side of the Portal become involved in the S.C.A.?"

Teaghue shrugged. "Many of us had to change specialties, I preferred to find out what market existed for what I had always done."

"You seem to have done well."

"Why would anyone engage in labor to do poorly?"

"Your workmanship is incredible, but I was referring to your business."

"As was I, good sir."

I looked down at him and saw him smiling. He obviously enjoyed talking about what he did, a trait that will endear you to any journalist. I tried to see any familial resemblance to the late Ossian, but I wasn't familiar enough with dwarven appearance in general. The kinky brown hair and beard, flat nose, and brown face were similar, but were also similar to just about every dwarf I had ever seen.

"A story, you say?" he asked. "On the S.C.A., my lord?"

"No. I am looking for background on a person named Ossian Parthalán."

I paused for a moment. I had no idea if Teaghue was a close relation to the dead Ossian or not.

"Go on." No overt reaction to Ossian's name, but I had the feeling that he knew Ossian. The way his humor seemed to fade, I suspected that he knew Ossian's fate.

"I cover city politics," I told him. "And I am looking for connections between him and the late Councilman Mazurich."

"Sad end, that," Teaghue said. He could have been referring to Ossian or Mazurich. "The councilman was a friend to me and mine. There was a feast when he died." He looked up at me. "You don't do poetry, do you?"

"No."

"Pity, a soul like Mazurich should have an epic written to him."

"Ossian thought highly of him, then?"

"Ossian Parthalán is not of any clan of mine and I shall not speak for him."

"But the councilman is well thought of in the dwarven community?"

"It was his work that found us homes, and labor worth pursuing. Without him, those of us that came from the Portal would be as rootless as the elves." Teaghue glanced away as if he was seeing something else. "Without him there would be no halls under Erie."

The "halls" he spoke of were the remnants of another industry collapse caused by the Portal's opening. The salt mines under Lake Erie, particularly those around the spit of land called Whiskey Island closest to the Portal, suffered some severe issues with "mana" that resulted in about a dozen deaths before the operation was shut down.

The dwarves ended up resident in those mines, apparently immune to the magical influence that tended to drive anyone else mad. I'd personally never paid much attention to the details of how that happened. At the time there was a federal blockade of the city, an economic meltdown, and a thousand other crises.

"He participated in the dwarven settlement in the mines?"

"He initiated it." Teaghue looked up at me with a suspicious expression. "You ask about dwarves and you do not know this?"

"Just trying to get your perspective," I lied. The fact was, I tried to avoid inhuman interest stuff that simply existed to announce, "See, it's magic here! See? We're special." It's a strange bias to have in this city, I admit, but I've always been more interested in the political ramifications of the Portal than its material manifestations. Usually, considering my seniority at the *Press,* and my particular beat, it wasn't an issue.

Usually.

Still it does tend to be a bit of a blind spot.

"I see," Teaghue said. I could feel the guy closing up.

"Can you tell me anything about Ossian's relationship with the councilman?"

"Ossian is nothing to me or mine. For the Councilman, he was a good man, ill-used."

"How so?"

"That is my perspective, Mr. Maxwell. Should you ever be interested in the purchase of quality arms or armor, feel free to return. Right now I have work to attend to."

Teaghue ended my interview by walking into the back of the shop, leaving me alone in the showroom.

A good man, ill-used.

I couldn't help but think, *Used by whom?*

CHAPTER FIVE

OF course, since *The Dwarven Armorer* was only two blocks away from Ossian's body shop, I swung my Volkswagen around to take a look at the place where the late Ossian Parthalán made his living.

Thor's Hammer wasn't much to look at. A brick garage with a rolling metal door, an asphalt lot with half a dozen cars in varying states of destruction, a high chain-link fence topped with razor wire. Only one of the cars gave a hint at what Ossian was capable of, a '68 Mustang that, from the back, was a mint cherry-red muscle car, and from the front was a rusted-out hulk. It was obviously a restoration job, not a wreck. The front of the car was jacked on its rims, the hood was gone, and the engine compartment was empty. The contrast between front and back made me wonder if dwarves actually were capable of magic.

I got out of my car and looked around, and I wasn't surprised to see the yellow police stickers sealing the garage door. It was the standard warning about a sealed investigation scene, along with a complex glyph that you did not want to break, unless you were into pain and felony convictions.

I had sort of been hoping to find a cop or two on the scene that I could talk to. No such luck.

I walked over to the side door opposite the chain-link and the lot, and stopped.

Someone *was* here.

Not cops.

The seal on the door had been torn open, along with most of the doorframe. The warning tag still smoldered with the aftereffects of the torn rune. The discharge should have dropped anyone opening the door.

However, judging from the splintered state of the door, whoever had smashed it was probably well past being affected by such nuisance enchantments.

I heard movement inside the building, and I flattened myself against the wall. Not being the action-hero type myself, I pulled out my cell phone and dialed 911.

"911. What is the nature of your emergency?"

"I'm at *Thor's Hammer* an autobody shop by West 50th and Detroit," I whispered into the phone. "There's been a break-in."

"Sir? I have tro . . . king you out."

I spoke a little louder, "Detroit and West 50th, break-in at *Thor's Hammer.*"

". . . t and Wes . . . at right?"

Christ, of all the times to get funky reception.

"Detroit and West 50th!"

". . ."

Nothing.

But the motion inside the body shop had stopped.

I decided that was not a good sign. I turned and ran back toward my car. Halfway there, a large panel of frosted glass windows exploded beside me. It happened suddenly, and about all I could do was throw my arms up to cover my face from the flying glass.

So I didn't see what yanked me inside.

I sailed in through the window, and slammed facedown into the hood of a Lincoln Town Car parked inside the garage. I felt the impact in every joint, as if every bone in my body had snapped in half. Even my teeth hurt. I rolled over and groaned, sliding down the slope of the hood. I couldn't even manage to get my arms up in front of me to defend myself.

Lucky me, I didn't need to. While I lay there, stunned, my assailant retreated out the window. I didn't get a good look at it, backlit by sun outside. However, what I did see made me think I didn't really want to get a good look.

Despite what the Cleveland Growth Association has to say about it, the born-again authors of my green evangelical pamphlet had a point. A lot of *nasty* things came out of the Portal. It's not all fairies and elves and unicorns. The thing that cleaned my clock would not make it into any convention brochures.

The face was a human skull covered by red glistening flesh, held in place by metal wires. It wore a trench coat that covered most of its body, and the fabric was spotted with stains from fluid that oozed from its exposed flesh.

When its hand gripped the edge of the window frame, I could see the tendons move, and the glint of metal.

Then the thing was gone.

I lay there until the sirens came.

Commander Maelgwyn Caledvwlch was, predictably, not pleased with me.

He walked up to me as a paramedic was giving me the once-over. Caledvwlch stood by the ambulance, watching as the medic waved some charms around my head and neck. The medic shook his head and said, "You'll be fine."

I rubbed my neck. "You're sure?" I still hurt all over.

"If you want me to, I can take you the Emergency Room."

I stood up and shook my head. "No, if you think I'm fine."

"Take some Advil."

"Mr. Maxwell," Caledvwlch announced himself as I stepped away from the ambulance.

"Commander Caledvwlch."

"How is it we find you assaulted in the late Ossian Parthalán's place of business?"

"I'm working on a story." I brushed some of the dirt off my clothes. "You should know, you showed me the picture."

"What did you expect to find here?"

"To be honest? Some cops who would be more forthcoming about Mr. Parthalán's death than you are." I looked into *Thor's Hammer*. It was easy now the window was gone, the view only obstructed by some yellow rune-stamped police tape draping the entrance.

My friend the zombie had been busy. He'd gutted the place. Filing cabinets had been torn open, the contents scattered everywhere. Tools, fragments of computer hardware, and broken office furniture littered the garage floor. A safe lay on its back next to the Lincoln, the door missing.

That made me rub my neck.

The Lincoln itself had been torn apart by this thing. The seats had been pulled out and shredded, the doors and fenders ripped off, bumpers on the ground.

Amidst the chaos, two things struck me:

First, the car had out-of-state plates, *California* plates. Not terribly common, even in the tourist-trap areas downtown.

Second was the number of people going over the crime scene.

Three carloads of forensic investigators was overkill for a B&E, even one by something like zombie-boy.

They seemed to pay particular attention to the fenders on the Lincoln.

"What was zombie-boy looking for?"

"I would make a suggestion, Mr. Maxwell."

"What?"

"That you leave this particular investigation to those with the expertise to undergo it."

I backed up a bit as Caledvwlch made a pass with his hand and folded his tall angular frame under the police tape. I called after him, not really expecting an answer, "Can you tell me why this investigation rates the personal attention of the SPU commander?"

Caledvwlch ignored me.

They had my statement, so there was nothing to keep me here. I did, however, slip out my phone and take a few discreet shots of the inside of *Thor's Hammer.*

Camera phones are a wonderful invention.

I revised my opinion of my phone when I'd driven to the Flats and had parked long enough to look at what I shot.

My phone was an expensive Cleveland model. That meant that it had some very hefty software that—in theory—could filter and do error correction to limit interference from the Portal's magical influence. Using a film camera anywhere around here would give you a picture, but the picture would be something out of Timothy Leary's id. Same thing with most pre-Portal electronics. Signals into any device—cameras, tape recorders, television, Xerox machines, cell phones, computers—tended to pick up hitchhikers generated by the mana around the Portal.

Of course, after over a decade of dealing with it, most of the problems have been worked out. If you duplicate a signal enough times, you can filter out a real image. It's just a matter of storage, bandwidth, and money.

And I had paid a lot for this phone.

For all the good it did.

The pictures were garbage. Demonic faces drooling at the camera, snakes coiling around twisted machinery, murky landscapes that looked as if David Lynch did underwater filming of the Cinderella castle at Disneyland. In one or two shots, I could make out parts of the Lincoln. That was it.

"Fuck it."

Just to check, I took a shot out the windshield.

Perfect. Murphy's law, I guess.

I was parked in a lot near the Club *Nazgûl,* trying to get a feel for the place before I stepped inside. Caledvwlch had called it a tourist club, but there are tourists, and there are *tourists.*

The building had been a warehouse in a prior life. Now it had been painted completely black. The only detail in the exterior came from subtle patterns done in glossy black, over the matte-black exterior. They looked like wards of some sort, which I suspect they were, since the city inspectors wouldn't let you inscribe anything really dangerous in a public place.

But looking at the outside gave me a good idea of the clientele they were trying to attract. My guess was the tourists who frequented this place probably came to this city alone looking to find some patron of the "dark arts." This place, I suspected, helped connect those wayward souls with mages who were more than happy to fulfill someone's faux-satanic heavy-metal fantasies.

Also gave the evangelicals a reason to reread "Leviticus."

The mages that cruised clubs like this weren't really black sorcerers, at least as far as city ordinances on necromancy, curses, and dangerous incantations went. Usually they were only a step up the food chain from the teenagers they conned. They didn't want to buy your soul. Just your body for a few nights—and if you had any drugs or cash, that would be nice, too. I reached the door, embossed in screaming black skulls, and thought of my daughter.

Maybe her mother is right . . .

I had the brief Dad argument with myself, one side saying how I really should give Sarah a lot more credit, the other thinking about all the kids that were given too much credit by their folks.

Is it different than anywhere else? There're predators everywhere. She'll be in more danger during spring break in Florida—

Maybe I should just lock her up when she gets here.

I grabbed a skull, pulled the door open, and walked inside.

The decor wasn't particularly innovative. Call it early Inquisition, though they one-upped Torquemada by putting in a dance floor. While my eyes adjusted to the gloom, someone in the back yelled at me, "Hey, we're closed today."

I blinked until I could identify the speaker. It took a moment because, until he moved, I thought he was a prop. The guy had a shaved head, a sleeveless black T-shirt, and a combination of tattoos and obnoxious piercings that would severely limit his career options.

"Hello, Kline Maxwell, *Cleveland Press.*"

The guy walked toward me, carrying a mop. "You a reporter?"

Add "not particularly bright" to my list of first impressions. "I understand you had some problems here last night."

"Fucking-A."

I'll take that as a yes. "Would you mind talking about it?"

"You going to put me in the paper?"

"You'll only be a named source if you want to be."

"That's cool." He set down the mop and held out his hand. "I'm Christian."

This kid got first place in line when they were handing out irony. I shook his hand. "Pleased to meet you."

"You're here about the dwarf, aren't you?"

"What's the story there?"

"Wish I knew. It's all fucked up." He pointed back toward a row of caskets on the other side of the dance floor. "I was working the bar. We'd just opened up at four. And this dwarf dude comes in and pays for one of the private party rooms upstairs." Christian pointed up into the vast loft space at a line of windows overlooking the dance floor. If the lighting were in full party mode, the rooms up there wouldn't be visible.

"Did you know him?"

"The dwarf? No, never talked to him and he wasn't a regular."

"You get a lot of dwarves?"

"A few, the little motherfuckers can get tanked . . ." Christian shook his head. "Anyway, this guy gets his room—"

"Alone?"

"Yeah, that's the weird bit. Those rooms are to party, you know? Hard to party alone."

But they'd be a good place to meet someone. Private, but in a public place. I wondered why the dwarf in question didn't ask me to meet him here.

Considering his fate, it was probably a good thing he didn't.

"What happened?"

"Place was just filling up at six, 6:30, then we start hearing the dude screaming. I mean nasty. Worst thing I ever heard." Christian leaned toward me. "The fucking Feds were already here."

"Undercover?"

He nodded. "Five guys pull guns and yell, 'FBI,' and run upstairs and find this guy chopped to pieces."

"How long between the scream and when they found him?"

"What, a minute. Less."

That was a lot to do to someone in a short time.

"Anything else, man? I got to clean up around here."

"Yeah, can you let me take a look at where they found him?"

The room Christian showed me was still sealed off by the cops. However, since they'd destroyed the door getting in here, the only barrier was some strategically placed yellow tape. That gave me enough of an opening to look inside and see the final resting place of Ossian Parthalán.

The room itself was designed for some ugly scenes. Chains dangled from walls and ceiling, waiting someone's bondage scenario. The table in the room also seemed to be a functional rack, right out of the Tower of London. One corner had a five-by-five metal cage, in case someone wanted to play Vietnamese POW.

All of it seemed a little tacky in the face of the real blood, and the outline marking the middle of the floor.

A white circle had been drawn on the floor, the outline of Ossian's body crossing a broken edge. Dwarves might not deal in magic, but this one had been trying to cast some protective spell. Apparently it didn't work.

I tried to take a picture, but my camera phone was having glitches again.

"I suppose it's too much to expect any security cameras up here?"

Christian laughed. "No, man, only in the parking lot, and the Feds got all of that."

I nodded. Not only was that kind of security expensive to maintain around magic-heavy sites, I suspect that it would kill a good part of the *Nazgûl's* business. The kind of party they were set up for wasn't meant to be recorded—except by the parties involved.

I carefully pushed the yellow ward-tape back so I could lean in a bit and get a better look.

"Careful there, man."

"I know what I'm doing." In theory, as long as I didn't actually break the line formed by the seal, I was okay.

I don't know exactly what I was looking for. I don't pretend I'm a crime scene investigator, and anything beyond the patently obvious was going to escape me. I needed a look at the actual case file, but since the Feds were involved, the chance of me getting someone to leak it were slim to none.

I looked at the doorframe, and one of the patently obvious deductions I was able to make was the fact that the Feds did, in fact, bust down a locked door. I could still see a size-twelve footprint next to the doorknob where the door had been kicked in. Kicked in hard enough to splinter the doorframe.

"No other way in or out?"

Christian shook his head. The upper floor was so quiet I heard his piercings rattle.

"This bothers me." I looked around the party room, at all the S&M gear. It took a second for me to pick up on exactly what it was. "You said everyone heard the dwarf scream, right?"

"Damn straight."

I stepped back from the opening and let the barrier swing back to a natural rest position. "Considering the kind of partying that goes on in these rooms, aren't they soundproofed pretty well?"

Christian's eyes widened as if I had just performed some mage sleight of hand. "Hey, that's right . . ."

"And the dance floor gets kind of loud, doesn't it?"

"Shit, then what the fuck was that noise?"

"Don't know, but I suspect that our dwarf was dead a while before you heard it."

CHAPTER SIX

"**C**ALEDVWLCH, you bastard," I cursed as I drove back to the office. The elf cop never really lied to me, but he had a habit of leaving out critical information. Information, such as federal involvement in whatever was going on.

While it might be coincidence that the FBI was staked out at the *Nazgûl,* I had a strong suspicion that the "unrelated matter" the Feds were investigating was unrelated only in so far as they weren't on a murder investigation.

Caledvwlch can be very literal when he wants to be.

And, if I needed anything more to convince me that the elf wasn't completely forthcoming—which I didn't—there was a matter of timing.

If Christian was right about his time line, then the Feds were busting down the door at the *Nazgûl,* about the time I was sitting down at the Old Arcade.

Caledvwlch was on my case with a crime scene picture within the hour. Even with a forensic mage and the authority of the Feds, no one could have identified the corpse, traced the phone log, and found me at my table in the Arcade in that space of time, unless the dwarf was under surveillance and his phone was already tapped.

So Ossian Parthalán was involved in something that the Feds were interested in. And to me it looked as if he was meeting someone in the bowels of the *Nazgûl.* Someone who scared him enough to attempt some sort of protective circle, however ineffective. The meeting goes badly, and if I trusted Caledvwlch's offhand estimate of the time of death—two hours ago when he caught up with me at seven—then Mr. Parthalán is eviscerated sometime shortly after five.

It's not until an hour later that someone—or something— screams, and the FBI breaks in and finds the dwarf's body.

You can do a lot in an hour, especially if you're adept at any black arts and have a sacrifice to work with. At the very least I suspected some highly illegal necromancy, especially when I thought of zombie-boy wading through the *Thor's Hammer* garage.

None of which explained the Feds' involvement.

And let's not forget zombie-boy . . .

When I got back to the office, Nina Johannessen was there, and I wasn't sure whether I was thankful or not. Her desk was off in one corner of the pressroom.

"Nina? You asked if anything strange happened to me lately?"

She looked up at me as I walked up to her desk. She set down a pen with which she was making some incomprehensible chicken-scratches on a notepad. I'd say it was all Greek to me, but there were clear traces of Latin and Hebrew around some of the symbols she was jotting down.

"Yes, I'm sorry about bothering you yesterday." She looked up and smiled. "Sometimes I feel a sense of urgency, and—"

"I don't know if it counts as Death or the Devil, but I've certainly scored one for 'new and threatening' since I talked to you."

"Oh." The smile left and her already pale skin lost whatever color it had to begin with. The sudden concern in her expression gave me the same sense of unease as hearing the word "Oops" in an operating theater. "What happened?"

"Well, I have a dwarf as the victim of a ritualistic homicide, and I had the bad fortune of running into an extra from the set of *Night of the Living Dead* when I checked out his place of business."

Nina leaned forward. "You ran into what?"

I shrugged. "I don't follow paranormal crap that closely. I wouldn't know what to call this thing."

"Describe it."

"A skeleton held together with raw meat and piano wire."

Nina frowned. "It did concern you, what I saw."

"What did you see?"

"Three trumps from the tarot."

Nina opened a drawer and pulled out an oversized deck of cards and after searching through it, placed three cards on the desk in front of her. One looked like a lighthouse snapping in half and tumbling a victim to rocks below, the next was a goat-legged demon framed by a pentacle and squatting on a rock where a pair of damned souls were chained, and the last was a skeletal figure in black armor, mounted on a horse.

The cards were labeled "The Tower," "The Devil," and "Death."

"The vision I had, was these cards—or embodiments of these three cards—"

I picked up the death card.

"That one, Death, isn't as bad as it looks, really." She sounded as if she was trying to convince herself. "It mostly represents change. The Tower is a much worse omen—"

"You use these to tell fortunes, right? If you were reading this," I tapped the desk with the card and put Death back with the doomsayer's triumvirate. "What would you tell me?"

"Death traditionally means change, the end of something and the start of something else. The Devil is pretty much a symbol of material desire, money and power. The Tower . . . ruin, destruction. A three-card spread tends to be past, present, and future." She looked down at the cards. "If I were reading this for someone, I couldn't leave out the net effect of the more mundane negative connotations. They're not good to see together like this."

"In a nutshell?"

"Someone with this spread has undergone a life change, one that set him or her on a path to pursue money, power, or lust, and that path is going to lead to destruction . . ."

The interpretation Nina just gave me could fit Mazurich. Possibly the late dwarf. I didn't like the thought that it might apply to me.

She was shaking her head as she stared at the cards.

"What is it?" I asked.

"Visions are never entirely what they first appear to be. That's the nature of the Oracle."

"What do you mean?"

"Reading it like a normal spread, it doesn't seem right to me." She shuddered slightly. "The skeletal apparition you described, it makes me afraid that what I saw was something more . . . *literal.*"

I laughed, "I don't think I'm going to run into the Devil."

"But you've already seen Death in at least two forms, haven't you?"

I looked at Death in his suit of armor, and thought of the zombie that had cleaned my clock, and of my friend, the dwarven armorer. A skeleton wrapped in metal . . .

Touché.

She gathered up the cards and replaced them in the drawer in her desk. "Tell me what's going on with you. I think you may need help."

"If you tell me something."

"What?"

"Why did you think the vision was about me?"

Nina looked up and hesitated a moment. "I just had a sense it was tied to you."

Now I'm not one to dismiss gut feelings, especially those of someone who made her living tied into the psychic network that wrapped this city. However, I am pretty good at telling when someone was flat-out lying. Most people just aren't that good at it.

"Come on, Nina, I know bullshit when I hear it."

"Part of the vision. In the Tower. I saw you."

"And that isn't good."

She shook her head. "No, it isn't."

I got the sense that she wasn't telling me the whole truth. However, whatever she had seen had obviously been disturbing. I could see the stress in her eyes, and to be honest I suspected she was avoiding something just because she found it too painful to go over. I made a decision not to press her on it, since she seemed more than willing to help me in the here and now.

That would turn out to be one of the worst mistakes of my entire life.

"Okay," I said, "see if you can help me make sense of what I'm dealing with here." I gave her the Cliff Notes version of the last thirty-six hours. She took her pad and made quite a few notes as I talked.

"So," I finished, "does any of this ring any bells? Have you come across anything that might connect with this?"

"I think you're right." She looked at her notes and frowned. "What you describe indicates someone trying to cast a protective circle. The circle was either unsuccessful or subsequently broken."

"You sound unsure about that."

"Dwarves do not cast magic—"

"That's what I thought. But there's a first time for everything, right?"

"It's not that simple. It isn't that dwarves don't. They *can't*." She shook her head. "Their nature makes them a suppressive force, diminishing the power of everything cast in their presence. For a dwarf to cast something, even the simplest protective spell, it would require energies beyond the ability of most mages."

"Well, apparently it didn't work."

"The point is, he thought it would, or why bother casting it?"

"Can't some rituals focus energy—"

Nina laughed. "Our dwarf would have to build up ritual potential for a week or two to cast anything—" She stopped laughing.

"What?"

"Well, if someone else cast a ritual, and embodied the power in some charm or fetish. That could give enough potential for him to make an attempt."

"I hear a 'but.'"

"Well, not only would such an object be inherently dangerous, it would require weeks of work by some mage simply to amass undirected power. A legal mage isn't going to do that, and I can't even imagine what the cost of that would be on the black market."

I wondered if something like that would be enough to interest the FBI. Maybe, but it didn't seem likely. While there was a thriving industry of black market mages around town, the nature of the crime made it inherently local. The nature of the radiation through the Portal meant that those mages' influence stopped outside the boundaries of northeast Ohio. The Feds tended to be more interested in things that might leave the state.

She shook her head. "No, it makes more sense if someone else cast the circle—maybe he met with someone besides his killer?"

"That's as plausible as anything else I have . . ."

"Now you sound unsure."

"If there was someone besides his killer around, why aren't there two bodies?" I shook my head. "Not enough information. Can you tell me anything about zombie-boy?"

"That name seems an accurate description, flesh animated by some necromancer—but there are some oddities about it."

"Only some?"

"The more decayed a body is, the more energy is required simply to have it move. Your zombie not only moves quickly, but shows more strength than I'd expect in even a freshly animated corpse. What you describe is certainly not fresh. And the wires and metal you describe are completely new to me."

"Any idea what the wires might be for?"

"A framework? A matrix to focus additional power? Armor, perhaps."

I wondered if she was intentionally referencing the Death trump.

She kept looking at her notes. "I can do some research on both of those. Find out if there are some magically plausible explanations I haven't thought of."

"Thanks."

She reached out and touched my hand. "Please, be careful."

"I always am," I lied.

I hadn't gotten out of the office before my extension rang. My mind was still churning with images of Death, the Devil, and the Tower when I answered.

A familiar voice told me, "My office, Maxwell. Now."

My boss, Columbia Jennings, wasn't the Devil, but she could give the witches from *Macbeth* a run for their money. She lorded it over the Metro editor's desk from an office filled with a chain-smoking haze, and if anyone ever had the balls to tell her this was a nonsmoking building, I hadn't heard of it.

When I walked into her office she looked at me and shook her head. "First off, don't shut off your cell phone while you're working. It makes me feel like you're avoiding me."

"What?" I pulled out my phone. "I didn't—" I looked at it and the screen was dark. Apparently I had. "Damn it. This thing's been acting up all day."

"Fix it."

I nodded.

"That's not what I wanted to talk to you about."

"I had that feeling."

"Shut the door."

When I did, she asked me, "Now, do you mind telling me how a story on the Washington mayoral campaign became involved with the SPU, a ritual murder, and the trashing of a crime scene?"

I shrugged. "Things got a little sidetracked."

"I gather."

"The dwarf was trying to pass me some information before he was killed. I'm just trying to follow up on it."

"Information about the Washington campaign?"

"Ah, no."

"What, then?"

I hesitated a bit before I said, quietly, "Mazurich."

"I didn't quite hear that."

"Mazurich, damn it. The dwarf claimed he knew the motive behind his suicide."

Columbia rolled her eyes at me. "I didn't figure you for chasing conspiracy theories."

"The dwarf was killed. That's a story in itself."

"And you became a crime reporter . . . when?"

"Look, I just want—"

"Maxwell, don't tell me what you want. You're one of the best paid reporters on the staff, you have a hell of a lot of latitude, but you don't get to make ad hoc decisions like that while you're on the payroll. This isn't some random op-ed piece. If the city public safety director starts calling me and asking what my reporter is doing, *I* should know why, at least."

"You're ordering me off this?"

"Please, lay off the journalistic martyrdom. You know you have to run this by me." She waved at a chair. "Now sit down, and convince me you should be doing this story."

She was right, of course. And she kept me there for ninety minutes, more, I think, to punish me than because she needed any convincing.

I left smelling like an ashtray, but with full editorial sanction.

CHAPTER SEVEN

THE next day was almost painfully clear and cold, the sky a near cloudless, razor-sharp blue. All of which made the atmospheric display over the Portal that much more spectacular. I was passing by on the way to City Hall, and when I parked my car it was hard not to look up and stare like a tourist.

The Portal is pretty much what it sounds like, a hole between this universe and the next about fifty feet in diameter. And while it was hidden from Lakeside Avenue by the retrofitted fortress that used to be Browns Stadium, its effect on the environment was visible for miles.

More poured out of the thing than magic and dwarves—it also contributed a permanent standing weather front thanks to differentials in temperature, pressure, and humidity between here and there. Today it was particularly active, building roiling black clouds stacked up for miles, swirling with hail, sleet, and lighting, all lit by piercing winter sun. Ice crystals fractured rainbows in the sky while the occasional bolt of lighting traced across the clouds.

When you told newcomers that the whole display actually had nothing to do with magic, they tended not to believe you.

As influential as the damn thing is, comparatively few people had ever seen it outside of those who actually passed through the thing. No photographs or video of it existed; the interference inside the stadium was too great for any software engineers to filter out. Even regular electrical appliances, floodlights, power tools, and forklifts began acting weird when they got within a few dozen feet of the Portal.

Other than those who had a close encounter with the object itself, the best image anyone had was artistic representations of the thing. None of which did it justice. Even the best drawings I'd seen made the thing look like a giant chromed Christmas ornament, a sphere reflecting the image of another universe.

Nothing I'd seen caught the sense of depth the actual phenomenon had, the feeling of looking deep into a direction that didn't actually exist.

I turned away from the storm and bought a copy of *USA Today* from one of the vending machines on the corner. Having been one of the people in the stands when the Portal was created, opening on the Pittsburgh thirty-five yard line, you'd think I'd be used to the damn thing by now.

I carried my paper and walked toward City Hall, serendipitously close to the epicenter of the last dozen years of city politics.

I took a station in the hall outside Council Chambers and opened the paper. The Supreme Court's discussion on the Portal jurisdiction had long slipped off the front page of the national consciousness. The news was dominated by Congressional debates on Medicare and illegal immigration. The President was on a trip to North Africa. And the cover picture showed about three hundred protesters circling an offshore oil platform in the Gulf of Mexico with yellow rubber dinghies.

I tended to get so focused on local events that it was nice to remind myself there was a world outside of Cuyahoga County. It helped me gain some perspective.

I read the paper for about fifteen minutes. Then the Council meeting recessed, and the members began filing out of the chamber. I folded my paper and waited for the current council president, Brenda Carlson.

"Thanks for meeting me on such short notice." I held out my hand when she came out to meet me. She smiled and shook it.

Carlson was just coming out of a marathon Council session, but she had the skill of not looking as drained as she must have felt. She had an easy smile, a red suit that appeared freshly pressed, and her hair was perfectly in place for any cameras that might be around.

By contrast, her late predecessor, Mazurich, used to come out of Council Chambers looking as if he had just been in a bar fight.

"Should I buy you a coffee?" she asked. "Or would that be a blatant attempt to influence the media?"

We left City Hall and found a booth in a coffee shop around the corner. I made a point of getting our coffee, despite her offer. I'm a purist and prefer my coffee unadulterated by sugar, cream, mocha, or whatever is Starbucks' flavor of the day. When I came back with our caffeine, she said, "I read your profile on Greg Washington."

"What did you think?"

"He's going to beat Clifton."

I chuckled. "Is that on the record?"

"It's common knowledge. Besides, no one on Council gets a warm fuzzy feeling when they think of Gabe Clifton."

"How about you?"

"Oh, I'll work with whoever the people of this city decide to elect." She smiled. "So is this what you wanted to talk about?"

"I'm afraid not. I'm here about Councilman Mazurich." I sipped my coffee and looked at her, trying to gauge her reaction.

"Dom? What about?" I could hear the suspicion in her voice. It didn't surprise me. I was the political attack dog on the *Press,* and I was pretty well known for unearthing ugly secrets.

"A couple of things. Primarily, why would a dwarf concern himself with why Mazurich killed himself."

"A dwarf?"

"A dwarf."

"Who?"

"The name I have is Ossian Parthalán."

"That sounds slightly familiar . . ."

I leaned back and set down my cup. "I was hoping you might help me with Mazurich's history. You worked with him the first five years after the Portal opened. You must have seen a lot that was going on."

"He was a good man." She was quiet a long time, staring into her coffee. "You remember, back when the Portal opened. . . . The power failures, the blackouts, the federal blockade—"

Of course, anyone who lived through it would never forget. The first year no TV at all, radio so intermittent as to be almost useless. Computers and other electronics would eventually fail as digital garbage filled their memories. It would be two years before the engineers started producing consumer electronics that would work properly.

I was lucky enough to be one of the few to have benefited, at least professionally, during the chaos. But even if the collapse of local TV and radio caused the proliferation of news dailies that gave me my job, I was still rational enough not to be the least bit nostalgic about it.

"Yes?"

"You remember that most of the city government locked itself behind a National Guard barricade?"

That was when Mayor Rayburn made his famous stand against the federal government coming in and taking control of the Portal, the U.S. Army blockaded the city against the Ohio National Guard, and—if it weren't for the intervention of Congress—the President might have ordered the first military assault on a U.S. city since the Civil War.

While it had been in the guise of protecting a natural resource, over the years it had come to light that Rayburn had been, in fact, negotiating unilateral trade arrangements on the other side of the Portal—and with the help of the governor and the Ohio National Guard, had helped orchestrate a regime change in the kingdom of Ragnan, the government on the other side.

The only thing that prevented a constitutional crisis at the time was badly written legislation on the part of Congress that effectively annexed the Portal and gave jurisdiction of all of its "contents" to the local government of the area the Portal sat in.

Only now, with a rewritten law and a new Supreme Court ruling had the Feds managed to finally gain control of the Portal, and the commerce through it.

"Yeah," I remembered City Hall, Browns Stadium, all of Lakeside, packed with kids in fatigues carrying machine guns, all trying not to look at the storm swirling the sky above the stadium. The image was something out of the Iraqi insurgency. "I tried to get into City Hall a couple of times, not much luck."

"Well, Dom actually went out into the city, he saw people, did what he could."

She told me stories of what he did do. He not only saw the people in his ward, he visited the camps where refugees from the Portal were being held.

That's where he first met the dwarves.

Without a common language, he couldn't speak to them, but he managed to notice something that had been missed by most of the other humans commanding the influx from the Portal.

Mazurich saw that, even in the midst of escaping a genocidal war and finding themselves in the midst of a (super)natural disaster, the dwarves still worked. With little more than the possessions they carried through the Portal and the material lying about the refugee camp, they were able to craft amazing things—textiles, jewelry, statuary. Even with no common language, the dwarves had started their own economy, trading with other refugees and even with their human guards.

Seeing what the dwarves did, and seeing the major problem of the day as the breakdown of infrastructure in the city combined with the panicked departure of much of the available skilled labor, Mazurich became Rayburn's ally in getting the nonhuman population legal recognition. Rayburn had high-level geopolitical motivations, mostly concerned with preventing a federal takeover of the city. Mazurich was much more practical. He saw the potential to integrate these new people into the city and get things working again. The dwarves were quick studies and picked up English—and shovels and jackhammers—all within a few short weeks.

Mazurich talked with the leaders of all the clans, always in an effort to try and meld the existing dwarven society into our own. It wasn't an easy task. Dwarves weren't solitary, and the clans tended to act as a unit—including in the acquisition of living space. Finding facilities to house several thousand dwarves in one place wasn't easy, especially for a race that preferred living underground.

Mazurich managed to pull it off, though. He managed to get the Port Authority and the county to buy up all of the remaining private property on a spit of land called Whiskey Island and designate it a relocation area for the dwarven population.

He managed to get his hands on the prime lakefront property and longtime political football by the simple expedient of political blackmail. There was still a federal blockade, and while the Feds were letting people out, no one was getting back in. In the space of a few months, Mazurich's dwarven contractors were pretty much the only game in town. Sewer, water, power, roads, name it and Mazurich's dwarven allies were maintaining it.

Keeping the dwarves happy became high on everyone's priority list.

And whatever the history, and whoever's ox was getting gored, Whiskey Island was a perfect solution for the dwarves. Not only was it spitting distance down the coast from the Portal, it was home to acres and acres of subterranean salt mines under the lake. Pretty much a perfect environment for the dwarves.

"I seem to remember some nasty stories coming out of the salt mines, before the dwarves moved in."

She frowned at me. "Are you trying to imply something?"

Actually, I wasn't. "I just remember some news stories from back then."

"Alarmist bullshit. It was the same stuff that was happening everywhere at the time—a salt mine just happens to be a dangerous place to panic."

"Uh-huh." I sipped my coffee, wondering exactly what she wasn't telling me. "What about recently? How were things with him and the dwarves?"

She smiled. "They loved him, he was practically one of their clan."

Mazurich managed to be human advocate and power broker to his new nonhuman constituency. His dwarves managed to form a bloc that was a political counterweight to Rayburn. They weren't particularly glamorous, but they ran the city, and because of them, Mazurich managed to keep the City Council tightly under his control. When you got down to the nitty-gritty, it *mattered* where your ward was on the priority list to get potholes fixed.

In return, Mazurich's own ward benefited greatly from dwarven labor. The technology park that lived over the remains of the old steel industry grew threefold, built by low-bidding dwarves. Dozens of new businesses set up shop, dwarven-owned and operated, ranging from one-dwarf operations like *Thor's Hammer*, to multimillion dollar R&D outfits like Magetech.

"Magetech? That's a dwarven operation?"

"Right in the heart of the Kucinich Technology Park. In fact, now I know why that name's familiar . . ."

"What name?" I was still absorbing the idea that Magetech had anything to do with dwarves. I had heard of it, of course. It was a magnet for venture capital. The next Internet boom and all that. The idea that it might be the first to viably apply magic to *any* modern technological process was like crack for investors. If anything, I would have expected a dragon or two to be involved.

But dwarves?

"Parthalán. That clan name. Their clan leader happens to hold the CEO position there, and a bunch of others sit on the board."

"No kidding . . ."

CHAPTER EIGHT

SURPRISINGLY, one phone call got me a meeting with the Chief Operations Officer of Magetech. It was unexpected enough that I had to reorder my whole day to fit in the sudden appointment. When I called to reschedule with members of Mazurich's staff, most of them sounded relieved.

Magetech was housed in a cluster of office buildings sheathed in mirrored glass. Even before I reached the parking lot, I could tell there was something unusual going on here. If you looked at the right angle, you could see something else in the mirror, something dark that traced glyphs and symbols that barely registered in the conscious mind.

The wards, if that's what they were, seemed only to register on my peripheral vision, and when I tried to look at them directly, my eyes hurt and I felt something between paranoia and dread.

I had to blink a couple of times to get the feeling to pass.

One of the annoying things about the world post-Portal was the fact you couldn't readily dismiss sensations like that. The sense that this was not a good place might actually have a concrete source outside my own subconscious.

Of course, dismissed or not, there was little I could do about the feeling anyway.

I pulled up and into the visitor parking area, feeling the uncharacteristic hope that this was a wild goose chase. As I stepped out of the car, I pulled my jacket close against the chill in the air. I walked up to the building, under a logo hovering in midair, and into a cavernous neo-industrial lobby: a few cubic acres of glass, exposed steel, and ductwork. Everything had been polished, so that even the rivets in the exposed girders gleamed.

Display cases lined the polished granite floor between the lobby doors and the reception desk. Floating in rune-carved Lexan cubes were artifacts of Magetech's R&D efforts. The objects were all pretty mundane and wouldn't have made much of an impression on someone who wasn't a Cleveland native; PDAs, cell phones, laptop computers, televisions, radios, digital cameras . . . so what?

The "so what" was the Portal. The mana flowing out from the world next door caused interference, severe interference, in every type of recording and communication media known to man. Magetech was jump-started by being the first to patent ways to correct for the problem. Because of that, Magetech got a piece of nearly every electronic device sold in Northeast Ohio.

I walked up to the reception desk. It was staffed by a woman who looked like a cross between a librarian and one of the nastier guards at a women's prison. She looked at me over the top of her glasses.

"Can I help you?"

"Kline Maxwell, *Cleveland Press.* I have an appointment with Simon Lucas."

"The *Cleveland Press,* I don't know—"

"It's okay, Nora," came a voice from behind me. "I approved it."

I turned and faced the Chief Operations Officer of Magetech. He was taller than I expected, and balder. There wasn't a lick of hair on his naked skull, and he was almost elven in his height and the way he moved. He held out a long-fingered hand and I shook it.

"Mr. Lucas?" I asked.

He nodded and looked toward the receptionist. "I apologize, Nora. Last minute addition."

Nora let out with an intimidating "Hrumph."

"Come with me, Mr. Maxwell."

Lucas led me past the reception desk, past a few corridors, and to a bank of elevators. "Nice setup you have here."

"These are just the corporate offices," Lucas said as he pressed the up button. "The heart of the operation is in Solon."

"Oh, I thought you had labs here?"

"Not for years," Lucas laughed.

The elevator slid open for us and we both stepped inside.

The interior of the elevator was all chrome and mirrors, and I again got the headache-inducing sense of seeing something out of the corner of my eye. As if something was written underneath the reflections, something old, arcane, and evil . . .

"Are you all right?" Lucas asked.

I realized I was rubbing my temple and I lowered my hand. "I'm fine. But I am correct? This is where operations started for you?"

"Oh, yes. On the location of an old blast furnace."

To my relief, the doors slid open. It was all I could do to avoid racing Lucas for the exit. Outside the elevator, there was a plush lobby where a glass wall opposite us looked out over the shorter buildings of Magetech corporate headquarters. Beyond that sat the rest of the Kucinich Technology Park, backed up by the Cleveland skyline.

The sky was clear enough that I could even see the cylindrical clouds marking the static weather front above the Portal itself.

"This way," Lucas said.

I followed him down a corridor dotted with portraits, most dwarven. I took out my notebook and jotted down names as I followed Lucas. No titles were provided, but I suspected I was looking at the founding members of Magetech.

Two of the portraits were of humans. The first, little surprise, was of Councilman Mazurich with tie uncharacteristically straight. The second was a man I wasn't familiar with at all. I suspected that meant that he wasn't a politician. The name on the engraved plaque was "Dr. Eric Pretorious."

I wondered what kind of doctor he was.

"Mr. Maxwell?"

Lucas stood by an open door, waiting for me. I stepped away from Dr. Pretorious and into Lucas' office. "So how did you come to be part of Magetech?"

Lucas closed the door after us. "I've always been a part of Magetech."

"Then why isn't your portrait on the founder's wall back there?"

"I do not work for that kind of recognition." He held out a hand toward a chair at a large oval conference table. "Have a seat."

The office was impressive, almost the size of the lobby downstairs. Two walls were glass, looking out at the Cleveland skyline, and everything was appointed in black-lacquered hardwood, chrome, and leather. It made me wonder what the CEO's office was like.

"You are here to talk about our history," Lucas said as he walked around me to fold himself into another chair across the table.

I held my notebook in front of me and nodded. "I'm doing a story about Councilman Mazurich's influence on the city."

"That was a tragedy," Lucas said. "He deserves a proper elegy."

At first, I thought Lucas misspoke. However, he didn't strike me as one to make a casual slip of the tongue. He was very controlled.

It made me think of what Teaghue Parthalán said, "A soul like Mazurich should have an epic written to him."

I nodded, "I've talked to dwarves that have the same sentiment."

Lucas leaned forward. "They told you much of the late Councilman Mazurich?"

"They expressed gratitude for the efforts he conducted on their behalf."

Lucas leaned back. "Impressive efforts they were. He did much to create their world on this side of the Portal."

"Such as helping to found this company?"

"Yes, the councilman was instrumental. He brought all the initial people together, including myself. He was adept at recognizing a problem, and seeing who might have potential solutions."

"The interference from the Portal."

"Our first viable product was a police radio and a walkie-talkie for the National Guard. Those first government contracts were the seed money that allowed all of this to happen."

I rubbed my forehead. The phrase "government contract" clicked one of the journalistic circuit breakers in my brain. "Was Mazurich involved in getting Magetech that kind of business?"

It was the obvious question, but it was also a loaded one.

Politicians, especially at the city and county level, were always open to the charge of conflict of interest. It would be hard to find a local official who didn't have an incestuous relationship with local business. That was the nature of the beast. As long as the politician in question wasn't *directly* involved in the decision to award largesse, there wasn't anything criminal to it.

But there's something called, "the appearance of impropriety." And, of course, it's the job of every corporate hack and politician to keep that "appearance" minimal.

Therefore I wasn't prepared when Simon Lucas said, "Again, he was instrumental."

I looked up from my notes, "Are you saying that the councilman helped steer contracts toward Magetech?"

Lucas smiled. The grin was predatory, and disturbing. As if Hieronymus Bosch did a hairless portrait of Jack Nicholson. Though the surreal appearance of Mr. Lucas might have had more to do with the office I found myself in. I got the continual sense of something trying to pry itself into my skull.

"Mr. Maxwell, the councilman did everything in his power to help our enterprise . . . Are you feeling all right, Mr. Maxwell?"

It was the damn reflections again. With all the lacquer and

chrome in the office, wherever I looked, evil gibberish tried to drill itself into my eye sockets. "I'm fine . . ." I closed my eyes and took a few deep breaths. "Did he benefit financially from those contracts?"

"Mr. Maxwell." Mr.Lucas steepled his too long fingers. "I assumed you realized he was part owner of this company."

He was still smiling. I couldn't read him at all. He had to know that he was dangling red meat for a political reporter like me. Mazurich was not just a corporate kingmaker, bringing all the principals together, brokering the deals that formed Magetech.

Lucas had just told me that he was a principal investor, and benefited personally from city contracts with the new company.

"Mr. Lucas, are you saying . . . ?" I sucked in a breath and looked down. I was getting a deep sense of vertigo.

"You do not look well. Let me get you a glass of water."

I nodded as I heard Lucas get up. In a moment I heard glass rattling.

"Are you saying that Mazurich helped award contracts that he benefited from?"

"Yes, he did." I heard water pouring over ice. "It was a different time, and Magetech was the only company available to do what needed to be done. As I said, he recognized a problem, and found solutions."

My brain was swirling inside my head. *He's just told me that our late council president was profiteering off the chaos from the Portal.*

I felt his hand on my shoulder. "I think you need to drink something . . ."

I nodded, weak and light-headed, the claws of a migraine just beginning to bite into my forebrain. "How much . . . ?" I couldn't actually complete the sentence. I closed my eyes, knowing that this wasn't right, that nothing about this was right.

Lucas asked for me, his voice low and breathy. "How much is his portion of Magetech worth?"

I could just manage a nod.

Lucas told me a figure that would make a dragon blush.

I opened my eyes to take the glass. My hand shook.

I looked down into the icy water and saw a skull in the ice, laughing at me. The glass slid from my hand and, while I remember hearing a shattering noise, I don't think I ever saw it hit the ground.

CHAPTER NINE

I'M not often prone to nightmares. I usually don't remember my dreams at all. This one, however, was a bad one.

I chase someone. I run through back alleys and scrap yards piled with engine blocks and old suits of plate mail. I run through the ruins of old steel mills and find myself at the Magetech complex, a maze of mirrored glass.

I hear a muffled voice calling for me . . .

"*Dad?*"

"*Sarah!*" I scream at the mirrored glass, and pound at the doors.

In front of me, the building implodes. It shatters as if there's no substance to it other than the mirrored glass skin. Shards fall and swirl around me, like a lethal snowstorm, flying daggers all reflecting my daughter's face.

"*Sarah!*" I call again, feeling my flesh cut to ribbons!

The shards swirl into a glass vortex, a chromed tornado falling into a spherical void that becomes the twin of the Portal itself.

I take a step forward, naked, bleeding and sliding on my own blood.

I am thrown back as a quartet of horsemen erupts from the Portal. Upon the pale horse that tramples me, I see a skeleton wrapped with raw flesh stitched together with steel wires.

The figure of death leans toward me, opens its mouth, and makes an electronic beeping sound.

Waking up didn't make the beeping go away.

I kicked off the covers, completely disoriented as to time and place. Three things managed to sink in the first ten seconds. I was in my own bed, my phone was ringing, and I couldn't remember how I'd gotten here.

I grabbed the phone, hoping for some clue to how I got back here.

No such luck.

"How could you put her up to this?" I could tell it was bad. Margaret had already skipped two preliminary octaves in the conversation and was a just a few sentences away from dog-whistle pissed.

Despite my disorientation, something about talking to my ex made it very easy to slide right into the argument. "You know I didn't put our daughter up to anything."

"You didn't tell her *not* to apply to those places."

"In case you haven't noticed, you're living a few thousand miles away—"

"There's a reason for that."

"—and when the subject came up, I told her to tell you about it."

"And make me the bad guy? That isn't fair, and you know it!"

I sighed. I try hard to be a good long-distance father, and I've done my best to keep Sarah from playing us off against each other. But somehow, that never seemed good enough for Margaret.

"Damn it, Kline, what am I supposed to do?"

"You're supposed to be her goddamn *mother*." I must have really been stressed out, because I was harsh enough to actually leave Margaret speechless. "You're the parent, you set the boundaries. You *are* the bad guy, by definition."

"I just want some support."

"What the hell do you think I've given you? Do you have any idea how often she tries to get me to tell her that you're being stupid and unreasonable? How many times I've told her *you're* the boss, and I'm not going to second-guess you. I'm not there—"

"You should have told her that she shouldn't have applied—"

"I told her she shouldn't have lied to you."

"You should have never let her fly up there."

"*I shouldn't have let her?*" My hand was trembling and my teeth were clenched so tight that my voice could barely come out.

"Kline?"

"I gave you everything you asked for, the divorce, custody, the nodding assent of every stupid soft-headed hysterical parenting decision you ever made— But I am *not* going to tell my daughter that I don't want to see her."

"That's not what I'm asking—"

"What, then? What are you asking? I'll tell you right now that there's nothing I'm going to tell her that will keep her from resenting our breakup."

"That's not what this is about!"

"So you've talked to her?"

"I've told her—"

"I know exactly what you've told her. Did you ask her anything? Like why she feels she has no chance discussing this with you?"

"This isn't a negotiation! She knows how I feel about this, and she went ahead anyway."

"Went ahead and what, Margaret?"

"You know what she did. She went behind my back—"

"—and was accepted into Kent State University."

She was quiet for a moment.

"You know how most parents I know find out about their kids going behind their back? A call from the cops. I want to know if you'd be coming down nearly as hard on her if that had happened. She applied to a college—you want to know how many parents would give anything to see that kind of rebellion in their kids?"

"Stop it! You don't understand."

I took a few breaths and released my grip on the phone. It was the first time in a few years that I had really lost my temper and let loose on Margaret, and it made me feel like an asshole.

Not that I was completely pure in this relationship. In my more self-aware moments I knew that a lot of my identity as a parent was tied up in being the reasonable one—an easy role when you're nowhere near the teenage epicenter.

"I'm sorry. I'm a little stressed out."

"A little?"

"She did wrong. I know it, and she knows it."

"What about her trip? She's coming to see you. She's been looking forward to this for a year."

My daughter's voice from my nightmare was ringing in my ears. "They're refundable tickets, aren't they?"

"I can't just cancel it."

"No, that would be a bit too much. But you can reschedule it, can't you?"

"You mean ground her for a month?"

"And send her over in January."

"You'd be willing to give up the holidays?"

I sighed. "I hate to say this, but it might actually work out better with my job."

"*Great.*" Somehow she was able to subliminally insert the entire history of our divorce in that one word.

"Let me know if you have any trouble changing the dates. I'll chip in any difference in the airfare."

"Thanks, but we have a good travel agent. I don't think it will be a problem."

"She's a good girl," I told her.

"I know."

"Tell her I love her."

"I will."

I hung up, feeling a mixture of relief and disappointment. I really had been looking forward to showing Sarah around the local tourist traps. But the nightmare image of zombie-boy was fresh in my head, and for once, Margaret's fears about mana-infested Northeast Ohio seemed perfectly reasonable.

Not to mention, I was still trying to figure out what day and time it was. I stumbled out into my living room, still holding my phone.

I squinted at daylight streaming in my windows. The angle of the sun made it early evening. I glanced in the kitchen and the clock on my microwave read 4:30 PM.

I sat down, shaking my head. I never slept during the day and waking up twelve hours off my normal schedule threw my whole equilibrium out of balance. I had no idea if I'd been unconscious for four hours, or twenty-four. My last conscious memory before waking up was talking to the COO of Magetech, Simon Lucas.

I checked my phone messages.

First call at 12:45, shortly after my interview with Lucas. "Hello, Mr. Maxwell? This is Nora Abrams at Magetech. Mr. Lucas wanted me to call and make sure you made it home all right. You were suffering a bad reaction, and we just wanted to check up on you."

"A bad reaction?" I muttered. "To what?"

At 2:00, Sarah had called. "Dad, I told her. She went ballistic, just like I told you she would. I just know she's going to cancel my trip up there. Call me or I don't know what I'm going to do."

My cell phone rang.

I usually turn the cell off when I come home. I try to keep the cell for work, and the landline for my personal life. Not that it works particularly well.

Probably I wasn't in any state to remember to kill it when I came home, if I was having blackouts. *Christ, what happened to me?*

I hung up the landline and answered the cell phone, mostly because my argument with Margaret was still running through my head at that point and I was half-convinced that it was my ex or my daughter trying the other phone because I had the home line tied up.

I wasn't thinking very clearly. Otherwise I would have looked at the caller ID.

"Maxwell?"

"Hello?" Male voice, odd accent . . . I shifted mental gears when I realized who it was. "Dr. Kawata?"

"Yeah, I ran those tests like you wanted me to. You need to tell me what the hell's going on here."

"What do you mean?"

"Oh, you want a list? I put that sample in the county's brand-new spectrometer. The one that's supposed to filter out all that damn background noise, and the bastard doesn't work. Readings as crazy as anything on the old equipment. I ran it a dozen times to average it all out, and you know what I got?"

"What?"

"Run-of-the-mill sodium chloride."

"Salt?"

"Salt. Plain old salt, crushed fine with a few trace mineral impurities."

"Shit. Why would someone send me salt of all things?"

"That's not the question, Maxwell."

"There's more?"

"Yeah, there's more. I want to know why I just spent two hours being questioned by the FBI about your little package."

"What?"

"What did you get me into, Maxwell? I'm a civil servant, I got a pension, I don't need to be mixed up in this type of crap."

I shook my head. I hadn't expected the FBI to catch up with this so quickly. "I'm sorry. I think the feds were investigating the person who probably sent that to me. I didn't mean to get you involved with anything."

"Well, you find any other mystery powders, have someone else look at it. I like my job too much."

"What did the Feds want?"

"Why don't you ask them? I'm sure they'll be talking to you."

Dr. Kawata hung up.

"Salt?"

I got dressed, trying to remember my interview with Lucas. I couldn't remember anything past dropping the water glass. However, the sense of unease around the Magetech complex still clung to me like the stale smoke around Columbia Jennings' office. Every time I thought of Lucas, I felt something sour in the pit of my stomach.

There was something twisted about the guy—and my feelings about him made no objective logical sense whatsoever. Anyone looking at a transcript of my conversation with him wouldn't see anything but a very cooperative and open interview subject. I knew, because I *had* that transcript. My notebook was covered with my handwriting. Notes I had no memory of jotting down

The guy had no problem answering every question I had, in detail.

"Maybe I was asking the wrong questions?"

The guy was way too open. He was telling me things about Mazurich's history with Magetech that no sane executive should be stating on the record to a political reporter.

I apparently had a more detailed conversation with Mr. Lucas than I remembered.

However, the highlights were clear from the prelude I could recall. I had conflict of interest in spades, and dollar amounts with enough zeros to give Gregory Washington's creative auditors an orgasm. The fact that Mazurich's assets were news to me meant that they were never publicly disclosed.

I flipped through my notes and saw a road map of Mazurich's secret finances, complete with quotes from Lucas that were marked as being on the record.

"What the hell?"

Lucas was giving me exactly what I should want.

For almost every line, I could think of at least two means of independent verification. With a few hours and a few phone calls, the right questions would have this story ironclad. I could easily reconfirm any quotes with Lucas before running the piece.

And I had a gut feeling that it was all completely accurate.

But that did nothing to dispel the sick sense of wrongness I felt about it all, and about Lucas in particular.

Stories aren't just handed out like that. And it was almost as if Lucas was intentionally sacrificing Mazurich, the founding father of his company. At the same time, he was allowing a PR catastrophe for Magetech. If I ran with this, people would call for hearings and investigations and . . .

It didn't make sense.

"This is why he killed himself."

Could it be a smoke screen? Throw something big at the reporter so he doesn't ask the really troublesome questions?

There was not a single thing in my notes about dwarves. Or zombies.

Or salt.

* * *

"Nina Johannessen, *Cleveland Press.*"

I sat down on my couch, phone in one hand, cold beer in the other. I pressed the bottle to my forehead and said, "Nina—"

"Kline? Are you okay? You haven't been at the office."

"I've been working."

"Something's wrong."

I hesitated, I wasn't sure if I wanted to go into something like unexpected blackouts with her. Instead, I changed the subject. "You told me you would look into some things for me?"

"Yes." I heard rustling in the background. "I've actually tracked down rumors of dwarven magi. Nothing concrete, but from the sound of it there might actually be that unfocused charm or fetish we were speculating about."

"What about zombies?"

"Have you heard any stories about a company named Magetech?"

I sat up, almost spilling my beer. "What?"

"Magetech, they have the patents on most Portal-adapted consumer electronics—"

"I know who they are."

"Well, they've been trying to come up with fusions of magic and industrial technology for years."

"What? Are you saying my zombie—?"

"I can't find anything matching your description, but there're stories about Magetech hiring dark magi, necromancers, real left-hand path people for some type of black projects lab."

"The kind of people who might be reanimating corpses?"

"Your zombie was too decomposed and too active to be an efficient use of mana, unless the metallic components were some sort of superstructure. And the investment in time and energy to create that wouldn't make sense, unless—"

"Someone was mass-producing it?" I shook my head. "Christ, there're more of those out there?"

"It could be an R&D project, or I could be drawing the wrong conclusions."

I shook my head. "No, it makes sense. If this thing was unique, why risk it on a simple B&E?"

There was a long pause on the other end of the phone. I got an uneasy feeling. "Nina, what aren't you telling me?"

"I don't know what . . ."

"Please, I smell bullshit for a living. What is it? Did you have another vision?"

Silence. I thought of my dream. The undead rider rising out of the shards of the Magetech complex.

"Is that how you thought to look into Magetech in the first place?"

"You know?"

I looked at the bottle, sweating in my hand. It was shaking. I felt a sick dread growing in my gut.

"What did you see?" I asked, "What did you hear?"

"The Oracle is sometimes unclear—"

"*I saw it, damn it!*" I slammed the bottle on the table in front of me. "I saw Death ride off your tarot card right out of the Magetech complex. I heard my *daughter.*"

"I'm so sorry, Kline. I didn't want to upset—"

"My *daughter,* Nina. Did you see her in your visions?"

A long painful pause. "Yes."

"Don't make me pull this out of you."

Her voice was shaking. "It could all be symbolic—"

"Cut the crap and tell me."

"I saw the Devil," she said, near tears, "and your daughter was in his hand."

CHAPTER TEN

NINA is probably right, it is all symbolic.

Even so, I did call Margaret back to make sure that we were on the same page and that Sarah wasn't coming anywhere near Cleveland for at least a month. I gave her some lame excuse, because I couldn't bring myself to say what really concerned me. I told myself that I didn't want to panic her, but it probably had more to do with the fact that I couldn't admit that she might be right about this city.

What really worried me was the idea that people who tried to cheat the Oracle tended to end up doing exactly what the ephemeral bitch wanted—from Oedipus to Macbeth.

The fact that both those examples were fictional didn't comfort me much. In my own life I had a brush with the Oracle that killed the soothsayer, and almost killed me.

All I could really think to do was keep my daughter as far out of the line of fire as possible, and do my job. If someone was about to threaten my daughter, my best course was to try and expose him, her, or it as fast as I could—and something was definitely up with Magetech.

I left my apartment, my hands still unsteady from my blackout and my talk with Nina.

I had one major contact that was wired into the supernatural goings-on in the city. And, while that might all be Nina's job, I had pretty much reamed her over the phone and I needed a nonconfrontational conversation. Now. So I tried calling Dr. Newman Shafran three times as I drove toward Case.

Case Western Reserve University was only about ten minutes' drive from Shaker Square, and my condo, so I was parking my Volkswagen in the metallic shadow of the Peter B. Lewis Building by six. Dr. Shafran still wasn't answering.

I couldn't tell if my growing sense of urgency was some lingering dread from my lost time, or the aftereffects of grilling Nina. I sat behind the wheel and tried taking a few deep breaths.

I made my living with my head and my ability to think clearly. I didn't like the feeling that someone might be messing with that. Combine my lost time with a supernatural threat against my daughter, and I had lost any real sense of objectivity.

When I got out of the Volkswagen, my destination didn't help my state of mind.

In the entire history of Cleveland architecture, the Peter B. Lewis Building would be the structure voted most likely to induce migraines and epileptic fits. It was hard to believe that someone managed to have a psyche twisted enough to conceive the thing *before* the Portal opened. My best attempt to describe it would be if Salvador Dalí ate a Silver Surfer comic book, and threw up.

After the Portal opened, it seemed to attract and twist energies so that occasionally the curved metallic shapes would throw out rainbow auras or plasmatic arcs of energy.

It used to house the College of Business Administration, of all things. Nowadays it had been adapted to the study of things more in tune with its surreal outlines.

When I closed the door of my Volkswagen, the metal skin of the building draped me in a crimson blast of static that shaded my vision for more than half a minute. I saw spots in my eyes, one of which resembled a massive dragon descending from the dusk-colored sky.

I blinked a few times and it was gone.

Dr. Shafran wasn't in his office, and I had to walk the non-Euclidean halls for about half an hour, asking random people where he might be. I was about to give up when someone directed me to one of the subterranean labs.

I walked down a shadowed hallway just in time to hear a small explosion and shattering glass. Having no idea what to expect, I ran down to an open doorway where brownish-green smoke was just beginning to roll across the ceiling.

"No. No. *No.*" I heard a familiar Eastern European accent as I rounded the corner. In front of me were ranks of lab tables with sinks and spigots for gas and oxygen. Two men flanked one of the tables in the middle of the lab; one easily seventy, the other in his early twenties.

On the surface of the table between them, a circle of runes was just fading from glowing yellow to a dull red. As the runes faded, a swirling mass of ugly, foul-smelling smoke rose upward from the table to spill against the ceiling. I heard exhaust fans working overtime to clear it.

In the middle of the fading circle was a pile of ash and broken glass.

"No." One last time, and Dr. Shafran threw up his hands. The younger man, a grad student I suspected, just looked at the ruins on the table. "This is not your mother's goulash recipe. Rituals are exact. The patterns must be maintained or the power you mass has no shape." He slapped the table, making the glass bounce a little. It was an impressive show of force for someone who looked like a German watchmaker and talked like Bela Lugosi.

The student shook his head. "It was a brand-new spell . . ."

"You cannot just throw words on a page or paint on a canvas and call it art!" Dr. Shafran took off his bifocals and pointed them at the student. "You must know the patterns you are changing, or this is all useless."

"But, sir,"

"Go, study what you just did here, and don't talk to me until you can explain what it is you did wrong."

Dr. Shafran stormed toward the door past me, then turned and said, "And clean this up."

The student looked at me as if he had just noticed I was there. I looked at him, then at Dr. Shafran walking down the hall. I faced him, shrugged, and told him, "Sorry," before I chased after Dr. Shafran.

"Doctor!" I called after him, running to catch up.

"What?" He sounded a little flustered. Then he turned and looked at me "I know you. Yes. Mr. Kline Maxwell."

"Yes."

"I got that grant request, thank you."

"Huh?"

"Our last conversation, dragons it was. Being quoted in a national story does wonders for the credibility of a scientist in an unpopular discipline." He waved me forward, toward the elevators. "Apologies for that display," he said as he gestured back toward the lab, where I could hear the student coughing.

"That's okay—"

"Somehow I cannot get through to the students that the presence of 'magic' does not invalidate the scientific method. Ten years of students, and how many have a solid science background? Three! A waiting list I have, and all astrologers, pagans, devotees of the

Golden Dawn. From all over the country. And can I even get a basic physics prerequisite written into the course descriptions? Pheh." The elevator arrived and he turned toward me. "That is not what you want to discuss, is it, Mr. Maxwell?"

"No."

"Come, then. Share a cup of coffee and let us discuss the subjects of future news articles and research papers."

He took me to a refreshingly rectilinear cafeteria with a set of tables and vending machines. It was an odd hour, and we were the only ones there.

I made an effort to back myself up and act like a journalist. I sipped machine black coffee as I gave Dr. Shafran background on my dead dwarf, and where he had led me to date.

Dr. Shafran steepled his fingers and nodded in the right places and prodded me with the occasional monosyllable.

I paid particular attention to the oddities about my visit to Magetech, and the rumors Nina had passed on to me. The moment I mentioned Magetech, he seemed more interested.

"Really? I was offered a position there, a long time ago."

"You?"

"My expertise, you see. I was uncomfortable, however, with their—" I noticed a pause, as if he was deciding how much to tell me. "Their nondisclosure arrangements. It is hard enough to publish as it is, to conform to some corporate bylaw as well would be intolerable. At the university I study as I see fit and publish as I see fit." There was a pride in his voice that sounded almost familiar. "But I'm acquainted with the man you mentioned that they did employ."

"Dr. Pretorious?"

"Yes, a great mind. It's a blow to my own vanity to admit that he was the first to begin the scientific quantification of the phenomenon we call the Portal, at this university in fact. You might say I inherited his position. He joined that private enterprise at the beginning, and I understand the decision has been quite kind to him—in the material sense."

Knowing the figures I had jotted down for Mazurich, that had to be an understatement. And Pretorious had the added benefit of not having to keep things under wraps to protect a public position.

"So do you know anything about what he worked on for Magetech?"

Dr. Shafran shook his head. "Like me, he is—or he was—a

scientist, a theoretician. The information the public sees coming out of Magetech is in the form of patents and end-user products. From that, you can see their engineering but not their research—and that is what would possess him. And anyone in my position will tell you that the time from pure research to practical applications is measured in decades."

"Could they be developing something like my zombie?"

"They could be developing anything, especially if they are employing black market mages. That begs the question, why would they?"

"Can you think of a reason?"

"There seems to be little chance of seeing a legal market for such an abomination, and I don't think the black market here is either wide enough or deep enough to support that sort of development."

"But someone did develop it."

"Which means that one of us is operating on a faulty assumption." I looked into my coffee.

"Now," Dr. Shafran said, "your mention of dwarves is interesting."

"You think so?"

"Well, as you've been told, dwarves, in a sense, are antithetical to mana. Where mana pools into areas of ritual and pattern, both physical and cultural, the presence of dwarves tends to push it away. I've had no opportunity to study the effect closely. Dwarves seem too wary to volunteer for any experiments."

"I wonder why."

"My guess is that there's some inherent biological or mental antipattern that affects the collection of mana. It makes them unique as far as intelligent nonhumans go. They don't need mana to exist."

"You mean they can leave the influence of the Portal?"

Dr. Shafran nodded. "They like to remain close to their clan, but I have heard of dwarves traveling as far afield as California."

"Now why would a dwarf go to California?"

"Disneyland?" Dr. Shafran smiled.

"About Magetech—" I looked down into my coffee again. I was uncomfortable leaving the realm of journalism for the personal. I barely knew Dr. Shafran. I didn't know if that made it easier or harder to tell him about my blackout.

"I've never blacked out like that before. Could someone have cast something on me?" I asked him after describing my interview with Lucas.

"Certainly someone could have, but you describe unease before you even entered the building."

"What does that mean?"

Dr. Shafran leaned back. "The mechanisms by which human beings perceive mana are not fully understood. Just as a camera or a telephone without filtering software can pick up signals from the mana force itself, so does your brain. But while the brain of a living creature is an infinitely better filter than any microchip, signals can and do sneak through. I suspect that you passed close to an intense source of mana you're particularly sensitive to."

"Why would it make me black out?"

"That may be a medical or a psychological question. But I might suggest there is some slight evidence that such static is not wholly random, and is responsible for what some New Age victims refer to as the Oracle."

Please, tell me he didn't just say that . . .

I rubbed my forehead. As much as I wanted Dr. Shafran to be pulling my leg, he didn't look like it.

"You're saying that I had some prophetic vision?"

"I am saying that you might have seen something you were not physically or mentally capable of absorbing at the time. I won't say much more than that, since far more people claim to see the future than I can credit."

I tried to grasp a little rational reassurance. "I would think fortune-telling and soothsaying is outside your scientific purview. Mana or not."

"Such things are unproven and untested in the lab. We have, however, conducted very interesting experiments that demonstrate that these energies can violate our commonsense notions of causality, just as they mangle our not-so-commonsense notions of physics, matter, and energy."

Well, that isn't very reassuring.

I stood up, shaking my head. I wasn't absolutely sure I had learned much . . .

"Are you all right, son?"

"This whole thing is making me uneasy."

"Is there anything else you would like to ask?"

I paused, and realized there was.

"What about salt?"

"Salt?"

"Salt. The dwarf sent me a sample of salt. What could be the significance of that?"

Dr. Shafran reached over and grabbed a saltshaker and sprinkled the white crystals on the table. "When you speak of salt, you speak of possibly the most potent mineral symbol in human culture. Physically, it is crystalline, and it is a longtime symbol of purity taking part in rituals millennia before the Portal existed. Its crystal structure, and the cultural significance surrounding it, makes it a perfect matrix to absorb the mana flow out of the Portal."

"What would that make the salt mines under Lake Erie?"

"Possibly the most potent concentration of mana on either side of the Portal."

It started making sense. So much mana in one place, no matter how dull someone was, the sheer force of all of that would leak through their mental filters. God help anyone who was sensitive or naturally adept. Of course, the mines became a disaster when the Portal opened.

"If dwarves are immune to the effects, they might be the only ones who *could* go down there."

Dr. Shafran nodded.

Christ, what happened when you refined the stuff?

CHAPTER ELEVEN

THAT disturbing sense of urgency kept me moving after I had talked to Dr. Shafran. My world felt out of joint, and I had the feeling that things were laughing at me from behind the reflection in my rearview mirror.

Be rational, damn it.

It was tied to the salt. The salt that I had given to Kawata, the salt that Ossian had given to me.

"This was why he killed himself."

Mazurich had led the dwarves into the salt mines. Mazurich and the dwarves had formed Magetech. The point of Magetech was to exploit the influence of the Portal, to apply twenty-first century science and engineering to it, or vice versa . . .

What kind of resource would that salt be?

I thought back to when I received the package. How my satellite and phone reception went, despite the filters for normal background mana. How Dr. Kawata complained about his brand-new spectrometer failing. The camera on my phone failing at *Thor's Hammer*, and at the *Nazgûl*.

The white circle around Ossian's remains.

Potential.

Implication.

Nothing solid . . .

I wanted to talk to Dr. Pretorious.

The man I called was a private investigator of a rather specialized variety. His name was Quintin Valentino, and he didn't stake anyone out, didn't take incriminating pictures, didn't even own a gun. As far as I knew, the guy lived in his office. But you could give him a first name and where the person worked, and he could come back with a credit report, tax records, arrest record, and résumé.

"Quint?"

"Kline, darling. How long has it been . . . ?"

"Too long. Can you look someone up for me?"

"On your account? Anyone you want."

"Name's Pretorious. Dr. Eric Pretorious."

"Please tell me you can spell that."

I gave him the spelling from my notes.

"Any other identifiers?"

"Worked at, probably part owner of, a company called Magetech."

"Well, that won't be too hard. Tomorrow soon enough?"

"Yes, fine."

I hung up my cell phone as I drove up one of Solon's snaking industrial pathways. Solon was one of the outer suburban nets that caught a lot of the industry shaken loose from the Cleveland metropolitan economy in the last quarter of the twentieth century. It was the closest of a cluster of suburbs whose combination of undeveloped acreage—read "farms"—and attractive real estate taxes attracted large box warehouses and factories like a presidential campaign attracted unreasonable promises.

I drove by windowless boxes made of concrete and corrugated steel, squatting in the midst of floodlit asphalt. Semi trucks backed into loading bays—industrial young sucking the teats of their mother. Every few moments, a tractor trailer would drive past me, going in the opposite direction. The side panels advertised kitchen cabinets, soft drinks, or auto parts.

At the end of the road sat my destination.

The Magetech factory/warehouse complex wrapped around the end of the street so completely that it was able to build its massive logo into the island in the center of the cul-de-sac.

I pulled into a small visitor's parking lot under the watchful eye of a security camera. I sat in my car and looked around, trying to get a sense of the place. The scale was huge. Easily several hundred acres. A half dozen separate buildings were immediately visible, each marked with standardized runes which could be wards, or could simply be some form of building markers. I could also see runes on the plowed surface of the main parking lot.

The lot was down a long driveway from the five visitor spots, wrapped in chain-link, and protected by a guard shack where a single uniformed dwarf sat, eyeing me suspiciously. The lot was mostly empty except for a quartet of charter buses, all bearing the Magetech logo.

As I got out of the Volkswagen, I saw thirty or forty dwarves dressed in overalls and hard hats exit one of the buildings and head toward one of the buses. I heard their guttural conversations drift my way, and slow to a stop as they reached the bus and more of them saw me.

It felt as if they all stared at me as they queued up to board the bus.

Okay, I'm out of place here. We've established that.

I wanted to see more of Magetech, and I was holding the hope that Mr. Lucas' uncharacteristic openness would filter down to the factory floor. Seeing the dwarves react to me made me second-guess that idea.

"Maybe I shouldn't be here," I whispered in a puff of fog.

I managed to shock myself by voicing such an unprofessional thought. I was still suffering from the aftereffects of my visit to the corporate office. I was expecting some evil premonition, some sort of nasty mana overload to raise the small hairs on my neck.

Fortunately, I didn't sense much of anything.

That made me wonder what was at the corporate office that made me react so badly. It couldn't be raw mana, considering what Magetech did here. I couldn't imagine there'd be *less* concentration here than downtown.

I took a few deep breaths, became a journalist again, and walked into the front office.

The name Simon Lucas was good for opening doors. Enough so that I had the sense that I was expected. After I showed my credentials and did a little strategic name-dropping, I soon had a bright-blue engraved visitor ID and a tour guide.

I was surprised that the foreman who got the job to show me around happened to be human—though he was as grizzled as any dwarf. "You keep that ID on you, boy, or security will hit you." He reminded me of an old shop teacher.

On our way to one of the factories, I got a glimpse of some of the security he was talking about. Not only were there double rows of razor-wire topped chain-link surrounding the compound, but they had some really impressive guard dogs. A Rottweiler is intimidating enough, but give one an extra two hundred pounds of muscle and an extra head or two, and you had a pretty good deterrent against industrial espionage.

My guide didn't need to tell me to stay on the path behind him. The first building I saw was an assembly plant. We walked along a path, safely behind a thick sheet of glass. My guide expressed some pride in the vast space beyond which was filled with a forest of industrial robots undergoing strange repetitive gyrations. He explained that the line I watched was the ultimate in flexibility, the same robots that put together cell phones one day could put together wide-screen TVs the next.

The flexibility was necessary, since ninety percent of Magetech's production was retrofitting third-party electronics. Most of what this line did was disassembly of some brand-name device, insertion of Magetech's patented hardware, and reassembly.

The robots themselves were unusual. I could see glyphs engraved along the arm, and most of them sat inside a protective circle of some sort. I looked closely, and judging by the swinging gestures and unnatural glow, a few were actually casting some sort of spell over the finished products—HP laptops at the moment.

I peppered the guy with questions, and, fortunately he didn't seem to mind answering them. A lot of what I asked was a matter of confirming background details. I didn't bring up Nina's rumors since I doubted that would be productive at the moment.

However, I looked down and saw a trio of dwarves working on one of the robots whose glyphs glowed an unhealthy green and I asked, "You employ a lot of dwarves?"

He nodded. "They can work safely around hazardous mana levels."

I looked down again at the shop floor, and the robot the dwarves worked on belched a noxious looking cloud of green smoke. "If it's not safe down there . . ."

"How can we be up here?" He knocked on the glass. "One of our developments, mana shielding. All the radiation is confined inside this building."

I looked at the glass, trying to see what he was talking about. "I didn't know you could do that."

My guide laughed. "A lot of what we do here would be impossible without it."

"How's it work?"

"Trade secret—suffice to say it came from the study of dwarven mana resistance."

"I see . . ." So, perhaps there was more to the fact that Dr. Shafran had no dwarves willing to be examined.

He took me around to see a clean room where chips were etched and enchanted, and a few warehouses where boxes waited to be shipped across northeast Ohio.

Everywhere dwarves worked, they gave me the evil eye. My guide made sure to steer me away from any employees. Judging by the way they reacted, I couldn't tell if the foreman was trying to hide something, or if he was protecting me.

It was late evening when I parked at my condo, trying to tell myself to take a break. The story would wait until the morning.

Fate, the Oracle, or just plain old bad luck had other plans.

When I stepped out of my Volkswagen and saw the lights on in my apartment, I knew there was a problem. I don't leave the lights on, as a rule. And as I slowly walked toward the lobby, I didn't see Willie, the doorman, anywhere around.

Not a good sign.

I hit the speed-dial on my cell phone; it rang once. "Cleveland Police Department."

I had a couple of thoughts about who might be knocking around my apartment, and was checking on the first possibility. "Can you connect me to the Special Paranormal Unit? Commander Caledvwlch, please."

The phone rang.

I got Caledvwlch's voice mail, which was just as well. "This is Kline Maxwell. It's ten after eight on Friday, I'm at my condo, and if you're not waiting in my apartment, either I'm about to be jumped or the FBI is about to haul me in for questioning about your dead dwarf."

I pushed my way into the lobby, and I wasn't particularly surprised when a gentleman in a dark suit stepped up to me and said, "Mr. Maxwell, come with me, please."

I hung up.

My apartment was Fed central. Half a dozen dark-suited men were poking around every corner of my condo, and judging by the state it was in, they had arrived a few minutes after I had left to see Dr. Shafran. They had easily put a good two hours into trashing the place.

They'd opened closets, rummaged through drawers, and right now they were in the process of pointing various arcane charms at the walls and the furniture.

"And what can I do for you?" I asked as my escort unceremoniously deposited me on my couch.

"Hey . . ." I stood up, only to be pushed back down by another suit.

I looked up at them. "You know, some sort of ID would be nice, not to mention a warrant."

"Still as cooperative as ever, aren't you, Mr. Maxwell?"

The voice was familiar, but I couldn't place it until the speaker walked into the living room.

"Blackstone?"

He hadn't changed much. Hair a little grayer, but he still looked more like a math professor than a government agent. He reached into his breast pocket and pulled out an ID for me. I gave it a cursory glance.

"'Counterterrorism?' New career track, or are you 'on loan' again?" Last time I saw him he was a semilegal spook working out of the euphemistically named "Threat Assessment Office." I'm not exactly sure what intelligence umbrella it worked under, but it was responsible for a fair bit of the cloak-and-dagger work around the Portal before the Feds got custody of it.

I guess it would have been too much to hope that the Feds winning that particular battle would put Blackstone out of a job.

"I have some questions for you."

I looked at the Feds ransacking my apartment. One of them found some dirty laundry I'd hidden and was busy dumping it on the floor, one dirty sock at a time. "I hope you have a warrant."

"We're here under authority of the Federal Special Administration Zone."

"Christ, Blackstone, that hasn't been used since the end of the blockade."

Blackstone shrugged and smiled. "I don't have to explain this to you, do I?"

What I said a while back, about repealing tax abatements, goes for extensions of executive power, too. Back in the chaos when the Portal opened, the federal government did a few crazy things—like ringing Cuyahoga County with tanks. In the midst of all that was an executive order that made the area within the Portal's influence a police state in the name of national security.

To my knowledge, it had never been tested in court, since the Feds never actually "occupied" Cleveland—Congress intervened before that happened.

I suspected that Blackstone was pushing things a bit.

"We're going to have a little talk," he said.

"Are we?"

"You're going to tell me everything you know about the dwarven operation."

I put my hand on my forehead and rubbed my temple. I could tell already that this was going to go really well. "Exactly which dwarven operation are we talking about?"

"You know better than to play coy with me. This isn't just provincial Cleveland voodoo involved here."

"Let me guess, it's a matter of national security."

"Let me spell this out for you. We know that there are humans involved in this ring. We know you had contact with Ossian Parthalán a few hours before he was assassinated, and that he sent you one package we know about. We've identified one cell in California, and just by coincidence we find that you've been out to the coast at least ten times in the past four years."

"Good Lord, Blackstone, my daughter lives there."

"And you've been a very attentive father."

"I don't believe this."

Blackstone sat on the arm of the couch, looking at me. Behind him, one of the agents started methodically rummaging through my DVD collection, popping disks into a laptop he had placed on the coffee table. "Help me, Maxwell. I don't really think you're involved in this. But I have enough now to pull you into the system, and then you're not coming back out."

"What is it you think I know?"

Blackstone smiled. "I'm giving you credit for being a good reporter. You'd obviously tapped the dwarf as a source. All I want is what he gave you."

The hell you say.

A little voice inside me told me that Blackstone wasn't going to be satisfied with the truth. What I actually knew was rather weak justification for the kind of muscle Blackstone was flexing here.

Blackstone was an asshole, and I didn't doubt that he'd pull me in just out of spite if he didn't like my answers. I couldn't even come up with some convincing lie. I didn't know what I'd be lying about.

The guy probably had a truth-detecting charm on one of his entourage anyway.

Plan B; play up what I did know and stall for time.

I looked at the guys tossing my apartment and said, "They aren't going to find any more. He only sent one package."

"So why send it?"

"To back up the information he was going to give me. A sample of what Magetech was working on."

I paused. That was a guess, and I didn't like guessing in front of the Feds. But it sank in without much surprise on Blackstone's part. I took it as a silent confirmation.

"That explains your visit there today . . ."

I looked around and had another guess. From the behavior of the Feds here, it was pretty obvious that this salt was considered some sort of contraband. If I played Blackstone right, I might gain as much information as he did from this interview.

"If I'm guessing right—" I continued on with the assumption that if I qualified the statement as speculation it wasn't pure bullshit. "—a sample of what he was shipping to California."

Blackstone should never play poker. His satisfied expression told me all I needed to know about my speculation. "Go on."

I thought of the car with California plates in *Thor's Hammer.* "Did the zombie get to the car before you did?"

Blackstone frowned. "I'm asking the questions here."

"Uh-huh. A little interdepartmental dispute with the local cops? They decided it was their evidence?"

"That's not your concern."

"The locals tend to get possessive about murder cases, don't they?"

Blackstone leaned forward. "Shall we continue with the matter at hand, Mr. Maxwell?"

"What do you want to know?" I said in my most helpful tone. I found it an easier pose to make, now that Blackstone had confirmed a nagging suspicion of mine; the suspicion that the Feds weren't fully cooperating with the local cops.

But then, what else was new?

"Let's start with the note. Who was Ossian Parthalán referring to? Why 'who' killed himself?"

Now there was an interesting gap.

"The way you were following our dwarf, I'm surprised you didn't have a tap on his phone—"

"Mr. Maxwell—"

"Apparently you didn't need a warrant."

"You are trying my patience."

"I'm cooperating."

"You're stalling."

You noticed. "Parthalán was hinting that the city government was involved. I never got to speak to him about it. He was killed before I got the chance. We were supposed to have a meeting the day he was killed."

"At the club?"

"No, the Old Arcade." I looked at him and decided to see how deep the schism between the Feds and the local cops actually went. "I found out he'd been killed when Commander Caledvwlch showed up and questioned me about it."

"What?"

"Maelgwyn Caledvwlch, head of the SPU. Special Paranormal Unit. If the dwarf's murder was part of a ritual, it falls into his jurisdiction—"

"Cut the crap. I know exactly who the damn elf is." He looked at a couple of the Feds who'd been watching our interchange. "I'm not even going to ask why we didn't know about this when it happened. I just want someone to follow up and find out what else is going on in the SPU we might have missed."

A pair of agents nodded and left.

"So, I take it this isn't a joint investigation with the local authorities?"

"Maxwell, do you really think—" Blackstone shook his head. "I don't think you realize how serious this is."

"Why don't you tell me?"

"You just told me that there were ties into the city government. What makes you think the local cops aren't involved?"

"Are you saying Maelgwyn Caledvwlch is dirty?"

"Good Lord—do you even remember how you met him?"

Yeah, I did. It wasn't really a comforting thought. To an extent, Caledvwlch's actions in the mess around the Aloeus murder weren't his fault, they were proxy actions for a crooked cop he'd pledged fealty to—but the law in this country doesn't make those kind of distinctions and the reason Caledvwlch wasn't in jail right now was primarily due to the DA's shallow investigation, and to the fact that, in the end, he handed the Rayburn administration the least politically damaging scapegoat conveniently dead and unable to testify.

I could say for sure that the elf played by the rules, but those rules were the ones he brought over from the other side of the Portal.

"What did you talk to him about?"

I don't know if I was relieved or not when I heard sirens approaching.

"Why don't you ask him yourself?"

One of the Feds searching my apartment stationed himself by the window and looked down at the street.

"What is it?" Blackstone asked him.

"Locals, looks like half the SPU."

"Shit." Blackstone looked at me accusingly.

I shrugged.

Blackstone shook his head. "Maxwell, you're either neck-deep in this, or you're incredibly stupid."

I didn't give him the satisfaction of telling him that those weren't necessarily mutually exclusive options.

Blackstone turned and walked over to the door of my apartment, just in time to confront a contingent of Cleveland police officers, Commander Caledvwlch in the lead. The elf towered over Blackstone, half his face obscured by the top of the doorframe.

"To what do I owe this pleasure?" Blackstone said.

"There is an ongoing murder investigation." Caledvwlch's voice was impassive as ever. "I am here to take Mr. Maxwell downtown for questioning."

"Mr. Maxwell is a material witness in a federal investigation."

"It seems we have a bureaucratic impasse, then." Caledvwlch pulled a cell phone out of one of the baggy folds in his suit jacket. "I will have to consult with the judge who issued the warrant."

"Actually," Blackstone said, "I think we're done here." He waved at his men, who started filing out of my apartment. He glanced back at me before he left. "I'll be in touch."

I'm sure.

Caledvwlch folded his way into the remains of my apartment, followed by a pair of police officers. He looked at me with his shiny metallic eyes and said, "It puzzles me that men create rules only so they can twist them out of shape."

"I will admit that feudal fealty is a little simpler."

"I have a warrant," Caledvwlch said.

I sighed. "So you are taking me in?"

"Only to make a statement." He handed me a sheet of paper from within his voluminous jacket. It wasn't an arrest warrant.

"You're looking for the letter?"

"Any correspondence that might have come from Mr. Ossian Parthalán."

"I'm afraid Blackstone beat you to it."

He nodded, and I suspected that he wasn't surprised at all. "If you would come with me and make a statement to that effect?"

He led me toward the door, and the other cops stayed in my condo. "What are they for?"

"Simply making sure that your fallible human memory hasn't forgotten anything." The two cops picked up right where the Feds left off.

I'd known Caledvwlch for a couple of years, and if you'd asked me to predict what his office would look like, I would have probably envisioned something as austere, sterile, and functional as an operating theater in a Trappist monastery.

I guess I was a little off the mark.

He sat me in one corner while he folded himself behind a desk that seemed a little small for him. The first detail I noted was that all the furniture was wood, very little metal at all.

It made sense. Elves reacted badly to iron, not just in elemental form, but alloys to a certain extent. I don't know the medical or magical basis for it. But, while elves only seemed to be injured by iron that broke through the skin, every one I've seen was wary of being exposed to the metal.

And, apparently, Caledvwlch wasn't a fan of IKEA. The desk and the chairs were rich antique hardwood. The kind of furniture that graced a policeman's office of Eliot Ness' vintage. On the polished mahogany of his desk sat a trio of bonsai trees in brightly colored ceramic pots. In one, a figurine of a Taoist monk sat on a rock grinning at some private joke.

On the walls I saw an eclectic collection of art, mostly Asian landscapes in ink washes.

"Mr. Maxwell."

I turned back to face him. "You wanted a statement?"

"You keep appearing in our investigation. It is time I had a clear picture of why."

I shrugged. "I think we're investigating the same thing?"

"If that is the case, I would be interested in exactly how the dwarven enterprise of Magetech is involved." Caledvwlch chewed the word with some visible distaste. I couldn't help thinking that it was for my benefit.

"You have something against Magetech?"

Caledvwlch spread his hands across the desk. "The dwarves are a noble race whose passage here was as perilous as our own. In the end, each of us chooses the paths we take. What connection exists between the dwarf Ossian Parthalán and the company Magetech?"

"I don't know. I was investigating Councilman Mazurich."

"And the material that Ossian Parthalán sent to you?"

"Salt."

Caledvwlch nodded, as if that was the answer he expected.

"Shall we review everything that happened since you received Ossian Parthalán's phone call?"

CHAPTER TWELVE

IT was well after midnight before I was completely disentangled from the legal system, tired, unenlightened, and more than a little annoyed. I generally don't like being leaned on.

Right now, though, I was walking out of the Justice Center and just wanted to get home.

It had started snowing while I'd been sequestered with Caledvwich. The snow muffled sound. While the bars and clubs were just getting into gear a few blocks away, where I was the night was—for a moment—dead quiet. It was eerie the way the snow swirled around. And briefly, framed by the silence, I saw a reptilian silhouette eclipse the upper part of the Terminal Tower.

Somewhere, a traffic light changed, and the silence was broken as cars shot by on the street in front of me, throwing slush at me and at each other.

We had only thirty dragons or so in the Greater Cleveland area. I wondered which one I'd just glimpsed. They'd been keeping a low profile, especially since the Feds took over the Portal. They were a set of creatures that made the Feds really nervous—and while they had rights, they only had them under Ohio state law.

Most of them had comfortably integrated themselves into the local economy, and—as powerful as they were—I doubted any of them wanted to be a test case for some sort of Fed crackdown. I was sort of surprised to see one flying downtown, even this late at night.

I turned my attention to the street and looked for a taxi.

I was lucky; one had started slowing down and pulling over, even before I started waving at it. I figured I must have looked forlorn and a little lost.

The Justice Center was probably a good place to pick up fares, with people being processed out of the system at all hours, so I didn't think much of it as I opened the door and slid into the back of the cab.

"Shaker Square, please," I told the driver as I leaned back in the seat. The cabbie had the heat somewhere in the high eighties, and the snow that had dusted my clothes melted instantly, soaking me through. I wiped my forehead, unsure if I was wiping sweat or melted snow off my face.

Now Shaker Square is pretty much due east of downtown, which happened to be the direction the cab had been traveling down Superior to begin with when it picked me up. I didn't think much when the driver took a right turn right after Public Square. There were a number of ways to get there, and I had enough cash on me that I wasn't that concerned about being gouged.

It was the second right, immediately after that one, that made me suspicious.

"Hey? I said Shaker Square—where're you going?"

That's when I glanced at the hack license. "Samanish Thégharin," next to a picture of a broad, full-bearded face. Dwarven.

The cab continued turning, circling the Soldiers and Sailors' Monument in the shadow of the Terminal Tower, until we ended up westbound on Superior.

"Do you mind telling me what's going on?" By this point there was no possible route that would explain where we were going. My cabbie had a destination of his own in mind. This was not encouraging given the profile of Ossian Parthalán's kinsman that Reggie had given me.

"Look, why don't you let me out, I'll take the bus."

Mr. Thégharin ignored me, as if he couldn't hear me at all behind the Plexiglas partition. I reached for the door, but the handles were absent. I apparently was going wherever Mr. Thégharin wanted.

I thought about smashing one of the windows to make my escape, but there were some scary-looking glyphs etched in the glass, and I didn't relish finding out what they did the hard way.

Before I worked up enough panic to make the attempt, the Detroit-Superior Bridge loomed up in front of us. A mass of concrete and blue steel arcing over the Flats whose far end was hidden by layers of blowing snow.

Instead of crossing the bridge, my dwarf swerved right. If he kept to the street, he'd head down to the Flats, but he pulled over toward a forest of orange barrels and blinking sawhorses. It seemed as if he'd plow right into the construction barriers, but barely visible shadows emerged from the blowing snow to move the barriers aside and let the taxi pass.

I glanced behind me and saw the same barriers quickly replaced behind us. Then a tunnel swallowed us in darkness.

The Detroit-Superior Bridge was a Depression-era project, built when the city still had streetcars, so it was built with two levels. The upper deck was designed for automobile traffic, the lower deck for the streetcar traffic. The lower level was shut up and mothballed when Cleveland got rid of its streetcar system. Despite a long series of proposals, and one major renovation, the lower deck remained closed for several decades.

It wasn't until recently, with the rise of tourism, that any plans for using the space reached the construction phase. The Regional Transit Authority planned to expand its existing light-rail line from the East Side and downtown, moving west toward Lakewood and Rocky River.

The western link would cross the Flats using the existing lower deck of the bridge. All of which was still five to ten years in the future.

But construction had already started. And, as was the case for about half of construction work in this town, a dwarven company had gotten the contract.

The cab rolled through a dark tunnel, past two sets of floor-to-ceiling chain-link fences that opened of their own accord. We passed pallets of rebar, concrete block, PVC pipe, and other items less identifiable to me.

Past the second gate, we pulled out onto the deck proper. It was a vast space, dotted by pillars marching off into the darkness. The far end was too distant for the headlights to make out, so it felt as if the half-finished railroad tracks marched off forever.

The cab rolled slowly down the center, between two pairs of tracks. Through concrete arches on either side, I could see the swirling snow obscuring the view of the Flats and the city.

Ahead of us, a group was waiting. A ring of squat figures was picked out in the taxi's headlights. They were dressed uniformly, as if they had all walked off the same job site. They wore brown coveralls, streaked with grime, heavy steel-toed boots, thick leather gloves, and hard hats. When they parted to let the taxi roll into the center of their circle, I saw that they all wore face masks or respirators.

I hoped the masks were more for anonymity's sake, rather than because of toxic particulate matter in the air.

The taxi came to a stop in the center of the circle, and the passenger door popped open for me. I didn't need a cue from my driver, Mr. Thégharin, to know what was expected of me. Despite my contrary streak, I am not completely self-destructive. I hadn't time to count, but there was a ring of about twenty dwarves circling this taxi. And, given the reputation they had for strength and martial ability—back home they didn't just *make* swords, after all—I doubted I could overpower any one of them.

Whatever was going on, I had a much better chance of talking my way out of it.

I stepped out of the taxi, and closed the door behind me. The taxi moved quickly enough that it almost knocked me over. It was through the circle, and the circle had closed behind it all before I had completely regained my equilibrium.

The glow from the headlights receded as the taxi continued on its journey toward the west side of the Cuyahoga. As the artificial light receded, it allowed my eyes to register the flickering orange light of candles surrounding me. Heavy black candles as thick as my forearm, and about half again as long, placed around the inner circumference of the ring of dwarves surrounding me.

I turned slowly until I faced the odd dwarf out. This guy was dressed the same, but he wasn't part of the group ringing me. He was bent over, backing around the inner circumference of the circle, chanting something quiet and guttural to himself as he poured something white out of a small canvas bag. He was completing a circle that separated me from the others, and he was just now walking across the space where the taxi had left.

I glanced behind me and saw that he had already passed the half of the circle where the taxi had entered.

The bastard has good timing.

I walked toward the one spot where the circle was incomplete. I didn't know a lot about magic, but I knew breaking a circle was a bad thing. If I wanted out of this, I needed to step out before this little ritual was completed.

The dwarf in the ring directly in front of me reached for his tool belt and took out a small mini-sledge and hefted it while looking at me. I stopped, looked around at my four-and-a-half-foot-tall audience, and asked, "Someone tell me what is going on here."

The only audible answer was the continued chant of the dwarf pouring the circle, who took a few steps across my path to complete it.

The hair rose on my arms and the back of my neck. I could smell the energy released into the air.

Like hell dwarves don't do magic.

A solid blue arc whipped around the perimeter of the circle, close enough that the force threw me backward. I stumbled and fell on my ass, roughly in the center of the circle. All around me, the air crackled as arcs leaped up from the circle, forming a blue hemisphere of energy about twenty feet in diameter—ending just short of the ceiling above me.

My pulse raced. I couldn't see this ending well.

"Mr. Maxwell," spoke a vaguely familiar voice.

I lowered my gaze to confront the dwarf who had completed the circle. Apparently, he was on my side of the circle when he finished. He took off his mask and I could recognize him.

"Teaghue Parthalán."

He walked toward me, his face grim. "Abandon the path you follow, Mr. Maxwell."

I pushed myself upright. We both now stood on a disk of concrete that seemed to hover in a universe of hazy blue. Nothing was visible beyond the barrier.

"Exactly what path is that?" I tried to keep my voice from shaking, and I wiped my palms on my trousers. I was still apprehensive, but the fact that Teaghue decided to talk to me was a little reassuring.

"The path the former brother of my clan had mind to set you on."

"It happens to be my job," I told him. It was my ornery streak speaking, and I counted it a victory of self-preservation that I didn't say the first five things that came to mind.

Teaghue shook his head and I had the odd impression that, wholly by accident, I had actually said the right thing. "You believe we do this lightly? But it has come to this. We must ask you to cease, for your sake as much as ours."

His attitude was not quite what I had expected.

"Is this a threat?"

The creases in Teaghue's face made his expression deep and impenetrable. His voice was cold. "It is a warning. A warning undertaken at great risk and no little expense. Ossian's misstep has drawn too much attention already. Should you suffer the same fate, the resulting chaos would be impossible to undo."

"Who killed Ossian?"

Teaghue stepped back and shook his head. "Do not ask that question."

I stepped forward. "Why?"

"You will draw *his* attention."

"Who?"

I was leaning over to talk to him, and with no warning, Teaghue struck me. His leatherwork glove hit the side of my face hard enough to knock me over. I fell back, spitting blood and cradling a broken lip.

"*Do not ask that question!*" Teaghue was obviously pissed, but there was an undercurrent there, one of very deep fear. I began to understand something—the dwarves were shilling for someone. It wasn't the dwarves who killed off Ossian, it was the Mr. Big who was running things. Ossian's attempt at contacting me made sense then; he wasn't turning against his clan so much as trying to get at Mr. Big.

I rubbed my mouth and looked at Teaghue. "If you tell me what's going on, I might be able to help."

Teaghue just shook his head.

I kept prodding. "Ossian must have thought so . . ."

"Ossian was a fool. Mazurich was a fool." Teaghue stepped up to me and grabbed my collar, and for the first time since we started the dialogue, I feared for my life. "And you are a fool, Mr. Maxwell. There are forces here you cannot contain and you would loose them on you and yours. The clans chose their path long ago, and turning back now would only destroy everything. Leave the authors of the Thesarch in the shadows."

"What do you mean?"

Teaghue backed to the edge of the circle. "We have done what good by you we can. Any further would do you ill." He muttered something and the blue around us dissolved, leaving me nearly blind in sudden darkness.

"Wait!" I said, getting to my feet again.

From a distance I heard Teaghue respond, "Abandon your path, Mr. Maxwell, it will only bring you sorrow."

Afterward, everything was quiet.

I stood and let my eyes adjust to the gloom. For a while it seemed that the rest of the world was reluctant to reveal itself. Slowly, as I listened, I started to hear the wind and blowing snow around the bridge, a distant siren, a lone car crossing the bridge on the deck above me.

When I could see well enough to feel safe taking a step, everyone was gone. The only sign of my strange interview was a white circle on the concrete, and a quintet of black candles outside its perimeter.

I looked at the circle on the ground and knelt by it. It echoed, on a larger scale, the circle drawn around the body of Ossian Parthalán. It was probably a stupid thing to do, but I ran my finger through the white crystals marking the circle, and touched it to my tongue.

Salt.

CHAPTER THIRTEEN

I TAKE a step forward, naked, bleeding, and sliding on my own blood.

I am thrown back as a quartet of horsemen erupt from the Portal. Upon the pale horse that tramples me, I see a skeleton wrapped with raw flesh stitched together with steel wire.

The figure of Death leans toward me, opens its mouth, and in it I hear the death rattle of Ossian the dwarf.

I turn and see the dwarf, spread-eagled and mutilated, lying on a vast mountain of salt. The dwarf's blood seeps into the grayish-white crystals, turning them orange, then crimson.

Live dwarves work at the base of the mountain, shoveling the bloodstained crystals into ore carts. They are all shackled to a large chain that is bolted to the base of a massive throne. I grab one and see the face of Teaghue.

"What are you doing?" I ask.

"It must be fed!" he says.

"What must be fed?"

The dwarf points his shovel at the throne.

I look, and the goat-faced Devil looks directly at me. Reaching out with a clawed fist, he says, "Behold the cost of defying me!"

The Devil opens his fist and I see . . .

I sat bolt upright in my bed, my whole body clammy from the sweats, my heart racing. I didn't remember what I had seen. I didn't want to remember.

I think I knew . . .

My phone rang.

I turned and looked at the handset, sitting in its cradle. It was still dark outside, and the little red LED cast an infernal glow over the whole bedroom. It blinked slowly with the insectile buzz, giving me intermittent views of my apartment, still devastated by the law enforcement invasion last night.

I don't get premonitions, but I didn't want to answer the phone. I sat in my bed and stared at it as the clock next to it blinked 6:01 AM at me.

It stopped. I don't know why, but I'd been holding my breath.

I slowly exhaled. If it were important, they'd leave a message.

The way my heart was racing, there was no way I was getting back to sleep. I got up and stretched.

The phone rang again.

"Oh, hell,"

I reached down and grabbed it. "Hello?"

"Kline? Thank the Goddess. I've been trying to reach you—"

She sounded severely stressed out, but I wasn't in a very forgiving mood. "Nina, it's six in the morning and I've only had three hours of sleep. Can this wait?"

"No, you're in danger. You can't let your daughter come to Cleveland."

"Look, me and my ex have dealt with that—"

"I've found out . . ." She trailed off.

"Found out what?"

"I can't over the phone. It's too dangerous."

"What's too dangerous?"

"Don't ask me any questions. Come to my house, where it's safe to talk."

"Nina, you have to tell me—" The receiver clicked and I was talking to a dial tone.

I rubbed my chin where Teaghue had hit me. I still tasted blood when I sucked on my lip. In Nina's protests, I had heard an echo of the dwarf: *"Do not ask that question."*

What could be so dangerous that to even ask about it was threatening?

Given the past three days, I couldn't readily dismiss Nina's warning. I just thanked God that Sarah wasn't going to be showing up today.

However, I almost called Margaret just to make sure. The only thing that stopped me was the fact it was three in the morning on the coast. Calling now would take concerned parenting to a passive-aggressive extreme.

So I didn't call.

I should have.

Instead, I turned on the light and surveyed the damage. "*Real* glad you're staying home, baby," I whispered.

Between the Feds and the local cops, the place had been devastated. Every drawer and closet had been opened, the contents piled at random on the furniture and the floor. The furniture had all been pulled away from the walls, cushions removed and stripped, and the less said of the kitchen the better.

I was in as bad shape as my condo. I had slept in my clothes, which were dotted with dime-sized splatters of blood from my busted lip. I stood up and went into the wreckage of my bathroom, hoping for enough unmolested toiletries to clean myself up.

West 25th and Vega was probably a decent neighborhood before the Depression. Now it was just one of those odd urban corners of Cleveland that gentrification and economic recovery had yet to reach. Vega itself was easy to miss—it was a one-way street that sat right on top of the I-90 on-ramp. Nina's house faced the Interstate.

I would have thought a full-time staffer would have been able to afford better.

Nina's address wasn't as run-down as its neighbors. The windows had glass, the paint had been done in the last quarter century or so, and the wrought-iron fence around the property was intact and relatively new.

Squinting through the blowing snow, you could almost ignore its neighbors and imagine how it looked when this area was upper middle class.

She met me at the door and pulled me inside. She looked as bad as she'd sounded on the phone. She wore jeans and a T-shirt, her eyes were red, her hair frizzy and yanked back in a severe ponytail. She looked more strung out than I felt, and I wondered if she'd had any sleep at all last night.

"I need to talk to you," she said as she pulled me into the house. I didn't get much of a look at the place. Victorian decor, lots of hanging fabric, lots of plants, the smell of incense.

"What about?"

"Shhh . . ."

She pulled me up a flight of stairs, past framed portraits of Buddha and Krishna, past a little statue of Shiva dancing, and into one of the upstairs bedrooms.

I stumbled in a few steps as she closed and bolted the door. She hung an amulet on the doorknob and said, "There."

Her voice echoed in the windowless room.

"Mind telling me what's going on?"

The room was empty. No furniture, no carpet, only a bare bulb in a light socket in the ceiling. Even the closet door was gone, leaving the closet an empty niche in one corner of the room.

On the hardwood floor was a large circle of glyphs drawn in a cursive feminine hand. "We should be safe in here," Nina said.

"Safe from what?"

Instead of answering, she pulled a tarot card out of her pocket and handed it to me. *The Devil* . . .

"What is this?" Fragments of my nightmare came to mind, looking at the card. The massive stone throne, the dwarves chained to its base.

"Behold the cost of defying me!"

"The visions are worse," Nina said to me. "They keep coming. They're warning you . . ."

"Warning *me?* What do you mean?"

Nina grabbed me. "They're *your* visions. Now, you're seeing them yourself. I saw them first because I'm sensitive, and I work close to you."

I backed up and shook my head. "Whoa, Nina, I'm no seer. I'm the most thoroughly mundane man you'll ever meet. I normally don't even report on the stuff."

She stared at me, "You've seen them."

I swallowed and looked down at the card.

"The Oracle can reach anyone, and being exposed to high concentrations of mana can bring on a sensitivity . . ."

"I haven't been . . ."

Bullshit, Kline. The dwarf mailed you a package of salt intense enough to throw Kawata's spectrometer out of whack. That ring at the Nazgûl *probably wasn't cornstarch, and you* tasted *a sample of what the dwarves were using last night, you Brainiac. God himself only knows what kind of power was flowing through Magetech corporate headquarters . . .*

I must have zoned out because Nina was shaking me. "Did you hear what I said?"

"What?"

"You can*not* let your daughter come here. Not before the Tower falls."

The Tower? I hadn't seen that yet.

"Fine, fine." I held up my hands.

"What?"

"I've told you, it's under control. We've already postponed her visit."

Nina's face went white. "She *was* going to . . ."

"One o'clock flight this afternoon."

"So close . . ." She turned away from me and started shaking.

"It's all right, we bumped her trip."

She kept shaking her head. "No."

I put a hand on her shoulder. "It's all right."

She spun around and said, "No, it isn't. *Call her.*"

"What?"

"Call her and tell her not to come."

"What is this, Nina? What does my daughter have to do with it?"

"She won't be safe as long as he—"

She stopped talking and the only sound was the house creaking and settling around us.

"As long as who? What?" I looked around. "We went over this yesterday. You said you discovered something. What was it?"

She stepped away from me, shaking her head. "No." She looked up at the corners of the room. The creaking was getting worse. Small trails of dust drifted down from the ceiling. It suddenly began to feel very warm in the house.

Nina's muscles went tense and her eyes rolled back in her head.

"Nina?" I reached for her.

Bad move.

My hand touched her shoulder and I felt a shock as if someone laid a two-by-four across my face. I slammed all the way backward into the far wall, cracking the plaster and bruising my kidneys.

"Annoying little bitch."

The voice coming out of Nina's throat was deep, masculine, and somehow, familiar.

The room darkened as the single light bulb began to fail. The light turned red as the glyphs on the floor burst into flame. *"Maxwell is mine, and you cannot keep me from him."*

I tried to push myself upright, but I felt a spasm of pain in my lower back and my legs slid out from under me. "Who are you?" I managed through clenched teeth.

"You know who I am. I am the answer to your question."

"What have you done to Nina?"

"Only accepted her invitation."

"Show yourself."

The laugh was inhuman and soul wrenching. *"I will show myself to you soon enough, when you come begging to serve me."*

"Let her go."

The thing laughed again, and the room was plunged into darkness as the flaming glyphs died out. The lightbulb flickered back on in time for me to see Nina collapse on the charred protective circle.

"Shit." This time I managed to get myself up on my hands and knees to get over to her. She was breathing okay, and my rudimentary knowledge of first aid allowed me to find a pulse.

"Nina? Can you hear me?"

She stared straight ahead, at the ceiling. I shook her shoulder gently. No response.

"God damn it."

I pulled out my cell phone and dialed 9-1-1.

Not wanting to deal with the Emergency Room, I didn't tell the paramedics about literally throwing my back out. I watched, more or less helplessly, as they examined Nina, and carried her out to a waiting ambulance. I called Columbia, knowing full well I'd get her voice mail on a Saturday, and left a message for her about Nina.

Then I called HR at the *Press,* hoping they had the right emergency contacts for her.

I didn't even know if she was married.

I sat in the Volkswagen for a long time before I could get my head around what had happened. This wasn't just Mazurich and a dead dwarf. Somehow this was tied to me, and my daughter.

It took a long time for Margaret to answer the phone.

"Hello?" Her voice was cracked and hoarse, I could tell that I hadn't woken her up. I heard someone in the background. I heard her stage whisper to someone, "It's her father."

I felt the bottom fall out of my stomach. "Margaret? What's wrong?"

"Kline, my God, I was going to call you—I'm still talking to the police."

No.

"What's the matter?"

She was whispering again, "No, he's my ex-husband, and he's in Cleveland."

"Margaret, what's the matter? Is Sarah all right? What happened?"

"We had a fight, a bad one . . ."

"Is she all right?"

"I think so, but—"

"But what?"

"She ran away."

My hand was shaking. This couldn't be happening. We had safely dealt with it.

Margaret was still talking. ". . .while I was asleep. I thought it was all settled. But she took the car. I don't know where she went. The police are here."

I felt like Macbeth watching the trees walking toward the rampart walls. "I know where she went," I whispered.

"What?"

"Send the cops to the airport."

"I don't understand. I canceled the flight myself. She couldn't—"

"Trust me," I said. "She's going to try and come here."

Margaret suddenly sounded suspicious. "How are you so sure?"

"Because that would be the absolutely worst thing that could happen."

"Kline?"

"Get the cops to check the airport. If we're lucky, the flight hasn't left yet. You can't let her come here."

"Now you're scaring me."

You should be scared.

"I have to check some things on my end here. Call me immediately once you find anything, okay?"

"She didn't tell you anything, did she?"

"I wish she had."

"I'll let you know."

"Thanks."

When I hung up, all I could think about was the last image from my nightmare; the Devil's hand opening, revealing the bloody, broken body of my daughter . . .

CHAPTER FOURTEEN

I FOLLOWED the ambulance to St. Vincent Charity Hospital. I had a desperate sick feeling that I was somehow responsible for what happened to Nina. When I came in asking about her, they stuck me in a little waiting room filled with hotel paintings, a phone, a box of tissues, and a Bible.

Great . . .

I called the *Press* again, but they hadn't had any luck contacting Nina's family. They'd already left several messages, but her only emergency contacts were her parents, who lived in Minnesota.

Another émigré to the exotic mana-soaked shores of Lake Erie.

I didn't know much about Nina's background, but I could guess at it. Mana likes ritual and pattern, and has a habit of infecting, or adapting to, existing codes and patterns. Anyone who had studied magic or the occult before the Portal opened had a leg up. A lot of people came here because their old magical studies suddenly had practical applications.

Nina had probably gone through the obligatory New Age experimentation in college. A little tarot here, a little cabalism there, some Golden Dawn everywhere . . .

Made me think of the students Dr. Shafran complained about.

I sat in a plaid lounge chair, picked up the house phone, and tried to call Dr. Shafran. I figured if anyone knew what the hell I might be dealing with, he'd be the guy.

No such luck. Of course he wasn't in the office. And I ran his voice mail out of tape three times trying to explain what I wanted. At the end of the third message, I tried to get a grip on myself.

"Okay," I said to myself, "panicking won't help anything. Act like a damn professional."

If the guy wasn't at work on Saturday, I'd get his home number. Easier said than done.

The guy wasn't just absent from normal directory assistance, even the people I knew in the phone company couldn't pull a listing for him.

In the end, I needed to call Quint anyway.

"What you got for me?"

"Kline, your doctor has a long file. You want the long version or the short one?"

I looked up at the clock and shook my head. "I have time."

Magetech wasn't a public company, but the pile of money Quint was able to trace was two zeros beyond what Mazurich had been hiding. Magetech had more patents than a Catholic schoolgirl convention, and the guy's name was on every one.

However, for someone researching the effects of magic on the world, Dr. Pretorious located himself safely outside its influence. He bought a house in a golf community south of Columbus about three years ago and secluded himself there. I had an address, as well as the market value of the residence—seven figures, and it didn't start with a one.

After Quint had worked backward through Pretorious' employment history, and a background check that the CIA would call anal, I asked him, "Could you do a quick look up of another doctor for me?"

"Name?"

"Dr. Newman Shafran, he works at Case Western."

"Hmm. You shopping around, Kline? These guys are probably too old for you."

"I'm just looking for a home phone."

Quint made a melodramatic sigh. "If you insist. Give me a moment."

I heard typing, then a muffled curse. "Can you spell that name for me?"

I did.

"Give me a moment." Quint muttered something unpleasant. As he muttered, a doctor walked into the room.

"Hold on," I said to Quint, who wasn't listening. I looked up at my visitor. "How is she?"

The doctor was an Indian man about ten years younger than I was. "Medically she's in no danger at the moment. I understand you were present during the attack?"

I nodded, lowering the phone. "Is she awake?"

The doctor shook his head, "I'm sorry. She's unresponsive."

"What's the matter?"

The doctor sighed. "There's no physical damage. She has suffered feedback from some magical event. I need the exact history of what happened—"

"Can't you transfer her out of the Portal's influence?" I asked. That was what they did with her predecessor when he was infected with semiconscious tumors that started sprouting little eyes.

"That's not a trivial treatment decision. Without analysis of the enchantment binding her, the effect of taking her out of a mana-dense area could be unpredictable. Can I have that history?"

I gave him what I knew, which wasn't much.

"Thanks." He put his hand on my shoulder, "We're doing what we can."

It didn't make me feel better.

When he left, I heard a small tinny voice say, "You bitch!"

I picked up the receiver, "Quint, you still there?"

"Tell me, Kline, are you just trying to make my life interesting?"

"Pardon?"

"Dr. Newman Shafran? Home number? The man doesn't exist."

"What, I've talked to him . . ."

"No phone, no credit report, address a PO Box. I can't even find the university records to match his doctorate."

"I don't understand. He works at Case. He's published scientific papers."

"Sure, dozens—but I swear he walks off the campus and ceases to exist. If I didn't . . ." he trails off. "I am such an idiot."

"What?"

"I was going to say, 'If I didn't know better,' but, of course I don't know better, do I?"

"Know what?"

"The man's an émigré from the Portal. Of course, no birth certificate, no paper trail prior to a dozen years ago. Hell, even his publications don't go back more than a decade."

"But he has a doctorate?"

"Threw me, too. This will be a little weird, you want me to keep digging?"

I shook my head, feeling a little uneasy about Dr. Shafran. I couldn't believe the man was from the other side of the Portal. He seemed way too much of the world I lived in. But all that was beside the point anyway. I didn't need to be going off on tangents. "No, Quint, leave it for now. There's another man who's more important. The name's Simon Lucas . . ."

* * *

When I left the cell-phone-free bubble of St. Vincent's, I had missed half a dozen calls. All from Margaret.

I called her back from the parking lot. Once I was in the Volkswagen, out of the snow.

"Where have you been?"

"The hospital, I had to turn off my cell—"

"Are you all right?"

"I'm fine, it was a coworker. Did they find Sarah?"

"Kline, our daughter has a future as a con artist."

I leaned back in the seat. "I was right, wasn't I?"

"The police found my car in the airport parking lot. She used her boarding pass—the one we thought I canceled."

"Thought?"

It turns out that my daughter was nothing if not resourceful. Margaret had, in fact, changed the flight dates. But she had done it via email, and apparently Margaret had never bothered to set the password on her e-mail. Sarah was able to look through all her email and pull up confirmation numbers and credit card info— enough to actually place a phone call to the travel agent last night, undoing Margaret's changes.

Apparently, doing everything on-line made it even easier for Sarah to impersonate her mother, since the agent had never actually talked to Margaret.

Once her boarding pass was valid again, all Sarah had to do was slip out early enough to make the flight. By the time the cops had caught up to the missing car, the plane had already been boarded.

I shook my head. "What is she thinking?"

"I don't know, Kline."

"You have the itinerary? Any layovers?"

"The cops already asked, no. It's a direct flight."

"What does she expect me to do? She has to know I'd put her right back on the next flight out, even if there weren't—"

I was about to say "*doom-laden prophecies.*"

"Weren't what, Kline?"

"A . . . a teenage susceptibility to self-delusion and denial. She really should have known better."

"Something else . . ."

"There's more?"

"She unplugged my alarm clock." She paused, and when I didn't immediately grasp the significance, she elaborated. "If I hadn't gotten up at four to go to the bathroom, if I had slept in, I might not have been able to get to you before the plane landed. She'll be there in less than two hours."

I exhaled.

"Well our little con artist is going to be lucky if I don't get my own ticket next to her on the way back."

Of course, Murphy's Law being what it is, the weather had to screw things up.

I was lucky to make it from St. Vincent's to Hopkins Airport in under an hour and a half. What had started as a light flurry managed to turn into a full-fledged blizzard before I had completely merged onto I-77 South.

Ten minutes before my daughter's plane was scheduled to arrive, I was just one of hundreds of people staring out the windows at Hopkins International Airport. Like everyone else, I was watching the sheets of white pounding the tarmac, and explaining to a cell phone just how the weather had screwed up everyone's life.

"Nothing?" Margaret said.

"No," I told her. "Pretty much every outbound flight's been canceled. I think I'm going to be lucky if they don't divert Sarah's flight to Akron or Columbus."

"That bad?"

"Bad enough that all the hotels around the airport were booked solid before I got here. I was lucky to get the Tower City Hilton."

"You couldn't just put her up in your condo like we originally planned?"

"Not a great idea, right now. Long story."

"It's what you're working on, isn't it? Are you getting death threats again?"

"In any case," I said, changing the subject, "our daughter has to know that things aren't business as usual. I'm not going to reward her by pretending this is okay. She's going to a hotel with me, and back out once the weather is clear."

"You're right," I heard her sniff over the phone. "I just can't help thinking we might have been too hard on her. It isn't like Sarah to do this—"

I know. "Suite 1123, Tower City Hilton. I called in the reservation when I was fighting this crap on the freeway."

"Okay," Margaret sounded uncertain. "I still wish she could stay with you."

"She *is* staying with me. It's a suite, two bedrooms."

"Look, that hotel must be expensive at the last minute. You should let me pick up part of the bill."

"Don't worry, I can afford it. If anything, we should take it out of Sarah's allowance."

"Kline?"

"What?"

"I know you're angry, but remember, she wanted to see you."

I rubbed my face. My jaw still hurt from where the dwarf had slugged me. "I know."

"Call me when her plane comes in?"

"Sure."

I hung up and looked up at the flight schedule. Twenty-minute delay so far.

"Sarah, what the hell were you thinking?" I whispered to myself as the delay rolled over to forty minutes.

CHAPTER FIFTEEN

WHEN she walked out the gate, I think she almost seemed surprised to see me.

"Dad?"

I walked up to her. "I think you have a bit of explaining to do, young lady."

"I tried to call you."

"Uh-huh, so you resort to car theft and fraud?"

"She wasn't going to let me come!"

I frowned. "Don't take that tone." I took the bag she was carrying. "Did you check anything? Do we need to go to baggage claim?"

"No."

"Then come on, let's get back to my car before the weather gets any worse."

She nodded and followed me through the terminal. After a few minutes she said, "I was looking forward to this trip for a year, then she said I couldn't go . . ."

"*We* said you couldn't go. Your mother does talk to me, you know. We bumped your visit to January because you needed to cool your jets for baiting your mother."

"It wasn't fair after planning—"

I stopped and turned to face her. "Do you have any idea what you just did? This wasn't breaking curfew, or pushing your mother's buttons. You broke the law, young lady. If your mother and I were more estranged than we are, I would be counted as an accessory. The only reason you aren't on a flight back to California right now is because there aren't any. I'd take you to a Greyhound station if I could trust you not to bolt at the first rest stop."

"Dad?" she was starting to tear up.

I sighed. "You have no conception how disappointed I am in you right now."

The floodgates were open now, and she pulled out the A-bomb of emotional blackmail. "I just wanted to see you, Dad. It just got so bad I had to go."

Uh-huh, you have the mother from hell.

"Yeah, I'm sure." I put my hand on her shoulder. "Well, lucky for you, you're going to have about twenty-four hours to get over it before I can send you back."

By the time we got to the exit, I realized that Sarah was not dressed appropriately. She wore jeans, a short-sleeved blouse, and a little leather jacket that existed solely to be a fashion accessory.

I tried offering her my trench coat, and she just folded her arms and said, *"I'm okay!"*

But even as she shook her head, I could see her staring out the glass at the layers of white falling down on the parking lot. She probably hadn't seen snow in person since she was five.

"You really need to wear something heavier than that. Did you pack something?"

"I'll be okay."

I bit my tongue. I knew enough to realize how easily a detail like appropriate winter wear might have been lost in the midst of the apocalyptic decision for her to come here.

She looked up at me. "You know, I saw a fashion show on satellite and they had a designer here who makes these killer jackets. It moves, like it's alive, and it changes color to whatever you think of . . ."

Great, and how much does that cost? "Honey, I don't think we're going to go shopping. Besides, you couldn't take something like that back home. It wouldn't work outside the influence of the Portal, and if it's heavily enchanted, leaving the influence of mana would probably destroy it."

I pushed through the door into the blizzard.

"W–well. If I got anything l–like that, you'd keep it safe for me? T–till I came back?"

"I said we're not going—" I looked at her, and saw eyes red from crying. I couldn't be a hard ass anymore. "Sure, honey."

I told myself that she was going to be safely in my sight from now up until I put her back on a plane home.

"D–Dad?"

"Yeah?"

"Give me your j–jacket."

I set down her bag and pulled off my trench coat and draped it ver her shoulders. Doing that made it sink in exactly how much ny girl had grown. I didn't feel distant from her, since we talked on he phone at least every other day, but I only actually saw her a few mes a year.

Giving her my jacket made me realize that she was only a hair horter than I was now. She could easily be one of the college in- erns at the *Press*—or a hostess at the bar where the old men of the aper went to talk about the interns without causing a hostile work- ng environment.

Sarah must have heard me sigh.

"What is it?"

"Just thinking about work." I picked up her bag and gestured to- vard the lot. "I'm parked over there."

"Oh, wow, is that a dwarf?"

I silently thanked God that her hands were too busy holding my oat on her shoulders for her to point. She was looking over at a taxi tand where a cab was idling, the driver waiting for a fare.

"Don't stare . . ."

It couldn't be, could it?

Cabs in this town were evenly divided between Jamaicans, rabs, and dwarves—and no, I don't know why Jamaicans drive abs in Cleveland, but they have since before the Portal opened. So e're at the airport, a dozen cabs lined up, of course there'd be warves.

It was pushing it to assume I really recognized this dwarf. No ay this was Samanish Thégharin, I was just being paranoid . . .

Our eyes locked and I told myself that I had only seen a bad dig- al photo on a hack license. That and the back of his neck.

The dwarf in the cab smiled at me.

Shit.

"Dad, you were telling *me* not to stare."

The cab pulled away, without a fare. He seemed to make a point f driving right past us, as if Mr. Thégharin wanted me to know for ertain who he was.

"Sorry, just happens that I know him." The sense of dread and rgency fell on me redoubled. I grabbed Sarah with my free arm nd led her toward my car. It was an effort to keep from breaking nto a run.

"*You* know dwarves?"

"Only a couple. I was just surprised to see him here." I tried to push the conversation away from Mr. Thégharin. "I know quite a few more elves."

"Yeah?"

"There're a few in the police department. They're an interesting bunch."

The drive back was agonizingly slow, because of the weather. Sarah was obviously disappointed. I guess, even under parental house arrest, she'd expected to at least *see* something of the mystic kingdom known as Cleveland, Ohio. And after all her planning, her first views were little more than swirling white and the occasional ODOT snowplow trying to keep the Interstate clear.

I was torn between thinking it served her right, and feeling sorry for her.

She made up for it by peppering me with questions, some of which I'm pretty sure she already knew the answers to. I guess it was her way of having a conversation with me, without talking about how she got here, or how much trouble she was in.

So most of the drive I spent answering questions about everything from the Portal to the local unicorn population.

"Fact is, most of the legitimate mages in town are employed by the government."

"So what do they do?"

"Mostly? They protect the public from the mages who aren't. There's a large black market around for all sorts of nasty enchantments. One of the priorities, ever since the Portal opened, is to try to keep a step ahead of the bad guys. From mass-producing protective charms to keep buildings and vehicles secure, to tracking down counterfeiters."

"Counterfeiters?"

"With the right materials, even a half-assed mage can easily make a physical copy of any small inanimate object. Such as a DVD or a twenty-dollar bill."

"There's a lot of that going on?"

"One of many reasons for a strain between the federal and local governments here. We're number two as far as IP piracy goes, right after China." I shrugged. "Fortunately, as long as the good guys catch the property before it leaves the Portal's influence, a forensic mage can detect the history of the material."

"What if it does leave?"

"Then you have a problem."

"I never really thought about that . . ." She looked out at the now.

"Well the movies and TV shows don't usually focus on the run-of-the-mill stuff."

"What about monsters? Griffins, dragons, that sort of thing? Are here a lot around, do you see any?"

I almost winced when I thought about griffins. I shook my head. There're only about thirty dragons around, and they tend to be too usy to accommodate journalists."

"What are they busy *doing?*"

"Nothing particularly sinister—not unless you're a left-wing Democrat." I looked across and saw Sarah's blank expression and laborated. "Dragons are fundamentally capitalists. They're into noney and power, and they're rather adept at acquiring it. They ame through the Portal, set up shop, incorporated, and started buying companies."

"You're kidding."

"You're picturing a dragon sitting on a mound of gold and ems? These creatures are intelligent enough to know that a pile of tock portfolios and board memberships mean a lot more in twenty-irst century America, even if they can only legally sign contracts nd own property in the state of Ohio. They may be huge and menacing, and breathe fire, but an army of well-financed lawyers can be lot more intimidating. And can venture a lot farther afield."

"You met a dragon, didn't you?"

I nodded. "Theophane. She bought out the top few floors of the P Building."

"What was that like?"

"Intimidating . . ." I talked on for a while about my meeting with ne dragon Theophane, two years ago. That was the last time my job ad gotten me involved deeply in nonhuman politics. And while I ept my voice light, I couldn't help but be apprehensive.

That time, when I dug into the history of elves and the death of ne supposedly immortal dragon, I almost got myself killed. And ne mess that resulted ended up killing a half dozen others, including a fellow reporter, and Caledvwlch's predecessor as head of the pecial Paranormal Unit—the latter decapitated by an eight-foot-ll stone gargoyle in the middle of my living room.

Not the best time of my life to be thinking about right now. The st couple of days held uncomfortable echoes, and it made me real-e that I didn't want my daughter anywhere around here. Not now, aybe not ever.

Margaret was right.

Sarah was going back first thing in the morning, even if I had to drive to the Pittsburgh airport to get her out. As my paranoia worsened, I doubled back twice, just to make sure no dwarven taxicabs were tailing me.

When I finally felt safe, I took an exit and drove downtown on surface streets.

"Where are we going?"

"The Tower City Hilton."

Sarah frowned, squinting out at the office buildings flanking us. "I thought I was staying at your place?"

"You aren't vacationing, young lady. This is just to put you up until I get you on a flight back to your mother? Understand."

"But I thought, now that I was here—"

"Sarah, you didn't think, or you wouldn't be here."

She gave me the silent treatment as I checked us in. I didn't try to press her. In the end I was simply too relieved to have her with me, safe. The crap happening around me was just too threatening enough so that I had the unprofessional urge to follow through on my threat to Margaret and book my own ticket back with her.

In the end, given the weather and the glut of outbound passengers, I was lucky to find one seat available on an outbound flight that was leaving anytime soon. I was really proud of myself when I found an 8:30 AM flight out of Akron. I reserved her a seat, somewhat fraudulently, with my *Press* AmEx card.

When I hung up, Sarah was leaning against the doorframe to her bedroom, staring at me.

"Dad, I'm sorry . . ."

I looked at her, and my dad sincerity detector wasn't quite working. I sighed. "You really need to think things out before you act, honey."

"You don't understand—"

"Sit down, Sarah."

She dropped into a lounge that faced me. "Dad—"

I held up my hand. "Let me give you the obligatory parental speech first." I leaned forward. "I'm not going to tell you that you aren't old enough to make decisions for yourself. That's the nature of the age you're at. This is the point where you make decisions that will affect the rest of your life."

"Dad—"

"Before you pull stunts like this, you need to decide if you're willing to live with the consequences. If your mother was the trou you make her out to be, it could have been a cop picking you up at the airport. Car theft, credit fraud, flight across state lines. Felony convictions don't make your life easier."

"Come on, Mom wasn't going to—"

"Call the police? Who do you think found the car at the airport? To be honest, if she went as far as pressing charges, I don't think I could blame her."

"Oh." She looked down at the carpet.

"For the life of me I can't understand why you seem to go out of your way to antagonize your mother."

"You don't live with her," Sarah said.

"No," I said, "and in less than a year you don't have to either."

"Dad, I feel as if she's trying to wall off a whole part of my life. Part of *me.*"

"What do you mean? We talk almost every day—"

She slammed the arm of the chair she sat in and stood up, shouting at me. "Damn it, Dad! This isn't about that! It isn't about you."

I leaned back. I was speechless for a moment, allowing my ego to absorb the statement. Not that I was dad of the year here, but I had been thinking . . .

"What is it about, then?"

Sarah shook her head, and I could see the tears starting. "I'm sorry. This isn't your fault." She ran to her room and slammed the door.

"Sarah?" I walked up to the door. "What is it?"

I could hear her crying.

I hesitated a moment and opened the door. She was splayed out, facedown on the bed. I could hear her say something like, "I'm sorry."

"What is the matter? Why did you run away here? Is there something at home I don't know about?" At this point I was visualizing nightmare scenarios that had been forbidden territory until now. "Is someone abus—"

She raised her head, sucking in an offended breath. "My God, Dad!"

"What am I supposed to think?"

She flopped back down on the bed. "I was born here," she whispered.

"What?"

"Mom doesn't understand. This all is part of my life, who I am."

I sat down on the foot of the bed. "So you run away here?"

"Don't I have a right to know where I come from?"

"Maybe there's a better way to deal with that, and your mother."

She sighed. "Maybe."

I placed a hand on her shoulder, trying to comfort her. She shrugged me away.

"Can I have some time alone?"

"Okay." I stood up. "Let me know if you want to talk."

"Uh-huh."

Apparently, she didn't want to talk. After about fifteen minutes of quiet sobbing, the jet lag caught up with her and she started snoring. I went in and took her shoes off and threw a blanket over her.

I had no right to, but I felt a little like crying myself. Not happy news when you find out that you're not the epicenter of your little girl's world any more. For all my attempts to be practical and realistic, the fact was that I still saw her as a twelve-year-old girl.

It just never occurred to me that anyone could feel that sort of connection to this place. The whole situation seemed too new for this to be anyone's ancestral homeland . . .

Sarah was what, five years old, when the Portal opened?

Another five years, there'd be a whole generation that had been born since the Portal. What kind of point-of-view shift would that make?

Case was going to need another Dr. Shafran or three.

These were the thoughts running though my head when my cell phone rang, a little after seven.

"Maxwell," I barked into the phone.

"Well, you like to get your money's worth, don't you?"

"Quint? You got me something about Simon Lucas?"

"Mr. Lucas is a busy little beaver. He's one of those guys that get a one-dollar salary on the books and gets paid options up the yin-yang."

"Worth a lot?"

"I counted easily over 150 publicly traded companies where his investment is into eight figures or higher."

"150 . . ." I tried to do the math in my head, but it had been a long day.

"All seems aboveboard. Including his immigrant status."

"Immigrant?"

"Yes, another one from the other side of the Portal."

"Great. It seems that Magetech has been very good to people."

"Mr. Lucas seems to have done the best, though he doesn't seem to figure largely in any paperwork Magetech had filed with any government agency. This guy is easily the highest compensated executive in the state of Ohio."

Pretty good for someone who was only close to the top of the Org chart, and one of the only humans in the rarefied upper atmosphere of the Magetech hierarchy. All the higher executives, and the board, were dwarven.

Oddest of all was where Mr. Lucas listed his residence.

All his financial records that Quint had been able to access, including some tax forms released to the SEC, listed Simon Lucas' residence on Whiskey Island.

According to all the man's records, he resided in the middle of the dwarven enclave, where the mana was so dense that human beings couldn't work there without going mad . . .

CHAPTER SIXTEEN

I GOT my wake-up call at five in the morning, and I was relieved to look out the hotel window and see a clear sky. I figured we had more than enough time to make it down to Akron and have some sort of breakfast at the airport before I put her on the plane. I dressed quickly, skipping a shower and a shave, figuring to let Sarah have the run of a clean bathroom before we left.

Dressed, I steeled myself for a tearful argument and knocked on the door to her bedroom.

"Come on, Sarah. Wake up, we have a plane to catch."

She didn't answer me.

"Sarah?" I pushed the door open.

The bed was empty.

"Oh, no." I stepped in. She wasn't here. Neither was her bag. "Shit, you're kidding me. Sarah?"

I ran out and threw the door to the bathroom open. "Sarah?"

Nothing.

She wouldn't just walk out . . .

"Why not?"

How the hell could I be that stupid? She as much as told me that she was running away to Cleveland, not to her father. She'd done everything but come out and tell me she would bolt.

I ran out into the hall, dashing the hope that she had just stepped out of the room. I was in the elevator, halfway down to the lobby, when I realized that my car keys were gone.

Better and better.

I walked out of the elevator and through the lobby, looking for her. No sign. *Christ, she doesn't even have a winter jacket.*

I found the concierge by the Euclid exit. "Pardon me, did you see my daughter leave?"

"Pardon."

"My daughter, she's seventeen, blonde, probably wearing a leather—"

"Oh, yes, an hour ago, I directed her to the garage."

I ran to the garage, dialing the police as I went.

"Hello?"

Margaret yawned and I realized that it must be three in the morning on the coast.

"It's Kline," I said.

"Oh," she was too calm. She must have been too asleep to hear the stress in my voice. "Are you at the airport already?"

Yeah, she was expecting me to call, wasn't she?

I looked around, for a moment too numb to say anything. I was sitting on the rail where my Volkswagen had been parked. A pair of police cars was here, which was a bonus for your average runaway case. I was lucky in that I had one string that I'd pulled as hard as I could.

"Kline? You *are* at the airport."

"She did it to me, too . . ."

"What?"

"Right up to lifting my car keys."

"Oh, my God."

I shook my head. "I was an idiot. She came out and told me she thought she was missing part of her past—"

"Yes, you."

"No, Margaret, this isn't about me."

"What are you talking about?"

"She didn't bolt from the hotel because she was desperate to see me. She ran here because she has some weird idea that this city is part of her heritage."

"I don't understand what you're saying."

"She told me that she thought you were 'walling off part of herself.' I don't think she was planning to see me at all."

"Where would she go?"

"I don't know. Does she know anyone out here? Any boyfriends?"

"Kline?"

"This is serious. Our daughter has just stolen *another* car and now I have no idea where she could be going. She has to have left some sort of clue. Something on her computer, email, letters, a diary?"

"What do you think—"

"I don't know what to think, but ransack her room and call me back when you find something— The police are here, I'll call you back."

"But—"

I cut her off as one of the strings I had pulled unraveled in front of me. Walking up the ramp of the parking garage, toward me and the two police cruisers, was the tall gangly form of Commander Maelgwyn Caledvwlch.

One of the hazards of name-dropping to a police dispatcher, the name in question might actually show up.

"Mr. Maxwell," he greeted me in his semi-Jamaican monotone.

"Commander Caledvwlch."

"I have become interested in your assessment of my priorities." He waved a long hand, encompassing the empty parking space and the pair of police cars. "I understand that your child removed your vehicle without your permission. But my understanding of human reasoning falls short when I discover that this requires SPU involvement. Can you enlighten me?"

I shook my head and put my cell phone away. "I got two answers for you, neither of them very good. Can we go somewhere private and talk?"

Caledvwlch took me to the back of a mostly-fiberglass minivan, which passed for an unmarked patrol car for the SPU elves. Not that any of them ever went undercover. It all had to do with headroom and iron content.

I eased into a seat with a groan and Caledvwlch managed to fold himself in next to me. I looked at him, the alien angles of his face framed by a ruff of hair and convoluted pointed ears. He watched me with metallic eyes with no visible iris or pupil. Behind the impassive expression I knew sat a sense of duty and fealty that made a fourteenth-century Samurai look like an anarchist.

I didn't know how he'd react to a father who was just freaking out and didn't know what else to do.

"The first answer," I looked at him. "Hell, it isn't one. I know how police prioritize things in this town. Runaway—especially one an hour old—isn't going to make it to the top of the list." I looked at Caledvwlch's face, no reaction. "If I just let it go with my daughter swiping my car, I'd be lucky if someone came and took a statement within the next twenty-four hours."

"The human phrase, I believe, is, 'to light a fire under someone's ass.'" He said it with no discernible emotion, and I wondered if it was possible he was mocking me.

"I am part of your investigation, however tangential. I just made sure everyone knew it."

Caledvwlch nodded and seemed to be lost in thought a moment or two. Then he asked me, "There was an incident, yesterday, with a colleague of yours."

I swallowed. I probably should have reported it to the cops. "Yes, Nina Johannessen—"

"She is in a coma. Did you know that?"

"Yes, I told the doctors what I could . . ."

"She is a seer, correct?"

"Yes."

"Did she see something about your daughter?"

I looked at Caledvwlch as I wondered exactly how much he knew. As usual, he didn't provide me any external clues. The elf would provide the play by play for the apocalypse with all the passion of a golf announcer.

"That was the other reason . . ."

I unloaded on Caledvwlch, probably the way any parent would unload on an available cop, even without any overt displays of sympathy. I didn't need his encouragement. I was prepared to hand everything I had over to him, however tangential, if it might have some distant relation to where my daughter might have gone.

I went over Nina's visions, the tarot cards, my nightmares, and how Nina said it was tied to my daughter. I told him about Nina's possession, and how whatever had taken control had the same voice as the Devil in my dreams.

"You should have reported that," Caledvwlch said quietly. "Possession of an unwilling victim is a first-degree felony."

"I know, but I called my ex after that, to check on Sarah, and that's when I found she'd slipped out of the house and got on a plane."

"You understand that you have just admitted to a criminal act?" Caledvwlch said. "At this time it is my duty to advise you of your rights."

"You're arresting me?"

"I am taking you to the station for a more formal questioning," Caledvwlch said. "A full statement now and I will not be prompted to take you in for failure to report a crime."

"What about my daughter?"

"Mr. Maxwell, as you informed the dispatcher, this is part of an ongoing SPU investigation."

* * *

Caledvwlch took me to an interview room only a few blocks away at police headquarters. While I'd suffered a few arrests in my career, I'd never been brought to the Special Paranormal Unit's interrogation room. Even when Caledvwlch "rescued" me from Blackstone, Caledvwlch just used a spare office to question me.

I didn't think it was a good thing that I now rated special treatment—and when a uniformed cop let me in, I was very glad that Caledvwlch hadn't felt the need to actually arrest me.

The room was constructed specifically to suit the needs of the Special Paranormal Unit, and those needs were, well, *special*.

First off, the room itself was designed like an operating theater, rather than a standard soundproof interrogation chamber—a cylinder with concave walls, with observers stationed behind one-way glass at the top of the room, looking down. The walls weren't layered in acoustical tile, but were concrete with gold symbols inlaid flush with the surface. When the foot-thick door shut behind me, the inlay formed multiple concentric circles ringing the wall from floor to ceiling.

In the center of the room was what looked like a dentist's chair. Looking at the heavy straps, I was rather glad that they didn't have me sit there. I got to sit at a more normal office chair that was one of a half dozen places at a metal table that formed a donut around the chair of honor.

When I sat, I said to Caledvwlch, "Nice setup you have here."

"Sometimes we must conduct difficult interviews." He waved at a plainclothes human who had joined us in the room. "Dr. Singh will be observing here, and may have some questions of his own."

Dr. Singh was a bald, white-mustached Indian man. He nodded a slight acknowledgment to me. I wondered who he was. I guessed that he was a forensic mage of some sort.

Caledvwlch sat down as well, "Shall we take your statement from the beginning?"

"Well, I talked to Nina—"

"Ossian Parthalán," said Dr. Singh. "Begin with his phone call."

"What?" I asked. "I went over this already, my daughter—"

"From the beginning," Caledvwlch said.

I looked from one to the other. "This has nothing to do with my daughter. It's the damn dwarves again. Damn it, we need to find her. What happened with Nina—"

"Mr. Maxwell," Caledvwlch raised his voice only slightly, but it was enough to cut me down in my tracks. The elf had held a gun on me before, but he had *never* raised his voice.

Caledvwlch stared at me with those cold metallic eyes, "This has everything to do with your daughter. Now, *from the beginning.*"

He didn't need to provide me with any more encouragement.

I ran down everything, step by step, since Ossian Parthalán called me to question why Councilman Mazurich shot himself. What scared me was when they had me back up and asked questions about my daughter.

"You received a call from California that evening," Caledvwlch said.

"Yes, Sarah." I repeated the conversation as I remembered it.

"Did she say anything odd?" asked Dr. Singh. "Possibly about her trip here?"

I shook my head.

"Did she ever mention contact with anyone from Cleveland?" Dr. Singh frowned.

"No . . ."

Caledvwlch continued. "So you examined this envelope, describe what you found."

But Sarah . . . I looked at both of them and couldn't tell if I should push it or not. How the hell could my daughter be involved in some sort of conspiracy here. It didn't make sense.

"This is the first time you've been contacted by dwarves?"

"Yes . . ."

Unless it wasn't Sarah.

What if it was me?

Blackstone had mentioned a connection to California. *Thor's Hammer* had a car in the shop with California plates. Dr. Shafran had said that dwarves, unlike elves or dragons, would be able to travel beyond the influence of the Portal, and he had even mentioned California.

She clearly wanted to come to Cleveland for reasons beyond visiting me. And Dr. Singh had practically repeated my own question to Margaret verbatim.

Did she have contact with anyone from Cleveland?

What was it she said in the parking lot? "*You* know dwarves?"

"You took pictures at *Thor's Hammer?*" asked Dr. Singh.

"They were garbage . . ."

"Yes, from the mana saturation." Dr. Singh looked at me. "Have you erased those pictures?"

"No."

"May I see them?" He held out his hand.

I cued the pictures up on the screen and handed my cell phone over. Caledvwlch soldiered on while Dr. Singh looked at my mana-spoiled pictures. He grilled me on my visit to the *Nazgûl* and when I mentioned taking pictures there, too, Dr. Singh looked up at me.

"Yeah, right after the others, just as useless."

Even as I recounted the story, I kept fixating on what Sarah had said.

"*You* know dwarves?"

It was exactly the way a teenager might phrase "*You* listen to hip-hop?" Or "*You* play video games?" All the inflection was on the bizarre concept that someone as old and out of touch as I was might have contact with something hip and new.

Dwarves?

What if Ossian Parthalán had more than one reason for contacting me?

Paranoia was running away with me. I had exactly zero evidence that my daughter had contacted any dwarves, ever. She was just upset. She'd come back within a few hours. All she wanted was to see this damn city . . .

Bullshit.

Even without the visions and Nina's collapse, I would have known that something was wrong. This wasn't how Sarah acted. Something serious had gone wrong with her life.

Caledvwlch walked me through my visit to Magetech, with Dr. Singh asking pointed questions about my blackout, and my catastrophic meeting with Nina. He grilled me on that, and on the subsequent arrival of my daughter, with no mercy. We went over what I remembered of each conversation over and over. Enough that I almost felt ready to break down the third time we went over my last drive with Sarah.

What kept me from losing it was the fact that Caledvwlch's questions about Sarah confirmed that he was operating under suspicions very similar to my own. He dwelled on her comments about the dwarf cab driver almost as much as I had.

When Caledvwlch drained me of just about everything I had, Dr. Singh stepped in. "You said you had nightmares, visions akin to what Mrs. Johannessen had told you about?"

"Yes."

"Describe them to me."

"What I remember . . ." I told him about Death galloping from the Portal, and the Devil enthroned above the dwarves.

Dr. Singh nodded and handed me my cell phone. "I took the liberty of messaging these pictures to the Cleveland Police server. I think you might want to look at them again."

"Huh? They're just random . . ."

No.

They weren't random. My heart leaped in my throat as I recognized the landscape of my dreams. The swirling mirrored glass and mounted Death. The mountain of bloody salt twisted around Ossian's corpse.

What did Dr. Shafran say? *There's some slight evidence that such static is not wholly random, and is responsible for what some New Age victims refer to as the Oracle.*

"Your own visions, are they?" asked Dr. Singh.

I nodded, unable really to speak. I had scrolled to the last distorted image. In the final picture, the goat-faced Devil leered at me, holding something broken and bloody in his outstretched hand.

Oh, God . . .

It took a moment to notice, but the last picture had a date-stamp that placed it well after my shots at the *Nazgûl.*

I had taken a picture of the Devil while I was at Magetech.

CHAPTER SEVENTEEN

B Y the time Caledvwlch and Dr. Singh were done with me, it was already eleven. Caledvwlch and Dr. Singh disappeared into some authorized personnel only section of the SPU, cutting me loose in the lobby of Police Headquarters.

The first thing I did was call back to the Hilton in the vain hope that Sarah had come back while I'd been with the cops. No such luck. I did what I could to quiz the cops on the duty desk about where things were with finding my daughter, but somehow, once my daughter was involved, I had lost my ability to finesse information from people. The questions I pounded the cops with had all the subtlety of a kick to the groin.

"Do you know *anything?*"

Predictably, all I got were half a dozen ways to phrase: "Go home, we're working on it."

That, and the fact that no one had spotted my car yet, was all I got. As I calmed down, I was rational enough to be thankful that they didn't have anyone escort me out.

I walked outside, squinting in the daylight, and called for a rental car. I didn't want to deal with any more taxis, though the dwarf in question was nowhere in sight. I sat on a bench outside the police station, feeling worse than useless.

Damn it, Sarah, how could you do this to us?

As if cued, my phone rang. It was an unfamiliar number, but a California area code.

"Maxwell," I answered.

"Kline."

"Margaret?"

"Where are you?"

"Outside the police station waiting for a rental to show up. Where are you?"

"I'm with William Jackson. You don't know him, but he's the father of one of Sarah's friends."

"You found something?"

"I don't know. But she talked about Cleveland, and magic, with Beth, William's daughter. They actually talked about rites and rituals, and a lot of other stuff I don't understand. It scares me."

Christ, Sarah . . .

"They talked about forming a coven. Beth had hidden all these books about the cabala, the seal of Solomon— That doesn't make any sense, does it? They live in California."

"There's probably more of that going on there now than there was before the Portal opened. The Portal is the best recruiting tool these New Age types have ever had."

I kept remembering the pamphlet, "God's Plan or The Devil's Handiwork?" and Club *Nazgûl.* I've worked in this town enough to know the taxonomy of mages better than the pamphlet's author. I knew that a wiccan coven was spiritually on a completely different planet than a Satanist.

Somehow, when it was my daughter, I didn't find the thought at all reassuring.

"She was planning this for a long time," I said.

Of course she would want to go to a college around here. She was one of those people who wanted to be on Dr. Shafran's waiting list. My daughter wanted to be a mage. "Does Mr. Jackson have any idea where Sarah might have run off to?"

"No," Margaret said, "but Beth has had a history of trouble. She broke down when we confronted her."

"What did she say?"

"They were 'practicing,' they wanted . . ." Margaret broke up, couldn't go on.

"They wanted what?" I asked. "Were they going to move here?"

A male voice came through the phone, "Mr. Maxwell? I'm Bill Jackson, Beth's father."

"Yes, thanks for helping my wife—ex-wife," I rubbed my temple. "What did Beth tell you?"

"They wanted to emigrate."

I dropped the phone.

That had never occurred to me. Even though that was the reason for the Portal, to travel between here and Ragnan.

For all the people that came through to our side, at least two of our own went the other way.

Even though the Feds tightened up immigration to our side of the Portal, thanks to an elimination of the worst price gouging by the city, there wasn't a shortage of people who had decided they didn't want to deal with this particular universe anymore.

Given the narrow aperture, it was rare to ever hear anything from our ex-pats again.

No, it didn't make sense. She'd need a passport, over two grand for passage . . .

And she turned eighteen next year and wouldn't need to have us sign off on a passport, or even tell us about it. If she was a student here, she might just buy a ticket with student loan money. Hell, Visa practically threw free credit at college students. And, when it came to that, over the past two days my daughter had shown no reluctance to steal credit card numbers.

Why?

Why would she want to abandon her mother, me, the entire planet, for a place that was literally medieval? I didn't know a lot of what was currently going on on the other side of the Portal, but of what I did hear, the words egalitarian, progressive, tolerant, and democratic were just the first on a long list of descriptive terms that did not apply.

Maybe I was just close enough to see the warts.

"Mr. Maxwell."

I dug my phone out of the snow with numbed fingers. "Yes sorry."

"Margaret said you wanted to know if they had talked to anyone from there?"

"Cleveland? Yes."

"Beth says that someone visited their coven circle—a couple of times. A short old man, she thinks his name is Parthalán?"

"Parthalán." I whispered.

A pair of cars drove up in front of me. The first car was a sky blue Solara. The driver got out and approached me. "Mr Maxwell?"

"Mr. Maxwell?" Jackson echoed in my ear.

The driver walked up, keys in hand. "I'm from Enterprise—"

"I have to go," I said into the phone, "but do me a favor and ask Beth for everything she remembers about Mr. Parthalán."

"I hope you find Sarah."

"So do I," I said as I hung up.

"This is Dr. Newman Shafran, I'm not in right now . . ." I was getting sick of the doctor's voice mail. I decided that once I wa done with Teaghue Parthalán, I was going to Case to hunt up the professor in person.

I sat in my rented Solara, parked about halfway up a cross street, just in sight of *The Dwarven Armorer.* The suit of plate still stood posed in mid-stroke, making me wonder how often Teaghue cleaned the salt off of it.

Shafran's voice mail beeped at me.

"Dr. Shafran. This is Kline Maxwell, and I need to know *exactly* what you've heard about dwarves going to California."

I hung up.

"Parthalán," I whispered.

He knew. He had to have known. It didn't matter if the dwarf that visited my daughter's coven— *My daughter's coven? Wrap your long-distance parenting head around that one.* In the end it didn't matter if that dwarf was Ossian, Teaghue, or some dwarf as yet unnamed. It strained coincidence to the breaking point to believe that it wasn't all connected.

Teaghue was the one dwarf still living who had made an effort to contact me. Even if it was a half-assed attempt to frighten me off a story.

I intended to return the favor.

My timing, however, sucked.

Before I'd even opened the door on my Solara, a trio of black Chevy vans shot by my car, skidding to a stop in front of Teaghue's shop, splattering gray slush all over his front display.

The doors slid open before they had fully come to a stop, and a dozen men in full Kevlar riot gear poured out of the two leading vans. As they rushed the building, I saw the letters "FBI" emblazoned in bright yellow across their backs.

Above us, a helicopter swooped down and started circling so low that I swore I could feel the downdraft from the rotors.

Ahead, beyond the vans barricading the shop, I heard the sound of wood breaking, then a small explosion. I couldn't see much past the vans, but white smoke began drifting up from the building. The door on the last van slid open, and Blackstone stepped out, talking on a cell phone. He stepped around the rear of the van, looking past the three vans at a commotion I couldn't quite see.

"You bastard."

In the best of times I didn't like Blackstone. Now he was stepping all over the one lead I had to where my daughter might be.

I jumped out of my car and started running toward him. I can honestly say I had no clue what I was planning to do when I got there. Events made up my mind for me, just before I reached him.

Something exploded out of the scrap heap next to Teaghue's shop. I saw a flash of motion, and then something large flew toward me, Blackstone, and van number three. I dove, knocking Blackstone out of the way, as a V-8 engine block slammed into the front driver's side of the van. The entire front end of the vehicle crumpled inward in a shower of safety glass. The whole van rocked back on its tires, the impact driving it back a foot or two.

"What the—" Blackstone started talking, spitting slush out of his mouth. I couldn't hear the rest of what he said, because gunfire erupted from every corner around me. It came from inside the building, and from all three vans.

The focus of all the gunfire was another zombie. The same wire-sewed flesh that had been in my nightmares. Like the thing that had wrecked *Thor's Hammer,* it was wearing a trench coat. It could have been the same one.

While bullets slammed into and through the thing's body, it picked up a wheel rim from the debris around it. It threw the rim like a lethal Frisbee, catching one of the armored Feds full in the face.

Blackstone had completely forgotten about me. He pulled himself up behind one of the vans and grabbed a walkie-talkie. *"Use the phosphor rounds! Burn the thing!"*

Phosphor rounds? That sort of thing was military ordnance, not standard SWAT equipment, even for federal counterterrorism units.

The gunfire stopped and I was able to hear a hollow *thump.* The sound was followed by a glowing trail that ended in zombie-boy's chest cavity.

The trench coat went up like a sheet of flash paper and the skeleton stood there, backlit from inside. The smell was horrible, like a cannibal hibachi grill.

However, zombie-boy wasn't easily discouraged. It actually reached inside itself, fished out the glowing round, and threw it back toward the building. Its throw was short and I could see several half melted wires dangling from its throwing arm.

Several more *thumps.*

I glanced back at the building, and saw a short silhouette climbing out of a window on the side opposite the scrapyard.

"Teaghue!"

I didn't even wait to see if anyone paid attention to me. I got up and ran.

CHAPTER EIGHTEEN

TEAGHUE ran straight for an alley, and I was right behind him. Above me I heard the helicopter.

I dodged trash bins and old tires as he led me behind several old industrial buildings. In the half minute or so it took me to catch up with him, I had time for one main thought.

The guy makes weapons for a living and is strong enough to coldcock me bare-handed. What do I do when I catch up with him?

Answer? *Fight dirty.*

Teaghue ran up a frost-covered pile of broken concrete, and jumped onto a chain-link fence ahead of me. He managed to grab the twelve-foot-high fence almost halfway up. He started scrambling faster than anyone with his length of limb had a right to. I ran up the concrete after him, knowing I had no hope of scaling the fence or making it over the barbed wire on top.

So, instead, I reached down and grabbed a chunk of concrete the size of a two-liter bottle. It was so cold it numbed my fingers.

I brought it down as hard as I could on the back of Teaghue's right hamstring.

He cursed something vile and guttural in his native tongue as he slammed into the fence. I brought my concrete-laden fist up into where a human kidney would be.

"What are you doing? You misbegotten bastard!"

He was hanging only by his hands now, scrambling to get a foothold. I jumped up and struck him on the side of his head.

He fell off of the fence, rolling, stunned, facedown, at the base of the pile of concrete. I fell down on him, before he could recover. I put my knee down in the small of his back and stopped with a jolt that sent the concrete sailing from my hand.

It had become slippery, mostly from my own blood. At this

point, I didn't feel much from my gore-stained hand as I wrapped
it in Teaghue's hair.

"Tell me where my daughter is."

"You don't know what you're doi—"

I slammed his face into the ice.

"Tell me where my daughter is!"

"You can't— *He* will kill us."

I pulled back on his hair while holding the back of his neck with
my opposite forearm. *"I'll kill you."*

"No," Teaghue sputtered.

I slammed his face down again, hard enough that my wrist made
unpleasant noises. I ignored the spasm of pain and repeated, *"Tell
me where my daughter is!"*

"He has her!"

"Who?"

"The one I cannot name!"

"Don't fuck with me!" I was shaking, and if I had a gun, *I would*
have killed him.

"No, he knows when you speak of him. There's no protection
here. None. A thought could bring him—"

Teaghue choked and sputtered. I felt his muscles tense, and he
began bucking against me as if he was having a seizure. I let go of
his head, and he began slamming his own face into the pavement.

"Teaghue!"

I got off of him and rolled his body over. His back arched and he
started groaning. The atmosphere around us darkened.

A bolt of energy arced from Teaghue to the fence, and I could
smell an awful mixture of static and brimstone.

Teaghue sat up facing me. His eyes were open, but they were
dead and sightless. His cracked lips smiled and he opened his
mouth to speak in a voice that was too familiar.

"Good help is so hard to find." Teaghue laughed, spraying gobbets of blood and mucus.

"What have you done with my daughter?"

*"If they hadn't tried to warn you, this all would have been
much less unpleasant."*

"What are you? Where is my daughter?"

"She is quite safe, and quite unaware of what is happening."
Teaghue laughed again. *"But, Mr. Maxwell, when I come to ask
something of you, it would be good to remember what I am capable of."*

Still grinning, Teaghue reached up to his face. Before I realized what he was doing, he had hooked his fingers into the orbits of his skull. His laughter quickly turned to screams.

"Great work, Maxwell," Blackstone fumed as a medic taped my injured hand. "Tell me one thing, did you save my life just so I could witness how you screwed up my investigation?"

Another set of medics was busy zipping Teaghue's remains into a body bag.

"Blackstone," I said, "my daughter is missing."

"Yeah," Blackstone watched them take Teaghue away. "And you think this helped her? What the fuck do you think you were doing? You, of all people, ought to know better. Corner a suspect with no backup, no kind of protection. Not even a goddamn rabbit's foot. You're damn lucky he didn't kill you."

I rubbed my bandaged hand. "Yeah, lucky."

"If you're not careful, you'll make me think you took him out on purpose."

"Blackstone, can we cut the crap? Am I disappearing into your little federal black hole? Or am I free to go?"

Blackstone paced around me, his shoes making sucking sounds in the slush. "As much as I'd like to put you on ice for the next decade or so—I think the people we want are going to try and contact you again." He waved over a couple of suits. "So I'm letting you go with an escort. Special Agent Francis, and Special Agent Levi," he indicated the two new people.

"Mr. Maxwell," they both said in unison. If it weren't for the fact that Francis was black, they could have been clones of each other.

"Follow him to his hotel room and sit on him." Blackstone turned toward me. "And don't worry about your apartment, we have a few agents keeping an eye on it for you."

I sighed.

"Oh, if you're wondering about local police," Blackstone handed me a sheet of paper, a copy of a fax stamped with a time early this morning. "I made a point of getting all the paperwork nice and tidy. We trump Caledvwlch's little circus of sideshow freaks."

I handed the warrant back and looked at my new federal baby-sitters.

My federal escort took me back to my hotel room. It was about this time that I had the sick realization that I hadn't called Margaret. There's only one thing worse than having to tell your ex-wife that your daughter might have been kidnapped—and that's not being the first to do so.

"How could you not tell me!"

Margaret was hysterical, and I wasn't doing the greatest job of keeping my own composure. I stood in the bedroom while my bookend Feds stood in the suite's living room doing a lousy job of pretending not to overhear us.

"What was I going to tell you? I had evil premonitions—"

"There are FBI agents in my house!"

"I know, they're here, too."

"Why would someone take Sarah?"

"We don't know for sure that anyone's taken her."

"Bullshit, Kline. You're a terrible liar." There was a pause. "I'm coming down there."

"Margaret, I know how you feel—"

"I want my daughter back! I'm getting on the next flight."

I rubbed my temples. "I don't think the FBI will think that's a good idea."

"Fuck the FBI."

"Please, Margaret, they're trying to find her." I almost choked on the phony sincerity of that line. I knew, intellectually, that Blackstone was trying to find Sarah, if only because of her tie to his investigation. But I didn't believe in it any more than Margaret did. "They're going to want you to stay there, in case they try and contact you."

"What if there's no ransom? If it's some psycho predator? You have black mages and Satanists—"

"I don't think that's what happened."

"How the *hell* do you know?

I swallowed. "I think they're trying to get to me."

"They? Who *are* they?"

"I wish I knew." I looked off into the living room. Francis, the black one, caught my gaze and quickly looked away. "But I think they're trying to blackmail me."

"Kline, if anyone hurts her because—"

"You should probably keep your phone line clear."

"In case they call," she said flatly.

"Or Sarah," I said, exhausting every remaining fragment of optimism.

She hung up.

I sat on my bed and stared at the receiver. I don't know what I expected . . .

We used to be married; shouldn't we be able to comfort each other?

I felt empty, used up, and helpless. I didn't know if my daughter was alive or dead, and there wasn't anything I could do about it. Worse, what I *had* done only seemed to have made things worse.

Margaret was right. Sarah was gone because of me, and if anything happened to her . . .

"Mr. Maxwell," Special Agent Levi stepped into the bedroom doorway. "Are you okay?"

"What do you think?" I slammed the hotel's receiver back on the cradle hard enough to set my hand and wrist hurting again.

"Can we get you anything?"

"No," I snapped.

As he turned away, I got a better grip on myself. "Hey—"

"Yes."

"Sorry for the outburst," I told him. "Not your fault."

"No problem, you're entitled." He shook his head. "If I thought that dwarf had taken one of my kids—believe me, I know where you're coming from."

"You have kids?"

"Six and nine."

"Around here?"

Levi shook his head. "A little too crazy for my wife, I'm out of Pittsburgh."

"Oh, been gone long?"

"Too long. I was hoping to be back for Christmas," he shrugged. "Doesn't look like it's going to happen."

He must have noticed my odd look.

"Oh, *I* am Jewish, my *wife's* a good Irish Catholic. We had to give our mothers grandchildren just to keep them from killing each other."

That made me feel guilty about my own divorce. Did Margaret and I have any issue that compared to that? Maybe Sarah was justified in wanting to be rid of both of us.

"Well, I hope you get back for your kids,"

"Me, too."

"And on second thought, can you order something from room service? I just realized I haven't eaten anything all day."

"Sure, what do you want?"

I lay back on the bed, groaning as the muscles knotted in my back. "Doesn't matter."

CHAPTER NINETEEN

I SPENT the next few hours running through every conversation I had with Sarah, trying to figure out exactly when I should have known, at what point I could have intervened to prevent this.

Damn it, Margaret, didn't you notice something? I wasn't there, you saw her every day.

Yeah, that was really fair, especially when it looked as if my daughter was enticed into something because she was *my* daughter.

Hell, if I wanted to backtrack blame, we could go all the way back to when the Portal first opened. At the time it had seemed reasonable that I would want to stay and cover the story of the millennium—and with every passing year, hindsight told me that it was Margaret who had been the reasonable one.

The times I wanted to feel better about the divorce, I told myself it was inevitable. I was too work-centered for the marriage to work. When I was being honest, I told myself that I had just let it happen. It had been what I really wanted, Margaret and Sarah far enough away that I could concentrate on what I was doing without worrying about them. Jump into my career full tilt, guilt free, and my only family concerns the periodic phone call . . .

Payback's a bitch.

Just waiting was killing me. I knew that I wasn't the first father to go through this, and that this wasn't the FBI's first experience with kidnapping, but it felt all wrong to me. They should be out there *doing* something. I should be out looking for my daughter, not waiting here for some sort of contact that might never come.

Besides, I doubted that I'd receive any contact while the Feds were baby-sitting me.

"I'm not doing myself any good," I whispered to myself. If I couldn't do something productive, I should do something distracting. I got out of bed and opened the door. Agent Francis was flipping through a magazine.

"Mr. Maxwell?"

"You think one of your guys at my condo could bring me my laptop? I should probably try and get some work done. I have a column due tomorrow."

Francis nodded. "If the forensic team's done with it, I don't think that will be a problem." He picked up the phone.

"And I think I left some of my notes on the coffee table."

"Sure— Hello, this is Francis, I'm with Mr. Maxwell. Yeah, he wants a couple of things from his condo if you're done with them . . ."

With my hand wrapped up, I was reduced to a two-finger hunt-and-peck. That was okay. That was the speed my mind was working at. I was lucky that what was due was an op-ed piece rather than anything hard. I just wasn't mentally up for that kind of fact-checking at the last minute. My notes from home might have a feature story on Mazurich buried in them, but I wasn't up to digging it out.

Instead, I fleshed out a half-written piece about the rising star of Gregory Washington and his apparent inevitable ascension to the mayor's office. It was only eight hundred words, but it was close to midnight before I finished it.

At least Columbia will be happy.

I e-mailed the story to her.

I almost logged out, but I saw an unfamiliar e-mail address in my inbox.

Thinking it was news of my daughter, I opened it.

"Someone wants to help you. Midnight at the Superior Viaduct."

"What?"

I glanced at the clock by my bed, and the digital numbers flashed 12:00 at me. "Great timing," I whispered. "Maybe tomorrow . . ."

I looked back at my laptop, intending to respond to the offer of assistance, letting them know I wasn't going to be able to attend any clandestine midnight meetings . . .

The e-mail was gone.

I tried to find the window on my desktop, I searched through the inbox, and the trash, and even tried downloading messages again, but it was gone.

The message didn't exist, but I knew I had read it.

"Shit."

"You okay in there, Mr. Maxwell?" Levi appeared in my doorway. The agents must have switched shifts.

"Yeah, I just deleted something by accident." What was I supposed to do? Tell the Feds about it? And what if the guy contacting me was gun-shy? If someone really had help to offer, could I screw that up?

Then again, what if I imagined it?

Right now I couldn't even prove that I had been sent anything. It could easily be fatigue catching up with me, granting me a little wishful thinking. I'd only seen it thirty seconds ago, and it was already too easy for me to dismiss it. Why should anyone else take it seriously—

Give it a break, you just don't want to tell them.

I *was* sure that I had read the message. And going to the trouble of sending me a self-erasing e-mail strongly suggested that the sender only wanted to deal with me. Given what I was involved in, it was likely that I hadn't even been looking at an e-mail, strictly speaking. The more I thought about it, the more likely it seemed that it was some sort of disguised enchantment, made up to look as if it was a normal e-mail. Mages had managed to send me messages that way, through electronic channels. It allowed some layer of camouflage—the mage can cast something on a server, or a switch box, or even wire conduit and the communication can go off at some preset time when the caster is nowhere near the site of the spell or the recipient.

The message had said midnight but didn't specify a date.

So I had two options. Either the proposed contact was past and I was SOL, or the instruction was a general communication protocol, and any date I visited the site at the specified time, something or someone would present itself. It was easy enough to set up some standing enchantment that would reveal itself at the specified time.

Twenty-four hours.

If there was even a fraction of a chance, I was not going to allow Blackstone's little army to screw it up. My daughter was a lot more important than his investigation.

"You should get some sleep," Levi told me through the door.

"I know." I yawned. Fatigue was finally starting to win over stress. Besides, I needed to get some rest if I was going to lose these guys and get to the Superior Viaduct for this meeting.

I shut off my laptop and tried to sleep.

CHAPTER TWENTY

I LOOK, and the goat-faced Devil looks directly at me. Reaching out with a clawed fist, he says, **"Behold the cost of defying me!"**

The Devil opens his fist and I see the image of my daughter, Sarah. Her body is naked, battered, and covered in gore.

"Dad," she manages to whisper.

"No." I run toward the Devil, but he pulls his clawed hand back and Sarah is gone.

"Show me to my adversary."

I begin to object, I don't know who the adversary is. But then the mists clear, and I see a tower hovering over the city, greater than any skyscraper.

"There!" I point.

A booming, inhuman laugh resounds. **"Your service will be rewarded."**

The Devil rises from his throne, and walks toward the tower. Moments later, after losing sight of the Devil, the tower begins to crumble.

"Sarah!"

I sat bolt upright in bed, plastered with sweat. Heart racing.

Daylight filtered through the drapes. And for a moment I allowed myself to relax. Then I heard the noise.

It came from the living room of the suite, a high-pitched electronic whine. It twisted and vibrated, and found just the right frequency to set my teeth on edge. My skin felt prickly, in a sensation that was becoming all too familiar.

I got out of bed, calling, "Agent Francis? Agent Levi?"

I slowly pushed the door open.

The two Feds were nowhere to be seen. The shades were all

drawn, so the only light was a blood-red glow from the television. What was on the screen was no normal broadcast. Somehow, despite all the redundant data transmission and all the built-in filtering, the television was picking up pure mana interference. The image was twisting and surreal, faces melting into a flaming blood pudding.

"Agent Francis? Agent Levi?"

One face emerged from the chaos on the screen, the goat face from the tarot, and my dream.

"Look upon my face."

Not a great idea, but I couldn't help myself. I locked eyes with the Devil-image and felt a shuddering wave of vertigo as the hotel room was wiped away by flames and blood as the Devil took my throat and pulled me into his presence.

He threw me to my knees and I faced the ground, coughing blood and staring at dirty brown soil.

"Behold, Mr. Maxwell."

I got to my feet and gasped. I was in a vast floodlit chamber, obviously underground. Behind me were vast spaces with unfinished walls, but in front of me the stone—the salt—was carved into incredible pillars, vaults, and arches.

Statues climbed over each other, toward the ceiling, and—like a cathedral—central to it all was a vast rose window that glowed with stained glass.

"The salt mines . . ."

"The lair of the dwarves."

I stumbled forward through a vast Gothic doorway. Before me was a great hall, with benches to seat hundreds. It was empty except for a single high chair next to an altar at the opposite end of the hall.

"Sarah!"

I ran toward her. She sat, eyes closed, hands folded in her lap. I almost reached her before a clawed hand yanked me back. *"No. Do not wake her."*

"What have you done?"

"Me? Nothing."

I reached for my daughter.

"Her conscious mind could not bear the sea of mana she sleeps in here. Should she wake, she would go mad."

"What do you want?"

"What you want, Mr. Maxwell? Publish your tale. Make public the dwarven trade in the substance of mana itself. Let it be

known that they traffic it beyond the shores of the Portal. Tell how your politicians profit . . ."

"Give me back my daughter."

"Do your job well, and she will be safely returned."

What the hell kind of blackmail was this? What kind of ransom? I didn't understand. Still, "Give me my daughter first."

The Devil chuckled and grabbed me by the shirt. *"Show some good faith, and I might."*

The world turned red and bloody again. I looked into the Devil's face and his eyes began to glow at me. *"You also know the cost of defying me . . ."*

The Devil's eyes became bright white, too bright to look at. My eyes watered and I shook my head.

"Mr. Maxwell?"

Someone was holding me down and I tried to push him off as the light went away.

"What the—" I looked around and the Devil was gone. Agents Levi and Francis were there, and the man holding me down and shining the light in my eye was a paramedic.

"Are you okay, Mr. Maxwell?" Levi asked.

"Yeah, I'm fine." I looked up at the medic, "What happened?"

"You had a seizure," said the medic. "For about fifteen minutes you were completely unresponsive."

I sat up. "I'm fine now," I said despite the fact that I suddenly felt dizzy.

"I think we need to take you to the clinic for observation."

"Is that necessary?" I looked over at Francis and Levi and their expressions told me all I needed to know. Whatever they had seen was severe, and the growing pain in my back told me I'd been doing more than lying around.

Levi looked over at Francis, "I'll go with him. You stay here in case there's some attempt at contact."

Attempt at contact? Boy, did you guys miss it.

They took me to the Cleveland Clinic where I spent a good part of the afternoon suffering through a series of uncomfortable and unnecessary tests. After which they deposited me in a private room, with Agent Levi stationed outside.

Great . . .

I needed to get out from under the FBI's thumb if I was going to have a chance to follow up on my phantom e-mail. I needed to think of something.

The problem was, all I had was a hospital gown and one of those stupid little bracelets. I don't know where my clothes had gone, and I didn't even have my cell phone. It took me a while to come up with even a stupid plan.

Fortunately, the clinic provided me with a phone.

"You're shitting me," Reggie said.

"Can you do it?"

"You're making me an accomplice."

"That isn't an answer."

"Damn it, you going to give me something for my byline out of this?"

"How 'bout my notes on Mazurich's secret slush fund. You can go to town."

"Christ, you *are* desperate. I'll be there in fifteen minutes."

It was fairly simple as escape plans went. Which meant that there were probably way too many things that could go wrong. Fortunately, I didn't have too long to dwell on it. By the time I had gotten the window to my room open, and brushed the snow off of the sill, I could hear Reggie's voice outside.

"I want to see Maxwell. I brought him a change of clothes."

"You'll have to leave that with me," said Agent Levi.

"Come on, how long has he been wearing the same stuff—"

I ran back to the bathroom, which was right next to the entryway. I wedged myself in the shadows, trying to be invisible, as Reggie walked into my room.

"Hey, Maxwell!" Reggie walked into the room and repeated, "Hey!"

With the bathroom and the front door open, I could just see Levi, sitting by the doorway. A paper grocery bag sat next to the chair. I had to smile when I saw that Reggie had scrawled "Kline Maxwell" on it in permanent marker.

"Hey," Reggie said, "where is he?"

Levi got up and walked into the room. "What?"

I watched him from behind as he looked at Reggie, then the bed, then at the open window. While his back was turned, I dashed out, grabbing the grocery bag.

"What the hell," I heard Levi say as I took the first turn I came to.

I tried not to run as I looked for a place to slip out of view. There were orderlies, nurses, and doctors, but everyone was in the middle of doing something, and no one yet seemed to have the spare time to notice me. Before any of them did, I saw another bathroom in the hallway, and I slipped inside.

Just like Reggie had said, the bag held a change of clothes. The fact that they were Reggie's clothes didn't really matter to me at the moment. The sleeves were short and the waist was loose, but at least the sneakers fit. Ratty as they were, he had even had the sense to bring a winter jacket, stocking cap, and gloves—all bearing the logo of the long-absent Browns football franchise.

I waited until the hallway was quiet, then I slipped back outside.

I took a very circuitous route to the parking garage, and found Reggie waiting for me in an idling Lincoln Town Car. He threw the door open for me and said, "You owe me."

"Yeah. I know."

He drove off, back toward downtown.

"There's one more thing," I said.

"Of course there is."

"I'd like to borrow your car."

Reggie gave me a withering stare for a moment. Then he said, "Of course, why not?"

CHAPTER TWENTY-ONE

SANITY would dictate that I lay low until midnight and my anonymous meeting. I managed to do that for nearly an hour. Then I broke down and started driving along the west side of the Cuyahoga. I wasn't clear on everything that was going on, but I was clear on where it was centered.

Whiskey Island.

What I would do when I got there was an open question. However, it was clear that Magetech's strings were being pulled from there. And if my demonic visitor was to be believed, my daughter was kept somewhere out there, in the mines.

As I turned away from Edgewater Park, on to Whiskey Island Drive, I was able to see the Cleveland skyline beyond the wooded confines of the dwarven peninsula. Whiskey Island was flanked to the right by the skyscrapers a mile away on Public Square, and on the left by the dark twisting clouds above the Portal.

Whiskey Island stabbed right between the two features as if it were a conscious metaphor for the division between the two worlds.

After passing through the Shoreway underpass, I paralleled the long-disused Conrail tracks that used to serve the port and the salt mines. I passed chain-link fences that were sagged and rusty, a few bore warning signs that I had never seen before. Big red letters "Fe" covered half the sign. Text in English warned "High Iron Hazard."

The English words were accompanied by a script that I believed was elvish.

Lots of things had occupied Whiskey Island at one time or another; nineteenth-century Irish immigrants, a defunct Coast Guard station, volleyball courts, a marina, the salt mines, of course . . .

And the Port Authority once ran an iron ore pellet terminal here. Decades of use probably saturated this area. I would not want to be an elf right now.

I shook my head. It was as if fate itself conspired to isolate the dwarven enclave.

The road got worse, the asphalt deteriorating the farther west I went toward the tip of the peninsula. It finally degenerated into a gravel track ending at a gateless chain-link fence. At one point I could have driven all the way to the largest marina on the Great Lakes—but that didn't exist anymore.

I got out of the Lincoln and looked around. I hadn't expected the way to be completely clear; I was at the back door, so to speak. All the traffic and new construction was concentrated on the southern edge and the western tip of the peninsula. The road I was on, like the train tracks, was mostly abandoned.

However, if my memory of my research was accurate, the salt mines were on the opposite side of the tracks from the old pellet terminal. At one point, they might have been visible from where I stood, but high concentrations of mana had some interesting effects on vegetation.

Past the chain-link, and the train tracks, stood a grove of trees whose twisted and gnarled trunks could have clung to the land here for a millennium. Could have, but didn't. This was one of a few areas where dark old-growth forests seemed to have erupted overnight, post-Portal. Somehow the twisted patterns of mana allowed centuries-old roots to climb over fifty-year-old train tracks. In one place a trunk as wide as the Lincoln grew through the open doors of a derailed boxcar.

The woods hid the southern sky, the naked winter branches as dense as any canopy. The only sound: my feet crunching gravel and the ominous creak as wind from the lake shifted the branches around me.

While the road was fenced off, the chain-link was in bad repair and showed no obvious wards. A man-sized gap was in the fence opposite the Conrail tracks, and led to a dirt trail that headed off where the road used to go.

"Okay, Kline, does this make sense?"

Yesterday I had chased a dwarf to his death. I had good reason to believe they held my daughter. Chances were they wouldn't be pleased to see me.

But Teaghue said that "he" had her. I didn't need to be a brain surgeon to figure out what demonic manifestation the late Teaghue Parthalán was referring to. Both in his last words and in the circle his fellows constructed for my benefit on the Detroit-Superior Bridge.

Add to that the image from my nightmares; the dwarves chained to the demonic throne, mining the massive mountain of salt . . .

"What are you doing?"

"It must be fed!"

However badly things went with Teaghue, I had a gut feeling that I might find some ally among the dwarves. Or at least some source of information.

That's how my rationalizations went as I slipped through the fence. Despite that, the fact was cold logic should have dictated that this was as dumb a move as chasing Teaghue had been.

A few steps past the fence, and the trees had me surrounded. I had to keep checking to make sure the path was still visible behind me. Enchanted woods had a habit of closing up behind people.

This one didn't seem to mind leaving me an escape route, though after a hundred feet, the path twisted around enough to make me lose sight of the fence and Reggie's car.

I stopped a moment.

This was one of the places in the area that no one had managed to map accurately since the opening of the Portal. All I had was some general geography. I was on a peninsula about a mile long, ranging from a third to a half mile wide. The western end, where it met shore, and where I had come from, had been the industrialized part, the east end had never really been developed and only had an abandoned Coast Guard station.

I was pretty sure that I was roughly in the geographic center, which would put me due north of the salt mines and the dwarven settlements.

However, the thick woods around me encouraged me to stay on the path, which kept going east—as far as I could tell.

I kept an eye to the right, looking for a clearing, or any passable way toward the mines. However, to all appearances, the plant kingdom had been completely triumphant. The Conrail tracks were totally overtaken. I saw railroad ties, and the rails themselves, embedded in large trunks ten, twenty, thirty feet up. Roots embraced and seemed to consume large fragments of concrete and asphalt. Corrugated steel poked out of snow-covered earth, only visible because the undergrowth had shed its leaves for the winter.

I knew the area was in was way too small to really become lost, but even in a space less than a mile square, I knew it wasn't safe to brave these kinds of woods. They tended to be larger on the inside than they were on the outside.

The light started to fail. Looking up, I saw the dappled white fragments of sky turn grayer. Another storm front moving in from the lake.

As if in response to my thought, thick white flakes began to drift down through the twisted branches above me.

"Fuck," I whispered, and my breath fogged around me.

In response I heard something rustle.

I froze.

The woods stayed silent around me. I couldn't tell if the sound I'd heard came from behind me or ahead of me.

I took a step.

Something crunched the gravel on the path behind me. It wasn't my foot.

I started moving. I tried to be quiet, but I could hear my shadow picking up the pace to match me. My heart raced, and the trees themselves seemed to feed into the sense of panic. I wanted to run, but I tried to reason with myself, *the point was to talk to someone, right?*

I wasn't Indiana Jones or James Bond; there wasn't any way I was going to free my daughter by stealth or force. The only thing I could do was to convince someone to hand her over. I had to talk to someone.

Now was as good a time as any . . .

I turned around and stood my ground, facing the last turn in the path behind me.

My stalker stopped moving before he came into view. If I listened now, I could hear his breathing heavy and deep. I could just see a wisp of his breath emerging from behind a tree.

I sucked in a breath, calmed myself, and put on my best journalistic game face. "Come on out, I just want to talk to someone."

I heard weight shifting on the gravel path. It sounded bigger than a dwarf. More like several.

I took a step forward. "Kline Maxwell, *Cleveland Press.* But, I think you know that, don't you?"

Something rustled again, a noise that took me a moment to identify.

"Come out and talk . . ."

Wings.

It came out, but it wasn't a dwarf, or even several dwarves. It leaped into the path in front of me, springing on feline haunches that were sized more for a Clydesdale, and stared me down with the head of a raptor that should have been extinct for a few hundred thousand years.

The griffin let out a screech that could probably knock lesser avian dead out of the sky.

Unlike a lot of critters that came out of the Portal, this was not something you could reason with. It was a wild animal. Most had a healthy fear of humanoids. However, this one was too hungry, too pissed, or just too nasty to be fazed by me.

It reared, and I did the only thing I could. I dove into the woods.

It wasn't quite the sanctuary it seemed.

I left the path, and the trees seemed to open up around me. Suddenly the stand of trees that seemed so closed in that a dwarf couldn't pass through widened to the point where a man could fully stretch his arms between the massive trunks.

While that meant I could run, unimpeded; it also meant that a pissed-off griffin could follow me. The only thing that kept me alive was the fact that the trees were just close enough to prevent it from pouncing or taking flight, and its bird-clawed forelegs were more designed for tearing prey apart, not chasing it.

That meant that I could barely keep ahead of it while running flat out. My only hope was to find some cover before I hit a clearing, or the water.

I hit all three at the same time.

After running through the unnatural woods for ten minutes beyond the point where I should have reached the edge of the peninsula, I broke out of the edge, somewhere on the northern shore. I faced a clearing stacked high with mountainous piles of dismantled steel machinery. A scrap heap a few dozen orders of magnitude beyond the piles next to *The Dwarven Armorer.*

I ran between stacks of girders too tight for my pursuer to follow. Behind I heard a screech and a rush of feathers. I could feel the griffin's hot breath on my neck as I wove deeper into the rusty iron maze.

I saw its shadow fly across the slice of sky visible above me. I leaned against a slab of metal and hyperventilated. My lungs burned and my legs felt like rubber.

You're a genius, Kline . . .

I closed my eyes and shook my head. At least I had my bearings again. I was standing in the last remnants of the Hulett ore unloaders—skyscraper-sized mechanical dinosaurs, four of which had dominated the pellet terminal for a good ninety years during the last century. They had been obsolete for a few decades when the Port Authority decided to dismantle the beasts—four of the six left in existence.

In the constant tension between redevelopment and preservation, redevelopment had won. Unfortunate, since political wrangling over this spit of shoreline, and the subsequent opening of the Portal, meant that the Port Authority never got to expand the docks here, losing even the existing facilities.

But the bones of this industrial fossil rested to the east of the old pellet terminal. So once I was clear of griffins, I could follow the shore and get back to the car. The shot of adrenaline from my confrontation was just what I needed to come to my senses and realize my limitations.

I waited a good twenty minutes until I was sure the griffin had given up on me. Then I tried to backtrack, which turned out to be less simple than it sounded.

I wove back through the maze of iron, toward what I thought was the edge, and I faced a dead end—a slab of iron an inch thick, dotted with rivets the size of my fist. I couldn't even see around it.

I turned around and worked my way back, and realized I had no idea which way to go. I stood at the intersection of five paths that wove through the ocher piles of iron, my feet sinking into thick, red slushy mud. My footprints led down four of the paths, in both directions.

"Shit." My voice came out in a puff of fog.

I looked at the piles of scrap and saw figures spray-painted on the pieces. I had ignored them, at first. Just ID numbers, probably left over from when the Historical Society had plans to reconstruct one of these monsters on another site.

That was right, as far as the white numbers went.

However, someone had also sprayed red and orange paint on the girders, marking arcane glyphs that actually hurt my eyes when I stared at them.

That couldn't be good.

I swallowed, and started to get the same creepy sensation I had gotten around Magetech. There, things seemed to hide beneath the reflections; here, it was as if something ugly hid under the pattern of rust flakes on the iron beams.

If I had my cell phone, I would have tried to call Dr. Shafran for advice. The little I knew about mazes like this, they usually forced you through the center in order to get out.

The problem was, like ancient Crete, there invariably was something nasty in the center.

However, I didn't have much choice but to play along.

I followed the path that wasn't graced by my footprints. I

slogged between twisted iron walls that tried to claw their way into my brain. I forced my gaze down, focusing on the path ahead of me. Every heartbeat felt as if the walls would close in and squeeze the life from me, even though in my narrow focus, the path became wider.

Each intersection, I could see one path that did not yet have footprints. Each time I took that fork.

My socks were wet, and every step I had the nasty sense that something was reaching up through the mud and touching the soles of my feet.

"And I was worried about the woods . . ."

I slogged on, following the logic of the untraveled road. The weight of the metal around me became a heavier and heavier pressure on the back of my mind.

Until I came to a dead end.

"Fuck!"

I looked up, and the sky itself was gone. I was in a cavern built of iron scrap. I could see, but the ruddy light was sourceless and nothing cast a shadow. When I turned around, I saw no footprints in the mud behind me.

"Shit. Are you out there?" I shouted. The words hung in the air, echoless. "Someone show themselves!"

The light in the air appeared to pulse. I was breathing hard, the air burning my lungs as badly as it had after I'd run from the griffin. Vertigo gripped me, the dizzying sensation that the world around me was dropping into free fall.

"I want my daughter!"

The glyphs spray-painted on the metal walls around me began to glow. It became harder for me to breathe, the air as thick as the mud swallowing my ankles. I tried to shout again, but the words came out as a wheeze.

The sourceless light slowed its pulsing, dimming to invisibility, leaving only the glowing glyphs surrounding me. The sense of falling continued and I was tumbling in a void, my muscles locked, unable to breathe, only able to see the burning glyphs that were like hot brands stabbing into the back of my skull.

Voices spoke a guttural language other than English. Somehow I understood the unseen speakers.

"The journalist."

"Yes."

"He must not be here."

"He is here."
"Who does he serve?"
"Who do we serve?"
"He has cost us too much."
"We have cost him too much."
"Can he do what we cannot?"
"He will or he will not. Those who look cannot find him here."
"He will return."
"When it is done, and all is lost—or won."

I sucked in a breath, shocking myself awake.

I was behind the wheel of the Lincoln. I was parked on some residential street somewhere. The sky was dark and it was just beginning to snow. I turned the key and the clock on the dash told me it was 10:30.

"What the hell?"

I had blacked out again. It was either another mana overdose, or it was some dwarven security system, or a little of both. I should probably count myself lucky coming through unscathed. I hoped to God I hadn't endangered my daughter.

No, the demonic bastard wants me. He needs the leverage . . .

I gripped the steering wheel, trying to calm down. Then I realized where I was.

The dwarves were trying to give me a message.

I was parked in front of the late Council President Dominic Mazurich's house. And on the passenger seat was a key on a St. Christopher key chain.

CHAPTER TWENTY-TWO

L ET it never be said that I can't take a hint.

Whatever was going on, I was getting the feeling that even if the dwarves weren't exactly on my side, they weren't on the side of my daughter's kidnapper either. Whoever was hiding behind the tarot Devil was at odds with the dwarves themselves.

"What are you doing?"

"It must be fed!"

Perhaps it was Magetech itself. It wouldn't be the first time a corporate entity took on its own life and started cannibalizing its workers and founders.

Whoever or whatever it was, the dwarves were afraid of even re-ferring to it indirectly. And given what happened to Nina and Teaghue, they had good reason. But it was clear that they didn't serve that master willingly.

So I made the assumption that I had been parked here to push me in the right direction.

I walked up the driveway to Mazurich's side door and tried the doorknob. Locked.

I looked for any obvious wards. I didn't see any, but if this was the house key, the St. Christopher medal was probably keyed to them. Even so, once I unlocked the door I stood and waited.

If any neighbor called the cops, or a warded alarm was tripped, I might get away with misdemeanor trespass if I was outside the house when they showed up. I gave them enough time to show up.

They didn't.

I let myself into Mazurich's house. I gagged a little. Death still clung to the air in here, as if an evil rot had sunk into the walls.

I stepped into the darkened house, unclear exactly what I was looking for. I left the lights off. The glass may not have attracted at-tention, but I wasn't about to press my luck. I let my eyes adjust until the glare from the streetlights outside was enough for me to navigate by.

I left the kitchen and entered the living room. A sectional couch, coffee table, not much else. Family photos crowded the mantel. Nothing out of the ordinary.

My foot crunched glass.

I knelt down and picked up the remains of a picture frame, a partly torn photograph fell from it. I set down the frame and picked up the damaged picture.

It was a digital shot, the strange ghosting marked it as probably coming from one of the first post-Portal cameras. Given the date on the back, and the subject matter, probably a prototype.

The picture showed Mazurich, Dr. Pretorious, a cluster of dwarves recognizable from their portraits at Magetech HQ, and Mr. Simon Lucas. The tear in the photograph split Lucas in two, and there was a heel print in the center.

I suppose that once suicide was the obvious cause of death, the cops stopped bothering with evidence. And the Democratic party machine, which drove most everything in the county, might have discouraged any close examination of the council president's connection to Magetech.

However, to be fair, I might just be a lot more comfortable with that kind of conspiracy.

I placed the photo on the mantel and headed upstairs.

Mazurich's house made me uneasy. It wasn't squeamishness as much as the look I was getting into Mazurich's personal life. I knew how much money this man had collected from Magetech. Even if the money was sheltered and hidden, one would expect to see some of that in the man's home. What someone chooses to spend money on is one of the keys to their character.

Mazurich hadn't done much of anything. It was almost as if he hadn't changed anything in the house since he separated from his wife. The impression came from the fact that every room seemed to have broken patterns. Pictures on the wall that formed lopsided, unbalanced designs. Matching end tables in a child's bedroom, but with no bed between them. Throw rugs on the wall-to-wall carpet arranged around furniture that wasn't there. Chairs facing blank walls . . .

I knew many, many people who put too much of themselves into their work. I counted myself among them. People whose residential address was little more than a place they went to go to bed. Their homes became shells. This felt worse.

Could a house be worse than soulless?

I wondered if I was suffering from the aftereffects of my ill-fated trip to Whiskey Island.

The master bedroom was the scene of the suicide. Here, the smell of death was the worst. Even though I could see that crime scene cleanup had been through here. The mattress was gone from the bed, leaving the naked box spring, and a large square of the wall-to-wall carpet had been cut away, baring the hardwood floor. In the streetlight glow from the window, there seemed to be a darker spot on the wood. Ink-black and shiny.

I stepped forward and the stain was gone. Some odd reflection, that's all.

Why am I here? What am I looking for?

I saw the bullet hole. It went into the wall above the headboard. Around it, the wallpaper had been stripped baring the plaster. More attempted cleanup.

I stepped forward and suddenly saw the wall spotted with gore, tufts of hair, shiny bits of—

I stumbled back and the vision disappeared.

"Okay, that wasn't the light."

I walked backward from the bed frame, toward the door. My heart raced.

The mana from the Portal used the environment around itself as an organizing principle. The patterns could be chemical, like the crystalline structure of the salt under Lake Erie; or ritual and cultural, like the New Age occultism that Nina had practiced. It could be geographic, such as in the mystical woods that had enveloped the North Chagrin Reservation; it could be architectural, like innumerable churches, or the maze the dwarves had made of the Huletts' remains.

Patterns could also be emotional, and psychological.

Such as this house, the mind of Mazurich, and the way he had killed himself.

The door slammed shut behind me.

"Shit." I whipped around and grabbed the knob and tried to pull it open. It was shut fast by something more powerful than the latch.

Something laughed behind me.

I turned around, back flattened against the door.

"Only the damned follow me here." Mazurich's voice was little more than a whisper. He sat above the bed, hovering above the box

spring where the missing mattress must have been. Blood flowed from his mouth, turning his chin and the front of his shirt a glossy black. His skull was shaped wrong, and when he moved, I could see that it was because of a massive crater in the back of his head.

He turned his face toward me and stared into my eyes. I couldn't look away. I knew the face. I had interviewed him innumerable times. I also knew he was dead, and the specter before me couldn't be him . . .

Just an image conjured up by the Portal.

"W—why did you kill yourself?" I tried to keep my composure. It wasn't easy.

Mazurich laughed again. When he lifted his head, I could see through his mouth to the wall behind him.

"You know, Maxwell. You'll join me in hell soon enough."

I shook my head, no.

"You will do His bidding, even if you fight Him."

"Who is he?"

"He has an infinity of names: the morning star, the bringer of light, the father of lies."

"He has my daughter."

Mazurich laughed.

"You are already lost."

"No," I whispered.

"You will give your soul for what He will promise you."

I screwed my eyes shut and clenched my fists. I tried to anchor myself against the fear. "What the hell are you?"

"What you will become."

"No," I shook my head. "You're the mana-animated guilt of a poor bastard that couldn't accept the decisions he made."

"You cannot fight Him."

"No," I whispered. *"You* couldn't."

A chill wind blew through the room, making my bones ache. For a moment I could actually feel my heart stop.

I opened my eyes, blinking, and the phantom was gone. No specter, no blood, and even the smell of death seemed to have receded.

The morning star,
The bringer of light,
The father of lies,
Lucifer,
The Devil.

Mazurich was a good Catholic, and if that's really what

Mazurich thought, I could understand how he might end up killing himself. I was shaken myself as I backed out of the bedroom.

What if the authors of that evangelical pamphlet had a point?

When I got back to the car, it was after eleven and I had another meeting to go to.

CHAPTER TWENTY-THREE

THE Superior Viaduct has an interesting history. It was one of the first rail connections between east and west across the Cuyahoga River, and one of the first moving bridges marking it as a precursor of dozens of drawbridges that would rise, fall, and swing across the river.

Nineteenth century trolleys crossed an arched stone approach toward a swinging iron trestle that would carry them west. The operation lasted only a quarter century or so, surviving at least one fairly significant disaster where a trolley plunged into the river, eventually to be replaced by higher, more modern structures at the beginning of the twentieth century.

The iron trestle of the bridge was shortly sold for scrap. But the arched vault of the eastern approach has remained for close to a century, a bridge to nowhere. Like the Huletts, it is one of many odd artifacts in the city that are subject to periodic debates that swing between development, restoration, and apathy.

With the viaduct, there was a brief development debate, but since the Portal opened the pendulum had swung solidly toward apathy. However, as far as meeting places went, it was probably the most public abandoned structure you could find—a raised open-air deck cutting through the heart of the eastern shore of the Flats.

While the East Flats were a little less hard core than the West— a fetish club like the *Nazgûl* wouldn't fit in with the restaurants and comedy clubs that clustered on this side of the river—the area was still choked solidly with people at quarter to midnight.

It reminded me why I haven't gone clubbing for over twenty-five years. I don't know what was worse, the five-mile-per-hour traffic, or the twenty-something pedestrians who believed that sidewalks were only a suggestion.

Fortunately, I still reached my destination ten minutes early. I parked Reggie's Lincoln by the barriers at the eastern end of the viaduct. I stepped out of the car and was just far enough away from the chaos and noise around me to hear my feet crunch in the snow.

The night was clear and cold, the only cloud was the fog from my own breath. The deck of the viaduct arced away from me, over the Flats, to dead-end at the river. Blocking my path, on the other side of the traffic barrier, was a tall chain-link fence. It had a gate, but it was padlocked.

I stood at the gate and looked at the deck. It was covered by a layer of snow, silver and unmolested under the glow of the full moon.

It looked like I'd got here first.

I wasn't about to break in. I could see a frightening array of wards scribed on the top rail of the fence. I didn't know what any of them might do, but I wasn't about to find out the hard way. I wasn't going to help Sarah by inflicting random curses on myself.

I stood by the gate and waited for my anonymous e-mailer to show himself.

I waited.

I checked my watch five times, each time sure that I'd been stood up, or that the phantom e-mail had really meant *only* last midnight.

However, every time, my watch told me that even less time had passed. It didn't feel possible. The ten minutes to midnight seemed to stretch to twenty. Everything seemed to crawl around me. Even the fog of my breath seemed hesitant.

By the fifth time I suspected there was something more going on than my impatience. My watch read 11:58:49, and I was convinced that I'd been standing here for way more than eight minutes.

I looked at the seconds and waited for the 49 to change to 50. And waited. In my head I counted to ten before the LCD winked over to 50. I counted fifteen to reach 51.

I looked up from my watch and realized that it wasn't just a wayward timepiece. The noise from the Flats was wrong, octaves lower than it should be, I couldn't pick out anything recognizable as a human voice, and everything was muffled and nearly subliminal.

Down the street where there were people, I could see movement, but barely. I looked down and kicked the snow at my feet, and saw it hang in the air for a short eternity before arcing slowly back to merge with the slush at my feet.

I looked back at my watch.

11:59:03.

I counted a full twenty seconds before the number flipped to 04.

Almost at the same time, the air around me rang with the sound of a gigantic bell. The sound was undistorted, and felt so close that I could picture myself right next to Quasimodo as he pulled the rope.

In front of me, of its own accord, the gate in the fence opened.

I looked around and all I could see of the world had stopped. The people at the end of the street showed no visible movement. By them, a glowing cigarette butt hung in midair where a leather-clad biker had thrown it toward the gutter. The Harley he rode was caught in mid-spray passing the college kids, the slush frozen in the air, halfway toward them.

There was another resonating bell sound, the gong vibrating the fillings in my back teeth.

My watch still read 11:59:03.

Something told me it was slow.

I expected it to be awkward to move, but whatever enchantment gripped me must have compensated for little things like air resistance, acceleration, and gravity. Whoever this was, he wasn't minor league.

I passed through the gate and walked across the snow-covered deck of the Superior Viaduct as the bell tolled again. Three down, nine to go.

Whatever distorted my sense of time began operating on my sense of space as well. The world around the deck of the viaduct began to twist, the moon coming impossibly close, and the neighboring Cleveland skyline receding into the far distance. The Flats below sank into a deep abyss while the river widened to rival the lake, swallowing the western shore.

The bell tolled four. And the air, cold and razor clear until now, began to spontaneously form mist, wrapping itself around me as I walked. The air became heavy, humid, and slightly warm.

Five.

I slowed my walk, because I knew that the viaduct dead-ended before the river, and I couldn't remember if the raw edge was fenced off or not. I didn't want to step off the end by accident. It felt as if I had easily traversed the length of it already.

Six.

Much longer than I expected, I couldn't trust my sense of distance anymore. If I was where I thought I was, I'd be midway across the river by now.

Seven.

I couldn't see my feet, or much of anything other than gray mist and a fuzzy glowing orb in the gray that showed where the moon must be. I could feel that I had left the snow cover. My feet fell on naked concrete. Or stone.

"We're not in Kansas anymore." The mist soaked up my words without the slightest echo, almost to the point where I thought I didn't actually hear them myself.

Eight.

The path I was on tilted upward and became uneven. I almost stumbled until I realized that I had come to a stairway. My heart was racing, my body was half convinced that any moment I would find the edge and take a fatal tumble into the river.

I had to tell myself that there were less grandiose ways to kill me off.

"Yeah, unless this is another hallucination."

Nine.

Pushing away unpleasant thoughts of bad trips and hostile illusions, I climbed the stairs. The mist began thinning almost immediately. After a few steps, I could see the moon clearly again.

Ten.

I stepped upward, out of the mist, and saw the moon eclipsed by something I had never seen on the Cleveland skyline. A cylindrical tower bisecting the swollen moon, with a height rivaling some of the tallest buildings downtown. The stairs I climbed, still shrouded in mists, weren't straight, but spiraled up the side of the tower, whose base seemed to have a foundation in the mists themselves.

Even though I had never actually seen it, the tower was familiar. *"Show me to my adversary."*

Eleven.

I finally stepped completely out of the mist; setting my feet on the first visible stone stair climbing up the edge of the tower. As I did, the mists themselves fell away.

I gasped.

There was no sign of the stair I had climbed to arrive here, or of any structure below the last two steps I had trod. The stair and the tower were anchored in nothing, suspended midair above the Cuyahoga River, about seven or eight hundred feet above the Superior Viaduct. The Cleveland skyline spilled out below me.

"The FAA has to love this thing."

I climbed up another quarter turn around the side of the tower and came face-to-face with a pair of ebony doors thirty feet wide and almost fifty high. An alien script wrapped every inch of their surfaces, glowing a blackish green in the moonlight. The hairs rose on the back of my neck, and the power here was thick enough for me to smell it in the air. It was like breathing hot static and adrenaline.

Twelve.

The bells came from inside the tower, and at the stroke of twelve, the huge doors swung out in front of me. They moved slowly, which was good because I needed to step out of the way to avoid being pushed off by them. Sidestepping the opening doors gave me a good look at how massive they actually were—the things were thicker than I was, and I needed to lose weight. Four-and-a-half feet thick at the base. The doors to this place took up more cubic feet than my entire condo.

I stood there at the entrance to the phantom tower as the doors completed their transit. Beyond was a massive hall that seemed to take up half the volume of the entire tower. Cylindrical walls shot away on either side, cased in marble, and hung with rich tapestries. Massive Gothic pillars formed concentric circles a third of the way in, reaching up to support vaults to a vast domed ceiling whose ribs at this distance seemed spider thin—though they probably rivaled the doors for sheer mass.

Thick rugs covered a flagstone floor arranged in a complex pattern that might have had some mystical significance. Iron sconces held torches illuminating the center space, and heavy chains suspended a vast iron chandelier—another object bigger than my whole condo—over the center of the room.

Sitting on the floor in the center of this vast room was the largest dragon I had ever seen.

The doors shut behind me before I fully realized I had walked inside.

"Welcome to my home, Mr. Maxwell. I am called Hephaestus."

Hephaestus was gargantuan, even for a species known for its size. A wall of reddish flesh, scaled and ribbed, towered over me even from a hundred feet away. His chest was almost as broad as the entry behind me. His forelegs, folded in front of him in a near catlike pose, were thicker and longer than my entire body and ended in clawed hands that could probably bat my Volkswagen around like a wad of tinfoil. Massive wings draped behind him, obscuring half of the huge chamber from me, and, perched on a towering serpentine neck was a triangular saurian skull that was the size of an Escalade.

His coloring ranged from a pinkish coral near the center of his chest, to a crimson so dark it was close to black along his spine and wings. He stretched his forelegs, and I could feel the movement in the stones beneath my feet.

"Come to me, I would talk to you."

I had only ever had one extended conversation with a dragon before. They tended to be solitary creatures, interacting with maybe one or two human proxies. They also were attracted to power, in its various forms, whether it be raw physical strength—which Hephaestus obviously had in spades—or the more intangible aspects such as wealth and knowledge.

Since they interacted with human society here, most concentrated on the purest distillation of power that we could provide—money. If you dug into the list of all the billionaires resident in Northeast Ohio, I would bet that once you dug behind all the shell companies and legal fictions, six of the top ten would have wings, claws, and little whips of sulfur smoke trailing from their nostrils.

"Unique home you have here,"

"Thank you," Hephaestus said. His booming voice had all the subtlety of a chainsaw being thrown into a wood chipper, but I could catch an inflection of pride. *"Not many have had the honor of an audience here."*

"It is impressive," I said, stopping about twenty feet away, which seemed a safe radius from any idle gestures. Also, with Hephaestus' head so far above me, it was about as close as I could get without tilting my head at an angle too unnatural for conversation. "And well hidden."

The floor shook as Hephaestus let loose with a rumbling bellows sound that, if I hadn't heard a dragon laugh before, would have scared the shit out of me.

Even so, I still backed up a step.

"Amusing choice of words, Mr. Maxwell. Hide? Indeed!" He lowered his head, circled his neck around me, and rested his chin on a clawed forefoot. I turned around to keep eye contact just as my gut began to realize that I was suddenly completely encircled by a wall made of dragon.

An instinctive step back and I was leaning against the curve of Hephaestus' muscular neck. I could feel his pulse in the small of my back, like a coal miner trying to pickax himself out of a hopeless cave-in. *"I do not hide, Mr. Maxwell. I merely make my home where men do not care to look."*

"Forgive my ignorance, but I've looked at this patch of sky every day for the last few decades, and I haven't seen this tower of yours. It's rather large to miss."

"Suffice it to say that, until tonight, you have been looking beside this spot, not at it. Most men have not trained their eyes to look in this direction."

"I seemed to walk it okay."

"When led, Mr. Maxwell. You could not see where you were going, could you?"

Despite the fact that Hephaestus spoke with a sonorous tone that vibrated my sternum and made Barry White sound like a castrati, I could swear that there was something almost impish in it. As if he took great pleasure in showing off his sky castle.

"No, I couldn't." I looked around. "Is this something like the Portal. Have I walked into some other reality?" I calculated my question carefully. The Portal had been a construct of another dragon, one named Aloeus. That was a fact that wasn't general knowledge, mainly because I wasn't able to get the details into print without having the story pulled by the forces that be. And while I had yet to write my book on how I found out that particular tidbit of information, I was pretty sure that Aloeus' handiwork was known among most of the nonhuman community. I also knew that if the elves could be defined by their reticence, dragons were almost as surely defined by their pride.

As I expected, bringing up Aloeus' handiwork encouraged Hephaestus to elaborate on his own. *"So close to understanding that you impress me. Like, but yet unlike. The Portal is simple, a hole in the wall, nothing more. No grace, no finesse. This, the creation of Hephaestus, is much more than that. A pocket of space that did not exist before my thoughts of it. A place that was not, but now is."*

My host was gracious enough to allow the implications of that to sink in. Could someone—something—create a whole universe from scratch? "How big is this place?"

"As large as suits my fancy at the moment."

"You didn't come through the Portal, did you?"

Again, the booming laughter came. The pressure made my skull ache as Hephaestus' neck vibrated behind me. It confirmed a suspicion that had been brewing ever since I walked in and saw him. There are not that many dragons in northeast Ohio. They might be secretive, but they also tend to stand out in public. A single appearance is enough to register deeply in the public psyche, especially for someone whose job is to cover the local news—"fuzzy gnome" or not.

The fact that Hephaestus was a new face to me, made me suspect that he did not come here through normal channels. At least that was more probable than the Feds suddenly loosening up the flow of nonhumans through the Portal.

"Astute you are, Mr. Maxwell."

I looked up at the tower above me; at the torchlight; the candles in the chandelier; at the tapestries I could see beyond the dragon's bulk, all of which could probably be titled "The Death of St. George" in one form or another; and it impressed me that exactly none of the twenty-first century seemed to have touched this place—

Other than myself.

"Jesus Christ, did you just *move* this place?"

"You are indeed worthy of my attention." Hephaestus lowered his clawed hand so his head hovered before me. *"Though it would be more accurate to say that I altered its orientation relative to various planes of existence, rotated its axis somewhat closer to that of your world."*

I stood there in silence for a few long minutes. I rubbed my face and realized that I hadn't showered or shaved in the past two days. My hand was shaking, and with the initial shock of meeting the dragon here wearing off, reality—such as it was—began to sink in.

"Why did you bring me here? Your message said you could help me. I need to find my daughter."

"Indeed, the predictable mortal concern for progeny."

His breath was hot, wet, and smelled of brimstone. His face was barely three feet from me—closer than I'd ever want to be.

"Can you help me?"

"In return for your help."

"What do you want?"

Hephaestus uncoiled from around me and sat upright. On his haunches, wings unfolded, his neck coiled almost to the chandelier. If it was possible, it was even more intimidating having his SUV-sized head sixty feet above me than when we were face-to-face.

"Mr. Maxwell, we have a common enemy."

Of course, I asked the obvious question. "Who is it?"

"I will not speak one of his names here, suffice it to say he has many of them." Hephaestus waved a clawed hand, and a line of torches lit along a stairway that spiraled along the inner wall of the chamber, behind the ranks of pillars. I hadn't noticed it before, and

because it was a human scale, much too small for Hephaestus, I wondered if it actually had been *there* before.

I turned back around, and Hephaestus was gone.

"What the—?"

A human voice, a *familiar* human voice, came from behind me. "Perhaps more the correct question might be *what* is it?"

I turned around and faced one of the last people I expected to see. *"You?"*

"Me," responded Dr. Newman Shafran, and the thick accent couldn't quite hide Hephaestus' glee at my surprise.

CHAPTER TWENTY-FOUR

"COME, come," Dr. Shafran took off a pair of thick round bifocals and used them to gesture toward the staircase leading up the wall. "To answer the question foremost in your mind, I am the Dr. Shafran you have known, and he is I." He looked at me with a glint in his eye, "as we are both the dragon Hephaestus."

That helped answer why Quint couldn't find a phone number for Dr. Shafran. The good Dr. Shafran might well cease to exist when he left the Case campus . . .

For once I had trouble coming up with a coherent question. "How, why . . . ?"

Hephaestus chuckled. "Please, let me take you to my library."

I followed him up the spiral staircase.

"To answer your concern, this mortal shell is propelled by my spirit which, along with the rest of my body has, in the terms I used earlier, rotated on its axis to be behind myself." He turned and smiled at me.

"Is there a real Dr. Shafran?"

"Oh, why be needlessly complex? Dr. Shafran is as real as you. Allow a scholar his alias."

We circled around the vast chamber once, and we were barely a quarter up the side of the wall. "Why do it?"

"What shocks you more, Mr. Maxwell? That I show such duplicity, or that I demean myself as much as to wear a man's shoes?"

I didn't know how to answer the question. The last thing I wanted to do was say anything that could come across as insulting. If anything, Hephaestus had managed to convince me that he possessed powers way beyond anything I had ever seen. I tried purposeful misdirection again. "I have seen remote-control golems before, gargoyles and undead—yours is the most real—"

Dr. Shafran touched me and the physical contact was enough to stop me talking. "Because it *is* real, Mr. Maxwell. This is my flesh." He let me go. "A gobbet of it, anyway."

We continued up the stairs as he talked. "Why should I reduce myself so? Because I can. To disguise the person of one's flesh so is beyond the means of any of my peers and it pleases me to do what others cannot. And it gives me an eye with which to view the men of your world. It allows me to watch, and to see . . ."

"See what?"

"The aforementioned enemy."

We continued to trudge up the stairs, and I began to see what looked to be an opening to the upper portion of the tower.

"What about my daughter?"

"Patience. You will see that our desires are one."

He led me upward and eventually we walked into a room that was as vast as the entry hall, the walls lined with shelves that held an endless supply of books ranging from simple scrolls to giant metal-clad volumes as tall as I was. The room smelled of incense, dust, and old paper. From the expression on Hephaestus' face I could tell that I was looking at a hoard as great as any pile of gold.

He walked over to a long table where a book was already open. He looked down at it and said, "Do you know much of the history of your sister land across the Portal?"

The Cliff Notes version of what I knew went something like this:

There's a realm of magic, elves, dwarves, fairies, and dragons. In the midst of this land enters mankind—i.e., my own kind, only scruffier. They found a land called Ragnan that slowly gobbles up everything around it. Among other things, the fact that men weren't immortal gave them a tactical advantage—they didn't care nearly so much about dying.

Ragnan becomes an authoritarian regime—human only—led by a god-king called the Thesarch, who seemed to have more authority than your average Pharaoh. He was helped in part by the fact that he was at the apex of the mana pyramid and could muster spells that could waste entire cities.

The last Thesarch was named Valdis, and he seemed particularly nasty and long-lived. Many of the nonhuman societies surrounding Ragnan crumble before Valdis and his enchanted human armies.

Then, a dragon named Aloeus throws a monkey wrench into the works by blowing open the Portal, opening the way between here and there. Out pours a tidal wave of magic and refugees, and—

among other political maneuverings—Aloeus manages to broker a deal that has the Ohio National Guard send a unit of armor and air cavalry through the Portal.

Valdis had a blind spot, not seeing the unenchanted, thoroughly mundane troops as a threat. Apparently, no one had shown him that things could be blown up very well without any mana at all. So, thanks to Aloeus, Mayor Rayburn, and the governor of the great state of Ohio, a coup ended the reign of the Thesarch, and started a rat's nest of political ramifications on our side of the Portal that was still working itself out.

So far, so good, from Hephaestus' point of view.

But there was more to it.

There always was.

"The explosion of the nation of men across the continents took generations in mortal eyes," Hephaestus opened a large atlas, showing alien lands in scripts I couldn't read. However, as he turned the pages, it was clear what was happening as the maps became dominated by a single color. "But for most immortals—dragons, elves— the pace of change came too fast to react. I watched many die."

"What about dwarves?"

"Mortal as well, but they lacked man's ability to master mana, and fell too often before it."

"I know of Ragnan's conquests—"

"Do you know of her ally?"

"Ally?"

Hephaestus walked over to a dark grimoire, bound in black leather that seemed to show remnants of facial features in the grain. He drew it off the shelf and placed it on the table between us.

"Not all immortals fought the Thesarch's rise."

Hephaestus opened the book and flipped though pages of arcane symbols until it opened on a full-page illustration. I wasn't really surprised to see—sitting on a stony throne, before a background of fire—the Devil from the tarot card.

"Shit . . ."

Mazurich, or what was left of him, was right. What I was dealing with was Satan himself. Or, at least as close a manifestation as the Portal could conjure up. The reign of the Thesarch was based on a literal deal with the Devil.

Or *a* Devil.

Appearance aside, Hephaestus wasn't describing Judeo-Christian metaphysics. He described a race of beings, few in number, older and more powerful than even the dragons. Beings that were so much of the mana they swam in that they often could forgo a physical form. The mana itself was a sense organ for them, making them near omniscient.

Demons and angels . . .

Their limited physicality, at first, made them little more than shadows in the conscious world. Creatures of dream and spirit, little known and little seen.

Until one of their number discovered a vulnerability in the mortal mind, a vulnerability that allowed him to cohabit the brain and the senses of a man—to give himself form . . .

And lust . . .

And desire . . .

"The vulnerability was two-way," Hephaestus said. "Its spirit could infect the body of a man, but it, in turn, became infected with the basest material drives."

"This thing allied with the Thesarch?"

"This thing *was* the Thesarch. It fed its human host with unimaginable powers, and in turn, human armies slaughtered immortals whose existence might drain the font of mana it now wanted solely to consume."

"Couldn't someone stop it? Others of its kind . . ."

"Were the first to die, consumed in rituals to extend the life of the first Thesarchs."

"But Valdis was killed . . ."

"And it infested the neighbor most convenient to it." Hephaestus shook his head. "Valdis was a host, nothing more. The latest in a long line."

"But the Thesarch was overthrown over ten years ago . . ."

"Do you know how long that is to ones older than I?"

Valdis, apparently, wasn't the only one who was surprised by machine guns, rockets, and high explosives. Our demonic spirit saw in the National Guard hints of powers that had never been conceived within the boundaries of Ragnan. So, instead of taking the mantle of Valdis' successor, it found someone anonymous to take it on its way to the other side of the Portal.

Why settle for one world, when two were available? And one was so much more interesting.

I shook my head.

"As powerful as this thing is, it can't live without mana, can it?"

"It is almost mana personified. It is as if you asked: 'Could matter exist without mass?'"

"Then how can it expect to take over this planet? The portion with mana is geographically infinitesimal."

"It has patience, and servants."

"What do you . . . ?"

I remembered my vision, the mountain of salt, the dwarves shoveling it while chained to the Devil's throne.

"They're smuggling salt."

"Spreading mana," Hephaestus said. "Every ritual that frees the mana trapped in those crystals, will leave some to sink into the earth. Every time, pulling the boundaries of the Portal outward."

I nodded, "He's holding the dwarves by the short hairs. They're living in what's got to be the place where he has the most powerful influence."

"And he's using them to spread that influence."

Patient bastard . . . "What do you think I can do?"

"I've been watching for his reappearance." Hephaestus folded his hands. "He is vulnerable on this side of the Portal while it is mana-poor. Until now, I was unsure that he was even here. Now I am." Hephaestus caressed the spines on one of his shelves. "Originally, I intended to shut off the Portal itself."

I swallowed.

"But the geology beneath your lake means that there may be enough mana to self-sustain now," Hephaestus frowned. "So I must change tactics. If these plans are disrupted, along with the distribution of mana, he may not be able to recover. Merely publicizing what is happening, the dwarves' smuggling ring, may be enough to cut him off from the mines, and weaken him enough to be defeated."

"You said you'd help with my daughter."

"Agree to this, and I can open a route to wherever she is. After which, you should both leave the area, go somewhere free of his influence."

I nodded.

"Do you agree?"

"There's one problem, Hephaestus."

"What is that?"

"That is exactly what he wants me to do."

I had managed to leave the dragon speechless.

CHAPTER TWENTY-FIVE

I FOUND myself back at the Superior Viaduct and Reggie's Town Car with little sign that anything had happened at all. It was four in the morning, and I only had my footprints going toward the end of the bridge and back to show that what I'd witnessed was more than hallucination.

It actually helped my sense of reality that my footprints passed through a locked and warded gate.

"What now?" I asked the chill night air.

Hephaestus/Shafran might be a powerful ally, but I didn't trust him entirely.

Actually, I didn't trust him at all. The dragon, like all dragons, was in it for himself. The fact that he so offhandedly mentioned shutting down the Portal was testament to that. That wasn't just shutting down the economic engine for the whole region. That would be condemning hundreds of thousands of creatures—including his fellow dragons—to death.

Someone about to throw away that many lives wasn't really that interested in Sarah. No way I could trust him to come though on any sort of promise to rescue my daughter. As far as I knew, there was only one being who had that power.

I let myself back into Reggie's car and pulled away into the Flats.

Before I quite realized where I was going, I found myself on I-77 heading toward Columbus. I think I was moving faster than I was able to think. At least faster than I was able to rationalize. The one thing I did know was that I was the only person I could trust to have my daughter's interests at heart. Not Hephaestus, not Blackstone and the Feds, and certainly not Old Scratch, the force behind what seemed to be going on.

And what was it that seemed to be going on?

Smuggling for one. The dwarves were mining salt out of their caves under Whiskey Island, salt that apparently was something akin to magic plutonium, a mana battery so rich in the energies coming out of the Portal, that it allowed the dwarves themselves to play against type and actually cast spells. A mineral potent enough that the Feds were worried about it being smuggled out of northeast Ohio.

If the salt allowed spell-casting of any sort outside the direct influence of the Portal, no wonder Blackstone and company were so panicked. Federal policy number one regarding the Portal was containment. There wasn't any nightmare scenario, from rampant counterfeiting to terrorism, that couldn't be made worse by mixing magic into it. In theory, given the plans and enough mana, a mage with the proper incentive could reproduce a nuke.

The idea that kind of power could spread elsewhere, not just domestically, but overseas, would give a lot of people in Washington sleepless nights.

That's not even addressing the political problems if nonhumans decided to leave the state where they had legal recognition. A dwarf might pass without much notice, but a dragon?

That was the first part of it . . .

Then there was Mazurich, who orchestrated placing the dwarven clans in the place they were currently exploiting. Nothing about his history implied anything other than a working-class alliance that would have made sense just about anywhere with any immigrant population. Mazurich became a dwarven advocate . . .

But somewhere Old Scratch got involved. I wasn't sure exactly when, but from Hephaestus' history I saw two possibilities. Old Scratch must have been drawn to the area of the salt mines from the start. Coming through the Portal to this "mana-poor" world, the way the salt mines apparently became a mana battery would have drawn his attention as soon as he arrived.

So he found the dwarves in residence, and somehow took over, infecting them as he had the rule of the Thesarch.

Or there was an even more sinister possibility—

If Old Scratch comes here very early, as Valdis is falling, or perhaps even before, he might be responsible for Mazurich's deal for the dwarves. Perhaps his intent was to have a captive population, tied to the mines, the labor needed to refine and distribute the mana he wanted spread across this new planet.

If Mazurich discovered this, that one of his greatest humanitarian achievements was at the behest of the Devil himself, the guilt may have driven him to kill himself.

This piece fit everything that had happened to date, except possibly the most important part, from my point of view—

Why did Old Scratch want me to run an exposé on the dwarven operation?

From every indication, he wanted me to blow the whole story wide open. Hephaestus wasn't the only one who was dumbfounded. I couldn't see any angle that made sense. All I knew was that whatever was going on, Old Scratch was manipulating things so I would make the situation public.

Then there was item number three . . .

Magetech.

It was part of the story, but beyond the financial conflict-of-interest story about Mazurich, I didn't know how.

It was becoming imperative that I know the whole story, because without it I was not going to know what was motivating Old Scratch. And I knew that, until I found out what the Devil wanted, I wasn't going to have much hope of getting my daughter back.

There were three sources I knew to go to for information on Magetech. The first, Magetech itself, had an evil effect on me the last time I visited. I had a feeling that it was a dangerous place, and the simple fact that it was saturated with mana meant that it was probably a hangout for Old Scratch himself. And, if I was avoiding concentrations of mana, directly approaching Dwarf Central at Whiskey Island was flat out, not to mention that—if I took Hephaestus at his word—it was Old Scratch's base of operations.

Last was a Dr. Pretorious, who had moved to Columbus, safely outside the influence of the Portal—also safely out of reach of Old Scratch.

It was after dawn when I had reached the southern outskirts of the state capital, and pulled up to Pretorious' house. Nothing much distinguished it. It was one large house in a development full of large houses. The only thing that might have marked it as odd was the fact that every window was shaded from the outside world. Even the vast windows marking the great room were shrouded.

In addition, the driveway up to the three-car garage was covered by an unbroken layer of snow. I began to worry that the doctor wasn't home.

I got out of the car and trudged through the snow up to the front door. I didn't see any sign of life. I rang the doorbell, and got no answer. I leaned on the button, listening to the electronic chimes inside the house.

Nothing.

I pounded on the door with little hope. "Dr. Pretorious? Dr. Pretorious?" My words came out in puffs of fog, and I began doubting that I had the correct house. I was going off of memory for the address. All my notes were in the hands of the FBI at the moment.

For a few seconds I wondered if Blackstone had beat me here . . .

"Dr. Pretorious!"

I tried the door itself.

Unlocked.

I let myself in, not knowing what to expect.

The smell hit me first, before my eyes adjusted. Food rotting, feces, ammonia . . . The heat was jacked so high that breathing the fetid air was like trying to suck air through a wet towel—a towel that'd been used to clean up the bathroom at a strip club. A cheap strip club.

As my eyes adjusted, I began to see eyes, dozens of eyes. Pupils reflecting light back at me. I froze when I heard something growl. I hyperventilated, thinking of all the nasty goblins, gremlins, and little beasties that crawled around dark places. I had to tell myself that I was too far from the Portal for that sort of thing, but I still held my breath until I could make out the feline outlines that went with the demonic eyes.

Cats. Just a shitload of cats.

"Fuck," I said, half relieved, half angry at myself. The word was enough to send about half the eyes scurrying deeper into the darkness.

I closed the door behind me, and stepped carefully around debris on the floor as I felt around for a light switch. I found a panel of three on the wall, only one of which worked. A light came on over the master staircase.

"Holy shit . . ."

The house was only ten or fifteen years old, cost a few million . . . In three years, Dr. Pretorious had managed to completely destroy it. Cat shit was everywhere. Wallpaper was stained and peeled off of yellowing walls. The carpeting had been shredded, the fibers pulled up into random piles all over the floor and the stairs.

The cats orbited me, staring, none closer than about fifteen feet. None of them seemed to be hurting for food, and the floor was scattered with empty cans and empty twenty-pound bags of cat food.

Deeper in the house I heard a television turned to Fox News or CNN. I could hear some talking head discussing trade relations with China.

I stepped carefully around the crap on the floor and headed toward the sound of the television. "Dr. Pretorious?"

The cats followed me, mewing and occasionally hissing if I passed too close. One that had been concealed under an empty pizza box lying in my path suddenly appeared in front of me, back arched, spitting, then jumped me. I had to bring my foot up to deflect it back toward the ground.

It shot away, and I escaped with a slightly unraveled sock.

I flexed my bandaged hand. Just being in this atmosphere was probably going to give me an infection. It was bad enough here having exposed skin. An open wound . . .

The den was actually worse. Lit only by the television, I saw a massive leather couch that looked as if it had had a losing argument with a rototiller. There had been built-in bookshelves, but most of the shelves had collapsed, spilling their contents on the floor, allowing the books to be shredded in a giant improv litter box.

There was someone watching the television, seated in a wheelchair. He looked about two or three times as old as his portrait. Hair uncut, beard unshaven, skin pale, spotted, and deeply lined.

"Dr. Pretorious?"

The old man continued to stare at the news.

"Dr. Pretorious?"

"Is it time already?" he whispered. His voice was cracked and brittle, as if he hadn't spoken in a long time.

"My name is Kline Maxwell, I'm from the *Cleveland Press* . . ."

"Is the seal broken? Have you seen a pale horse?"

Shit, the guy's lost it. He's nuts.

"I wanted to talk about Magetech."

He turned toward me, and his pupils were wide and cloudy with cataracts. I doubted he could see anything. "I don't talk about that."

"You were a scientist, you helped found the company."

He shook his head violently. "I don't talk about that." He stared at the television again. He switched to another news channel where a Republican Senator from North Carolina was talking about an upcoming Supreme Court nomination.

I looked at him, and the television, and asked, "What are you looking for?"

"A sign. A sign he is coming."

"Is he part of Magetech?"

He was quiet for a long time, before he said, "I didn't know." He turned toward me. "Tell them I didn't know."

Filthy as the floor was, I knelt down so I could be on the same level as he was. "If I'm to tell them, I need to know your side of the story."

"I don't talk about that."

"Because you're afraid of him."

"He will come, for all of us."

"Let me know what you did." I reached out and touched his shoulder. "You've been beyond his reach for three years."

"You don't know anything."

"Then tell me."

CHAPTER TWENTY-SIX

IN fits and starts, it came out.

Early on, Mazurich understood that someone needed to reconstruct the physical infrastructure of the city, or any political gains made by Mayor Rayburn and the statehouse would be hollow. Roads, buildings, sewers, those were all immediate, and led to the alliance between Mazurich and the dwarven immigrants.

Beyond those first steps was the creation of Magetech.

Shortly after the first city contracts were signed with the dwarven clans, and before they had found a homeland in the mines under Erie, Mazurich was approached by another immigrant from the Portal. Simon Lucas had been one of the growing numbers of human immigrants to come from Ragnan.

While Mr. Lucas was new to our world, he had an excellent command of English and some compelling arguments. Cleveland was in danger of becoming simply an extension of Ragnan. Science and technology couldn't be allowed to retreat in the face of the Portal. On the contrary, the disciplines developed in this world, in the absence of mana, could be used to create an understanding and manipulation of mana beyond anything imagined in Ragnan.

Mr. Lucas persuaded Mazurich, especially as it became clear that, like the dwarven contracts to maintain the roads, it had been left to local companies to solve the problems in the technical infrastructure, the interference of magic in everything from the communications signal from cellular phones to digital cameras.

Mr. Lucas helped arrange the settling of the dwarven clans under Whiskey Island, and in turn the dwarven clans, rich with funds from city construction contracts, invested their funds with Mazurich and the new Magetech start-up.

Mazurich bought several technology companies that had been

collapsing under the stress of the Portal. And he brought in Dr. Pretorious.

"The engineers and programmers studied our technologies, how to make them work. I studied mana . . ."

A lot of mana.

Dr. Pretorious was probably exposed to more mana than any human in history. He had free access to the product of the dwarven mines for his experiments, and over a period of seven years studied how to use it in an industrial setting.

"Infused into alloys and crystals, wires and circuits—the basis for self-perpetuating machines, enchantments that replicate with no human intervention. Mana concentrated to the point it sustains its own creation." He stared at the television. "We conceived of things that could make the heavens tremble and the stars fall from the sky. We manufactured means to open the gates of hell itself . . ."

"Simon Lucas."

"The Devil himself," Dr. Pretorious said. "I don't talk about that."

"You need to tell me, what is he trying to do? What does he want?"

He continued to stare at the TV, as if he could actually see it. I looked at it and saw coverage of a winter storm in Chicago, headed toward us. The color seemed off . . .

On the bottom, the scroll blurred and started repeating "I don't talk about that . . . I don't talk about that . . . I don't talk about that . . ."

All around us, cats began crying. The feline wail became louder and louder, as if we were suddenly in the midst of hell's own choir.

"The sign," whispered Dr. Pretorious.

The picture on the television blurred into a mass of swirling color, splattered blood, and laughing half-fleshed skulls.

I shook my head. "No, we're not close enough to the Portal."

I heard shattering glass from behind me. I turned to see a pair of shadows walk into the den. In the ruddy glow of the television I saw raw flesh, stitched over bone with steel wire.

"I've been waiting for you," said Dr. Pretorious as he turned his wheelchair around.

"What are they?"

"Our children," he said, facing the two zombies. One reached for the old man, and I did what was probably one of the top ten dumbest things I have ever done.

I grabbed for the zombie.

Not only that, since I'm right-handed and obviously wasn't thinking, I grabbed its wrist with my injured hand. The words "bad move" are an immeasurable understatement.

My grip sank into rotten flesh, and I could feel bone and wire—and touching the wire was like touching a high-tension line. The creature didn't even need to shake me off. When the metal cut through the dressing on my hand, and touched skin, I felt a resonating blow of energy rip through my body. It tore through me with such force that, for a moment, it was as if my perceptions had been blown free of my flesh. I could see my own body fly backward though the air and slam into the remains of one of the bookcases.

I blinked away phantom images of shattering Magetech and Death from the tarot . . .

Zombie One grabbed Dr. Pretorious by the neck and lifted him out of his wheelchair.

The other one headed toward me.

I tried to push myself upright, but my hands slid on books and cat feces and I couldn't do much more than push myself a little backward. I heard a strangled gasp from Dr. Pretorious. Then the other one grabbed me by the shoulders.

Again, terrible forces flew through me, twisting my vision outside of myself.

Then the impact of a window snapped me back to the here and now. The window gave way around me, the heavy drapes entangling me were the only thing keeping me from being flayed alive by flying glass.

I landed, stunned, in a snowdrift, in front of the house.

Every move I made sent daggers of pain through my arm and my back, but I scrambled to get free of the drapes wrapping me. As I did, I heard the sound of sirens coming closer.

I pulled the drapes free of my face and my upper body, and saw my zombie, framed by the window. Steam rose from its raw flesh as it climbed out of the window, toward me. The sunlight reflected off the metal wrong, as if the metallic stitching holding this thing together was reflecting back a completely different light.

The air around it was blurry and out of focus, as if I was looking at a heat haze around it. However, I suspected it was more from the concentration of mana powering this thing, than from any mundane energy.

I half crawled and half rolled out of the drapes, and managed to push myself to my feet. In that time, the zombie was already halfway toward me, and the other one was climbing out of the window.

This cannot be happening in Columbus . . .

But it was clear. Magetech had managed to encapsulate the forces flowing from the Portal, and create a self-powering magical effect. Those things were radiating mana, almost as if they were Portals themselves, spewing magical radiation enough to interfere with the doctor's TV.

I made a limping dash toward the Lincoln, barely ahead of the zombies. I reached the door just in time for the first police car to skid to a stop at Pretorious' cul-de-sac.

"Freeze!"

I stopped moving, even though I knew that the cops weren't shouting at me. I heard one of them say, "Holy shit." And the undead twins shifted their attention to the police. Two uniformed cops took position on the other side of their patrol car, and started firing.

Bullets tore away chunks of flesh and clothing, but otherwise didn't impress the two zombies. One of the cops tried to call something in on the radio, but I could hear the mana interference from where I was.

I dove into the Lincoln.

These bastards might have unnatural speed and strength, but the physical tensile strength of flesh, wire, and bone had to have limits.

"Sorry, Reggie," I muttered as I shifted the Lincoln into gear.

Now we were a little more evenly matched.

I fishtailed in the driveway, pointing the nose at the two zombies, and beyond, at the police car. The cops were backing away, reloading, and the zombies were almost at the patrol car itself.

I floored it.

The wheels whined and spun in the snow under me, and for a moment I thought I wouldn't move at all. Then the tires bit through to pavement, and the Lincoln shot forward, the momentum carrying it across the snowy lawn.

At the last minute, as the zombies turned back toward me, I spun the wheel hard left. Across the snow that had the effect of turning the car sideways without any slack in its forward momentum.

I sandwiched the zombies between the passenger sides of the two vehicles. I heard screeching metal as all the glass on the passenger side shattered. And the upper half of one of the zombies flopped through the front passenger window.

As it reached for me, I shifted into reverse and floored it. The rear right tire screeched on pavement, and I could smell melting

ubber as the Lincoln and the patrol car began rotating counter-
lockwise.

It grabbed my sleeve as I frantically shifted in and out of reverse,
rying to unlock the Lincoln from the patrol car.

The rear window shattered, as Zombie Two broke through.

I floored the accelerator in reverse, shooting backward into the
ul-de-sac, trailing the rear passenger side fender of the patrol car.

I slammed the brakes, and Zombie Two fell backward off the
ear of the car. I hit the accelerator again, and the Lincoln bumped
p twice as I rolled over the zombie with front and back tires.

The other one was pulling itself in through the passenger win-
low. I shifted into drive and floored it, over the other zombie, side-
wiping the patrol car again. This time the force of the impact tore
Zombie One loose.

I pulled the Lincoln to a shuddering stop as three more patrol
ars shot down the street toward us.

Fortunately, the battle was over. The zombies were still moving,
ut their limbs were shattered to the point that no one was in any
langer unless they came within biting distance.

From behind me I heard a bullhorn fighting static.

"Step—bzzt—of the car, kee—bzzt—in sight!"

I didn't need to hear what they were saying to understand it. I
tepped out of the car and, without anyone asking, knelt on the
round, and placed my hands behind my head.

The first two cops only paid me nominal attention; they were
nore interested in the impossible piles of dead things that were
quirming in the middle of their subdivision. As I waited, I watched
ats jumping out of Dr. Pretorious' house, running away from the
arnage.

It took about four hours for the Columbus cops to process me.
'he guys were nice enough about it; I'd saved two of their guys
rom the *Night of the Living Dead* road show. However, I still was
vitness to a murder, and I'd committed God only knows how many
noving violations in someone else's car with no actual ID.

Thankfully, while Reggie was pissed, he wasn't pissed enough
o tell the cops I'd stolen his car. So they fingerprinted me, took a
ew mug shots, and took my statement.

The statement was the longest part, and I probably wasn't quite
s forthcoming as I should have been. Not that I was actively un-
uthful, I was just preoccupied as I began to understand Old
cratch's motives.

Hephaestus was half right. . .

I told the cops how I borrowed the Lincoln because my own ca had been stolen. By my daughter. Which was the subject of anothe police investigation. Yes, I'd seen those zombies, or a zombie lik them, involved in another break-in at an auto shop in Clevelanc They could contact Commander Maelgwyn Caledvwlch of th Cleveland Police for more details.

I left out everything about my meeting with Hephaestus, be cause I didn't know how deep Old Scratch's lines of informatio went, and the more I thought about it, the more I became certai that the old dragon was the only real bargaining chip I had.

All in all, I was busy marking time until Blackstone showed u He didn't disappoint me.

He marched into the squad room where a Columbus detectiv was interviewing me, leading a small army of Feds. He waved hi ID around like a club. "Okay, Maxwell, you're coming with us."

My detective stood up. "Sir, we're in the middle of an investiga tion here."

"Not anymore."

"I need some authority—" The phone on the detective's des began ringing.

"That would be your chief."

The detective answered, "Yes. Yes. But—yes. Okay. I will"

Blackstone waved at me. "Good Lord, Maxwell. What the he were you trying to do?" He turned toward the detective as the ma hung up. "You'll coordinate with Special Agent Thompson here" Blackstone waved at one of the interchangeable Feds. "He'll colle all your case files and arrange transport of all evidence."

Looking beaten, the detective nodded.

"Come with me," Blackstone said to me.

I stood up. "You really know how to make a good impression.

Blackstone grabbed my arm. "This isn't a game."

"You think I don't know that? It isn't *your* daughter."

Blackstone hustled me out of the police station.

CHAPTER TWENTY-SEVEN

BLACKSTONE threw me in the back of one of their vans and we drove off back toward Cleveland. Blackstone sat in front.

After a while, when I had firmed up my plans in my head, I asked, "I guess it would be too much at this point to let me go under my own recognizance?"

"Maxwell, I hope that's just your sorry attempt to be funny."

I stared out at the freeway, where the snow was already becoming heavy. "What do you want, Blackstone?"

"I want you to go to your hotel room and *stay* there."

I shook my head. "No. Not that, what's your goal here? What is your ultimate mission . . . ?"

"Do I have to spell it out for you? We need to bottle up this dwarven smuggling operation, shut it down."

"And beyond that?"

"We're the first line of defense between the things released by the Portal, and the rest of the country."

"Why don't we pull over at the next rest stop?"

"Christ, Maxwell, you think—"

"We need to talk."

Blackstone looked at me, then at his driver. After a moment of thought Blackstone told him, "Do it."

Blackstone led me away from the idling van until we were standing next to the main building of the rest stop. The snow was heavy enough that the Interstate was invisible from where we stood, and the noise from the idling van was nearly inaudible.

"What?" Blackstone snapped, his voice coming out in a puff of fog.

"Look, I know you've been trying to keep a lid on the Portal for a long time. But you saw what happened in Columbus. The genie is out of the bottle."

"If we get a handle on this type of trafficking—"

"Those things were self-powered. This goes beyond the dwarves and their magic dust. There's a technology out there that could let *anything* walk free of the Portal and go *anywhere* . . ."

"I'm not an idiot, Maxwell," Blackstone said. "I saw that mess. What are you getting at?"

"What if you could do more than shut down the dwarven operation? What if I could hand you the company responsible?"

Blackstone laughed. "You have an inflated sense of your investigative prowess. You think I don't *know* where this is coming from? You think I can just walk in the lobby on your say so? Your friend Dominic Mazurich wasn't the only politician paid off by Magetech. Unless you can give me something ironclad, I don't think we need to go on."

"What if you had someone inside, who would give you everything?"

"Define 'everything.'"

"Evidence against the dwarves, testimony against Magetech, and the specs on their research."

"Did Dr. Pretorious tell you something?"

"Are you interested?"

"What are you asking for?"

"Twenty-four hours without an escort."

Blackstone stared at me. "How do I know you're not bullshitting me?"

"You don't. But am I asking too much?"

"I'll give you . . ." Blackstone looked at his watch. "Until nine AM tomorrow morning."

Not quite twenty-four hours, but I wasn't about to push it. "Okay," I said. "Now, does someone have my clothes from the hospital?"

Blackstone was as good as his word. By three, I'd gotten my own clothes, my wallet, my cell phone, and the keys to my rental car. Once I was back in my rented Solara, I scanned through my messages.

Three from Margaret, two from Reggie, one of which was mostly profanity, and one from Dr. Shafran asking if we should meet again.

Yes, I thought, *we should.*

But not before I met with someone else.

First, I called Margaret back. For the most part I let her cry on my shoulder since that meant I didn't have to go into much detail over what was happening here. I kept it short and vague—the Feds were still waiting for some kind of contact, and I was about to call someone who might know something about Sarah's whereabouts.

By then, I had driven around to the West Side technology park where Magetech housed its corporate headquarters. I didn't want to actually walk into their buildings again—a blackout would be a bad thing at this point.

I pulled my Solara to a stop in the parking lot of a small windowless bar that looked as if it predated the technology park by a few decades. The place was called "Slapp-Happy's" and looked as if it had just opened for the day.

I walked in and glanced at the television over the bar. The zombies had made the national news. I saw CNN running pictures of Dr. Pretorious' development. The video only started going funny when they approached one of the zombie parts or the battered remains of Reggie's Lincoln.

Great . . .

I didn't need to hear the audio to see where the story was going to go. The idea that the weird stuff in Cleveland was no longer completely confined would burn through the national news like a California brushfire. Paranoiacs like Blackstone would suddenly seem a lot more credible . . .

I was beginning to understand the point of the zombies.

The point was what was airing right now through one of Magetech's electronic satellite filters.

I took my cell phone, but I made a point of walking back to the pay phone nestled back by the bathrooms.

From there, I called Magetech.

Ten minutes later, Mr. Lucas slid into a booth across from me. "You look surprised to see me, Mr. Maxwell."

I shook my head and drank my club soda. "No, it's just your appearance is so . . ."

"What?"

"Mundane."

"How should I look, Mr. Maxwell?"

"I think we both know what you are, Mr. Lucas. Can we skip the pretense otherwise?"

"You have me at a disadvantage."

"I don't think so." I sipped my club soda. "I want my daughter."

Mr. Lucas leaned back in the booth. "I am sure she is quite safe."

I nodded. "I'm sure. She wouldn't be worth anything to you otherwise." Lucas stared at me, and I could see the hint of the Devil in his expression. Though I was probably imagining it.

"It took me a while to figure out what you wanted," I continued. "What you were trying to do with me. Sure, use me to sacrifice the dwarves and—posthumously—Mazurich. But why threaten me to do something I would have done for you with the right information? But that's how it works. I agree and you might let me see her, but it isn't over then, is it? You want an advocate, someone in the media. You'll hold her hostage as long as you think I'm useful . . ."

"Mr. Maxwell, why are we holding this conversation?"

"Your plans are coming together nicely. Spread the mana and you spread your influence. The dwarves were nickel and dime, weren't they? You don't need them anymore. Magetech has gone beyond the mines, hasn't it? You have the means to create mana now, and how better to spread that as far as possible than to have it fall into the hands of the U.S. government?"

"Mr. Maxwell—"

"You want Blackstone to take it over. You want all of this in the hands of DARPA and the DoD. Who else would exploit it quicker, farther, and with no regard to cost. They'll spread the mana for you faster than the dwarves ever could."

"—I don't think we need to continue."

"But I want my daughter back," I said as Lucas stood up, "and I have something you want."

Lucas stopped and turned toward me. "What?"

"Information." I sipped my club soda and waited. My heart was racing. Deals with the Devil were a little out of my league.

He looked me up and down. "Shall we accept for a moment, your premise?" He slid back into the booth. "Hypothetically, shall we decide I am the fiend you believe me to be? That I have access to your missing daughter? Fine, Mr. Maxwell. But I might point out that such a fiend would easily be able to detect falsehood."

I'm counting on it, Old Scratch . . .

"Might I assume that, for all of Magetech's advancements, it has not been able to uncover the central mystery of the Portal itself? How it formed, how to form something like it?"

"Make that assumption."

Thank you, Mr. Lucas, but that is pretty self-evident. You had to use the Portal to come here, and if you could create them at will, nothing would stop you from opening new ones wherever you wanted, and spilling Ragnan's mana all over the planet.

"So the dragons kept at least one secret from you."

Lucas didn't look happy. "*You* have this knowledge?" he snorted at me.

"I know where it is." I swallowed. I was reaching the most dangerous point of the conversation. Even now, I was second-guessing myself, but I made a point of remembering my vision. Death, the Devil, and the Tower crumbling to earth. I was *meant* to do this.

"Where?"

"It is in the possession of a dragon named Hephaestus."

"*Hephaestus?*" It wasn't just a look anymore. I could feel Lucas' emotion, in waves of force coming off of him that rivaled what I felt when I touched the zombie. I had to concentrate to avoid losing focus and falling into some new nightmare visions. "Where did you hear this name?"

I had expected a reaction, but this was more than I had hoped for. "You know him, then?"

"He has chosen to be my adversary, and for that I will suck the power from his marrow." He reached over the table and grabbed me. The power came off him in searing waves. It tore into me, timed with my pulse, carrying with it images of fields strewn with skulls, pyres the size of small cities, dragons falling out of the sky, and the endless march forward of the Thesarch's army.

"You are Valdis," I whispered.

"Show me to my adversary."

"My daughter," I croaked. "Bring me my daughter and I will show you to his doorstep and lead you inside."

He let me go. And slowly the power drained back into its human shell. "Beside this prize, anything else you might give me is less than nothing. Give me this and you shall have your daughter."

I nodded. "Forgive me if I don't trust you. I want my daughter first."

"You try my patience."

"But you know I'm telling you the truth. Give me my daughter back, and I will give you what you want."

Lucas nodded. "I see that you believe this to be true. So I will do as you ask."

"Bring her to the Superior Viaduct tonight at five minutes to midnight."

"Remember, though, she will be hostage to your continued intention. I expect you both to accompany me to Hephaestus."

I nodded, not trusting myself to speak.

Lucas left me at the booth, and I had to sit and calm down for several minutes. I desperately wanted a drink, or five, but a clouded head was the last thing I needed. I was about to betray someone, *something*, incredibly powerful, and the last thing I needed now was to tip my hand.

When I felt calm enough, I walked back to the rear of the bar and called Dr. Shafran.

"Yes," he answered his line this time.

"It's Maxwell. We do need to meet again. Tonight at midnight."

I spoke with him another ten minutes, hoping I was doing the right thing.

Sarah, I'm going to get you back, baby.

Whatever I have to do.

CHAPTER TWENTY-EIGHT

"*Show me to my adversary.*"
I begin to object, I don't know who the adversary is. But then the mists clear, and I see a Tower hovering over the city, greater than any skyscraper.

"*There!*" *I point.*

A booming, inhuman laugh resounded. **"Your service will be rewarded."**

The Devil rises from his throne, and walks toward the Tower. Moments later, after losing sight of the Devil, the Tower begins to crumble.

The image of the crumbling tower haunted me as I sat in my rented Solara, waiting for Lucas and my daughter. I was plagued with the recurring thought that I didn't know what I was doing. Desperation was driving me to risks I never would have contemplated before.

I was playing with my daughter's life, and I didn't know if I could go through with it. All I had to validate my decision was a hallucinatory vision, one that may have been open to interpretation.

As people have said to me before, the Oracle is a bitch.

Outside the car, the snow was getting worse. A blizzard moving down from Chicago, combining with lake effect, cut down visibility to about twenty yards. Occasionally, the wind would pick up and it would drop to nil.

Ahead of me, the twin cones of my headlights aimed toward the bridge, fixing on the gate. Caught in the beams, the snow moved sideways.

The clock on my dash read 11:49.

"Show, damn you . . ."

Slowly, a twin pair of headlamps became visible in my rearview mirror. They approached and came to a stop behind the Solara. I couldn't even make out the outlines of the vehicle.

Bracing myself, I stepped out of the car, and walked back toward my guest. The wind bit into my exposed skin, the flying ice like an army of tiny pikemen charging my skin as if it was a fleshy Bastille.

As I walked around behind the Solara, I started to see the vehicle that had driven up behind me. A Volkswagen Beetle.

My Volkswagen Beetle.

"Sarah!"

I ran to the car, sliding in the treacherous footing. I almost fell face first into the side door as I clawed through a layer of ice to find the door handle. I pulled the door open, wrenching my bandaged hand, and showering myself with fragments of snow and ice.

I stood by the open door, dumbfounded, staring into the idling car.

It was empty.

The clock on the dash of my Volkswagen read "11:54." As I watched, it flipped to "11:55."

"Mr. Maxwell?" came a voice from behind me.

I spun around to see Simon Lucas standing in the halo of my Volkswagen's headlights. The snow swirled around him, but didn't seem to touch him.

I backed away from my car, slamming the door. "Where's my daughter?"

"She's safe, Mr. Maxwell, I assure you."

"You were supposed to bring her."

He smiled at me with a stare that burned into every organ in my body. "I decided I should provide you with an incentive to avoid any second thoughts."

"No." This couldn't be falling apart on me now. "That wasn't the deal." I ran at Lucas, a move that beat me grabbing the zombie for dumbest move of all time.

"You do not dictate terms to me."

I didn't see him move, but there's a good chance he didn't. One moment I was running toward him. The next I was bouncing off the windshield of the Volkswagen. The windshield spider-webbed below me as my right elbow smashed through. Briefly all I was aware of was the pain streaking up my arm. It was so intense that somehow I missed the moments where I rolled off the hood onto the snow-covered street.

I blinked, and I was on my knees. Spitting snow as I held myself up with my left arm. My right arm, clutched to my chest, was shooting pain so bad that I still couldn't focus on where I was, or what I was supposed to be doing.

I blinked, and the snow seemed to be slowing its fall.

"Do not presume. No servant is too valuable for me to destroy." I heard footsteps walk around in front of me. A pair of shiny leather shoes stepped into my field of vision. They were unmolested by snow or salt. As were the legs of the sharply creased trousers above them. *"On your feet, Mr. Maxwell."*

I pushed myself unsteadily up, one-handed. The pain in my right arm became more concentrated and localized, and I realized that something had dislocated or broken in my elbow. "Fuck."

"You pathetic little man. You think that is the limit of pain?" Lucas walked around me, not seeming to be completely in the world. *"With a thought I could place you in torment for a thousand years, focus your existence on a single eternal moment of agony."*

It was easy to see why this guy, as the Thesarch or as Simon Lucas, could command so many people. How the hell could you fight something like this?

"You offered me something I desire. You live now, your daughter lives now, only to provide this to me. Tell me."

I glanced through the window of the Volkswagen. Snow had just started blowing in through the broken windshield. The clock on the dash read "11:57."

"You want to find Hephaestus, and his hoard of knowledge, you only need to wait."

"I have no taste for riddles."

"The Portal to his lair will open at midnight." I looked up at the snow, which had near frozen in the air.

"Portal?"

"How do you think he hides from you so well?"

I received an inordinate amount of gratification from the surprise on Lucas' face. It had been a strategic omission on my part, partly because I had been trying not to give much away when I thought I had some chance of Lucas bringing my daughter.

The other part is I didn't want Old Scratch here to have too much time to prepare. The bastard might hold sway over every crevice that held mana, but if he wanted to pass through a Portal, everything I had learned told me that he had to do it in person.

And as I expected, his first impulse was not for a face-to-face. The Simon Lucas who faced me, untouched by snow, was not

Old Scratch. Lucas nodded at me, folded his arms across his chest, and shimmered briefly.

Then he was gone.

"Lucas!"

The unmoving snow was silent around me. I leaned back against the Volkswagen and unzipped my coat enough so I could slip my right arm in for some support. As time slowed around me, and the endless minutes crept along, I got a sick feeling that I might have lost my daughter, that I had done something to make Lucas doubt me . . .

But at "11:59" according to the Volkswagen's dash, a shadow fell out of the sky. Something huge and bat-winged passed over me, and thudded on the roof of the Volkswagen, shaking it back on its shocks. I stumbled away from the car, turning, half expecting to see Hephaestus before me.

My new guest wasn't quite that big.

"Your service is rewarded," it said from on top of the Volkswagen. It was twice as tall as a man, even seated on its haunches. It had the head of a goat—but a goat that was a carnivore. Fangs curled over its black lips, and its chin was streaked with blood. Its skin was reddish purple and bristled with black hair that became denser as it grew down from a near naked chest, to become a shaggy pelt down its hooved legs. *"Few mortals are privileged to meet my flesh."*

I backed up as the Devil extended a leg to step off of the car.

"I thought you didn't have a physical body."

"I desire one, so I have one." It drew its claws across the side of my car. They effortlessly pierced the skin and tore through the quarter-panel. *"Should I be confined to the proxy senses of my servants? What is my power if I cannot taste the blood of my sacrifices with my own tongue?"*

It looked down on me with eyes that were now completely inhuman.

"Better to sup on Hephaestus' soul."

Around us, the snow had frozen in midair and the mist from my breath hung unmoving between us.

Inside the Volkswagen, the clock flipped over to "12:00."

The bell tolled one, and the gate opened in front of the Solara.

"Now, show me to my adversary."

CHAPTER TWENTY-NINE

THIS time, the way was harder, and time seemed to progress even slower. The snow had drifted up to my knees in places and my legs burned with the cold. My breath fogged, and I could feel it freeze on my cheeks.

And with every step, I felt the presence behind me. A massive weight I could sense, as if it was about to envelop me. A heat that offered no warmth, the sound of a heavy breath that smelled of carrion, the sound of muscle and skin moving. But when I looked behind me, I saw nothing. Some enchantment hid the demon from my sight.

I only looked behind me once. He corrected me by drawing one of his claws across my back, one of the same ones that had cut through the skin of my Volkswagen. My clothes were nothing to it, and it cut, burning, through to my shoulder blade. The wound wasn't disabling, but it hurt like hell, and the wind found another stinging patch of skin to attack.

As the blood froze on my shoulder, I heard a whisper in my ear. *"Do not turn again. Do not show you are followed."*

I didn't even nod. I just trudged forward.

"Good."

It may have been my imagination, but I could feel the desire from this thing behind me. This close, I couldn't escape the sense of a black sucking need that seemed to overwhelm even the waves of power that surrounded the thing. It was as if I was leading the personification of lust, in just about every depraved connotation that word had. The kind of lust that made child molesters and serial killers seem civilized.

I knew this thing behind me had come from the Portal, and was just another in a long line of immortal entities to take up residence in my city. I knew that its physical presence was a self-creation, almost certainly modeled on the belief and customs it found here. It probably found that—like the ritual-imbued position of the Thesarch helped amplify the power of mana—taking a predefined demonic role was a shortcut to even more power . . .

I knew all this.

But when my feet found the first of the stairs, I knew in my heart that what followed me was the Devil himself. I was walking a path to certain damnation and I didn't know how to stop.

Even though the passage to the base of Hephaestus' tower took an eternity, we came upon the great ebony doors too soon for me.

The tower struck twelve.

The doors remained shut.

I could feel the fury rising behind me. The power of it passed me in waves, and I could almost see it wash against the doors. I thought I could see a tint of blood-red ripple across the black-green script.

It happened again, and it wasn't my imagination.

Waves of glinting red washed across the script in pulsing waves, emanating from the base, where the doors met. Behind me, I heard a laugh. *"The great Hephaestus hides behind his walls like a child."*

Visible now, he stepped past me, to face the giant onyx doors. On them, the script now glowed a pulsing red. With wings outstretched, the demon was almost as large as the doors themselves.

"I've come for you, dragon. And I will not be denied."

The script glowed a solid red, as if the door's core had become molten. Something urged me to back down a few steps.

"Your wards do not deter me," it said as it reached out and touched the door. The demon's touch unleashed a holocaust. Balls of flame erupted from the door, and instead of blowing outward, wrapped themselves around the demon, shrouding him in a fire burning red, then yellow, then white. The air filled with the smell of roasting flesh as the demon's skin began to blister and peel.

The demon laughed.

It kept laughing as more fire erupted from the door, sheets of flame and energy pouring into the spot where the demon stood. The flames were so hot that I could smell my own hair burning, and my eyes watered to look at it.

I backed down a few more steps.

Still it laughed.

The demon's flesh roasted away, leaving a carbonized skeleton that soon disappeared under the heat of the rippling fire. Still the flames enveloped the demon, erupting from the doors faster and faster.

Still the laugh.

The door slowed, sputtering, the script fading from white-hot to a dull red. Before it stood a pillar of fire in the shape of a demon. The flaming image stretched its arms, and from the flames came a voice.

"So like a dragon, to focus on the body."

I don't think it spoke English anymore. I don't think it "spoke" in any real sense.

The flaming arms embraced the door. I heard something sizzle and pop, and long cracks crawled across the glowing script of the doors, the cracks glowing hotter and emitting steam. The doors groaned and screamed as if they were living things.

I took cover flat against the stairs before the doors imploded in a shower of gravel, smoke, and red-hot ash. For a moment the entrance to the tower was wrapped in an impenetrable cloud. As it settled, the fire was gone, replaced by a demon form made of crackling red-hot onyx. Enchanted alien script still glowed on the surface of the stone, but the words somehow had become disturbing, obscene.

It flexed a new onyx claw.

"I think I like this better."

It stepped though the smoking hole that had been the grand entrance. I took the stairs upward, slowly, until I could see the great entrance hall. The onyx demon walked into the chamber spreading its arms and wings, facing upward.

"Show yourself, dragon!"

"DEFILER!" The nonword screeched through the tower, tearing directly into my brain. The force of it caused the great pillars to crack. Then, arcs of green twisting energy burst from the pillars, converging on the demon. The whipping tendrils buzzed and hissed with power so dense I needed to lean inward just to stay upright. My singed hair danced with static.

The script on the demon's skin now pulsed green as the tendrils danced across the surface of its body, pulsing in time to the buzzing energy. More tendrils exploded from the surface of the wall, blowing free plaster and marble, leaping from pillar to pillar, to slam into the onyx creature.

The demon groaned as the buzzing became a roar. Its back arched, as the substance of its body began to shake. The black-green glow pulsed more intensely as the tendrils, whipping and dancing, pulled the thing off its feet. The demon, body shaking and whipping around with the tendrils of energy, rose until it was in the center of the great room.

For a moment, it seemed as if Hephaestus was about to win.

Then the onyx demon froze in the midst of its seizure. The green tendrils of energy suddenly seemed to stretch and vibrate like elastic bands. The green in the demon's skin faded, and began pulsing red. The red leaked from the script carved in its skin to bleed into the suddenly taut, linear bands of energy connecting it to the walls of the room.

When the red reached the walls, the walls exploded. A cascading disintegration of fire, stone, and smoke, that rolled counterclockwise around the inner surface of the chamber tearing off every finished surface, crumbling stairs, burning tapestries, and imploding pillars. The force of it blew me back, rolling across debris, causing blinding pain in my shoulder and arm.

I blinked the pain and smoke out of my eyes and found myself facedown at the edge of the tower stair, looking down through blowing snow at the faint image of the Cuyahoga River.

I slowly rolled on my back.

The great entry hall had been blown apart. The interior had been razed to the outer stone walls, the great pillars blackened stumps, every surface steaming, the floor blasted, cracked and covered with ash.

If anything, Old Scratch seemed even bigger.

"Tasting your flesh will please me."

"OBSCENITY!" The sense of the word shook the tower to its nonexistent foundation.

The ceiling erupted. The arching dome collapsed, shedding blocks the size of large SUVs to crash into the floor around Old Scratch. The demon knocked some of the stones aside as they fell, sending one smashing through the skin of the tower wall to tumble into an imperceptible infinity between us and the Cuyahoga below into a dimension I couldn't point out.

Something screeched from above, and the dragon Hephaestus flew down out of the descending rubble, flames belching forth to fill the room below him. The great lizard fell through smoke, and rubble and the burning remains of the library above. The wings of the dragon stretched from wall to wall in the remains of the great hall.

Hephaestus reached down into the pool of fire with taloned hands and scooped up the demon's body and slammed it into the floor. As the flames cleared, I could see the crater formed by the blow. In it, I could just see the remnants of crumbled bat wings.

Hephaestus slammed the demon down again.

Even though I saw a black leg snap completely off, I knew that Old Scratch wasn't beaten. Couldn't be beaten.

As if it sensed my thought, the demon started laughing.

Hephaestus brought the broken remains of the demon up for another blow, and the demon's arm shot out impossibly far, impaling the dragon's chest. Gouts of blood sprayed from the wound as the demon dug into the dragon's body.

A spasm racked the giant form, and Hephaestus crashed to the ground. The impact shook the floor, and as I looked up, I could see great cracks forming in the edifice of the tower itself, as if the dragon was part of the building's structural integrity.

Hephaestus' grip went slack on the demon, and the onyx creature, broken, humpbacked and laughing, attached itself to the dragon's wounded chest like a twisted lamprey. It wasn't even a laugh anymore, it was more a perverse childish giggle.

"Oh, yes. Such a feast. I shall wear this flesh."

The area around the wound began glowing red as the demon burrowed, spreading blood and gore. Above everything I could hear the fabric of the tower split and crumble.

Hephaestus' great head lay on the ground, and it shifted slightly to focus one gigantic eye on me. And, I could swear I saw the dragon smile, right before the great body vanished.

"What?"

The demon, suddenly alone in the center of the tower, tried to stand, but its body was half formed, fleshy and larval.

"Brace yourself, Mr. Maxwell." Dr. Shafran ran toward me, diving. He grabbed me and we rolled off the edge.

Suddenly in free fall, I tumbled under the tower. Dr. Shafran was gone and the wind whipped by me as I fell toward a river I knew I'd never reach. Above me, the great tower fragmented, the upper stories falling. For a moment it was exactly the image on the tarot card.

I felt more than heard the demon's voice, *"No!"*

The tower itself began twisting, the broken remnants turning in on themselves, the space it occupied whirlpooling in on itself as if everything was being sucked through a cosmic drain. The whole edifice folded into nothing.

Something swept by me and a clawed hand bigger than I was

scooped me out of the air. Something twisted, and Hephaestus and I were flying over a normal Cleveland skyline.

A draconic chuckle shook the fillings in my teeth and made m injured arm ache.

"And he said I focus too much on the body."

CHAPTER THIRTY

M Y desperate plan had worked better than it had a right to. It
had relied too heavily on Old Scratch's weakness—a desire
to dominate that went beyond any reason. I had been betting that
giving the demon the chance to defeat a longtime enemy would pre-
occupy it, and it wouldn't consider the fact that, if Hephaestus created a Portal to a private retreat, it could just as easily close it.

However, almost everything had gone like clockwork. I had led
him to Hephaestus' doorstep, and my strategic revelation of the
tower's nature caused Old Scratch to show up "in person" without
giving the bastard the time to consider the possible consequences.
Arrogance and overconfidence led the way from there to
Hephaestus' doorstep. And while the dragon's continued assault on
the demon's physical body might not have been effective in terms
of damaging his adversary, it was a pretty damn good distraction,
preventing Old Scratch from picking up on the fact that he was in
the middle of a trap, and it was closing shut on him.

It helped that I had told the dragon what was coming when I
phoned him in his Dr. Shafran form.

As we flew through the biting winter air, I screwed my watering
eyes shut.

There was only one major flaw in the execution of my plan.

"Sarah . . ." I whispered.

My arm hurt as the dragon laughed again.

"Damn it! I lost my daughter!" I spat at the gigantic creature that
dragged itself through the air.

"You believe I do not honor my agreements?"

Hephaestus rose above the Cleveland skyline, dodging downtown skyscrapers and the federal building as he aimed toward the
Erie shoreline west of the river.

"What are you doing?"

Hephaestus laughed again, as the ground below whipped by faster than I could make sense of it. The dragon aimed like an arrow right at a spit of land that stuck out paralleling the shore.

As we shot by it, I saw a cluster of dwarves by the roadside look up toward us. Ahead and below, on the icy surface of the lake, something appeared, a sphere unfolding from the same nameless dimension the tower had been sucked into.

"Wait, I can't go——"

We hit the sphere, and the wind ceased. Our motion had stopped, and we were no longer flying over the lake. We were in a cavern, a familiar one . . .

A vast floodlit chamber, a vast space of unfinished walls leading toward a carved building formed into incredible pillars, vaults, and arches. I could study the statues this time, and I could see dwarven bodies twisted into all forms of obscene agony.

"This was his cathedral."

Unlike my vision, the space wasn't empty. Dwarves crowded around the front stairs of the facade, facing us. They all stared at Hephaestus as he set me on the ground.

I looked at the dwarven faces, and saw fear.

I limped forward.

One of the dwarves stepped forward. I recognized Samanish Thégharin, my cab driver. "You cannot be here."

"My escort says otherwise."

"A human cannot live in these halls," Samanish grabbed my jacket. "Leave for your own sake, and before his wrath comes down on us all."

I pulled away. "*He* is gone."

"What?" Samanish's eyes widened.

"The one you will not name. The one whose existence poisoned the mana in these halls. The one who dedicated this hall to himself."

"I am here for my daughter." I started walking toward the great Gothic arch ahead of me. After a moment the dwarves parted in front of me. As I closed, I could see the facade crumbing. The statues seemed to dissolve into powder, the stained glass fading and flaking into gray dust.

Hephaestus must be enjoying himself.

I could feel the mana around me, subliminal, at the corner of my awareness, like at the Magetech complex. This time, there was no foreboding to it, no evil weight . . .

Perhaps that was as good a sign as any that Old Scratch was gone.

I stumbled forward through the vast Gothic doorway. Before me was the great hall, its benches filled with hundreds of dwarves watching me. Obscene decorations crumbled around us as I limped up the aisle toward the high chair next to the altar.

As I reached the chair and reached for my daughter, the altar crumbled.

"Sarah!"

She yawned and stretched, blinking. "Oh, shit, Dad?"

"Are you all right?"

She looked me up and down, eyes wide. "All right? Dad? What happened to you?"

"Let's get you home." I led her out of the cathedral with my good left hand.

Not one of the dwarves moved as I took her out of the cathedral, which was in the midst of becoming little more than another unfinished cavern. "What's happening, where am I?"

"You might not remember it, but you were kidnapped."

"What?" she gasped as we walked through the doorway. Ahead of us, past a semicircle of dwarves facing the remnants of Old Scratch's cathedral, the massive form of Hephaestus sat on his haunches, arms folded. His great Escalade-sized head nodded down toward us on the serpentine neck.

"Do I not keep my word, Mr. Maxwell?"

Sarah shook her head. "Oh. My. God."

"Thank you," I said. "I owe you."

Hephaestus snorted. *"Nonsense. You provided defeat for my adversary of an aeon. The books are balanced."*

"It's talking to you," Sarah whispered.

"And it is a pleasure to meet you as well, Miss Maxwell."

Sarah gasped and grabbed me. It was all I could do to keep from wincing when my injured arm moved. "It's okay," I said through clenched teeth. "He's a friend."

"Shall I take you from this place, or do you prefer to walk?"

I looked at the dwarves surrounding us and swallowed. "Perhaps we should go."

I took a few steps forward, and Samanish Thégharin stepped between us and Hephaestus. I stared down into his wrinkled face and felt my good hand ball into a fist. "This isn't a good idea," I told him. "I'm taking my daughter."

"Please," he said. "Forgive us."

"Just let me go——"

He rested a wrinkled leathery hand on my arm. "We saw what happened to our greatest benefactor. Mazurich's death is the shame of all our clans. We did not want you to follow him. Ossian, Teaghue, they tried to push you off the path He was driving you down. It cost us, and we found it cost your daughter as well." He looked at Sarah. "This wasn't our intention, but when He saw we tried to influence your father, He made us take you."

I removed his hand. "It's over now. I just want to take my daughter home."

"You've broken the chains binding our clans," he said. "Honor demands we repay you."

I looked across at the dwarves. All I could think was, what a damn mess. Even if I didn't break the story, it was probably too far gone for anyone to stop. Samanish Thégharin thought I delivered them from bondage, but I doubted that anyone beyond the people in this cavern would accept what they had done under that bondage. I looked around and thought of the trials, the scandals, and the innuendo that would decimate these clans.

Will you thank me then?

Fact was, I don't always love my job . . .

"Is there anything we can do?"

"Yes, actually, there is . . ."

EPILOGUE

ON top of everything else, dwarves make good medics. I had a decent cast on my arm as I dove Sarah back to our hotel. She started apologizing profusely when we passed the remains of my Volkswagen. I told her, honestly, that all that mattered to me was the fact I got her back.

I called Margaret and had the pleasure of handing my cell phone over to Sarah. I didn't even wince when Sarah started going on about how her dad was friends with a dragon.

I called St. Vincent Charity Hospital, and was relieved to find out that Nina had come out of her coma. I had hoped that with Old Scratch's influence gone from the local ether, she might wake up, but I hadn't been sure.

The snow had stopped, and the roads were clear, so we got back to the hotel by 8:40. I wasn't that surprised when I opened up the door, and saw Blackstone and Special Agents Levi and Francis.

"Well," Blackstone said, "if it isn't the prodigal fucking journalist."

"You're early," I said.

"Yeah, and I'm having some doubts," Blackstone said. "I see you found your daughter."

"Who the hell are you?" Sarah snapped at him. "What are you doing in our hotel room?"

"Mr. Blackstone here," I said to her, "is our local federal pain in the ass." I nodded at the two others. "His friends are Special Agents Levi and Francis. FBI."

"Assigned to your kidnapping, Miss Maxwell," said Agent Levi. From his expression, I think he took my little walk out of the hospital personally.

"Oh," Sarah said.

"Francis?" Blackstone said. "Will you and Levi take her in the other room and get a statement. And for God's sake, keep an eye on her."

"Dad?" Sarah looked at me.

"It's okay, they're cops. And I need to talk to Mr. Blackstone."

"Damn right you do," Blackstone said.

I watched Francis and Levi lead Sarah out of the room. When the door closed, Blackstone looked at me. "Okay, I'm not heartless. I know you scammed me so you could get your daughter. If it was me, I'd probably pay anything to get her back. But now she's back, and you better come clean with me. What did you pay, and to whom, to ransom her?"

I limped over to one of the chairs and eased myself down into it. I sighed.

"Christ, what happened to you?"

"Blackstone? I told you, you're early."

"Don't start playing games now, I could—"

There was a knock on the door. Blackstone stared at me.

"You gave me until nine AM."

The door knock sounded again.

I smiled at Blackstone, "Maybe you should get that. It's nine o'clock."

Blackstone looked at me, shaking his head. "I don't believe this," he muttered as he walked over to the door.

He opened it, and a line of solemn-looking dwarves walked into the room. "What?" Blackstone said.

The first dwarf stepped forward and nodded his head in a short bow. "I am Gwentarian of the clan Parthalán. I bring the board of directors of Magetech, Inc. We wish to offer the federal government a deal."

Blackstone turned toward me and said, "You bastard, how long have you been sitting on this?"

"You better get negotiating," I told him. "These guys are used to making deals with the Devil."

S. Andrew Swann

MOREAU OMNIBUS   0-7564-0151-1
(*Forests of the Night, Emperors of the Twilight, & Specters of the Dawn*)
"An engaging, entertaining thriller with an exotic cast of characters, in an unfortunately all too plausible repressed future."
—*Science Fiction Chronicle*

FEARFUL SYMMETRIES   978-088677-834-7
"A novel as vivid as a cinema blockbuster loaded with high-budget special effects." —*New York Review of Science Fiction*

HOSTILE TAKEOVER *omnibus*   0-7564-0249-2
(*Profiteer, Partisan & Revolutionary*)
"This is good old-fashioned military SF, full of action, colorful characters, and plenty of hardware." —*Locus*

DRAGONS AND DWARVES: NOVELS OF THE CLEVELAND PORTAL   978-0-7564-0566-3
(*Dragons of the Cuyahoga & Dwarves of Whiskey Island*)
"Skillfully done light adventure with more than a dash of humor."—*Science Fiction Chronicle*

BROKEN CRESCENT   0-7564-0214-X
"A fast-paced, entertaining tale of the boundary between magic and science." —*Booklist*

To Order Call: 1-800-788-6262
www.dawbooks.com

Sherwood Smith

Inda

"A powerful beginning to a very promising series by a writer who is making her bid to be a major fantasist. By the time I finished, I was so captured by this book that it lingered for days afterward. I had lived inside these characters, inside this world, and I was unwilling to let go of it. That, I think, is the mark of a major work of fiction…you owe it to yourself to read *Inda*." -Orson Scott Card

INDA
978-0-7564-0422-2
THE FOX
978-0-7564-0483-3
KING'S SHIELD
978-0-7564-0500-7

And now available in hardcover:
TREASON'S SHORE
978-0-7564-0573-1

To Order Call: 1-800-788-6262
www.dawbooks.com